T0318828

God Has Spoken

God Has Spoken

Theresa A. Campbell

www.urbanchristianonline.com

Urban Books, LLC
97 N18th Street
Wyandanch, NY 11798

ISBN 13: 978-1-60162-681-3
ISBN 10: 1-60162-681-9

First Trade Paperback Printing December 2014
Printed in the United States of America

10 9 8 7 6 5 4 3 2 1

Distributed by Kensington Corp.
Submit Wholesale Orders to:
Kensington Publishing Corp.
C/O Penguin Group (USA) Inc.
Attention: Order Processing
405 Murray Hill Parkway
East Rutherford, NJ 07073-2316
Phone: 1-800-526-0275
Fax: 1-800-227-9604

I dedicate this book to my mother, Maxine A. Allen.

You are a beautiful woman of strength, courage, and faith.

Thank you for your love and encouragement and for always reminding me that it's not over until God has spoken.

Acknowledgments

"Every praise is to our God . . ." (singing and dancing). Lord, thank you for taking me on this wonderful, soul-fulfilling journey. I have faith that you will finish the wonderful work that you have started in me!

Thanks to my biggest fans, my brothers, Warren Osbourne and Gregg Allen, for rooting me on when I need it the most. You guys are the best!

How do I say thanks to my editor who brings out the best in me in writing? Mrs. Joylynn M. Ross, you rock!

Warmest thanks to all the readers who supported my first novel, *Are You There, God?* and are holding this one in their hands. I know you have a lot of choices out there, and I appreciate you giving the "little guy" a chance. God bless you!

"God has spoken plainly, and I have heard it many times: Power, O God, belongs to you."

Psalm 62:11

New Living Translation

Prologue

"They are hypocrites! Big fat liars! Traitors!" Dupree yelled furiously as she hammered her fists into the leather couch on which she perched. "Tiny! Officer Gregg! You are disgusting! I hate you!" She spoke as if both parties were present.

Sitting on the other couch across from Dupree, Jas, Dupree's friend and roommate, nervously nibbled on her thumb.

"All these years I wondered if my mother was dead or alive. And all this time she was here in Kingston, living the big life without any concern about the daughter she left behind or the woman who had raised her," Dupree said angrily.

By now Dupree's voice had raised a few octaves higher. She jumped up off the couch and began pacing the carpeted floor like a restless monkey.

"We suffered, Jas. My aunt is confined to a wheelchair and is living with strangers, while Tiny is here living it up." The word "Tiny" was said with distaste and disrespect. "Then she thought if she gave me a job and an apartment to live in, everything would be okay. I don't think so, Tiny!"

Dupree's voice grew higher and louder with every word she spoke. Her eyes lit up with fury as she pounded her right fist into the open palm of her left hand. "Oops." Dupree placed her right hand over her mouth dramatically; her eyes widened as if a light bulb just went off in her head. "I forgot that she is no longer Tiny." Her hands now rested on her small waist as she rocked back and forth on her heels. "She is now the big shot executive, Mrs. Eleanor Humphrey. Who knew?"

Jas watched her friend helplessly.

"And what about the *kind* police officer who suddenly decided to help me after I was almost raped and murdered? The *Good Samaritan* who paid my college tuition for me to attend NYU next spring? That's right. *He* is my *father*. Yup, meet the great and wonderful, Officer Gregg," Dupree spat nastily.

"Where were you, Daddy, when we struggled to find food?" Dupree screamed. "Where were you when I needed money to pay for my college entrance exams? When I had to work from sunrise to sunset so my aunt and I could survive?"

"Dupree, please try to take it—"

"I don't want to take it easy!" Dupree turned fiery eyes on Jas before she continued on the warpath. "Where were you, Daddy, when the man I trusted like a father brutalized me? Huh? Where were you when I needed *my* father? Nowhere." Dupree answered her own question. "*That's* where you were, Officer Gregg. You were *nowhere* to be found."

Jas slowly stood up and carefully approached Dupree. Dupree ran into her friend's arms and began sobbing on her shoulder.

"Even Tony, who I thought was my best friend, deceived me," Dupree said of Anthony Gregg, Jr., the boy she'd just found out was her biological brother.

It was the last summer of high school during Daily Vacation Bible School (DVBS) as Dupree got ready to watch the play, Little Baby Jesus, *when Tony asked to sit beside her and officially introduced himself.*

"Well, Pree, my name is Anthony Gregg Jr., but please call me Tony," he whispered in her ear.

Dupree knew who he was because his parents and grandparents were longstanding members of her church. Dupree and Tony were about the same age, attended and graduated from the same high school, but they had never officially met before.

"And mine is Dupree, not 'Pree,' so please call me Dupree," she replied testily.

Instead of being insulted, Tony threw his head back and laughed out in delight.

Tony was very polite and friendly and expressed an interest in getting to know Dupree.

"I just want to talk to you some more and get to know you," Tony had said to her after she refused the ride home that he had offered after the play.

"Why?" Dupree asked. No boy had ever shown interest in her before, but there stood a handsome, rich, popular boy wanting to get to know her.

"You seem like a nice person, and I just want to be your friend," Tony said sincerely.

"Let me tell you something, pal," Dupree began, pointing her finger at his face, "if this is some bet or game you and your obnoxious friends are trying to play with me, you better keep right on steppin' because I am not that type of girl. Got that?"

"No no no, this is no game," Tony stammered, his sincere eyes pleadingly interlocked with Dupree's fiery ones. "I have seen kids teasing and making fun of you at school, but you never got in a fight with them. At first I thought you were just scared, but then I realized that you were just taking the higher road. You behaved like a good Christian girl should, and I think that makes you the bravest of them."

Dupree lowered her eyes to the ground as the anger slowly tiptoed away. She was at a loss for words.

"Perhaps some other time." Tony's smiling voice snapped Dupree's head up. She shyly smiled at him and nodded before she turned and walked away.

At first Dupree wasn't sure what to make of Tony, but she finally let her guard down and interacted with him more. They sat together at DVBS, laughed, and talked about silly things and began spending more time together. It wasn't long before a great friendship developed between Dupree and her new best friend, Tony.

"Okay, let it all out," Jas said as she gently rubbed Dupree's back. "Let out all the pain."

Dupree followed her friend's instructions and continued to vent. "Mrs. Eleanor Humphrey aka Tiny, where were you when I trusted the first man I thought loved me and he betrayed me?" Dupree whispered into the back of Jas's neck. Her body felt drained and weary as the fight gave way to despair. "Where were you, Tiny, when I needed my mother?"

Jas held her, and the two friends wept.

"Where was I when my daughter needed me?" Mrs. Eleanor Humphrey sobbed on her husband's shoulder as they lay in the middle of their king-size bed. "I have failed her and Aunt Madge. Oh God. I didn't even know that my aunt had a stroke years ago and was confined to a wheelchair. What kind of person am I?"

"Sweetheart, you had it pretty rough yourself in the beginning," Dwight said in her ear as he soothingly ran his fingers through her long, straight hair. "This is not your fault but the monster who took advantage of you."

By now Dwight was getting worked up as he talked about Officer Gregg, Dupree's natural father.

"Baby, I was also a willing participant." Eleanor lifted her head and turned wet eyes to her husband.

"You were a misled child," Dwight spat as he raised himself into a sitting position. "He was a grown man and should have known better. You are a good person. Back then, you were Tiny, the young, confused fifteen-year-old girl. Today, you are Mrs. Humphrey, the woman I am proud to call my wife. If I'd been there to protect you back then . . ."

"Okay, okay, sweetheart. Please calm down," Eleanor said. "I know how much this upsets you."

"*Upset?* I'm *furious!*" Dwight shouted. "I still would like to get my hands on that scumbag. And he called himself a police officer. There to protect and serve. Well, he served himself all right."

Eleanor gently reached up and pulled her husband back into her arms. He inhaled and exhaled deeply a few times, allowing his tensed body to slowly relax in her embrace.

"I'm going to run you a warm bath," Dwight said to his wife a few seconds later. "By the time you get out, I'll have something ready for you to eat." He popped himself up on one elbow and looked down at her with concern.

His wife mutely stared back at him with sunken, solemn eyes. Leaning over, Dwight kissed her softly on the lips before he hopped off the bed. Walking quickly, he entered the adjoining bathroom.

I have to make my daughter understand, Eleanor thought. *I have to explain to her and Aunt Madge why I left and stayed away.*

"Okay. I'm ready for you." Dwight's voice interrupted the thoughts in Eleanor's head. "Lift up that cute little butt so I can slide you out of this skirt." Dwight attempted some humor.

His wife gave him a small smile and helped him undress herself. He lifted her into his arms and took her to the huge bathtub, where he gently lowered her into the warm, sudsy, scented water.

"This feels so good," Eleanor purred in pleasure. "You knew just what I needed." She touched his cheek with the back of her hand. "Like always."

"Yeah, this will help you to relax," Dwight said. "Later, we need to figure out where we go from here."

"I have to make my daughter understand." Eleanor began tearing up again.

"Baby, I strongly believe that the Lord is going to work out everything for you and Dupree," Dwight replied tenderly.

His wife searched his handsome face for any doubt, but saw only his love and confidence staring back at her.

"I love you," Eleanor whispered. "I don't deserve you."

"No. I'm the one who doesn't deserve you," Dwight replied softly. The couple smiled at each other, their strong love transparent in their eyes.

"I'll leave you to enjoy your bath," he said. "When I get back, we'll have dinner."

Eleanor watched him walk away and sighed wearily. "What am I going to do now?" she said to the silent room as she slid down lower in the bathtub, suds reaching up to her mouth. Eleanor remembered asking that same question many years ago and the response she got had sent her on a journey to hell.

Chapter One

Tiny's Story

Falmouth, Trelawny, Jamaica, West Indies, Year: 1978

"Tiny!" Aunt Madge shouted, her squinted eyes looking out the window into the darkness of the night. "Tiny! Chile, you better get in this house right now."

Her small voice echoed over the small boarded houses sitting on the outskirts of Falmouth, Trelawny, before disappearing into the night. Aunt Madge paused and listened but only her heavy breathing filled her ears.

"Lord, please, give me the strength to deal with that chile," Aunt Madge mumbled as she moved away from the window and anxiously paced her small one-bedroom home that she shared with her niece. "I swear she is going to be the death of me. I bet she is with that little force-ripe woman, Dolly."

Oblivious to the calling of her aunt, a few miles away, fifteen-year-old Tiny and her best friend, Dolly, sat on Dolly's dilapidated house steps sipping orange juice and rum from two big, chipped enamel mugs without a care in the world.

It was almost midnight, and the countryside was pitch-black except for the small flittering lights from the peenie wallies that danced in the humid air. Dolly Bell aka Rockin' Dolly as she liked to call herself was also fifteen years old. She shared a home with her thirty-year-old absentee mother, who spent more time at her boyfriend's house than home with her only child.

Dolly was a big-boned, light-skinned girl with a voluptuous figure. She had men of every age, shape, and size panting after her, and she used this to her advantage. She slept with numerous men for money and material goods and changed her lovers as frequently as she did her underwear. Tall or short, fat or slim, young or old, leg or no leg, Dolly wasn't partial. But her specialty was older, married, or committed men, who did anything to be with the overgrown child and everything to keep her silent. This earned her the nickname "Battabout" in the small community. Battabout was a Jamaican term for a loose woman.

"Old Jezebel!" the bitter women who had shared their men with Dolly would shout from afar when they'd see her in passing. This, meant as an insult, was taken as a compliment by Dolly.

"You got me confuse as ain't nothing old about me," Dolly would respond, spinning around to show off her bootylicious body. "Ask your man and he'll tell you." Dolly laughed and sashayed away in her four-inch platform sandals, her huge behind held hostage in the tight miniskirts or booty shorts she favored, rolling from side to side in victory.

"Aunt Madge is probably having a fit that I'm out so late." Tiny giggled and belched loudly. "Oops. Sorry."

"You are so drunk." Dolly threw her head back and laughed out loud. "The warden is definitely going to kill you when you get home," she said in reference to Aunt Madge.

"Oh, please." Tiny sucked her teeth and rolled her eyes before taking another sip from the mug. "This is some good stuff right here." She lifted up the mug in salute.

"Yeah, we just finished two bottles." Dolly giggled and daintily swung her long braids over her shoulder. "Tomorrow I'll get some more from my baby, Blacker."

"Your baby, huh? Wait until Mrs. Blacker catches you," Tiny said and doubled over in laughter. The alcohol that swam in her veins made everything even funnier.

"Girl, I'm not scared of Mrs. Blacker," Dolly replied. "She's the missus, and I'm the mistress. It's all good."

"Chat bout!"

The girls high-fived and whooped until tears ran down their faces, their loud laughter disturbing the silence that blanketed the night.

"Okay. Now let's get back to your lesson of love," Dolly said when the laughter died down. "Look at me and learn, girlfriend. Professor Dolly is here for you."

Tiny giggled and gave Dolly her undivided attention.

"Now when a man looks at you, bat your eyelashes like this." Dolly flicked her eyelashes rapidly as she demonstrated. "Then you slowly swipe your tongue across your lips and flash that bright smile."

Tiny blushed and hung down her head in embarrassment. "I won't be able to do anything like that," she mumbled.

"Tiny, look at me," Dolly demanded in a stern voice. "This is nothing to be ashamed of," she said after Tiny's doelike eyes met hers. "Remember, you are doing this so things will get better for you *and* the warden."

Tiny nodded shyly and glanced away. Dolly had been giving her these lessons of love for a few weeks now.

"Do you want to get away from this boring back-a-wall place?" Dolly asked Tiny as she used a match and lit the marijuana spliff she held in her hand. She slowly took a long drag and blew the smoke in the air. "Well, do you?"

"Yes," Tiny said in a meek voice. "But I've never done anything like that before."

"Well, there has to be a first for everything," Dolly replied. "I'm going to Kingston as soon as Big Dread sends for me." Her eyes lit up as she stared off into her make-believe future. "I'm going to become an actress and star in plays at the National Pantomime."

The Jamaica National Pantomime was located in the Ward Theatre in Downtown Kingston since 1776. The Pantomime depicted bright, colorful costumes, upbeat music, festive, magnificent sets, supertalented casts, and uplifting themes.

"I want to go to Kingston too," Tiny whispered.

"There is nothing wrong with doing what you have to do to get a better life." Dolly continued to lecture her eager student. "This is survival of the fittest. A girl has gots to do what she gots to do. You better take my word."

Tiny gazed adoringly at her wise friend as Dolly's words left their prints on her immature, impressionable heart. Like a dry sponge in a bucket full of water, Tiny sucked up everything.

And that was why Aunt Madge did everything in her power to end the budding friendship between the two girls. She had tried unsuccessfully to set Dolly on the straight and narrow road.

"Baby, the Lord loves you and is very displeased with your behavior," Aunt Madge said to Dolly one day when she saw her in town. "You must remember that your body is the living temple of the Lord, and you should keep it holy."

"It's a temple all right," Dolly remarked with a smirk. "I have men bowing down in worship." And she rudely sucked her teeth before she walked away, leaving Aunt Madge staring at her back, her eyes filled with pity.

"I have to keep that girl away from Tiny before she corrupts her too," Aunt Madge mumbled. "I can't afford for my niece to go astray. Please help me, Lord."

Aunt Madge's sister Ellen died while giving birth to Tiny and since the child's father had also passed away before she was born, it was left up to Aunt Madge to take care of the baby. She raised Tiny like her own daughter.

"I want you to stay away from that girl," Aunt Madge warned Tiny. "She is bad news." But her words went in one ear and out the other. Tiny thought Dolly's life was exciting, unlike her own, so she ignored her aunt and clung to Dolly. This was a very big mistake that would cost her more than she bargained for.

Chapter Two

"I'll catch you later, Dolly." Tiny waved good-bye before she floated light-headed up the dark, narrow track toward the main road. She and Dolly had spent most of the evening and night drinking rum and smoking marijuana, so she was as high as a helium balloon.

As Tiny walked in the shadows of the night down the main road toward the dirt track that would take her home, her firm behind peeped out of the very short shorts that Dolly had lent her earlier that evening. She was too wasted to remember to change back in the long, wide, floral dress that Aunt Madge had made for her.

"You are a lady, and I want you to dress like one," Aunt Madge often reminded Tiny. "You don't need to expose your body for every Tom, Dick, or Harry to see. You must always keep your body properly covered."

Tiny hummed a song as she took slow, calculated steps on the side of the road. Suddenly, bright lights illuminated the blackness, and she stopped and turned around, shielding her blinded eyes with her hands. The car slowly drove up and stopped by her feet. Unafraid, Tiny strolled over to it and leaned in through the open window to peek inside. Her eyes instantly lit up as she stared at the handsome young man behind the wheel.

"Well, hellooo, Officer," Tiny greeted, her smile spreading wide from one ear to the other as she gazed at his uniform.

"Good night to you," the police officer replied. "What are you doing walking by yourself this late at night?"

"Oh, I'm not scared." Tiny giggled and batted her eyes at him as she had just been taught.

He laughed out in amusement and surprise as he looked at the tall, beautiful young girl. He knew that Tiny and her aunt attended his church. Although he had never spoken to her before, Tiny seemed like a quiet, respectable girl. This was clearly not what he was seeing before him.

"Get in and let me give you a ride." The police officer pushed the front passenger door open and Tiny giggled as she slid into the seat.

"Promise you won't arrest me," Tiny said as she turned toward him, the short shorts riding further up her slim, toned thighs, exposing more skin.

The police officer stared for a brief moment before he shook his head as if he was getting out of a trance. He then started the car. "I'm Officer Gregg," he introduced himself after they drove off. "Officer Anthony Gregg."

"I'm Tiny, and I loveeee a man in uniform," Tiny flirted. Officer Gregg blushed and laughed nervously. He knew what Tiny was doing and as a thirty-four-year-old man, he should have put a stop to it. After all, she was only a child, but he felt flattered by the attention.

"So are you going to give me a ride tomorrow night as well?" Tiny leaned into him, her breath stank of the marijuana and rum.

"You know I could arrest you for smoking and drinking, right?" Officer Gregg grinned at her.

"Arrest me, please," Tiny said in a baby-like voice as she held up her small wrists to his face, giggling uncontrollably.

Officer Gregg laughed and slapped her playfully on her naked thigh. "I think this is your stop," he said moments later. He pulled over beside the track that would take Tiny home. The two sat in silence and stared at each other before Officer Gregg cleared his throat and glanced outside his window.

"Well, good night," he said as he avoided Tiny's eyes, missing the disappointment that reflected in them.

"Bye." Tiny popped the car door open and stepped out. As she bent forward and opened her mouth to say something else, the car sped off like a bat from hell, disappearing into the night. Officer Gregg was trying to run away from trouble, but would he be fast enough?

"What do you mean what do you do now?" Dolly looked pointedly at Tiny. "Tiny, this is it! This is the break you have been waiting for. Don't you see?"

Tiny stared at her innocently. Today she was sober and terrified out of her mind as she recounted her encounter with the dashing police officer the night before.

"Dolly, I'm not seeing anything right now. Aunt Madge was so mad last night when I came home practically naked and stoned out of my mind," Tiny said.

Dolly laughed out loud. "I'm surprised the warden didn't have a heart attack and die."

"That's not funny," Tiny snapped. She was very disobedient to her aunt, but she loved her unconditionally and could not imagine a life without her.

"Sorry. Sorry. Shoot, a girl can't even make a little joke." Dolly pouted and rolled her eyes at Tiny.

"Don't joke about anything happening to Aunt Madge. She is the only family I have, and she loves me," Tiny replied.

"Okay. Let's get back to you and your police boyfriend," Dolly said excitedly.

"He is *not* my boyfriend. Dolly, the man is more than twice my age, and you know he's married," Tiny said. "For heaven's sake, he and his wife attend my church."

"That's even better for you," Dolly replied eagerly. "Now, listen to me, and you and the warden will be set for life. I have seen Officer Gregg, and the man is fine like wine. Plus, he is rich. Tiny, the Lord has answered your prayer."

"He has?" Tiny asked naively.

"Yes, He did. This is what you are going to do." And Dolly laid out the foolproof plan in great detail.

The next day Tiny went to the public phone in town and called Officer Gregg at the police station. She told him she wanted to meet up and talk to him later that night. Instead of putting Tiny in her place, he agreed to the meet the young girl in the first classroom of Building One over at the high school.

"I'll just go and have a talk with her," Officer Gregg said to himself. "The poor child looked as if she is going through some stuff and probably just needs some fatherly advice."

But advice was the last thing on Tiny's mind that night. Arriving at the high school before Officer Gregg, she cautiously crept through a small opening that someone had cut in the wire fence at the back of the school, then hurriedly entered the semidark classroom. The moonlight streaming through the open windows reflected the shadows of the trees on the wall. High on the strong weed that Dolly had given to her earlier and slightly tipsy from the cups of cheap wine that she consumed to boost her courage, Tiny sprang into action. She spread a flimsy blanket on the teacher's desk, before slipping out of the borrowed minidress she wore. As hollow footsteps grew closer, Tiny hurriedly went and lay down on the desk, showcasing her birthday suit.

"What are you doing, girl?" Officer Gregg asked in surprise as he stood by the open door of the classroom. "Are you crazy or what?"

Tiny smiled as his bulging eyes roamed hungrily over her bare body.

"What do you think I'm doing, Officer?" she replied with a wink and swiped her tongue seductively across her glossed lips as Dolly had shown her. Her glazed eyes beckoned him to come closer.

"I'm leaving now," Officer Gregg whispered, still rooted to the same spot he stood, his eyes fixed on Tiny. "I thought you just wanted to talk. Looks like this right here says it all."

Officer Gregg closed his eyes tightly, shaking his head from side to side, mumbling incoherently to himself. Finally, he turned to leave. "I'm out of here," he said loudly and took a few steps away from the classroom. But suddenly he stopped and almost in slow motion, turned back around. As if they had a mind of their own, Officer Gregg's feet quickly took him back to the classroom door. He knew he should have just turned around and gone home to his wife, but he became a victim of his lustful flesh as he stepped into the classroom, closing the squeaky door behind him. As he looked at Tiny's perfect young body, he knew he just had to have her. So against his better judgment, he went to her.

Tiny giggled as she watched him approach as if in a spell. The plan was in action.

Chapter Three

As Officer Gregg hurriedly stripped off his uniform, Tiny watched him in fascination. However, her eyes grew wide in alarm when the tall, masculine, naked man walked toward her. Fear washed over her exposed body, instantly evaporating the alcohol and marijuana out of her system. She began to tremble slightly. Tiny was now a scared, innocent, virgin girl, playing a grown-up game with a very sexual, mature man.

"Hmmm, maybe this wasn't such . . ." her voice trailed off when she felt the heavy weight of Officer Gregg weighing down on her. With her eyes tightly closed, Tiny flinched at the sharp pain that swept through her body, frightened out of her mind. This was no longer a game.

Early the next morning, Tiny dragged her sore body over to Dolly's house. "I did it." Tiny looked at Dolly solemnly.

"Girl, I'm so proud of you!" Dolly replied enthusiastically, oblivious to Tiny's dreary mood. "Welcome to the club." Dolly grinned sheepishly. "You are a grown woman now."

Tiny hung down her head, shame plastered on her face. "I think I made a big mistake, Dolly."

Dolly stared at Tiny. "No, you didn't. You are just feeling that way because it was your first time," she informed her friend. "Things are only going to get better from now on."

Tiny nodded her head, ignoring the feeling of apprehension in her gut. "You are right. Everything will be just fine."

"You better believe it, girl," Dolly replied amusingly, and the two friends high-fived each other. "Sit back, relax, and enjoy the ride."

Tiny did exactly that and what a ride it was. "So, will I see you tomorrow night?" Tiny asked Officer Gregg a few nights later as they both hastily pulled on their clothes after having sex.

"Not tomorrow. My wife and I are having dinner with my in-laws who are visiting from New York."

Tiny pouted like the child she was and sucked her teeth in disappointment.

"Hey, don't be like that." Officer Gregg, now fully clothed in his stiff police uniform, crept up behind her and kissed her lightly on her neck. "I'll see you the day after, and I'll have something special for you as always."

Tiny's eyes gleamed like fireworks, and she smiled in anticipation. After giving her virginity to the dashing policeman almost two months prior, the need to be with him had only intensified with each passing day. So like clockwork the two would meet for their quick, nightly sex encounters in the same classroom in the high school.

For this, Officer Gregg rewarded Tiny with nice gifts and money. Some of the money Tiny hid at home for her move to Kingston; the rest was spent by her and Dolly on weed, alcohol, and skimpy clothes.

Officer Gregg, on the other hand, knew what he was doing was wrong and that he had a lot to lose, including his wife. Also, as an officer of the law, what he was doing went against everything his profession represented, but he couldn't stop himself. Tiny was like a drug, and he was addicted to her. To have such a beautiful, young girl vying for his attention and who wanted to be with him every day was a big boost to his ego. It was almost like he was back in high school, sneaking out of the house to be with his girlfriend.

Aunt Madge watched in horror as her little girl changed for the worse right before her eyes. "What's gotten into you, chile?" she asked Tiny one night when she came home wearing a tight bodysuit and stank of weed. "Where did I go wrong with you?" Tears ran down her face as she looked at her niece trying to act like a woman.

Tiny's eyes welled up as she watched her aunt's small shoulders shake as she cried. She knew her recent behavior went against everything Aunt Madge had taught her, but she was young and having fun. What was the harm in that?

"I'm sorry, Aunt Madge. But I'm just having a good time," Tiny informed her.

"Good time? Is *this* what you call having a good time?" Aunt Madge asked. "I guess you are also going to stop going to school like your partner in crime?"

"No!" Tiny quickly assured her aunt. "I'll never do that, Aunt Madge. I promise."

And Tiny kept her promise. How she did it was a mystery, but she managed to be a good student by day and a hellion by night.

"Remember, what tastes sweet in your mouth burns the belly." This was one of Aunt Madge's frequently used Jamaican proverbs that sliced through Tiny's worried mind a few weeks later. The silence filled every creak and cranny of the pitch-black classroom as Officer Gregg's labored breathing slowly returned to normal.

Tiny felt his body moving away from her, but she quickly wrapped her small arms around his neck and forcibly held on to him. She knew she couldn't allow him to leave until she told him her news. With her eyes tightly closed in fright, Tiny stuttered as she tried to speak, but no words came out. She wished she could take a draw from a strong marijuana spliff right about then. Where was Dolly when she needed her?

Now impatient and frustrated with her actions, Officer Gregg reached up to unclasp her hands from around his neck and was surprised at her strength as Tiny held on.

Still visibly shaking but determined to be heard, in a small but clear voice she whispered softly in his ears, "I think I'm pregnant."

Officer Gregg froze in shock as he saw his entire life flash before his eyes. He was as good as dead, for surely his wife was going to kill him.

"You're *what?*" he shouted. "You *can't* be pregnant. Weren't you on the pill?" he asked.

Tiny looked at him blankly. She had no idea what he was talking about. Dolly didn't tell her anything about any pill.

Officer Gregg stared down at the naïve naked girl under his body and felt sick to his stomach. It had just dawned on him that he had been abusing this young girl for a few weeks now. And to make matters worse, he never took the necessary precaution to protect them both. Now here she was, a child who was going to have a child: his child. But maybe, just maybe, there was a way out of this awful situation.

"You can't have this baby. I'll give you money to go to Kingston and get an abortion. No one has to even know you were pregnant."

Tiny looked at him as if he had lost his mind. Her mother had lost her life to give her life, and she would rather die herself than to kill her baby.

"I am *not* killing my baby," Tiny screamed. Her anger gave her the courage to go against his wishes.

And then it happened.

Officer Gregg snapped and changed into a terrifying animal right before her eyes. In a flash he jumped to his feet, reached over, and grabbed her by the neck, lifting her small naked body like a ragdoll high into the air.

"Oh, yes, you will," he growled. "One or both of you will have to go, some way, somehow, and I am going to make sure of it." Then he began to squeeze the life out of her, literally.

I'm going to die now, Tiny thought as she kicked wildly and scratched at his face. Things had not turned out the way Dolly said they would.

Tiny thought back to the conversation she'd had with Dolly earlier that day.

"Pregnant? Oh my God! Girl, you done hit the jackpot now," Dolly screamed excitedly as she jiggled around her yard. *"I bet he is going to divorce that old goat he is married to and marry you."*

"You think so?" Tiny asked in a small voice. *"I love him so much, Dolly. I know this started out as a plan to get money, but I really do love him."*

"What's love got to do with this? As long as you get the paper, it's all good," Dolly replied.

But Tiny shook her head stubbornly. Without the weed and booze, her naivety shone through like a full moon on a dark night. "I love him," she repeated forcefully. "And he loves me too."

Dolly looked at her and shook her head. Tiny still had a long way to go in this business, but she was a good student and Dolly refused to accept defeat. "Fine, you love him. Listen, tonight you must tell him about the baby. I bet he is going to suggest you move to Kingston until his divorce. As a matter of fact, we can both move as planned. I'll be like y'all's nanny or something." Dolly squealed in excitement. "This is so cool. It will be you and him and me and Big Dread. Hey, maybe we can all be roommates. What do you think?"

Tiny rolled her eyes at Dolly and worriedly chewed on her bottom lip. "So everything will be all right?" she asked Dolly.

"Girlfriend, everything is everything," Dolly said with full conviction.

Not!

As the room spun around and around, Officer Gregg's grip on her neck tightened. Tiny felt light-headed and knew she was about to lose consciousness. Suddenly her head seemed to explode as she was flung roughly into the wall, where she bounced off like a ball before landing facedown on the dirty concrete ground. Pain exploded in every available artery in her body. Choking and coughing, she desperately sucked some much-needed air into her burning lungs. Tears poured from her red eyes as she whimpered weakly, folding her aching body into a protective ball. She wasn't sure why he didn't kill her, but she knew she needed to get away from him quickly before he changed his mind and finished the job. But she was hurting too much and was too weak to move.

Tiny felt her aching head jerk back as Officer Gregg grabbed a handful of hair and snapped her head off the floor. She felt the cold metal of the gun pressing into her neck, and she screamed in terror. "Please, don't kill me," Tiny pleaded. "I'm sorry. Please."

"You better not call my name to anyone!" Officer Gregg screamed into her ringing ears, spit flying out his mouth. "If you do, I *will* come back and kill you. In fact, I will kill your precious Aunt Madge first. You wouldn't want anything to happen to her now, would you?" he threatened.

Tiny shivered in fear.

"Would you?" Officer Gregg growled.

Tiny shook her head and winced at the pain. He waited a few seconds before he loosened his tight hold on her hair and stood up before hurriedly pulling on his clothes.

Officer Gregg then stormed out of the classroom without a backward glance at the wounded young girl he had almost killed. Tiny breathed a sigh of relief after the rackety door slammed shut. Pain she had never known before pierced her body from head to toe, but she found the strength to roll over onto her back, and then into a sitting position. Even her shallow, labored breathing sent arrows of piercing agony through her body, but down on all fours she slowly crawled to an old metal chair close by. Feebly hanging on to its unsteady legs, Tiny painfully stood up and wobbled over to a window that overlooked the tall bushes where he usually parked. Trembling in fear, she peeked outside, noticed his vehicle was gone, and breathed a sigh of relief.

She had no idea how she made it out of the classroom to her house, but Aunt Madge's scream echoed in Tiny's bloated head as she crumbled into her aunt's arms before she lost consciousness.

Aunt Madge whimpered in despair as she lifted Tiny into her small arms. Walking gingerly over to Tiny's twin bed which was directly across the room from hers, she carefully laid her down before dashing into the bathroom. Reaching under the face basin, Aunt Madge quickly grabbed her medicine chest of homemade remedies and medicines before rushing back into the room to attend to Tiny's injuries.

"Tiny? Baby? Come on, sweetie, open your eyes for me." Aunt Madge gently slapped Tiny's bruised cheeks and watched as she blinked her eyes rapidly, before she slowly stole a peek through her swollen left eye.

"Baby, it's me," Aunt Madge whispered. "You're going to be all right." The tears poured down Aunt Madge's face as she sat on the edge of the small metal bed looking down on her niece's bruised body.

"Where are you, Lord? If there is a time that we need you, it's now," Aunt Madge prayed with her hands raised high in the air. "Help us through this trial. Please, I'm begging you."

Tiny cried softly as she watched Aunt Madge praying for her. *I can't let anything happen to her.* Tiny thought to herself. *I have to take this secret to my grave.*

"Tiny. Tiny." Tiny realized Aunt Madge was talking to her. She opened her busted lips to speak, but it was too strenuous, so she allowed the silent tears to speak for her.

"Baby, were you raped?" Aunt Madge asked worriedly but Tiny shook her head. Aunt Madge breathed a sigh of relief. That was one less problem to deal with.

"Sweetheart, I cleaned the wounds with my bay rum and cerasee medicine and applied some heated kerosene oil and gauze," Aunt Madge told Tiny. "Tomorrow I'm going to take you to the clinic for a checkup, then we're going straight to the police station to file a report."

Tiny's eyes grew wide in fright as she shook her head from side to side. "No no no," Tiny murmured in panic.

"What do you mean by no?" Aunt Madge asked puzzled. "You were attacked. We can't let them hooligans get away with it. By the way, do you know who attacked you?"

Again, Tiny's eyes bulged in terror, and she shook her head in distress. She could not afford for Aunt Madge to go to the police because she was attacked by a police officer. He was one of them. They would be on his side. She couldn't win. There was no use . . . no use at all.

The next day Aunt Madge gave in to Tiny's refusal to go seek treatment, telling her aunt she felt okay, that it wasn't that bad. So Aunt Madge applied some more of her home remedy and let Tiny stay in bed. Tiny still refused to go to the police station.

"I bet it was Dolly those people were after and attacked my poor niece in retaliation," Aunt Madge muttered to herself, refusing to accept what Tiny had become. "Maybe Tiny will now stay away from that little she-devil."

And Tiny did, but not for the reason Aunt Madge thought. A few days later, Tiny dragged her still bruised body to Dolly's house, only to be informed by her mother that Dolly had left the day before for Kingston.

"And I hope she never comes back," Dolly's mother said with apparent relief in her voice.

Tiny looked at her with disgust before she walked away. She wasn't sure who she was more upset with . . . Dolly for leaving without even a good-bye or her no-good mother who did not care what happened to her teenage daughter.

Over the next few weeks as Tiny's tummy grew, she used a piece of an old sheet and wrapped it tightly around her swollen belly until it was as flat as a board. She attended school as normal and every afternoon she was home helping Aunt Madge with chores around the house. Aunt Madge was elated to finally have her niece back.

"I wish Dolly all the best wherever she is," Aunt Madge said one morning to herself. "Tiny can now move on with her life, and I won't have to worry so much about her again."

Aunt Madge's words couldn't be further from the truth.

Chapter Four

"Lord, have mercy!" Aunt Madge yelled as she dropped the bucket of water she held in her hand, water splashing everywhere. "Tiny, what is that?" She pointed at Tiny's swollen tummy as if it wasn't obvious.

Aunt Madge was outside when she heard the spatter of water in the bathroom and knew Tiny was having a bath. As it was her turn next, she dipped the big, plastic bucket in the water drum and carefully took it into the bathroom. There she got the shock of her life when Tiny's pregnant belly greeted her at the door.

Tiny's wet body slid down into the bath as she began to sob. "I'm sorry, Aunt Madge," Tiny said. "I'm so sorry that I let you down."

Aunt Madge ran out of the bathroom, horrified.

The roller-coaster ride Tiny had been on for the last five months had literally left her nauseated, light-headed, and drained. She had watched in alarm as her body changed in preparation for motherhood. Not knowing what to do or where to turn, Tiny decided to hide her secret for as long as possible. But not anymore. "Maybe it's for the best that Aunt Madge finds out," Tiny whispered as she looked down on her big stomach. "I can't do this anymore."

Even though she knew she was in a lot of trouble, a sense of relief flooded Tiny's body. She no longer had to tie a sheet around her stomach, enduring the discomfort all day. No more lies, no more secrets. Well, maybe a few secrets . . . like the identity of her baby's father.

Aunt Madge grabbed the light pink sheet from Tiny's small bed as she ran past, wrapping it tightly around her waist before she proceeded outside. This was a practice by the older generation of Jamaican women; to ban their bellies and bawl as an expression of the tremendous grief they bear. With her hands on her head, Aunt Madge marched circles around the yard as she howled like a wounded, rabid dog.

Tiny watched her aunt through the window and cried even harder, her wet body now wrapped in a towel. To see Aunt Madge in so much pain was almost more than she could bear. As Aunt Madge's cries grew louder, so did Tiny's.

Finally, Aunt Madge knelt down on a large rock that pierced at her knees, but her heart was in too much pain to care about physical pain, and she began to pray. "Lord, this is too much for me to deal with," Aunt Madge began. "I done fail that chile there, and now her life is completely over. Please give me the strength, dear God."

As Aunt Madge prayed, a sudden calm washed over her as the Holy Spirit gave her comfort. Suddenly, Jeremiah 1:5 came to her troubled mind. *"Before I formed thee in the belly I knew thee; and before thou camest forth out of the womb I sanctified thee, and I ordained thee a prophet unto the nations."*

"No one is a mistake," Aunt Madge whispered as she digested the verse. "I might not like the way and time this baby was conceived, but God knows best." Slowly Aunt Madge got up off the ground and went back inside the house, where a terrified Tiny was now hiding in the closet.

"Tiny, come out, sweetheart," Aunt Madge said as she sat on the edge of her bed facing Tiny's.

Hearing the love and affection in Aunt Madge's voice, Tiny poked out her head from the closet, her brows knitted in confusion. Tiny saw the warmth in Aunt Madge's eyes and knew although she was disappointed in her, she wasn't going to forsake her.

Tiny quickly exited the closet and took a seat on the bed, facing Aunt Madge, her protruding stomach resting on her lap.

"Who did this?" Aunt Madge asked as she pointed to Tiny's stomach. "Who is the father?"

Tiny's eyes grew wide in fear. "I . . . I . . . I don't know," she lied.

"What do you mean you 'don't know,' Tiny?" Aunt Madge questioned. "Are you afraid of him?" she asked after seeing the fear in her niece's eyes. "Did he threaten you or something?"

Tiny whimpered softly, her eyes tightly closed, shaking her head from side to side. She folded under her lips and refused to say another word.

Aunt Madge gave a big sigh. "I am not happy about this," she began. "And quite frankly, I don't even know how we are going to get through this. But I'm going to trust the Lord." Tiny stared at her apologetically. "It will be hard, but God never makes a mistake."

Tiny jumped off her bed and ran across the room. She hugged her aunt, the only mother she knew. For the first time in months, Tiny began to have some hope.

The next morning as Tiny stared down on her engorged tummy, she knew she could not go back to school. It was an era when pregnant girls were not allowed to stay in school, and Aunt Madge had forbid her to tie down her tummy because it was harmful to the baby. So Tiny stayed hidden at home, missing the last year of high school.

Tiny had also stopped going to church. She did not have the heart to deal with the whispering, the pitiful stares, the tongue-lashing, and the nasty gossip. But most of all, she was scared to see Officer Gregg and ashamed to look at his wife. Tiny was aware that she was the talk of the small town. Aunt Madge was also being labeled as a bad mother, and this put Tiny in a deep depression.

"My niece, please don't listen to what people say about you," Aunt Madge told Tiny one morning before she left for the market. Aunt Madge was a small-time farmer who sold her yams, bananas, sweet potatoes, breadfruits, sweet corn, ackees, oranges, mangoes, and grapefruits at the market in town. "The only opinion that matters is the Lord's." Aunt Madge did everything to get Tiny out of the funk but to no avail. She cooked all her favorite dishes, but even her delicious meals tasted like cardboard to Tiny. She ate just enough for the baby's sake, got very little sleep, and worked around the house from morning to dawn, pushing her swollen body into exhaustion.

The nights ran into days and days into nights, until late one afternoon Tiny's life was interrupted by the sharpest and worst pain she'd ever felt. "Woiee!" she screamed as another pain shook her body. "Lord, have mercy. Aunt Madge, I'm dying." Tiny thrashed her legs around frantically on her bed, her arms waving wildly in the air as one contraction after another assaulted her body. Her thin nightgown clung to her body and was drenched in sweat.

"You are not dying, sweetheart. You'll get through this. Just take deep breaths until I get back," Aunt Madge replied. "I have to run and get Miss Mandy." Miss Mandy was an elderly midwife who had delivered many babies for the women in the community for over three decades.

Tiny watched helplessly as Aunt Madge rushed out the door. She needed her aunt to stay by her side, but she knew she had to get the midwife. They could not afford to go to the hospital.

Across town at the Falmouth Hospital, a dedicated Officer Gregg was with his wife who just also happened to be in labor. The same night that Tiny had told him she was pregnant, when he finally got home, his wife also informed him that she too was pregnant. However, where he had tried to kill his teenage mistress, he lifted his wife high into the air and squealed with happiness. That was very good news . . . unlike Tiny's.

Now, months later, surrounded by her doctor, nurses, and her dedicated husband, Mrs. Gregg was getting ready to give birth to her first child.

Alone at home, Tiny whimpered in pain as another contraction hit. Her frightened eyes stared helplessly into the ceiling as she pleaded for God to take her out of her misery. "Woieee!" Tiny screamed again as she twisted and turned on the small bed, sweat pouring down her face. "I can't take this anymore. Aunt Madge!"

A few minutes later Aunt Madge burst through the door and rushed over to Tiny. Tears filled her eyes as she watched her niece bathe in anguish. Miss Mandy wobbled in after her and went straight to work.

After a few agonizing hours in the small semidark one-bedroom house, little Dupree came into the world at 10:30 p.m. on January 25th, 1979.

And around that same time, on January 25th, Anthony Gregg Jr. was born. There was a big celebration at the hospital by the proud father, the delighted grandparents, relatives, and friends of the newborn.

One mother was elated while the other was tormented. Was this a premonition into the lives of these two innocent children?

Chapter Five

"Waaaaah!" the baby yelled as she kicked her tiny legs in the air. "Waaaaaah!"

"Tiny! Tiny!" Aunt Madge shouted from the outside kitchen. "The baby is crying, chile."

Tiny ignored her as she sat in the yard under the hibiscus trees, staring out into the bushes below the house.

"Tiny, go and feed the baby." Aunt Madge's voice traveled from the kitchen into the yard.

Tiny sucked her teeth loudly and rolled her eyes. With her arms folded around her tummy, she stretched out her legs and nestled her head against the bark of the tree.

Aunt Madge came out of the kitchen as the baby continued to cry and looked at Tiny. "Girl, don't you hear the baby crying?" Aunt Madge asked sternly. "She is hungry and probably needs to be changed."

Tiny continued staring mutely at the bushes without even glancing at her aunt. With a deep sigh, Aunt Madge shook her head and wiped her wet hands on the apron around her waist. Without another word, she turned around and walked up the steps, into the house to attend to the baby. This was fast becoming a regular practice.

It was five days since Baby Dupree was born, and Tiny hadn't touched the baby once. In fact, she totally ignored the child. Aunt Madge could not understand what was going on.

"I think she just needs some time to get used to being a mother," Aunt Madge had said to her good friend, Mother

Sassy, just the day before. "This is a big adjustment for her."

"Hmmm, if you say so," Mother Sassy had replied skeptically. "As far as I can see, there is no bond between Tiny and that baby. She even refused to name her own child."

And that was true. When Aunt Madge had asked Tiny what name she would give the baby, Tiny turned her head away without a response.

"How about Dupree?" Aunt Madge had suggested enthusiastically. "I think that's a very unique and cute name."

Tiny shrugged her shoulders and rolled over on the bed, pulling the sheet over her head.

But Aunt Madge was optimistic. "Everything is done in due time," she said to Mother Sassy. Aunt Madge wondered when that time would be due.

The next day as a weary Aunt Madge walked along the narrow, dirt road to the house, balancing a big basket on her head, the screams of the baby reverberated in the air. That day was the first time she had left Tiny and the baby alone to go to the market. With a deep frown on her face, Aunt Madge quickened her steps. As the baby's cries grew louder, the weariness forgotten, Aunt Madge broke out in a trot. Placing the overloaded basket by the front door, she hurried into the house.

A foul smell assaulted her nostrils as she entered. Aunt Madge quickly walked over to the distressed baby lying in the middle of the small bed and realized the odor was coming from her. "Tiny! Tiny, where are you?" No response. Aunt Madge's eyes scanned the room for Tiny, but she was nowhere to be found.

In record time Aunt Madge changed the baby's diaper and lifted her tiny body into her arms and over her shoulder.

"Shhhh." Aunt Madge rocked the screaming baby gently as she prepared her formula. Tiny had blatantly refused to breast-feed after the baby was born.

"Tiny, you have to breast-feed the baby," Aunt Madge had told her moments after the baby was born. "Not only is breast milk the best, but we really can't afford to buy baby feed." But her words went in one ear and tumbled out the other.

"Okay, my little one, here we go." Aunt Madge sat on the edge of the bed with the baby in the crook of her arms. She placed the bottle into the baby's mouth and the hungry child latched onto it. As Dupree sucked greedily, the tears welled up in Aunt Madge's eyes. She realized that the baby hadn't been changed or fed for the entire day. "I wonder where that girl went leaving the baby alone," Aunt Madge mumbled.

Meanwhile, Tiny sat on top of a huge rock that towered out of the middle of the river. The sound of the running water beat into her troubled mind. Her shoulders shook as she cried uncontrollably.

"I can't do this anymore," Tiny murmured. "I just can't go on like this."

Shortly after Aunt Madge left Tiny alone that morning, the baby began to cry. Tiny took one look at the little, wiggling creature on the bed and shrieked in fright. Right before her eyes, the baby transformed into a monster. Gnashing its long, sharp teeth, the big, bulging, red eyes spun around wildly in its elongated head. The short frog-like legs thrashed around as it snarled at her. Tiny's feet came alive as she fled from the house and down the hill, her eyes wide in terror. Dodging through the bushes and ducking around trees, Tiny ran toward the river. She had to get away from that scary thing.

As if in a trance, Tiny swiftly waded through the waist-high water, the angry strong current pulling at her feet.

Upon reaching the tall, large rock, she slowly clawed her way to the top. With her legs folded under her body, her clothes soaking wet, Tiny shivered as she sobbed. She looked down at the seemingly small trees below and the little houses in the far distance and breathed a sigh of relief. She was safe from the creature.

And there Tiny stayed for the entire day; hungry, agitated, crying, and mumbling to herself.

"Twinkle, twinkle, little star, how I wonder what you are," Aunt Madge sang as she paced the floor, gently rocking the baby in her arms. A few minutes later, she placed the sleeping child on her own bed. As she changed the soiled sheet on Tiny's bed, she kept looking at the doorway, willing Tiny to walk through it. But she did not.

Night fell like a black bedspread over the countryside and Aunt Madge began the worry. She lit the small kerosene oil lamp and waited. With both hands on top of her pounding head, she restlessly paced the small house and prayed fervently.

"Tiny!" Aunt Madge shouted through the opened window into the night. But the only sound she heard was the echo of her own voice. "I have to find her," she muttered. "Please, God, don't let anything happen to her."

Aunt Madge took one look at the sleeping baby before she went and pulled on her shoes sitting at the top of the steps. Softly pulling the door closed, she walked outside into the kitchen. Aunt Madge quickly grabbed the bottle torch she kept in a corner and lit it with a match. The bright flame illuminated the darkness as a strong kerosene scent filled the air.

Peering through the night, Aunt Madge slowly made her way down the hilly terrain that led to the field. One hand held the torch over her head while the other clawed at the bushes to prevent her from falling.

"Tiny!" Aunt Madge screamed over and over as she made her way through the trees that slapped at her face. No response.

Finally, Aunt Madge heard the sound of water and knew she was near the river. She swallowed the lump that rose in her throat as she fearfully made her way toward the running water.

"Tiny! Tiny, where are you?" No response.

Standing at the edge of the river, Aunt Madge held the torch higher over her head, looking around frantically. Suddenly she spotted something up ahead in the middle of the river. Unable to see what it was, she stepped out into the water. Scrambling toward the object, her heart hammering in her chest, she struggled to keep her small body upright against the fast-moving water. As Aunt Madge got closer, a lone figure curled up on top of a towering rock came into her view. It was Tiny.

Relief washed over Aunt Madge. "Baby, come on down," Aunt Madge said gently as she stared up into the haunted eyes of her niece, barely made visible by the lighted torch. "It's going to be okay."

Tiny shook her head and rose unsteadily to her cramped feet. With her arms outstretched at her sides like a pair of wings, her eyes dancing crazily in her aching head, she stepped closer to the edge of the rock.

Aunt Madge gasped. Her heart leaped in her chest. "Tiny. Please don't," Aunt Madge pleaded. "I won't leave the baby with you anymore."

"It's not a baby," Tiny's raspy voice rang out. "I don't want to take care of it." She took another step closer to the edge.

"No! Tiny, please don't do this," Aunt Madge begged. "Please." Aunt Madge glanced down at the shadowy water tugging at her body and shuddered. Beneath her feet and all around her were sharp rocks of various sizes and shapes. Also, the water wasn't deep enough for a dive from that height. If Tiny jumped, she would no doubt break her neck.

"Tiny. Tiny. Listen to me, sweetheart." Aunt Madge edged closer to the foot of the rock, rapidly blinking away the tears that clouded her vision. "Don't jump. Please, I'm begging you, don't do it."

"I can't take care of it." Tiny's voice was a little above a whisper, her vacant eyes still staring out in the distance. "Please, don't make me."

"I won't," Aunt Madge replied. "I'll take care of her."

"You promise?" Tiny asked in a childlike voice, her wide eyes locked with Aunt Madge's terrified ones.

"I promise, baby," Aunt Madge affirmed with a small smile, her free hand extended to Tiny. "Have I ever broken a promise to you?"

Tiny fidgeted as she looked down undecidedly at the outstretched hand.

Aunt Madge's legs trembled as she waited nervously. "Please, God, don't let her hurt herself," Aunt Madge prayed softly under her breath. "Please, bring her down safely."

A few agonizing seconds went by before Tiny slowly crawled down the rock, landing with a small splash in front of Aunt Madge. Instantly Aunt Madge's arm reached out and pulled Tiny in a tight embrace, crushing her shivering body to hers.

"Thank you, Lord," Aunt Madge said. "Thank you." Tiny's warm tears wet her neck as they stood in the middle of the river crying.

"Aunt Madge." Tiny pulled away slightly from her aunt to look into her eyes. "Do you know that thing is not really a baby?" she whispered as if she was revealing some classified secret. "It's an alien that's trying to kill me."

Aunt Madge's mouth popped wide open. She saw the crazy look in Tiny's eyes and became alarmed. "What?" Aunt Madge squeaked, her breathing labored as she took deep gulps of cool air.

"Yes." Tiny leaned in closer to Aunt Madge's ear. "As soon as you left for the market this morning, it tried to eat me."

"It did what?" Aunt Madge croaked.

"Oh, yes. Don't you see, Aunt Madge? It's going to kill us. I think we better kill it, before it kills us," Tiny said.

"The devil is lie!" Aunt Madge exclaimed. "Sweetheart, don't you go anywhere near the baby . . . hmmm . . . it. Remember the Bible says thou shall not kill. You get it?"

Tiny nodded absently as if in a stupor.

"Come on, baby." Aunt Madge took ahold of Tiny's hand, and together they wobbled out of the water onto the riverbank. Wearily, they walked back home.

"The poor chile is acting crazy because she is not taking good care of herself," Aunt Madge said to herself later that night after Tiny went to bed. "I have to make sure she gets more rest and eats proper food."

With the problem diagnosed and a treatment plan decided on, Aunt Madge felt a little lighter in her spirit. But two days later, exactly a week after Baby Dupree was born, Aunt Madge found out that her prognosis wasn't a good one.

Chapter Six

Tiny shivered slightly as she sat in the back of the bus staring out the dirty glass window. Clutching her knapsack close to her chest, she watched the trees and houses dash by as the bus zipped toward Kingston City.

Earlier that morning, Aunt Madge had taken the scary little creature to Mother Sassy's before she left to plant yams in the field. True to her word, Aunt Madge never asked Tiny to tend to the baby again. Instead, she made arrangements for Mother Sassy to care for the baby when she was at work.

Soon after Aunt Madge left, Tiny withdrew her knapsack from under the bed where it was hidden. Yanking the zipper open, she reached in and pulled out a wad of money. It was the money that she had saved from her affair with Officer Gregg. This was to have taken her away from the country to an exciting life in Kingston, but that was before she got pregnant.

Tiny's mind flashed to her old friend Dolly. "I wonder if Dolly is still acting in Kingston," Tiny said aloud. Suddenly a plan began to formulate in her mind. Tiny giggled excitedly. She hurriedly stuffed a few pieces of clothes and other personal items into her bag and in a few minutes she was ready to begin her new life. But first she had to make a stop.

As Tiny took slow, calculated steps up the long driveway, she barely glanced at the beautiful flowers and manicured trees along the way. Her sobered eyes stayed locked on the huge, magnificent house looming before her. "I have to do this," Tiny repeated over and over. "Aunt Madge is going to need some help with the little, scary creature."

Still unsure but fully determined, Tiny walked up the steps to the huge mahogany door. She knocked and waited, nervously wringing her hands together. Not getting a response, she knocked harder as an unexpected wave of anger invaded her body. "So you are going to kill me, huh? We have nothing while you and your wife have everything," Tiny muttered furiously.

Suddenly the door opened and a smiling Mrs. Gregg stood before Tiny with her little bundle of joy in her arms. "Hello. May I help you?" she asked Tiny pleasantly as she gently rocked the baby.

Tiny's mouth opened to speak, but no words came out. Puzzled, Mrs. Gregg stared at the young lady standing before her. She vaguely remembered Tiny from church and wondered what she was doing at her front door.

"He said if I told anyone that he is the baby's father that he would kill me and my aunt," Tiny said quietly as she stared unblinkingly at the beautiful woman before her.

"Excuse me?" Mrs. Gregg was perplexed. "What are you talking about?"

"Please, I'm begging you, talk to him. Aunt Madge is going to need some help with the creature. Hmmm, I mean the baby."

Mrs. Gregg's eyes widened as the impact of Tiny's words slammed into her gut. "Little girl, are you saying that you have a baby and *my* husband is the father?" she asked.

Tiny nodded her head and looked down at the floor. The courage she felt a few seconds ago was slowly creeping away. "I'm sorry for everything," Tiny mumbled, her eyes still fixated on the floor.

"You *are* sorry! Look at me when I'm speaking to you, little girl!" Mrs. Gregg screamed.

Awakened by his mother's loud voice, the frightened baby began to cry. But Mrs. Gregg was too angry to tend to him right then. "Now listen to me and listen carefully." Mrs. Gregg took a few calculated steps toward Tiny, and the terrified girl stepped back in fright. "Take your bastard child and go and find the idiot who knocked you up. Leave me and my family alone." Her face became ugly with anger and hatred as she continued on her warpath. "If you ever go around spreading these lies about my husband, *I* will be the one to have you and your aunt killed!"

Tiny whimpered in fear. She turned away from the livid woman and quickly ran down the steps into the yard. Taking a frightened glance over her shoulder, Tiny screamed, her enlarged eyes glued to the big clay flowerpot flying at her head. Ducking in time, it zoomed by her, smashing in pieces near her feet. "Help!" Tiny yelled as she dodged another flowerpot that exploded in front of her.

"Help?" Mrs. Gregg shouted furiously. "You need help, huh? I got something for you." With the shrieking baby draped over her shoulder, she grabbed another flowerpot with only one hand. Bitterness poured from her eyes as she took another shot at Tiny, hoping to have a better aim this time.

Tiny was yelling and hopping over sharp pieces of flowerpot as she tried to make a getaway. Constantly looking over her shoulder, she finally made it to the walkway where she sprinted away from the house and the pissed-off woman as fast as her legs could go.

By the time Tiny got into town, her blouse was soaking wet with perspiration. Huffing and puffing, she bent over with her hands on her knees, sucking deep breaths in her exhausted lungs. Now there was no doubt in her mind that she had to leave the community and she could not return. She knew if Officer Gregg did not get her first, then surely his crazy wife would.

Tiny hopped on to the next bus heading for Kingston and went and sat in the far back with her head held low. She did not want anyone who knew her or Aunt Madge to see her. Luckily for her the bus filled up quickly with passengers and in less than ten minutes she was moving away from a haunted life . . . and unbeknown to her . . . into a hellish nightmare.

Chapter Seven

The bus zoomed into the noisy bus terminal in downtown Kingston. Tiny stared wide-eyed through the window at the craziness outside and began whimpering in fear. It was her first time in the big city. "Maybe I made a mistake," she whispered fearfully. "But I can't go back home. Officer Gregg or his wife will kill me if I do."

"Lady, are you getting off the bus or coming with us to the garage?" the conductor shouted at Tiny.

As if coming out of a trance, Tiny looked around the bus and realized she was the only one left on it. Slowly she made her way down the aisle and stiffly stepped off the bus, clutching her knapsack to her chest.

Her bright eyes expanded even more when she saw the hundreds of people rushing about in every direction, the loud animated voices ricocheting in her head. Tiny placed a hand on her forehead where a massive headache was brewing.

"*Beeeeppppp!*" Tiny jumped back in fright as the side of a fast-moving buggy car swiped by her leg.

"Get out of the road, fool," the rude driver shouted at her before plunging on ahead, his hand planted firmly on his horn causing numerous people to jump out of the way to avoid being run over.

Tiny stood on the pavement trembling in disbelief. "But I wasn't in the road," she said to herself. "I was standing on the sidewalk." But she would soon realize that no one cared. It was every man for himself.

Still visibly shaken, Tiny asked a passerby for directions to the Ward Theatre and hurried off down North Parade to find Dolly. *Wait until Dolly sees me,* Tiny pondered. *She's going to be so surprised.*

Soon Tiny stood outside the huge doors of the big, white building of the Ward Theatre, staring up at the symbol of Jamaica's rich cultural heritage in awe.

"May I help you, ma'am?"

Tiny turned around and noticed a short man standing a few inches away from her. He had a mop and a plastic bucket in his hands.

"Yes," Tiny replied and walked closer to him. "I'm looking for my friend who works here."

"Well, the theatre is closed to the public today," the man informed her.

"What?" Tiny felt her stomach drop. She hung her head, wondering what she was going to do then.

"The casting director is inside working." The man's voice snapped back Tiny's attention to him. "He's been working here for over twenty years. I'll get him for you. Maybe he knows your friend."

"Thank you so much," Tiny replied with relief in her voice. "I'll wait here for him."

The maintenance worker hurried through a side door, disappearing from Tiny's sight. Moments later he returned with a tall, light-skinned, distinguished-looking man.

"Hello, I'm Mr. Edison," the man introduced himself to Tiny. "How may I help you?"

"Hi. My name is Tiny, and I'm looking for my friend, Dolly Bell," she said as she stared at him anxiously.

"Hello, my name is Dolly Bell, but I'm fabulously known as Rockin' Dolly. And I am about to become your biggest star ever," Mr. Edison mimicked Dolly. He flung his arms in the air dramatically, spun around, then posed with his hands on his waist.

Tiny threw her head back and laughed out loud. "Yup, that's Dolly," she said with a deep sigh of relief. "When is she coming to work?"

"Well, she doesn't work here. In fact, she never did," the casting director informed Tiny. "After her audition I suggested she take some acting lessons and come back in a few months. But, of course, she wanted to star in her own play right then. So she stormed out of the auditorium in anger."

Tiny stared at him with her mouth wide opened. Dolly was not working there? Lord have mercy on her now.

"But I did see her a few days ago," Mr. Edison added.

"Really? Where?" Tiny's face lit up. There was some hope after all.

"My cousin was visiting from Westmoreland and I took him to a club in New Kingston." Mr. Edison looked away from Tiny, his face flushed. "Hmmm, Rockin' Dolly works there."

"Yes! Thank you, sir," Tiny said excitedly. "Can you please tell me how to get there?"

"Sure. Wait here and I'll go and write down the address for you," he replied before walking off. He came back shortly and handed Tiny a piece of paper. "The club opens around eight p.m.," he told her. "The buses are over there, across the park." He pointed with his index finger. Tiny turned around and looked in that direction. "Tell the conductor that you are going to New Kingston. He'll let you know when you reach your stop."

"Thank you very much, sir." Tiny had a big smile on her face. "I'm going to surprise her."

"I bet she will," Mr. Edison mumbled before he walked back inside the theatre.

She waved good-bye to the kind maintenance man who was trimming some trees at the side of the theatre before she skipped away.

Tiny decided to do some sightseeing around Parade before heading to New Kingston. The bar wouldn't open until later that night anyway. Weaving around carts of roast corn and jerk chicken, Tiny stopped by some vendor's stalls with jeans pants, colorful blouses, fancy dresses, shirts, and fashionable shoes. As she licked an ice-cream cone, Tiny looked on in fascination, her face tinted with excitement and curiosity.

Walking past the shops, restaurants, and stores, Tiny stared in amazement when she came to the two-story building which was Jamaica's Supreme Court. "Wow, this is awesome," Tiny said in a low voice. "I think I'm going to love Kingston."

Downtown Kingston was a huge part of the Jamaican economy. As Tiny stared up at the old high-rise buildings that rose up in the sky, she purred in pleasure. The streets were crammed with hardware and wholesale stores filled with anxious, screaming, shoving consumers while the buses and cars narrowly navigated their way around the masses in the marketplace.

Sitting in the middle of the chaos is the famous Victoria Park. This was in honor of Queen Victoria of England. Tiny remembered reading about this park in a book that Dolly had lent her, and she grinned in excitement as she looked up at the statue of Her Majesty Queen Victoria.

As she wandered around the huge park, Tiny gasped at its beautiful landscape, which included a wide variety of flowering plants and trees such as the royal palm, the lignum vitae, and the national tree of Jamaica, the Blue Mahoe. Nature lovers fanned out everywhere while small kids ran around playing. Everyone was enjoying the park, including Tiny. She found a cool place under a big tree. Lying on her back in the grass, she closed her eyes contentedly. A few minutes later she was sound asleep.

Tiny's stomach grumbled in protest as the hunger kicked in. Slowly opening her eyes, she stretched her hands over her head and yawned. Night had fallen, and it was dark under the tree where she slept. Moving her body into a sitting position, Tiny glanced around and noticed that the park was almost empty. The dim light from the few working street lamps scattered around fought against the darkness as the large trees now cast eerie shadows on the ground. It was a huge contrast to the scenes earlier that day.

Reaching out her hand to the side, Tiny fumbled around for her bag but felt nothing. Alarmed, she jumped to her feet and frantically looked around, but there was no bag. She closed her eyes and took a deep breath. Surely her mind was playing tricks on her! She opened her eyes and looked down at her feet again, but the bag wasn't there.

In a panic, Tiny ran around the park hysterically searching for the bag. Tears ran down her face as she looked under trees, crawled under benches, dug down in Dumpsters, felt around in the grass, and checked behind the fountain walls, but there was no bag. The bag was gone.

Exhausted, Tiny sat on a bench and wept. All her money and clothes were in the bag. Now she had nothing. Her stomach grumbled again, and Tiny felt a cramp in the bottom of her tummy. *What am I going to do?* she wondered. She had only planned on getting some rest before taking a bus to New Kingston to look for Dolly. Instead, she had fallen asleep for hours while someone stole her bag.

Tiny got up and sluggishly walked out of the park into the street. Wandering around, she noticed a handful of buses and a few cars while the shutters of most of the businesses were closed. The crowd from earlier was gone, and the few people remaining were packing up to go home.

As Tiny dragged herself up the street, she passed a small car parked by the side of the road. The left front door was open, and a man dressed in all-white stood in front of it.

"Hello, beautiful. How ya doing?" the animated driver asked, a toothpick dangling from the corner of his mouth.

Tiny paused, shrugged her shoulders, then walked away.

"Wait!" the man shouted at her back. "Hold on a minute."

Tiny stopped and turned a long sad face to the man, her teeth gnawing away at her bottom lip.

"What's the matter, baby?" the man asked. "Come here. Tell me what's going on."

Tiny took a few steps toward the man. She had no money and needed a ride to get to Dolly. Maybe this kind gentleman would help her. "Someone stole my bag in the park with all my money. Now I don't know how I'm going to get to my friend in New Kingston," Tiny said solemnly.

The man noticed the look of despair on Tiny's face and instantly his face lit up. "Maybe we can work out a little something," he said to her, licking his lips as his hungry eyes roamed over her body. "A beautiful girl like you will have no problem getting a ride."

Tiny looked at him horrified as it dawned on her what he was implying. "Are you suggesting that I sleep with you in exchange for a ride?"

"Listen, baby." The man leaned his back against the car. He crossed his ankles and folded his arms. "It's obvious you have no money. You have something I want, and I have something you need. Yeah, exchange is no robbery." Grabbing his crotch, he winked at Tiny.

Tiny's mouth popped open in shock. Without another word she turned and hurried away, the man's mocking laughter trailing after her.

Once again in the park, Tiny sat on a bench squeezing her legs together. Her full bladder wasn't cooperating. Unable to hold it any longer, she crept behind a tree and sheepishly looked around. Bending down, she quickly relieved herself and hurried away. After a while, Tiny sat in the grass, her back against a tree. This one was directly under a street lamp, but it gave her little comfort. She noticed a homeless man sleeping on a bench across from her and another a few feet away under a dark tree. At least she wasn't alone. "I'll just stay here until morning," Tiny said aloud. "Tomorrow, I'll ask someone for directions and walk to the club to find Dolly. Then everything will be all right."

As the hunger pain slammed into Tiny's body, she ignored it as her mind flashed back on Aunt Madge. Tears welled up in her eyes. "I love you, Aunt Madge," Tiny whispered. "Please forgive me, but I just had to get away."

Chapter Eight

Back in Falmouth, Aunt Madge was on her knees by Tiny's empty bed praying. "Dear God, I place my little girl into your capable hands. It's a cruel world out there, Lord. But I know with you watching over her, Tiny will be all right. Please bring my baby back home to me safe and sound. I decree and declare that the devil shall not hurt a single strand of hair on her head. In your holy and mighty name I pray. Amen."

Aunt Madge held onto the bed and pulled herself up off her knees. Feeling tired and drained, she went and sat on a small three-legged stool by the window, staring out into the black night, her mind consumed with Tiny.

"So where in Kingston is Tiny going?" a church sister had asked Aunt Madge earlier that day in the market.

"Kingston? What are you talking about?" Aunt Madge responded as she weighed out the yam for the woman.

"I just seen Tiny take off on a bus heading for Kingston."

The yam fell from Aunt Madge's hand. "What? You must be mistaken," Aunt Madge replied nervously as she searched the woman's eyes, pleadingly. "Tiny is home getting her rest."

"No, ma'am. I know Tiny since she was a baby, and it was her on that bus." The woman saw the shocked look on Aunt Madge's face and realized she didn't know about Tiny's little trip. "Sister Madge, I'm so sorry. I thought you knew."

Aunt Madge felt her feet wobble. Worry etched across her face as she quickly lowered herself onto the stool by her stall. Where was Tiny going in Kingston? Who was she going to? Was she coming back?

"Are you okay?" the woman asked Aunt Madge with concern. "Can I get you anything?"

Aunt Madge shook her head and shakily rose to her feet. Without a word, she grabbed another piece of yam off the stall and handed it to the woman, waving away the money she held out to her.

As if in daze, Aunt Madge cleared off her little stall, packing away everything in the big straw basket. Rapidly blinking away the tears, she hoisted the heavy basket on her head before walking away from the market in distress.

Shortly thereafter, Aunt Madge arrived home. Leaving the basket at the top of the steps, she hurried inside the house. She still held some hope that her church sister was wrong. After all, it had been said that everyone has a double somewhere out there.

"Tiny! Tiny!" Aunt Madge shouted, down on all four looking under the beds. "Where are you, Tiny?" she cried as she looked behind the doors. "Baby, are you in here?" she said as she searched in the bathroom. But the house was empty.

Still not giving up, Aunt Madge ran back outside. Dashing into the kitchen, she looked around anxiously. No sign of Tiny.

Dear God, maybe she went back to the river, Aunt Madge thought. A lump the size of a baseball rose in her throat. Coughing and wheezing, Aunt Madge bent over, sucking deep breaths into her lungs as she struggled to breathe. Composing herself, she headed for the river.

"Please, God. Don't let Tiny do anything foolish," Aunt Madge prayed as she slipped and slid down the rough trail, grabbing at the tall grass on either side of her to prevent a fall. Walking quickly through the field, fear oozing through every pore, she headed toward the sound of running water.

The hot Jamaican sun kissed her face as she stood at the edge of the river. Using her hand to shield her eyes, Aunt Madge peered across the water where the huge, tall rock loomed into the sky, unoccupied. It looked as if Tiny had indeed left for Kingston. But although her mind was confirming the obvious, Aunt Madge's heart refused to accept it.

"Tiny! Baby, where are you?" Aunt Madge chanted as she walked the riverbed. Looking behind trees, in deep ravines, around big rocks, in tall grass along the riverbank, she searched for Tiny. Traveling east, west, north, south, mile after mile, Aunt Madge combed the surrounding area. But no sign of Tiny.

A little over an hour later, totally exhausted, Aunt Madge slumped down on a rock, her aching, swollen feet stretched out in front of her. She now knew in her heart that Tiny had really left. It was then that the floodgates opened. Aunt Madge rested her throbbing head in her hands resting in her lap and bawled. Deep, wrenching sobs vibrated through her entire body.

Tiny was gone. It was like an echo in Aunt Madge's brain as she slowly walked back home. Her little girl had done run away.

Aunt Madge was still crying when Mother Sassy brought home Baby Dupree later than evening. "She's gone," Aunt Madge informed her longtime friend as she took the baby from Mother Sassy's arms. "Tiny ran off to Kingston."

Mother Sassy wrapped her arm around her friend's shoulder and the women cried together. A few minutes later, they prayed together before Mother Sassy left to go home.

"Looks like it's just you and me now," Aunt Madge said to the baby that night as she rocked her to sleep. "But I will never stop praying until your mother comes home."

And praying she did. Aunt Madge pounded on heaven's door, beseeching the Lord to send guardian angels to watch over Tiny. Unbeknownst to her, Tiny would need all the protection she could get. She was a little guppy swimming in a pool of sharks.

Chapter Nine

Tiny's head dipped. Alarmed she sprang awake, her eyes scanning her surroundings suspiciously. After receiving the indecent proposal from the rude man, her radar was up. She couldn't afford to fall asleep. She had to stay awake until daylight.

It was the wee hours of the night. The park was dark and eerily silent. Tiny spotted a few more homeless people scattered around on benches and under the trees. Taking a deep breath, she slowly allowed her body to relax.

Yawning, she rolled over on her side, the grass tickling her face. With her head cushioned by her hands tucked under her neck, she stretched out her long legs and stared into the night. A smile crept up on her face as she thought about seeing her friend, Dolly, again after all these months. Yes, tomorrow everything would be all right.

Tiny's head nodded again. Blinking her eyes rapidly, she struggled to stay awake. Through tired, slanted eyes she peeped at the trees in her blurry vision. Her chest rose and fell rhythmically. Soon, long eyelashes draped closed over droopy eyes, and Tiny fell into a deep sleep.

Moments later, her eyes popped opened and widened in terror at the faces looming above her. A scream started in her throat but was muffled by the huge hand covering her mouth. She tried to move her arms, but they were pinned to her side. Desperately, she tried to kick her legs, but they wouldn't move. She attempted to twist her body but could barely move. Tiny was pinned down to the ground.

Helpless, the tears leaked down the side of her eyes, wetting her neck before disappearing in the grass behind her body.

"Well, well, well. What do we have here?" the menacing voice boomed in Tiny's ear. "I think Santa is a little early this year." A chorus of harsh laughter rang out into the night. A cold chill ran down Tiny's spine.

Visibly shuddering, her panic intensified, again, Tiny tried to move her body, but to no avail.

"Relax!" the command echoed in her ear. "You give us a hard time, and I'll put a bullet in your skull. Understand?"

But Tiny writhed even more. Twisting this way, turning that way, she felt her body loosen a little against the human restraints. A burst of energy washed over her, and she kicked out her right leg, making contact with something soft. Angry expletives reverberated in the air.

Baff! A hard fist connected with Tiny's left eye, snapping her head further back into the grass. Pain exploded in her head as she thrashed wildly in the grass. Arms frantically tried to hold her. But she bit into the hand over her mouth and screamed in terror.

Tiny was slapped repeatedly. Her face was on fire. Undeterred, like a wildcat, she clawed and yelled. "Help! Help! Somebody, help me!"

Then the scream lodged in her throat. The heel of a hard boot clamped down on her windpipe. Pressing and crushing. Blows and kicks rained all over Tiny's body from every direction. Whimpering in agony, she closed her eyes, finally welcoming the big black spread that came down and covered her. Tiny slipped into unconsciousness.

Aunt Madge woke up gasping for breath. Cold sweat washed her from head to toe. Her nightgown clung to her body. Glancing across the room, her eyes fell on Tiny's empty bed and her eyes were instantly filled with tears. Slowly she pulled her body away from the baby who was curled up asleep at her side. Placing one foot on the floor, then another, she stood up and tiptoed over to Tiny's bed.

Something wasn't right. Aunt Madge felt it down to her bone. Kneeling by the bed, she began to pray again for Tiny.

Pain ripped through Tiny's body. Moaning, she sluggishly opened her eyes but only one gave her a blurry vision of a mocking face before her. The other was swollen shut.

"Welcome back," said the cold voice in her ear. "I thought we lost you there for a minute."

Whipping her head to the left, then right, Tiny saw that her hands were pinned to the ground by two men. Horrified, she looked down at her feet that were spread apart and pinned down by two other men. A feeling of dread filled her body. "Please. Please don't hurt me," Tiny whispered through dried, cracked lips. "Please."

"Oh, we don't want to hurt you, baby," said the cold voice again. He was obviously the leader of the group. "Not if you cooperate with me and my boys."

"What do you want?"Tiny asked. She refused to acknowledge the obvious. "I don't have any money. Someone stole my bag earlier today."

"Looks like you are having a bad day," the leader teased. "Luckily, we are here to make it better for you."

Their sinister laughter echoed throughout the park. Tiny closed her eye against the tears that leaked down her face. Hope was rapidly slithering away.

I'm sorry, Aunt Madge, Tiny thought. *I didn't know it would end like this.*

Tiny's eye popped open when she felt something wet running down her cheek. Bile rose up in her throat as the gang leader swiped his slimy tongue across her lips. She turned her head away. Angrily, he grabbed her face and spun it back toward him.

"I don't want to hurt you." Spit tickled her face. "But I will if I have to." His bad breath filled Tiny's nostrils and she gagged.

His rough hands grabbed her breasts and squeezed hard. Tiny let out a loud scream before his hand covered her mouth. Struggling against the human restraints, Tiny was unable to move as the other four men held her down. Breast milk soaked through her bra and wet the front of her thin blouse.

"Well, what do we have here?" The gang leader's eyes lit up as he grinned in appreciation. With one hand still covering her mouth, the other hand pulled a pocketknife from his waistband. Leisurely, he ran the knife down Tiny's face, across her throat, then over her breasts.

Tiny sniveled in fear. She tried to plead with her attackers, but her words were muffled.

The sharp blade of the knife sliced Tiny's blouse opened. Shortly after, she felt a small breeze fanning against her exposed breasts as her bra was cut away. Eager hands kneaded her sensitive breasts.

"No!" Tiny shouted in her head, straining against the hold on her body but to no avail.

The gang members chuckled and jeered as they eagerly watched their boss. As customary, he would get the first go at Tiny before she was passed on to them.

Next, Tiny's jeans were cut away from her body. Tiny tried kicking her legs, but they anticipated that move and held her firm. Poor Tiny was no match for these five strong men.

The knife continued its journey as it moved up her legs. Seconds later, her panties dropped at her side. Except for the pair of sneakers on her feet, Tiny was naked.

"Wicked! *That's* what I'm talking about," the gang leader yelled. His eyes grew big as they feasted on Tiny's nude body. "Boys, we done hit the jackpot tonight."

Humiliated, with her eyes tightly closed, Tiny prepared for the worst.

"Turn her over," the leader commanded.

Tiny was flipped over like a pancake. Her buttocks were up with her face kissing the grass.

Someone slapped her hard on her bottom, and Tiny wailed like a wounded animal. Then Tiny felt her legs pulled even further apart, before a hard, smelly body was on her back. "Help!" Tiny shouted before the hand was clamped over her mouth.

"Just relax, baby." The foul breath fanned her face as he slipped a hand under Tiny's hip, raising her bottom higher in the air.

Tiny felt the man's aroused body brush against her bare bottom and she knew she was about to be gang-raped and killed right there.

This was it.

Chapter Ten

Suddenly the sky exploded with what sounded like thunderous fireworks. The guns sang hoarsely. The loud sound resonated into the air. The ground rattled. "What the heck?" said the gang leader lying on top of Tiny before he jumped to his feet. Almost tripping over his pants wrapped around his ankles, he hurriedly pulled them up to his waist. Lunging for his 9 mm gun that lay in the grass at his feet, he ran and ducked behind a bench close by.

Almost simultaneously, his boys let go of Tiny's legs and arms. Alarmed, they too grabbed their guns and ran to take cover behind some dark trees, returning fire.

Tiny squealed out in fright. She covered her ringing ears with her hands but was too paralyzed to move. Her mind was stuck on feeling the private parts of the man pressing against her own nude body. Just as he was about to rape her, the shots rang out. Tiny didn't know who was shooting or why, but they had obviously saved her from being raped.

Unbeknown to Tiny, as soon as the gang of thugs entered the park that night, most of the homeless people grabbed their meager belongings and carts and fled. They knew trouble was brewing and wanted nothing to do with it. Except one man, who hid behind a tree and watched as Tiny was attacked. Horrified, he sneaked away and ran out to the main road, looking up and down the street for the police who sometimes patrolled the area.

Minutes went by and he saw no one. The homeless man knew Tiny didn't have much time, and he by himself was unable to help her. Still wandering the nearby streets, he refused to give up as he looked for help.

Suddenly the lights of a car turned a corner up ahead. He ran toward it and breathed a sigh of relief as the police car came toward him. Waving his hands wildly in the air, he flagged down the car that stopped at his feet.

"What's the matter, man?" one of the police officers asked.

"A girl is being attacked in the park," the homeless man informed the officers. "The men have guns. I think they're going to rape and kill her."

"Officers requesting backup at Williams Park, downtown!" the other police officer shouted over his radio. "Woman is being attacked. Men are armed and dangerous."

Pulling off at lightning speed, the car hugged the curb and disappeared toward the park. The homeless man wandered in the other direction, hoping they would make it in time to save the nice-looking young girl.

Police officers fanned out over the park with guns drawn. Dodging from tree to tree, they cautiously looked around for the area where the attack was taking place. Soon one of them saw a girl being held down by four men, while another man dropped his pants, fully exposing himself.

The officer ran back to a safe distance and relayed the location to the other police officers. Quickly they surrounded the gang members, blocking them in.

Laughing and giggling, the gang was unaware that they were being watched by the police. The anticipation of raping Tiny filled their thoughts and mind. The police officers watched as the gang leader got on top of a helpless Tiny. Then one of the police officers fired a warning shot in the air. Soon his colleagues were doing the same.

Scrambling for cover, the surprised gang members returned fire at the police, and a gun war between the two groups ensued.

A bullet whizzed by Tiny's head. Trembling in fright, she rolled over to her side and glanced around but saw nobody. Getting up on all fours, Tiny crept alongside a row of trees, her head hanging low. Shortly after, she peeked up and saw the side exit of the park leading to the main road. If only she could make it to the road.

Rapid gunfire filled the air. The hair on Tiny's head stood up straight when someone howled in pain. "Lord, please protect me," Tiny said aloud as she dashed from the park. Bolting through the opened exit, she took off down Kings Street naked as a jaybird.

Zooming past closed stores and businesses, Tiny continued running for her life. Her breasts flapped heavily against her chest, breast milk seeping down her body. Fear splashed across her face like a neon light. Inhaling deeply and exhaling loudly, Tiny didn't let up until she came to a small community of tiny board and zinc-fenced houses.

Panting like a dog in the middle of the street, Tiny bent over with her hands resting on her knees, sucking air into her starved, burning lungs. A few minutes passed before she stood up and checked out the area. She saw no sign of any human life. Walking slowly along the side of the semidarken streets, her hands covering her breasts, Tiny was conscious of her nakedness. "What am I going to do now?" she whispered as she looked around in fright.

Pop! Pop! Tiny dived through an opening in the zinc fence closest to her, landing facedown in the dirt. With her hands over her head, she whimpered, fearing her attackers had tracked her down.

Soon the distinctive sound of a car came rolling by her. The car backfired as it zipped down the street. Shaken, Tiny took a deep breath before hesitantly getting to her feet.

Dusting dirt from her face and the front of her body, she glanced around, noticing that she was in the backyard of a small house. Running from an ackee tree at one end of the yard to a mango tree at the other end, was a clothesline. Hanging on the line was freshly washed clothes. Tiny burst out in tears but quickly bit her lips. Either the house occupants were out at the time or they were sleeping. In any case, she didn't want to be seen.

Moving like a shadow in the night, Tiny approached the clothes hanging on the line. She noticed some men's trousers, shirts, and shorts. Her eyes then landed on some women's dresses a few inches away. Silently, she reached up and pulled off one of the dresses. The clothespins fell to the ground at her feet. Walking along the clotheslines she looked for some underwear but saw nothing. Tiny went back and took off a pair of men's shorts from the clothesline.

Slipping the dress over her head, it fell a little above her knees. Tiny then pulled on the shorts. The elastic waistband surprisingly fit her small frame. Out of nowhere her mind flashed back on a popular Bible verse that Aunt Madge recited frequently, First Chronicles 16:34, "O give thanks unto the Lord; for he is good; for his mercy endureth for ever."

Chapter Eleven

Feeling a little better now that she had some clothes on, Tiny skulked around the side of the house. The roof of the neighboring house provided a dark silhouette which looked safe enough to hide until daylight.

Sitting with her back against the outer frame of the house, her chin resting on her bended knees, Tiny closed her eyes. Her tummy growled, but she ignored it. Before long, the night's activities caught up with her and Tiny nodded off.

"Good morning, Jamaica! Thank you for tuning in to the Jamaica Broadcasting Corporation. This is JBC, your favorite radio station."

Tiny's head jerked up in alarm at the DJ's voice that came through an open window above her head. Wincing at the crick pain in her neck, she used her right hand to massage it. It was daylight. The beautiful rays from the sun could be seen over the top of the trees in the distance. It was also time to go before she was discovered. Obviously, someone was awake inside the house.

Tiny tiptoed to the backyard. Scanning the area, she saw no one. Silently, she made her way back to the opening in the fence that she had jumped through. Squeezing her body through the tight space, she found herself on the sidewalk.

The street was now bustling with activities unlike a few hours ago. Vendors rushed their carts loaded down with goods toward the Parade market. Vehicles zoomed up and down the road, and small businesses were opening their shutters.

"Good morning," Tiny said to a kind-faced woman who was passing by. "Can you please tell me how to get to New Kingston from here?"

"Oh, dear Lord. Are you okay?" the woman asked as her eyes ran over Tiny's bruised face in alarm. "What happened to you, baby? Do you want me to take you to the hospital? Want me to go and get the police?" She fired one question after the other at Tiny.

"No no no," Tiny said quickly, shaking her head. "It looks worse than it is. Really, I'm fine." She looked at the woman with one bloodshot eye, the other was partially closed.

"You don't look fine to me," the woman pressed on. As a mother of five daughters, her motherly instinct refused to drop the issue. "I think you need medical attention."

But Tiny shook her head and turned to walk away.

"Okay, okay," the woman's voice stopped her. "New Kingston is a little distance away. You will need to take the bus."

"Oh, I can walk," Tiny said. "It won't be a problem."

The woman looked Tiny up and down. Her eyes narrowed as she began to put the pieces together. "You are not from around here," the woman noted. "Where are you from?"

"Trelawny," Tiny mumbled as tears filled her eyes. She looked away from the woman.

"Sweetheart, look at me," the woman said. Her brows were knitted with concern as her eyes met Tiny's. "Please go back home. This is no place for a beautiful, innocent, country girl like you."

"I can't go back," Tiny whispered. "They are going to hurt my aunt if I do."

"Come on." The woman grabbed Tiny's hand. "I'm taking you to the police station. You are going to tell them who threatened your aunt and why you had to run away from your home."

"No!" Tiny's voice was laced with panic. She pulled her hand out of the woman's. "Please. I just need to get to my friend who works in New Kingston."

"Fine. What does your friend do?" the woman asked skeptically.

"She works at a club there," Tiny answered.

"So you are going to be staying with her?" the woman asked with apprehension. She was still bothered by Tiny's situation.

Tiny nodded her head. "Once I get to her I'll be okay."

"All right then." The woman reached into her handbag and pulled out some money, which she handed to Tiny. "This is enough to get something to eat and for your bus fare to New Kingston."

As if on cue, Tiny's stomach grumbled its appreciation. Embarrassed, she took the money. "Thank you, ma'am." Tiny expressed her gratitude. "I promise I'll be okay."

"I'm still praying that you will go back home soon," the woman told her. "You don't want to jump out of the frying pan into the fire. Come on, let me show you where to get the bus." Again, she took hold of Tiny's hand and they walked toward the bus stop.

Approximately an hour later Tiny hopped off the bus on Knutsford Boulevard in New Kingston. Her eyes traveled up the modern, high-rise buildings as she took in the hustle and bustle of the busy financial sector. But unlike the day before when she gazed wide-eyed at everything, Tiny wasn't that impressed with her environment any longer. She knew that despite the glitz and glamour, danger was also lurking around the corner.

Tiny got directions to the club from a passerby and hurried toward Dominica Drive where it was located. It was early morning but maybe someone was there who could give her some information on Dolly. "Please be open," Tiny mumbled as she walked. "Please, God, let there be someone in that club who can tell me where to find Dolly."

But there wasn't anyone. "CLOSED" read the sign hanging on the front door of the "Champion Girls" club. Tiny's shoulders dropped in frustration. She would have to wait until eight p.m. when it would be opened.

Tiny felt a sharp cramp in her tummy, a reminder that she hadn't eaten in hours. Slowly she walked away from the club onto Trinidad Terrace. Across from an insurance building, she noticed a small restaurant. Crossing the street in a hurry, Tiny opened the restaurant door and went inside. The strong smell of the Blue Mountain coffee, fried dumplings, ackee and saltfish, and other tantalizing dishes tickled her nostrils. Her stomach growled in anticipation.

A few customers stared at Tiny curiously as she quickly walked to the back of the room, her head hanging low to the floor. Taking a seat in a corner with her back toward everyone, her face to the wall, Tiny picked up the menu off the table. She decided to order the cheapest thing on the menu. Before long a waitress came over and took her order, barely glancing at Tiny's injured face. Returning fifteen minutes later, she placed the food on the table in front of her. "Enjoy," the waitress mumbled before hurrying off to attend to the next customer.

A groan escaped Tiny's lips after she took a big bite of the fluffy fried dumpling. Biting, chewing, and swallowing, the four dumplings disappeared in record time. Tiny sat back contentedly in her chair and took a few sips of the hot mint tea. A loud belch resounded in the room. She quickly looked down at her empty plate embarrassed. She felt eyes digging into her back, but she ignored them as she drank the rest of her tea, draining the cup.

Moments later, Tiny stood up and walked to a register at the front of the room. "How much is it?" she asked the cashier.

"Two dollars."

Tiny took out some money from her jeans pocket and counted out the two dollars, leaving her just a few dollars to spare. She exited the restaurant and stood on the sidewalk in uncertainty. What was she going to do until eight p.m.?

Tiny was exhausted and quite frankly, her body was still aching from the beating she took the night before. Now that she had something to eat, some sleep would be nice. She decided to just walk around and look for somewhere to sit and wait.

Back on Knutsford Boulevard, Tiny noticed some long benches under big trees alongside the busy main road. Walking across the soft, manicured grass, she wearily sat down, stretching out her long legs. It was broad daylight, and she felt safer. As she watched the vehicles zooming up and down the road, people scurrying in every direction, her eyelids grew heavy.

Maybe I should go home. But just as quickly as the thought entered her mind, the angry face of Beverly Gregg filled her mind as well. She saw Officer Gregg's furious eyes as he almost choked her to death, and finally she remembered the teeny creature that came from her body. Tiny shuddered. No, she could not go back home.

Moments later, Tiny groggily curled up on the bench, her knees pulled toward her chest. Soon she succumbed to the exhaustion, her troubled thoughts put to rest . . . at least for a while.

Chapter Twelve

Tiny woke up suddenly. Her heart pounded in her chest. Wide-eyed she jumped to her feet and frantically looked around. She was by herself under the tree.

Night had fallen. New Kingston was brightly lit and still full of life. The workday had ended for most, and it was now time to have some fun. Tiny walked down to the street and asked a lady passing by for the time. It was eight thirty p.m.

Yay! It was time for her to see Dolly.

Excitedly, Tiny made her way back to the club, which was just on the other street. As she got to the front door, the sign now read "OPEN." Finally.

Tiny pushed the door inward and was welcomed into a semidark room by vociferous voices. The melodious sound of Beres Hammond streamed from loud, hidden speakers declaring to everyone, "I'm in Love with You."

Small, round tables with occupied chairs were scattered about. Thick, heavy smoke slithered in the air from the cigarettes and cigars that dangled from their mouths and fingers. As Tiny looked around she noticed the large mugs of beer and glasses filled with gold and white liquid. Also, most of the patrons were men with only a few women hanging around. Where was Dolly?

Tiny walked toward the counter at the front of the bar. Three women and a man dressed in black were behind it, scampering around as they poured and mixed drinks. Rows and rows of liquor and wine lined the wall behind them.

"Excuse me," Tiny said as she waved her hand, trying to grab their attention.

"Yes?" the man snapped impatiently as he paused to look at her.

"I'm looking for Dolly. Is she here?" Tiny asked hopefully.

"Later." The rude one-worded man walked away. He grabbed a bottle of Wray & Nephew White Overproof Rum off a rack and hustled over to the other side of the bar.

Tiny was ecstatic as she made her way to the back of the bar. She heard a few whistles and catcalls, but she ignored them. At least she found Dolly. Sitting at an empty table, Tiny waited.

It seemed like forever to Tiny as she waited for Dolly. She twisted her neck around and around to loosen the crick in it. Tapping her fingers on the table she glanced around the crowded room again. No Dolly.

Suddenly the dim light went out, throwing the bar into total darkness. Tiny gasped and her heart leaped in her chest. She quickly jumped to her feet as she peered into darkness. The previous night flashed in her mind, and she began to tremble uncontrollably.

She had to get out of here. But her steps were halted by the loud cheering and shouting that echoed around the room as the front of the club lit up with multicolored lights. Tiny stared in amazement at the small stage that she hadn't noticed before.

And there she was. Tiny's mouth dropped open as Rockin' Dolly danced her way onto the stage; naked as the day she was born. Her big breasts flip flapped as she pumped and grinded to the music.

The club exploded in even more cheers and applause.

"Simmer down: can you hear what I say? Simmer down," said the voice of Bob Marley and the Wailers over

the yelling. But Rockin' Dolly was just too hot to take heed. She spun around, her back facing the audience and the two basketballs behind her began to jiggle. Up. Down. Together.

The crowd went wild. Dollar bills rained down on the stage like confetti at a New Year's party.

"Go, Rockin' Dolly!"

"Rockin' Dolly, marry me!"

"I love you, Rockin' Dolly."

Dolly grinned in response as she gyrated to the music. She whirled around and gravitated closer to the front of the stage, the sparkling light washing over her pretty face.

"Lord, have mercy," Tiny whispered behind the hand covering her mouth.

Dolly did a split. One leg was pointed to the east and the other to the west. Bending over backward with her long braid fanning out behind her, Dolly swayed in slow motion. Her small waist going around in circles, she ticked, she tocked.

The club roared in excitement.

Next, Dolly leaped to her feet like a frisky colt and spun around, giving the crowd another fabulous back view. *Clap! Clap!* Her butt cheeks slapped against each other rhythmically. *Clap! Clap!* A few of the men began clapping their hands in sync to her buttocks, yelling and screaming in absolute delight.

Tiny covered her face in embarrassment, peeping through her fingers.

The Rockin' Dolly show continued for another ten minutes before Dolly hurried around the stage, picking up her money. Finally, she exited through a side door, leaving behind a thunderous applause of aroused men.

The dim light came back on and the waitresses and waiter hurried around refilling empty glasses for the now thirsty men. Tiny shakily stood up and made her way outside. She would wait for Dolly there.

With her back braced against the wall, she took deep breaths as she tried to wrap her mind around what she had just seen. Dolly was definitely starring in her own play. But it certainly wasn't the Pantomime.

She heard the voices followed by giggles before the club door opened. Out came Dolly wearing a little, tight minidress with a huge, tall man with long, thick dreads down his back. They both had marijuana spliffs hanging from their mouths.

"Dolly," Tiny said as she walked toward them, her eyes searching Dolly's face.

Dolly's eyes widened in surprise as they met Tiny's. "Oh my God. Tiny, is that you?" Dolly asked as she ran to her. The two friends hugged. "What happened to you?" Dolly asked after she pulled away and looked at Tiny's face. The bruises were still evident on her face and she was sporting a black eye.

"It's a long story," Tiny replied, embarrassed. "I'll tell you about it later."

"Ahem," said the man behind them.

"Oh, I'm sorry." Dolly smiled and walked back to him. Grabbing him by the arm, she gently pulled him forward to meet Tiny. "Tiny, this is my baby, Big Dread," Dolly said proudly. "Remember I told you about him?"

"Hello," Tiny said as she looked at the huge man. For some strange reason, a feeling of distrust and dislike for him filled her body.

"Hi, beautiful," Big Dread replied as he pulled away from Dolly and walked closer to Tiny. "Where have you been hiding?" His long, yellow teeth smiled at Tiny as he slowly ran his index finger down her cheek.

Tiny took a step back and looked over his shoulder at Dolly, confused.

"Don't pay him any mind, Tiny," Dolly laughed loudly. "Big Dread is just messing with you."

"That's right, Tiny. I mean no harm," Big Dread said with a wink and swiped his long tongue across his thick, black lips. "Any friend of Dolly's is a friend of Big Dread." Tiny looked at him skeptically but nodded her head. She didn't like him one bit.

"So are you going to be staying with Dolly and me?" he asked with a smile as he looked over Tiny from head to toe. "Some people say three is a crowd, but Big Dread says, the more, the merrier." His yellow teeth flashed again in the night.

"Is that okay, Dolly?" Tiny asked looking over his shoulder at her. "I really came here to stay with you. Well, at least for a little while."

"Girl, please." Dolly cut her eyes at Tiny and flicked her right hand in the air. "You know you are always welcome wherever I am."

Tiny grinned and ran over to hug her friend. "Thank you, Dolly," she whispered in her ear. "I really do appreciate it." Tiny choked up as she pulled away from Dolly. She didn't have to sleep outside again that night.

"Now that we have that settled, let's go and get the party started," Big Dread whispered in Tiny's ear from behind.

Tiny jumped away from him in fright and spun around to face him. "Party? What party are you talking about?" she asked him suspiciously, her eyes locked on his face.

Big Dread took two big steps toward Tiny until he was standing merely inches away from her. She felt a chill run down her spine but stood her ground. Her head shot up determinedly to stare into his small, beady eyes.

"Big Dread has big plans for you, baby," he said to her. "You are little bit on the skinny side, but Big Dread doesn't specialize. With some good Big Dread loving and proper food, I'll fatten you up in no time." He reached out and grabbed one of Tiny's breasts and squeezed real hard.

Tiny gave a yap. As if it had a mind of its own, her hand lifted up and connected with his face. Big Dread's head snapped back, more from the shock of being hit than the force of Tiny's hand.

"Tiny, what's wrong with you?" Dolly screamed loudly.

"So you like to play it rough, huh?" Big Dread growled before he grabbed Tiny by her neck with one hand, lifting her off the ground. "Okay, let the games begin."

"Let me go!" Tiny screamed as she kicked wildly, her hands slapping at his face harmlessly.

"Baby, please let her go," Dolly pleaded as she softly patted Big Dread on his behind. "She isn't worth it, darling." But Big Dread ignored her.

"I was going to take care of you and even make you perform with Dolly," Big Dread said angrily. "But now I am going to teach you never to disrespect Big Dread again." He tightened his hold around her neck.

Tiny wheezed as she struggled to pry his hands away from her throat. Her eyes rolled in her head. She felt light-headed as the little strength she had left slowly drained away. *My God, I am going to die in Kingston after all,* she thought.

Chapter Thirteen

"Big Dread, please let her go," Tiny faintly heard Dolly below. She sounded like she was underwater. "Come on, baby. You don't want to go back to prison for killing her. She is not worth it."

Big Dread shook his locks as if he was coming out of a daze. Slowly he loosened his hold on Tiny's neck before he lowered her to the ground. "I should have killed your skinny behind," he snapped angrily. "But I'll get you next time."

Tiny bent over with one hand on her knee and the other massaging her throat as she sucked air into her stinging lungs. She coughed and choked, struggling to normalize her breathing.

"Tiny, what's wrong with you?" Dolly asked angrily as she bent over to stare into Tiny's face, unconcerned by what her man had just done to Tiny. "He only wanted to have some fun with you, Miss Goody Two-shoes."

Tiny looked at her in shock.

"By the way, where is your little bundle of joy?" Dolly spat nastily. "Did the hog eat it for dinner?"

Tiny stood up straight, her eyes filled with tears at the venom coming out of her friend's mouth.

"Dolly!" Big Dread yelled angrily. "Come over here right now."

Dolly rushed over to Big Dread, her eyes were filled with fear.

"As for you, don't even think you are setting foot in Big Dread's palace," Big Dread barked at Tiny. "Unless you want to come and apologize to Big Dread." He grabbed his crotch and stared pointedly at her.

Tiny turned away in disgust. Just the thought made her nauseous.

"Fine, then we are out of here." Big Dread's voice snapped back Tiny's attention to him.

Tiny look at Dolly pleadingly, tears now running down her face. "Please, Dolly. I'm sorry."

Dolly rolled her eyes and sucked her teeth. "Looks like you are on your own, Miss Thing," she informed Tiny. "You better go back to the country where you belong. Nobody disrespects myyyyyy man."

Big Dread grabbed her by the arm and dragged her down the street, leaving Tiny staring at their backs in dismay.

"What am I going to do now?" Tiny asked herself. "It looks as if I am going to be spending the night outside again." Using the back of her hand, Tiny wiped the tears from her face as she pondered her situation.

"It's no use to cry over spilled milk," Aunt Madge had told Tiny on many occasions. "It's best to count your loss and move on." And that's exactly what Tiny decided to do. She would find another place to sleep tonight, somewhere busier and safer. Then come morning she would figure out her next move.

Tiny walked back over to Knutsford Boulevard that was jumping with action. Bright lights, people everywhere, vehicles going up and down the street, and loud noises helped liven up the place. Tiny glanced around at her surroundings, looking for a place to rest for the night.

"Half Way Tree Road!" a bus conductor shouted from a parked bus across the street. "Anyone ready for Half Way Tree Road?"

Tiny looked up and down the busy road until there was a gap in the flow of traffic. She quickly crossed the street over to the bus stop.

"Half Way Tree, pretty lady?" the conductor asked Tiny as she approached the bus, his body blocking the opened door.

Tiny nodded her head. "How much?" she asked him. She only had two dollars left.

"Only two dollars for you," the man replied as if he'd read her mind. Tiny took the money from her pocket and gave it to him. He moved away from the door, allowing her to get into the bus. Tiny walked down the aisle, ignoring the curious looks before taking the only available seat left in the back.

Since the bus was filled with passengers, they were off. It was a short ride that took only fifteen minutes and before she knew it, Tiny was getting off the bus on Constant Spring Road.

Half Way Tree was similar to New Kingston with the crowd of people rushing about in every direction, loud, honking vehicles zooming up and down the busy streets, large towering buildings and bright lights.

Tiny walked around solemnly. Her tummy growled as the aromas from the street side vendors' jerked chicken, roasted corn and mannish water tickled her nostrils. She was hungry again and tired. She had no more money or anywhere to sleep that night.

As she dragged her feet along Half Way Tree Road, Tiny came upon a little park in the middle of the square. It had a few wooden benches, the huge, deep, water foundation was dry as chip, and a few big trees scattered around. It definitely wasn't Jamaica's finest park, but it was in a busy location where she would be safe until morning.

Tiny walked over to an empty bench off to the side of the park and sat down wearily. She people watched for what seemed like hours, ignoring the gnawing of her stomach, before her eyelids began to get heavy. The night air was thick and humid. She curled up on the bench with her hands under her head as a substitute pillow. Before long she drifted away.

Fluffy, Mouse, and Breezy, three of Half Way Tree's homeless drunks, stared down at the young sleeping girl in awe. It was after three in the morning and most of the businesses were closed. The once busy streets were now bare and eerily silent, the vendors and commuters long gone. The excitement of a few hours ago had evaporated like a cigarette puff.

"She pretty," Fluffy slurred with a one-toothed grin. "I want to kiss her." He burped loudly.

"Shhh," Breezy glared at him. "Don't wake her up yet until we're ready for action." He took a swig from the flask in his hand, his crossed eyes looking in opposite directions.

"I want to be first," Mouse whispered, scratching at the boils all over his body. "I'm the smallest one." At barely five feet and weighing ninety pounds soaking wet earned him his name.

"Both of you follow me," Breezy ordered before he staggered away from Tiny. Clearly the leader of the group, Fluffy and Mouse followed him over to the dry water fountain. Slowly they fumbled their way over the edge into their hollow concrete bed. During the day they panhandled on the streets of Kingston. At the end of the day they combined their earnings to get a small bite and a lot of alcohol. At night, they usually made their beds in the bottom of the fountain and spent the night.

"Mouse, you will go first," Breezy instructed. "I will go next, then Fluffy."

"Why do I have to go last?" Fluffy sulked, his fat, beefy face looked like a pitiful bloodhound. He even drooled like one.

"Because I said so." Breezy turned a lazy eye on Fluffy, who hung down his head in fear. "Here, take a hit of this liquid gold." He passed the bottle to Fluffy, who took a few sips, before passing it over to Mouse. The three men drank until the bottle was empty and they were as drunk as skunks.

"I'm ready to go," Mouse slurred. He tried to stand up but fell back down on his behind. Breezy and Fluffy giggled as they slowly stripped down out of their filthy clothes. Their body odor could have knocked a person unconscious.

"Okay, here we go again." Mouse stood up unsteadily to his feet. He cursed repeatedly as he fought to take off the dirty pieces of rags that he wore. Soon he was naked, his little, wrinkled penis almost invisible.

Breezy and Fluffy looked at Mouse and covered their mouths to stifle their laughs. They didn't want to wake Tiny who was still sleeping nearby.

Mouse slipped back over the edge of the fountain, landing unsteadily on his feet. Cautiously he took a few steps toward Tiny, his red eyes lit up in anxiety. Suddenly he stopped, his eyes bugged out of his head. He closed his eyes tight and smiled to himself. That was some really good stuff that Breezy gave him. It even had him hallucinating.

Mouse opened his eyes and this time he screamed in terror, instantly sobering up.

"Help me! Breezy! Help!" Mouse screamed as he sprinted back over to the water fountain and jumped in.

"Shhhh! Shut up before you wake her up." Breezy snapped a hand over his mouth to muffle his screams. "What's the matter with you, man?"

Mouse stared at him with wide eyes, trembling like a leaf. "Giants. Giants. Giants," he muttered over and over, pointing in Tiny's direction.

"I think the liquid gold was too strong for him," Fluffy said to Breezy. "His little body couldn't handle the good stuff." The two men laughed.

"Okay, let me go and do a man's job." Breezy burped loudly. "Mouse, you go and take a nap. Be careful of the giants." Breezy and Fluffy covered their mouths to smother their laughter.

Breezy grinned in anticipation as he climbed over the fountain and cautiously approached Tiny. He stopped and looked back over his shoulder at Fluffy who gave him a thumbs-up. As he turned back around, Breezy's crossed eyes began spinning crazily in his head. He opened his mouth, but no words came out. *Good God, Mouse was right.*

Standing before Breezy on either side of the sleeping girl were two large, warrior giants. They seemed to be at least eight feet tall with long, sharp swords in their trunk of arms. Their bright red eyes glared at Breezy.

"What the heck?" Breezy finally turned around and ran past the fountain and out through the side exit, yelling, "Goliaths! Goliaths!"

Fluffy, surprised and alarmed by Breezy's behavior, hopped out of the fountain and ran after him, quickly followed by Mouse.

Tiny woke up startled by the screaming. Frightened, she jumped up and looked to see the back of a naked man running away from the park. Suddenly it hit Tiny what could have happen while she slept. But what ran them off, she wondered as she looked around her. A homeless man was across the street asleep under a shop piazza, and another figure was bundled up down the street, but she saw nothing or no one who had helped her.

Maybe it's my guardian angels, Tiny thought. If only she knew how right she was.

Chapter Fourteen

Tiny spent the rest of the night awake, scared to go back to sleep. Soon Half Way Tree woke up and began to get ready for another busy day. People began coming out in numbers, the taxis and buses were going up and down the streets, and businesses were opening up their doors. It looked as if it was going to be a productive day for most . . . except for Tiny.

Tiny was hungry and needed to use a bathroom. Her body was stiff from the beating she had taken the night before and from sleeping on the hard bench. She had no money. She walked out of the park onto Constant Spring Road, looking for a public bathroom. Luckily she came upon a restaurant that was already packed with early-morning customers getting their breakfast.

Tiny slipped inside, looking around for the restroom. She noticed it at the back of the restaurant and silently made her way down to it. No one paid her any mind. She slipped inside the small bathroom and locked it. She was happy to see that it was clean.

Tiny quickly relieved herself, then went over to the face basin where she rinsed out her mouth and washed her face. As she looked at the swelling that was still visible on her face and the discoloration around her eye, Tiny teared up. "What did you do to deserve this? What are you going to do now?" she asked her image in the mirror. No reply.

"Hello?" Someone knocked on the door, snapping Tiny out of her thoughts.

"I'll be right out," Tiny replied. She quickly walked over to door and opened it. Tiny smiled apologetically at the woman glaring at her before she hurried back into the restaurant. The smell of the delicious food caused her tummy to grumble. As she passed by a vacant table, Tiny noticed a used plate with a piece of leftover bread. She glanced around skeptically, inching her way closer to the table. Slowly she reached out and grabbed the piece of bread into her hand. With her head hanging low, she hurried out of the restaurant.

Once outside, Tiny stuffed the bread into her mouth and gulped it down in three quick bites. This just whet her appetite and soon an idea began to form in her head.

Tiny slipped back into the restaurant and stood among the other patrons as if she was waiting to place her order. Looking around on the sly, she noticed a few tables with leftovers. She slid over to the first table and quickly scooped up the piece of dumpling off the plate. The other table had three large pieces of bacon. Tiny smiled happily.

"Hey! You!" Tiny looked up to see an angry man yelling at her as he walked toward her. In panic, she rapidly maneuvered her way through the restaurant and ran outside, her hands filled with leftovers.

"That was close," Tiny said before she stuffed the food in her mouth. She walked over to Molynes Road, chewing, as she looked around for another restaurant. She came upon a small, beautiful, bamboo-styled hut. Excited, Tiny hurried inside and stopped suddenly. Her eyes scanned the room to see that the few patrons inside had stopped eating and were staring at her suspiciously.

"May I help you?" a cold voice asked from behind the counter. Tiny quickly turned around and ran out. That didn't turn out as she expected.

Tiny spent most of the morning slipping in and out of restaurants, pastry shops, and bakeries, snatching up crumbs and leftovers. In most cases she was chased away, but a few times she got lucky and was able to get a little something in her stomach.

Tiny spent the day wandering the streets. When she got tired, she found somewhere to sit and rest, then she was off again. She walked the malls, looked into store windows, and people watched. For the most part she was ignored. Just another homeless runaway in town.

As night fell, Tiny became worried. She needed somewhere to sleep. She couldn't go back to that park. Wandering around aimlessly, Tiny walked out on Maxfield Avenue, and noticed up ahead a few police cars parked on the street in front of an old, brick building. It was the Half Way Tree Police Station. Curious, she hastened her steps and hurried over to the building.

Standing at the entrance of the walkway to the building, Tiny noticed a heap of junk vehicles piled up in an isolated, semidark area at the back. Most of these vehicles were involved in an accident or confiscated by the police. Looking around skeptically, Tiny sneaked around to the side of the building and made her way over to the abandoned vehicles. With her head hanging low she walked over to an old car at the furthest back. She grabbed the old metal handle of the right back door and pulled. *Ta-da!* It popped open.

Squeezing her small frame through the door, Tiny crawled over onto the backseat and pulled the door shut behind her. The car smelled stuffy, old, and moldy. She reached over and slightly rolled down the window at the front, welcoming the stiff, humid air that rushed in. With her knees pulled up to her chest and her arms under her head, Tiny curled up on the backseat of the car. Here she felt safer than she had been since she came to Kingston. After all, who would try to attack her at the police station?

***

The day after Tiny ran away, Aunt Madge sat at the top of the small steps with Baby Dupree nestled in her arms. Her worried gaze looked over the fields below and into the forest of trees visible in the distance. "Where are you, Tiny?" Tears leaked from her eyes.

As if sensing the sadness of the moment, Baby Dupree began to cry and kick her little legs. Aunt Madge stood up slowly and put the baby over her shoulder. As she rocked the baby, she sang one of her favorite hymns, "Amazing Grace." *"T'was grace that taught my heart to fear, and grace my fears relieved."* Pain washed over her body from the crown of her head to the soles of her feet. She felt helpless but knew in her heart that the only thing she could do at that moment was to continue knocking on heaven's door for the protection and safe return of her niece. It was all in God's hands now.

Chapter Fifteen

It had been one month since Tiny arrived in Kingston. She was in very bad condition. Her hair was filthy and matted on top of her head. The once bright, colorful dress was now dirty brown and torn in a few places. When hunger hit she would dig up scraps from garbage bins and swiped crumbs and leftovers from restaurants, but that wasn't enough to sustain her. She began to lose a considerable amount of weight from her already slim frame. Her hollow eyes protruded from her haunted face. She was starving and dehydrated. Life as Tiny knew it was quickly disappearing as she fell into the routine of being a homeless, depressed runaway.

For the last three days Tiny was unable to move out of the old car she had been sleeping in at the police station. Pain like she had never felt before rained upon her body like piercing bullets. Her stomach was on fire.

As Tiny lay in her own feces in the back of the old car, shivering, a cold sweat washed her body from head to toe. Her teeth rattled in her head as she muttered incoherently to herself. With her eyes tightly closed, Tiny surrendered herself to death.

Mama Pearl hummed a gospel song as she took small steps up the walkway of the police station toward the front entrance. Her big handbag was slung over one shoulder, while her two hands held firmly the large paper box containing the potato pudding she carried.

Mama Pearl was well-known at the police station where her oldest son, Gerald, worked as a cop. She was loved and respected by all the cops who were all referred to as "my son" or "my daughter." She visited her son frequently, carrying dishes of her delicious cooking; oxtail curry goat and her special potato pudding. It was always more than enough for one person, and many of the other cops had gotten a taste at one time or another.

As she neared the door, Mama Pearl glanced over at the familiar heap of junk cars at the back of the station and stopped suddenly. She could have sworn she saw something moved.

"Hmmm, probably a stray cat looking for mice," she muttered to herself. She took another step forward but stopped again. Her eyes went back to the old cars, her brows rose in confusion. "There is something back there that the Lord wants me to see," Mama Pearl said to herself. "Papa Jesus, I'm not sure what it is, but I'm going to be obedient, sir."

Mama Pearl tiptoed slowly toward the old cars, her steps hesitant but determined. The first few cars she looked into were empty. She continued toward the back when a bad odor filled her nose. With her face twisted up, Mama Pearl took deep breaths as she continued walking.

A scream lodged in her throat as she approached the last car. "Oh, dear Lord," Mama Pearl whispered in shock. Two pieces of sticks, resembling legs, were hanging out the opened back door. Her heart slamming against her chest, Mama Pearl walked closer and saw the scrawny, young girl shaking uncontrollably in the backseat. She smelled like rotten garbage. Tears filled Mama Pearl's eyes.

Mama Pearl quickly rested the box in her hand on top of the car and leaned inside to look at the young girl. Suddenly, two pair of red, haunted eyes stared up at her, piercing her soul.

"Help me," the weak voice begged a little above a whisper.

Mama Pearl gasped loudly and pulled her head out of the car. She cushioned her weak body against the car as her jelly feet felt as if they were about to crumble. "Lord, dear Lord," Mama Pearl muttered. "Dear Lord, dear Lord."

Mama Pearl was not a stranger to the homeless people scattered all over Kingston. She was a long-standing viewer of the poverty that hit so many Jamaicans and only seemed to get worse, day by day.

Her heart bled as she turned and stared at the sick child again. She looked as if she was a minute away from death's door.

Tiny rambled some gibberish and moaned in agony as sharp needles pricked her all over her ice-cold body. Her teeth chattered, and her eyes rolled around listlessly in her head.

As if she was coming out of a trance, Mama Pearl hobbled away from the car toward the entry door of the police station, screaming for help as loud as she could.

Two cops standing close by the door heard the screams over the chaos going on inside the station and ran outside with their guns drawn. They looked around frantically but only saw Mama Pearl hurrying toward them, waving her hands wildly as she yelled to them for help.

"She needs help!" Mama Pearl shouted. "Come help me get her to the hospital."

"Get who, Mama Pearl?" one cop asked as he looked around puzzled. He saw the usual traffic of people on the street going back and forth, but nothing out of the norm.

"She's in the car." Mama Pearl glared at him. "She will die if she doesn't get help right away." She turned around and pointed to the heap of junk cars behind her.

The two cops rushed past her as they cautiously approached the cars, their guns still held tightly in their hands. They were greeted by a strong odor, then the scrawny legs sticking out of the backseat of the old car.

"Lord have mercy," one whispered when his eyes focused on the girl whimpering like a wounded cat. "Run and get the key for the car," he said to his colleague who had his hand over his nose. The police officer ran off to do as he was asked. "And grab a blanket from the bunk room," he shouted at his back.

"We have to move fast," Mama Pearl said as she walked up to stand beside the police officer. "She needs medical attention as soon as possible."

The officer holstered his gun and walked closer to the car. "Sweetheart, we are going to help you," he said to Tiny as he breathed through his mouth. "Stay with me, my dear." He glanced impatiently over his shoulder and saw the other officer running back with a big blanket in his hand.

"Here you go." The police officer handed over the blanket. "I'm going to start the car." He sprinted off and headed to a police car parked in front on the street.

The police officer reached into the car and threw the blanket over Tiny, from her neck down. Carefully he rolled her over into the blanket and lifted the body of bones into his arms. Trying not to gag at the foul odor that filled the small, cramped space, he slowly pulled out from the car with Tiny securely wrapped in his arms.

Walking quickly with Mama Pearl hurrying beside him, he carried Tiny to the running car with his partner sitting in the driver's seat. The back door was opened. He carefully slid into the backseat with Tiny still nestled in his arms, while Mama Pearl grabbed the front passenger door open and hopped in.

"Drive," Mama Pearl instructed in her no-nonsense voice after she closed the door.

"Yes, ma'am." The officer hit the siren and pulled off at a high speed toward University Hospital of the West Indies. In record time the tires were squealing to stop in front of the emergency room. He put the car in park, flung his door open, and hurried to the back of the car to open the door for his colleague.

Mama Pearl quickly opened her door and got out. Waving her hand wildly in the air, she shouted for help. Seconds later a nurse and a doctor pushing a stretcher rushed toward them. The officer carefully got out of the car with Tiny held tightly in his arms and carried her over to the stretcher. He lowered her onto it and stepped back so the medical staff could take over. Unshed tears filled his eyes.

Tiny was rushed inside with Mama Pearl right on their heels.

"I'm sorry, ma'am, but you can't go in there," a nurse passing by said behind Mama Pearl when she tried to slip into the room that Tiny and the medical personnel had disappeared into. "That room is off limits."

Mama Pearl rolled her eyes and turned around to face her. "I need to know if she is going to be okay," Mama Pearl said, her voice laced with concern.

"Is that your daughter? Don't worry, she's in good hands," the nurse said in a friendly voice. Mama Pearl didn't correct her mistake. "While you're waiting why don't you come and fill out the necessary paperwork?"

Mama Pearl stared at her with panic in her eyes. "Paperwork?" she asked.

"Yes. We need your daughter's name, medical history, your information for the billing, and so on."

"Hmmm, I . . . I . . . I can't deal with that right now," Mama Pearl stuttered. "I'll take care of it later."

"But—"

"I said later," Mama Pearl said sharply. "I'm not going anywhere until that child is okay, so I'll be right here."

"Okay, ma'am," the nurse said respectfully. "Come and have a seat in the waiting room. Someone will be out soon to give you an update on your daughter."

Mama Pearl nodded her head. She wearily dragged her feet into the waiting room and sat in a plastic chair close by the door. With her eyes tightly closed, she rested her head against the wall and began to pray for the young, sick girl. She knew Tiny needed all the prayers she could get.

Chapter Sixteen

"Hello? Ma'am?" Mama Pearl's eyes popped open to see a doctor wearing a white coat leaning over her. "I'm sorry to wake you, but I wanted to give you an update on the young lady you came here with."

"Yes, sir." Mama Pearl jumped to her feet. "How is she? Is she going to be all right? Can I see her?"

"Slow down, one question at a time," the doctor said with a smile. "I'm Dr. Warren, and I'm sorry that took longer than anticipated." The doctor looked Mama Pearl from head to toe, noticing the neat hair pulled back in a thick, grey bun and a clean, pressed, red flowing dress with matching soft, leather shoes.

"She isn't related to you, is she?" Dr. Warren asked Mama Pearl.

"No, I don't know her," Mama Pearl admitted with a sigh. "I found her in an abandoned car at the police station."

"That's what I thought." The doctor nodded his head. "I could tell that she was homeless."

"So what's the matter with her?" Mama Pearl asked. "Is she going to be all right?"

"Ma'am, you are not related to her, so I'm not supposed to disclose that information to you."

"What? I found her. *I'm* responsible for her now," Mama Pearl said forcibly. "The Lord led me to her for a reason, and I'm not going to turn my back on her. I'm all she has right now."

Dr. Warren folded his arms across his chest and looked at Mama Pearl with apprehension. "Well, she is homeless, or at least it seems like that's the case," he began. "I guess you are her temporary guardian, huh?"

"Yes, yes, I am," Mama Pearl said quickly, nodding her head. "Please tell me what's going on."

"We are optimistic," Dr. Warren replied as he stared into Mama Pearl's worried eyes. "She is suffering from diverticulitis."

"Thy what?" Mama Pearl asked puzzled.

Dr. Warren smiled and explained. "Diverticulitis. This happens when the diverticula or pouches formed in the wall of the colon get inflamed or infected. The feces get trapped in the pouches, and this allows bacteria to grow there. This can lead to inflammation or infection."

"Oh, I see," Mama Pearl said a little skeptical. "So is this 'divert' thing serious? Can it kill her?"

"Diverticulitis can perforate and can cause death," Dr. Warren answered. "Some of the symptoms include belly pain, usually in the lower left side, that is sometimes worse when you move. There is fever and chills, bloating and gas, diarrhea, nausea, and sometimes vomiting. Also, not feeling like eating is common," he patiently informed Mama Pearl.

"Lord have mercy." Mama Pearl covered her mouth with her hand. "That's some very serious stuff, Doc. What are you doing to help her?" Mama Pearl's face was etched in worry.

"Well, we did some x-ray and blood tests. We are still waiting on the results of the blood tests that we should get back later tonight or in the morning, but the x-ray shows that she has an abscess that is infected. I'm afraid we'll have to do surgery." Dr. Warren's eyes filled with sympathy.

"Thank God I found her." Mama Pearl shook her head in amazement. "If that abscess had burst inside her . . ."

"Yes, I'm glad you found her in time," Dr. Warren agreed. "She could have stayed there and died. Do you have any more questions for me?" Mama Pearl shook her head. "Okay, I need to go so we can get the surgery done."

"Thank you, Doc," Mama Pearl said with a grateful smile. "Please, don't let anything happen to her."

"We'll do our best," he replied before hurriedly walking away, leaving a cloud of uncertainly behind.

Mama Pearl wearily lowered herself back into the chair. She felt a headache coming on, but she ignored it. Her heart was consumed with the young girl who was suffering behind those closed doors. "She's in your hands now, Lord," Mama Pearl said as she glanced up at the ceiling. "I ask that you stay in the operation room with her and give her the victory."

"Mama, are you okay?" came Gerald's worried voice beside Mama Pearl before she was pulled into a big, tight hug.

Mama Pearl nodded her head and clung to her son. God, it felt good to have someone there with her.

"I just got back to the station after leaving a crime scene and the officers told me what had happened," Gerald said as he gently rocked his mother in his arms. "How could something so terrible happen to that girl? Is she going to be okay?"

Mama Pearl gently pulled back and looked into the concerned eyes of her oldest child. "They are going to do surgery. Her colon has an infected abscess that could rapture and kill her."

"How awful," Gerald said with deep emotion. "Don't worry, Mama. This is a good hospital. She's going to be okay."

"I hope so," Mama Pearl said sadly.

"Mama, you look tired." Gerald touched her cheek affectionately. "Let me take you home to get some rest."

"No," Mama Pearl said adamantly. "I'm not going anywhere until I know that child is okay."

"I'm off duty, so I can come back and check on her," Gerald persisted. "Remember your doctor said you have to take it easy, Mama." His voice was filled with concern for his sixty-year-old mother who suffered from high blood pressure.

"I feel fine," Mama Pearl replied stubbornly. "I want to wait awhile, okay?"

Gerald gave a big sigh and nodded in defeat. "A little while, and then I'm taking you home, even if I have to throw you over my shoulder," he said playfully, pointing his index finger at his mother. "Or do you want me to call Sydney, Alwayne, Robert, and Omar?" he added with a smirk, referring to his other four brothers.

Mama Pearl rolled her eyes, a little smile flickering at the corners of her mouth. What would she have done without her boys?

Chapter Seventeen

Mama Pearl was a widow and mother of five sons. Gerald, the oldest, was a cop; Sydney, the second son, was a high school principal; Alwayne, the middle son, was a lawyer; followed by Robert, who was a college professor; and Omar, the youngest, was a bank teller.

After the sudden passing of her husband when the boys were very young, life for Mama Pearl was hard. Raising five boys without a father would have forced many women to give up, but not Mama Pearl. She cleaned houses for the rich folks who lived in the affluent areas of Kingston, from sunrise to sunset, and took good care of her boys. They all went and graduated from college, an opportunity she never got.

"There is nothing I can't do with God on my side," Mama Pearl would respond when asked how she did it. "If God brings me to it, He'll bring me out of it."

Mama Pearl lived in a beautiful house in Meadowbrook that her sons bought her a few years prior. She was a devoted Christian and was very active in her church. A kind woman who would offer meals to her neighbors, strangers, and even the mentally ill. She loved and cared for people. She was a mother of her community. It wasn't a coincidence that the Lord led her to Tiny.

Gerald and Mama Pearl waited a few more hours before they were told that the surgery was successful and Tiny was moved to a room. She was given strong pain medication and antibiotics and was sleeping restfully.

"I'm afraid she won't be getting any visitors tonight," the nurse had informed them. "Please come back tomorrow." A reluctant Mama Pearl nodded and allowed Gerald to take her home.

The next morning, Omar dropped off Mama Pearl at the hospital, bright and early. She got very little sleep the night before as her mind was too consumed with the poor young girl.

"I'm going to park and meet you inside, Mama," Omar said through the open window to his mother before he drove off toward the parking lot. At twenty-one-years-old, Omar was the only son who still lived at home.

Mama Pearl waved and hurriedly walked into the hospital, carrying a large basket containing ackee and saltfish, fried dumplings and cornmeal porridge.

"Good morning. I'm Jackie. How may I help you?" the chirpy receptionist greeted Mama Pearl when she walked up to the information booth.

"Good morning, Jackie. I'm Mama Pearl, and I'm here to see a patient," Mama Pearl replied.

"Okay. What's the patient's name?" Jackie asked with a bright smile.

Mama Pearl paused and looked at her. She had a little problem because she didn't know the girl's name. In fact, she knew nothing about her at all. "Well, I'm not sure."

Jackie looked at her skeptically. "You don't know who you're visiting?"

"No, I don't." Mama Pearl shook her head. "I think she's homeless. I found her yesterday, and we brought her here. She had surgery last night."

"Oh, okay. Her," Jackie said as if she had just solved the mystery. "I know exactly who you are talking about. Our Jane Doe in Room 200." In fact, the entire staff in that section of the hospital already heard about the homeless girl who had almost died in the abandoned car. "You are the lady who found her?"

Mama Pearl nodded her head. "Yes, that's me."

"You helped save her life," Jackie said with admiration.

"No, the Lord saved her life," Mama Pearl corrected her. "Our steps are ordered by the Lord. Don't ever forget that."

"Yes, ma'am," Jackie replied humbly. "Please go straight through that door over there and turn right." She pointed and showed Mama Pearl where to go.

"Thank you," Mama Pearl said gratefully and walked in the direction she was shown.

It was early morning, but the hospital was already bursting with activities. Porters pushed wheelchairs and stretchers up and down the aisles. Nurses, doctors, and medical assistants were scurrying from one patient room to the next.

As Mama Pearl passed the nurse's station, no one paid her any attention. She walked down the narrow corridor looking at the room numbers until she came to Room 200.

Mama Pearl entered the room to find a doctor and a nurse standing over Tiny's bed, looking down at the chart in the doctor's hand. They looked up at her when she entered.

"May I help you?" the doctor asked.

"Yes, I'm here to see her." Mama Pearl pointed to the still figure lying in the bed.

Tiny had tubes and wires running from her nose and arms that were connected to beeping machines. Her eyes were closed, her breathing shallow.

"How is she doing?" Mama Pearl asked as she looked at Tiny with fear in her eyes.

"I think she has passed the worst," the doctor replied as he looked down on Tiny. "We removed the abscess, but she has a bad infection in her colon and is in a lot of pain. So we are giving her some very strong pain medication and antibiotics which is why she's sleeping right now. She's a lucky girl."

"Luck has nothing to do with it," Mama Pearl said softly. "Trust me, I know. This child has someone beating on heaven's door on her behalf."

They stood for a moment looking down on Tiny until Mama Pearl broke the silence. "I carried some breakfast for her, but I guess she can't have it."

"No, ma'am," the doctor said quickly, noticing the basket in Mama Pearl's hand for the first time. "She'll be fed intravenously for a while, then put on a strict liquid diet for a few days."

"Okay, whatever it takes for her to get better," Mama Pearl said with a sigh. "I'll be here every day to see her, so I have enough time to give her some good food."

"Hmmm, I think she'll be moved to the Kingston Public Hospital soon," the doctor informed Mama Pearl.

"What? Why?" Mama Pearl looked at him as if he had lost his mind.

"Well, she is homeless, and this is . . . well . . . They will take care of her at the public hospital."

"Excuse me?" Mama Pearl was appalled. She walked over to a small table in the corner of the room and placed her basket on top of it. Turning around, she walked back over and stood in front of the tall doctor, who towered over her by more than a foot, one hand resting on her hip. "You are *not* moving her *anywhere*," Mama Pearl stated angrily, her finger pointed up at the doctor. "Do you hear me? She is staying right *here*."

"What's going on?" Omar asked as he stepped into the room. He looked from his upset mother to the bewildered doctor, back to his mother. "Mama?"

"They want to move her to KPH," Mama Pearl spat. "Treating her like she's nobody."

"No, that's not what this is about at all," the doctor explained to Omar. "I was just explaining to your mother that her care here will be expensive, so—"

"So I'll take care of her medical expenses," Mama Pearl said with determination.

"You will?" Omar stared at his mother in surprise. "Mama, can I talk to you for a minute outside?"

"There is nothing to talk about, Omar," she responded as she stared directly into his eyes. "The Lord led me to this child to help her, and I am going to do *exactly* that."

Omar sighed and shook his head in surrender. He knew when his mother's mind was made up there was nothing anyone could say or do to change it.

"That's absolutely wonderful!" They both turned to look at the doctor, who had a big, stupid grin on his face. "You made the best decision ever. We provide the best services here at this hospital. In fact . . ." He bit his lips after Mama Pearl took a few steps closer to him.

"Okay, why don't we go and take care of all the paperwork?" the nurse who had been silent all this time finally spoke. "Ma'am, sir, if you both could please follow me?" She waved her hand in the direction of the door and walked toward it. Glancing back over her shoulder to make sure Mama Pearl and Omar were behind her, she led them out of the room and over to the administrative office.

Chapter Eighteen

Tiny lay still on the bed, while her heavy eyes lazily swept the room. Ever so slowly, she moved her body slightly to the left and suddenly it went numb as waves of pain flooded her being. Taking deep breaths with her eyes tightly closed, she waited for the pain to subside. Soon the tears started running down her cheeks. "I miss you, Aunt Madge," Tiny whispered. "I'm so sorry for everything that I have done." Deep sobs shook her body, triggering another bout of intense pain, physically and emotionally.

"Please don't cry, my dear," Tiny heard a warm voice say above her. "It's going to be okay."

Tiny's crying tapered off as she glanced up to see an elderly lady standing over her bed. The smiling face looked vaguely familiar, but for some reason she couldn't tell from where. She had seen so many different faces as she wandered the streets.

"I'm Mama Pearl," the lady said as she pulled the chair closer to the bed and lowered herself into it. "What's your name, sweetie?" She reached over and took Tiny's hand into her own, her eyes fixed on Tiny's face.

Tiny looked at her nervously.

"It's all right," Mama Pearl assured her. "I'm not going to hurt you. I've been waiting two days to talk to you." Mama Pearl gently rubbed the hand she held in her own.

"Two days?" Tiny's weak voice sounded like music to Mama Pearl's ear.

"Don't you remember me?" Mama Pearl asked, and Tiny shook her head. "I found you in the old car and took you here."

Tiny closed her eyes, but only the image of a blurry face popped in her mind.

"That's okay," Mama Pearl said gently. Tiny looked at her. "You were too sick to notice what was going on around you."

"Thank you," Tiny whispered. "I thought I was going to die and was actually looking forward to it."

"Don't you dare say that!" Mama Pearl was shocked. "The Lord has a great future in store for you . . ."

"Eleanor," Tiny offered. "My name is Eleanor, ma'am."

"Aunt Madge, why does everyone call me Tiny?" Four-year-old Tiny pouted out her lips, her small hands folded across her chest. "I'm not tiny, I'm a big girl."

"Yes, you are, sweetheart." Aunt Madge smiled as she reached down and lifted Tiny into her arms. "When you were born, you were so tiny and cute, I began to call you 'Tiny' and everyone started to do the same." She kissed Tiny on her cheek. "But your real name is Eleanor, and you are a big girl. And I love you." She tickled Tiny's side, and the child began to laugh uncontrollably.

Unshed tears filled Tiny's eyes at the memory. It was at that moment that the name "Tiny" officially died and Eleanor was resurrected.

"Nice to meet you, Eleanor." Mama Pearl's voice brought back Eleanor's eyes to her face. "A beautiful name for a beautiful girl."

Eleanor smiled shyly. She was beginning to like the friendly lady.

Over the next five days, Mama Pearl visited with Eleanor every day. Each of her sons also stopped by at one time or another to meet the young girl who had captured their mother's heart. Their hearts also went out to

Eleanor. That morning as Mama Pearl passed the nurse's station on her way to Eleanor's room, she was stopped by a nurse. "Excuse me, Mama Pearl?" the young lady said affectionately. They had all become familiar with the feisty, loving, elderly lady. "Yes, my dear?" Mama Pearl quickly walked over to her. "Is something wrong with Eleanor? Did she take a turn for the worse? I thought she was doing well?" With each question, her voice rose higher in panic.

"She is fine, ma'am," the nurse assured her. "I was asked to tell you when you arrive that you are needed in the administrative office."

Mama Pearl frowned. She wondered what the problem could be. She had given them a down payment for Eleanor's medical care and would be paying the balance when she was discharged, courtesy of her five sons who were footing the bill. "Okay, I'll go over there before I go to see Eleanor." Mama Pearl turned around and walked briskly to the office.

"Enter," a small voice responded to her knock on the door.

Mama Pearl turned the door handle and entered the small office.

"Mama Pearl, it nice to see you again," said Mr. Lake, the billing administrator, as he stood to his feet behind his desk. He had met Mama Pearl when she was there to set up the account for Eleanor. "Please have a seat, ma'am." He waved his hand toward an empty chair facing his desk.

Mama Pearl grunted, her lips fused tightly together as she walked over to the chair and sat. "What's this about?" she asked in a stiff voice. "You need another payment? What?"

"I just wanted you to know that it's time for Eleanor to be discharged," Mr. Lake said gently. "In fact, we are planning on doing so tomorrow."

"You are discharging her tomorrow?" Mama Pearl asked in a stunned voice.

"We have done all we can for her here," Mr. Lake explained. "She still needs to fully recover but nothing that cannot be done at home. We will give her pain medication and antibiotics. With some rest, plenty of water, and a high-fiber diet which includes fresh fruits and vegetables, Eleanor will be okay."

Mama Pearl was dumbfounded. She knew Eleanor could not stay in the hospital forever, but she thought she had a few more days to figure out a few things.

"There is a girl's home in Papine that is willing to take in Eleanor," Mr. Lake added. "It's a place for homeless girls like her."

"Absolutely not," Mama Pearl said firmly as she stared into his eyes. "She is coming home with me."

Mr. Lake silently looked at her over the top of his eyeglasses that rested on the tip of his flat nose. "Mama Pearl, are you sure? You have already done so much for this young lady . . . but taking her in your home?"

"I'm sure," Mama Pearl said unwavering. "I'll be here tomorrow to get Eleanor and to settle my bill with you."

"You are an amazing woman," Mr. Lake said with admiration. "I have a strong feeling that Eleanor's life is about to change for the better. God bless you both." He stood up and extended his right hand to Mama Pearl.

Mama Pearl got to her feet and shook his hand. "Thank you for everything you have done for her." She turned around, walked out of the office and out of the hospital, her mind racing. *I'll be back to see Eleanor later. Right now it's time for a little family meeting.*

"That's not going to happen," Sydney said point-blank to his mother. "We are not going to allow you to do that. Right?" He looked from one brother's face to another.

"That's right," Alwayne replied in a firm voice, and the others nodded in agreement. "Don't even think about it, Mama."

Mama Pearl was sitting on her couch in her living room, surrounded by her five sons. She had called a family meeting for that afternoon to tell them that Eleanor would be moving in with her. She wasn't surprised by their behavior; after all, Eleanor was a street kid that she knew nothing about.

"I have made my decision, sons," Mama Pearl said calmly. "I know in my heart that this is what the Lord wants me to do."

"Mama, the Lord doesn't want you to bring a stranger in your home to live," said Robert. "I mean, you are already paying a huge hospital bill for this kid after saving her life. Isn't that enough?"

"You mean, *we* are paying a huge hospital bill," Gerald muttered.

Mama Pearl gave him a sharp look. "If it was any one of you, I would want someone to do the same for you," she said. "Eleanor is a kind, sweet girl who is going through a lot right now, and we are going to help her." Emphasis was placed on the word "we."

Omar rolled his eyes, leaned further back into the couch, his hands folded across his chest. "She is a kind, sweet girl," he mimicked his mother.

"Boy, watch your mouth." Mama Pearl turned sharp eyes to him. "Don't think you are too grown to talk any way to me. You hear me?"

"Sorry, Mama," Omar replied sulkily. "But you don't know if this girl is dangerous. What if she attacks you, and no one is here, huh?"

"Omar is right, Mama," Sydney said. He reached over from beside her and took his mother's small hand into his own, staring deeply into her eyes. "I don't see why she can't go to the girl's home and you visit her there, Mama. Don't get me wrong, I have met her, and I feel for her, but the fact remains we don't know her enough to move her in here with you."

"Omar lives here too," Mama Pearl pointed out.

"But I'm not here all the time, Mama," Omar responded. "I do work, and I have a social life, you know?"

"Please, Mama. Listen to us," Robert added affectionately. "We love you, and we are going to protect you, no matter what."

Mama Pearl smiled as she looked from one handsome face to the next. These are her sons. Her little boys were now strong, independent, educated men who loved their mama, four of whom were husbands with children of their own. Tears leaked down her face as she looked at them with pride.

"Oh, man. Mama, please don't cry." Gerald who was sitting to her right pulled her into a hug. The other sons edged closer, their faces filled with concern.

"I'm okay," Mama Pearl said as she sat up on the couch. She sniffed and used her hand to wipe her eyes. "I'm just so proud of all of you. I want you to know that." She smiled at them. "You all know I'm not irrational, right?"

They all nodded their heads.

"And you know I have never been wrong once when I tell you that the Lord has asked me to do something, right?"

Again they nodded their head.

"So work with me on this, my sons. I know that this is what I should do, and I'm going to do it. You can stop by as often as you want and check up on us. But this is something I need to do."

The room was arrested in silence. The brothers looked at each other, deep in thought, their concerns still alive.

"All right, Mama," Alwayne finally responded and took a deep breath. "We are still not too sure about this, but we are going to go along . . . for now."

"And don't think we're not going to be monitoring the situation," Gerald warned in his cop voice. "She makes one bad move, and I'm throwing her little behind in jail." Mama Pearl laughed out loud, clapping her hands together excitedly. Even though she never needed her sons' approval for Eleanor to stay with her, she wanted them to support her decision. They were still skeptical, but she was hoping that eventually they would realize that she was doing the right thing. In fact, she hoped that they would come to care for Eleanor as she had in such a short time.

"So, Gerald, my darling, what time will you be here tomorrow for us to go and get Eleanor?" Mama Pearl asked too sweetly.

"Oh, man," Gerald groaned. His brothers and mother laughed loudly.

Life was definitely going to be interesting from now on.

Chapter Nineteen

"Wow. This is so beautiful," Eleanor said under her breath as Gerald pulled his car into Mama Pearl's driveway. With her head hanging out the car window, she looked at the beautiful house in awe. Modest in and of itself but to Eleanor who lived in a one-bedroom house all her life, this looked like a mini mansion.

Gerald got out of the car and walked around to open the front passenger door for his mother. He then proceeded to open the back door for Eleanor who sat in the backseat.

"I'll get the door," Mama Pearl said and hurried up the driveway to open the front door.

"Here, take my hand," Gerald said and held out his hand to Eleanor.

Eleanor took ahold of it, and he slowly helped her out of the car.

"Now lean on me and walk slowly," he instructed. "I know it still hurts when you move, so please be careful."

Eleanor smiled at him gratefully and allowed him to help her inside the house.

"She's in here, Gerald," Mama Pearl shouted from a bedroom in the back.

Gerald walked behind Eleanor as she took baby-like steps toward Mama Pearl's voice. As she entered the room, Eleanor stopped suddenly, causing Gerald to bump into her back. She was at a loss for words as she looked around the nicely decorated room. To say the room was beautiful was an understatement. The tears she had been struggling to hold back came rushing out. Eleanor leaned her back against the wall and sobbed. Deep, heart wrenching sobs that caused her abdomen to hurt, but she was oblivious to the pain.

Gerald and Mama Pearl looked at each other. They weren't sure what to do.

"Eleanor, it's okay, sweetheart," Mama Pearl said soothingly as she walked over to her. Her big, welcoming smile pulled at Eleanor's heartstrings. "Please come and lie down before you hurt yourself again."

Eleanor continued crying, her eyes searching Mama Pearl's face questioningly.

"It's all right, Eleanor," Gerald said and cautiously walked over to her. "I can imagine how overwhelming this is for you." Gerald felt like an eel for the way he behaved when his mother told him that Eleanor would be staying with her. To see Eleanor's reaction to being inside a room where she would be staying was priceless.

Gerald looked over at his mother, and she smiled at him as if she had read his mind.

"Thank you again for doing this for me, Mama Pearl," Eleanor said as her crying tapered off. "I . . . I . . . I'm so grateful." She hiccupped. "Excuse me."

"You are welcome, my dear," Mama Pearl said warmly. "Please, come and lie down." She took ahold of Eleanor's hand and led her over to the full-sized bed. "Tomorrow I'll show you the rest of the house."

Eleanor sat on the edge of the bed. She slipped her feet out of the flip-flop slippers that Mama Pearl had brought for her to the hospital that morning. Slowly, she swung her body onto the bed, flinching at the sharp pain in her abdomen, her face looking up at the ceiling.

Mama Pearl quickly fixed her head on the fluffy pillow before pulling the clean, floral, cotton sheet over her body. "Your bathroom is right there." Mama Pearl pointed to a closed door. "If you need help with anything, please ring this bell."

Eleanor turned her head to look at the little bell sitting on the bedside table. "Thank you, Aunt Madge." Eleanor smiled. "I think I can manage."

Mama Pearl and Gerald looked at each other. "Who is Aunt Madge?" Mama Pearl asked curiously.

Eleanor's eyes bugged out of her head. "What . . . What are you talking about?" She nervously twirled the sheet between her fingers.

"You just called her 'Aunt Madge.' Who is that?" Gerald said as he stared down on Eleanor in the bed. "Is that your aunt? Is she alive? Where is she now?"

"Gerald, please slow down." Mama Pearl gave him a stern look. "We are going to let Eleanor get some rest now. We can talk about this later."

Eleanor nodded her head, avoiding their stares. After Mama Pearl and Gerald left the room, she closed her eyes tightly. *This can't be real,* Eleanor thought. Over the last month she was beaten, almost raped twice, ate scraps and leftovers, even out of garbage bins, slept in an old abandoned car, got sick and lay in her own feces praying for death. Now here she was, lying in a clean bed, in a nice house, warm, safe, and comfortable. She had never had her own room before.

"Is this you, God?" Eleanor whispered, looking up at the ceiling. "Thank you, Lord." The tears returned and joyfully glided down her cheeks.

Chapter Twenty

Eleanor quickly pinned the wet clothes on the clothes-line. This was the last batch, and she was finished for the day. She wanted to surprise Mama Pearl with dinner when she got home from church. Easter was just a few days away, and Mama Pearl was on the planning committee for the Easter festivities at church. "I need to make sure everything is perfect as we celebrate the resurrection of my Jesus Christ on the third day after His crucifixion," Mama Pearl had told Eleanor. In order to accomplish this goal, she spent a lot of time at the church.

Eleanor still found it difficult to comprehend how her life had changed over the last two months she had been living with Mama Pearl. For the first week, Mama Pearl ignored her protests and waited on her, hand and foot. She adhered to the doctor's advice of a strict liquid diet, making her every different type of soup: chicken, chicken foot, red peas, beef and gungo peas. Not to mention the different types of mouthwatering porridge: cornmeal, oatmeal, green banana, and rice. Mama Pearl was on a mission to get Eleanor well and healthy, and it worked, for the most part.

Fully recovered, Eleanor decided to earn her keep by doing household work. She washed, cleaned, cooked, and went grocery shopping. Mama Pearl's sons were astonished at her transformation. "She must have lived with someone who taught her to do these things," Robert said one day to his mother when he came to visit. The house was sweetly perfumed with the brown stew chicken that Eleanor was preparing in the kitchen.

"Yes, I knew that girl didn't belong on the street. She doesn't want to talk about her past," Mama Pearl told him. "I've tried to get her to tell me where she's from, but she would either start to cry or run to her room to lock herself away."

"Wow, I wonder what had happened to cause her to choose the street than stay home?" Robert asked puzzled.

"We will probably never know," Mama Pearl replied, shaking her head. "But she will never be on the streets again. Eleanor is becoming a part of this family." And she was.

Eleanor felt great, physically. However, mentally, she was a mess. Most of her nights were restless as she twisted and turned, fighting against her demons. She had nightmares of the scary creature eating Aunt Madge. She would see Aunt Madge weeping at losing her niece. Aunt Madge sitting up at nights, looking through the small window, watching for her to come through the door.

I need to go home, Eleanor often contemplated. *I miss Aunt Madge.* But as soon as the thought popped up in her mind, so did the images of the gun held to her head and the flowerpots flying through the air toward her. "I can't go back now. Officer Gregg is surely going to kill me now that I told his wife about the scary creature. No, I have to stay away, not only for myself, but for Aunt Madge as well."

Eleanor knew that there were secrets that she had to take to her grave. Mama Pearl treated her like the daughter she never had. Her sons and their families had finally come around and began to treat her like family as well. And while she shared herself physically, Eleanor shut herself away from the world emotionally, like a snail that came out for a while, then retreated back into its shell, hiding away from the world.

***

It was Eleanor's birthday, May 26, 1979. She was sixteen, but her troubled mind made her feel like sixty. As the sun rose that morning, Eleanor got out of bed and walked over to her bedroom window that overlooked the backyard. The breadfruit and mango trees in the yard appeared blurry as the tears ran down her face.

If she was home now in Falmouth, the smoke would already be pouring out of the small outside kitchen which was really rough, uneven boards held together by long, sharp nails with some naked sheets of zinc as the roof. Aunt Madge would be cooking her favorite breakfast of roasted breadfruit, ackee, saltfish, and chocolate tea.

"Oh, Aunt Madge, will you ever forgive me?" Eleanor whispered. "I made such a mess of my life. If only I had listened to you instead of Dolly. Why did my life have to be this way?" Eleanor rested her forehead against the glass pane and wept. Months of suffering, aches, and pains came rushing out like a tsunami. "Please, help me, Lord," Eleanor cried. Her slender body shook with the intensity of her pain.

"Eleanor! Eleanor! Are you okay?" came Mama Pearl's panicked voice from outside the door, followed by a loud knocking. "Sweetheart, please let me in."

Eleanor turned around and looked at the closed door in terror. Instantly she stopped crying and wiped her wet face with the edge of her nightgown.

"Eleanor, I heard you crying and just want to make sure you're okay," Mama Pearl said in a concerned voice. "Please, let me help you."

Eleanor stared at the door like it was a poisonous snake. What was she supposed to do now? She took a few small steps toward the door, then stopped. Rocking back and forth on the heels of her feet, she nibbled on her thumb as she contemplated her situation. She had no idea she was crying that loud for Mama Pearl to have heard her. This would only lead to a slew of questions which she wanted to avoid. On the other hand, Mama Pearl would not just go away. She cared about her and would not let up until she knew Eleanor was okay.

Without a further thought, Eleanor walked to the door and unlocked it. She pulled it open to see Mama Pearl and Omar staring at her with worry.

"Come here, my dear," Mama Pearl said and drew Eleanor into her ample bosom. As Mama Pearl rocked her gently, she soothingly rubbed her back. "It's all right now," Mama Pearl said softly into her hair. "You are going to be okay by the grace of God."

Omar stood and stared awkwardly at Eleanor and his mother. He had no idea what to do or say to help make things better and this frustrated him. "Eleanor, can I get you a glass of water?" he asked gently.

Eleanor raised her head and looked at him in surprise. She could tell from the day she moved in that Omar wasn't pleased with her being there. While he hadn't been outright rude, he certainly wasn't welcoming either.

For the first few days, he had watched her like a hawk. If she was in the living room, as soon as she walked out, he would walk in. Eleanor once hid behind the door and watched as he took inventory of his mother's fine china, antique pieces, and other valuables that she had collected over the years. "My God," Eleanor had whispered under her breath, "he is checking to see if I've taken anything." Embarrassed, she tiptoed into her room, refusing to let the tears swimming in her eyes fall.

However, before it got better, it got worse. It was laundry day. Eleanor sat on a small wooden stool separating the clothes into two piles; color here and white there. As she pushed her hand into the pocket of a pair of jeans pants belonging to Omar, she felt a piece of paper. Puzzled, she pulled it out and stared in shock at the twenty-dollar bill in her hand. Suddenly it hit her like a pivot jab to her stomach. "He's trying to set me up," Eleanor said aloud. "He wants to tell Mama Pearl that I stole his money so she'll put me out of the house."

Eleanor sat as still as a statue, the money crumbled into her tight fist. Her eyes narrowed into slits as the anger rushed through her pores. "I am *not* going back to live in the streets, so help me God," Eleanor said aloud. "The Lord sent Mama Pearl to help me, and I'm not going to let Omar ruin this for me."

Eleanor stood up, huffing and puffing. Furious, she marched up the back steps into the house. As she approached Omar's bedroom door, the urge to kick it entered her mind, but Mama Pearl was in her room taking a nap. Instead, Eleanor knelt down and shoved the twenty-dollar bill under the bottom of the door. Standing up, she dusted off her hands as if she had just touched something vile, turned on her heels, and walked back out of the door.

Later that evening Eleanor watched from her hiding place behind the couch as Omar walked toward his bedroom. She saw him open the door, then looked down at his feet. Suddenly Omar looked up and glanced around questioningly. Seeing no one, he reached down and picked up his money. Eleanor smirked as she saw him lower his head in shame before entering his room and closing the door.

"*That's* what you get for trying to set me up," Eleanor muttered to herself. "I may be a lot of things, but I'm not a thief."

The next few days were uncomfortable between Omar and Eleanor. However, it was as if an unspoken understanding had been formed between them. Omar eased up on Eleanor, and she continued to work hard to prove herself worthy of living there. It didn't take long for Omar to let his guard down and begin to see Eleanor as a part of the family. As the days went by, he started to think of her as the little sister that he never had.

"Eleanor?" Mama Pearl's voice snatched her off memory lane.

"Huh?" Eleanor asked as she looked at her puzzled. "Oh, I'm sorry." She turned to Omar and smiled apologetically. "Yes, I would like a glass of water. Thanks."

Omar nodded and hurried away.

"Come and sit down," Mama Pearl said and led Eleanor over to the bed. Eleanor sat on the edge with her hands folded in her lap, looking down on the bedside rug under her feet. Mama Pearl sat down beside her, placed her hand around her shoulder, pulling her closer to her body. "Do you want to talk about it?" Mama Pearl asked. "Maybe I can help you."

Eleanor shook her head, still refusing to look at her.

"Here you go," Omar said as he entered the room. He handed the glass of water to Eleanor and took a few steps back into the corner.

Eleanor put the glass to her mouth and drank greedily. "Thank you," she said looking from Omar to Mama Pearl. "I'll be all right now."

But Mama Pearl decided to try one more time. "Eleanor, I know you are going through some stuff, baby. But today, you seem to be in more pain than usual. What's going on?"

"It's my birthday." It slipped out before Eleanor realized what she had said.

"It's your birthday?" Omar asked surprised as he took a few steps closer to her.

"It's your birthday?" Mama Pearl squealed and jumped to her feet. "Happy birthday, Eleanor!" She reached down and pulled Eleanor to her feet and into her arms again.

Mama Pearl was big on birthdays. She believed it was the day that the Lord first allowed His people to take their first breath; therefore it should be celebrated and appreciated. Even when she struggled to find food for her boys to eat while they were growing up, she commemorated each of their birthdays. Whether it was a homemade cake with a lit candle in it or a cheap toy from the store, she taught her children to appreciate the day she gave birth to them. Eleanor would be no exception to the rule. After all, she was now family.

"We are going to have a party," Mama Pearl said excitedly. "Omar, you have to go and notify your brothers immediately."

"No!" Eleanor shouted. Omar and Mama Pearl looked at her with their mouths opened. "Sorry, but I don't want a party. Please."

"Why not?" Omar asked. "We always celebrate birthdays in this family."

Eleanor smiled at his reference to her being in the family. "Thank you, but not this year, okay?" She looked at them pleadingly, yearning for their understanding.

"Okay," Mama Pearl said in a low voice. "We won't have a party, but I'm going to make all your favorite dishes today and invite over just the family for dinner."

Eleanor opened her mouth to protest, but Mama Pearl raised a hand in warning. "No. I don't want to hear it. It will be a small, informal dinner with us. No party, no excitement, just dinner."

Eleanor gave her a knowing look but nodded her head in defeat. She was quickly learning that it was hard to win against Mama Pearl.

"Yay!" Mama Pearl shouted like a child.

Omar laughed out loud, and Eleanor couldn't help the smile that crept up on her face.

"So what's for breakfast?" Mama Pearl looked at Eleanor with a big grin.

"So what's for breakfast?" Aunt Madge had asked Tiny last year. The memory flashed in Eleanor's mind. There it was again. That pivot jab to her gut. Subconsciously, Eleanor wrapped her arms around her waist. She took a deep breath in and let it out slowly. "It's roasted bread-fruit, ackee, saltfish, and chocolate tea."

"Great, I just happen to have everything here for the birthday girl," Mama Pearl said happily. "Omar, why don't you call your brothers and tell them about dinner?"

"All right, Mama," Omar replied and turned to walk out of the room. He turned back around and walked over to Eleanor. "Happy birthday, Eleanor." He gave her a quick hug, before he turned on his heels and strolled out of the room.

"Okay, let's get the party . . . hmmm . . . I mean the breakfast started." Mama Pearl looked at Eleanor sheepishly.

Eleanor shook her head and gave her a warning look, a little smile tugging at the corners of her mouth.

"Okay, okay, I'm going," Mama Pearl said with a big grin on her face as she backed out the door, closing it shut behind her.

Eleanor looked at the closed door and sighed. It was going to be a long day.

Chapter Twenty-one

"Happy birthday to you," Aunt Madge sang softly as she sat on the three-legged, wooden stool in the kitchen with Baby Dupree gurgling and wiggling in her arms. "Happy birthday, dear, Tiny. Happy Birthday to . . . to . . . to . . ." Aunt Madge dissolved into tears. Her small body vibrated at the heavy sobs pouring from her.

As if on cue, Baby Dupree began to cry too, kicking her little, chubby legs.

"Shhhh, hush, baby," Aunt Madge sniffled as she rocked the baby. "It's your mother's birthday today and I don't even know where she is or what she's doing."

Baby Dupree, now four-months-old, gradually stopped crying and stared up at her grandaunt as if she understood what she was saying.

"But I know she is alive," Aunt Madge continued talking to the baby in a teary voice. "I can feel it in my soul. My niece is alive because I trust my Lord to take care of her."

Aunt Madge groaned and stood up as if she was in pain, balancing Baby Dupree over her shoulder. Walking into the living room, she went and sat around the small table with the baby in her lap. Sitting in the middle of the table were her prized crockery dishes containing mouthwatering ackee and saltfish and thick, yellow slices of roasted breadfruit. A small kettle pot of hot chocolate tea completed the menu. Tiny's favorite breakfast.

Although she had no appetite, Aunt Madge placed a small serving of food on her plate and poured out some hot chocolate in her mug. Baby Dupree grabbed at the plate, and she shoved it further back on the table, out of her reach. "Dear Lord, today is Tiny's sixteenth birthday, and I want to take this time to thank you for her," Aunt Madge prayed. "She is not in my sight right now, but she is in yours. Please, I'm begging you that wherever she is, let her know that I love her and my arms are wide open waiting for her to come home. Please provide her with food, shelter, and clothes, my Lord. I ask that you protect her from the arms of the devil, so anything or anyone that rises up against her cannot prevail. Please keep my baby in your arms until I see her again. These and other mercies I ask in your holy name. Amen."

Taking small nibbles of food, Aunt Madge stared out the window as a sudden peace began to fill her soul. She had no idea where Tiny was or what she was doing at the moment, but she felt in her spirit that she was okay. "Thank you, Holy Spirit," Aunt Madge said aloud. She pushed back her chair from the table and stood up with the baby. "Your mother is all right," Aunt Madge said and tickled the baby's side. Baby Dupree giggled happily, drool running down her chin. "Yes, she is. Yes, she is." And Aunt Madge did something she hadn't done in a long time. She looked up to the heavens and smiled.

"Happy birthday to youuuuu!" A thunderous round of applause and cheers resonated around the room.

Eleanor hung down her head, totally fixated on the floral tablecloth on the table. "Thank you," she said shyly.

"You are welcome, my dear," Mama Pearl said cheerfully from across the table. "I'm so glad that we get to spend this day with you."

Eleanor looked up at her and smiled.

Earlier that morning, as promised, Mama Pearl had prepared her favorite breakfast and served it to her in bed. "Room service for the birthday girl," Mama Pearl had announced as she walked into the room, balancing the tray in her hands. She placed the tray at the foot of the bed. Giving Eleanor a kiss on the cheek, Mama Pearl then walked out of the room, closing the door behind her. Eleanor was left alone to her breakfast. But Eleanor wasn't fooled. Mama Pearl knew she needed that time alone, and she was grateful that she understood.

"For you, Aunt Madge." Eleanor raised her fork with a piece of breadfruit in the air, tears and snot running down her face. "For loving and supporting me, even when I messed up. I love you so much."

Eleanor was sure the food was scrumptious. The smell alone was mouthwatering, but each bite she took tasted like a piece of cardboard. She didn't deserve this. No, not after what she had done. However, she forced herself to eat the meal that was lovingly prepared for her. She had hurt too many people; Mama Pearl wouldn't be one of them.

"Are you okay, Eleanor?" asked Mama Pearl's seven-year-old grandson, Troy, snapping her back to the present. "You look sad."

"Oh. I'm okay, Troy." Eleanor gave him a big smile and a wink. Troy giggled in response.

Eleanor looked around the dining table at the smiling faces that came to dinner for her birthday. The guys were there with their wives and children. The table was laden down with piles of food: curry goat, jerked chicken, escovitch fish, rice and peas, steamed vegetables, lemonade and carrot juice. They had just sung "Happy Birthday" and were getting ready to eat. It might not have been an official birthday party, but it was pretty close to one. These people deserved to know how much she appreciated all that they were doing for her.

"First, I want to say thank you, Mama Pearl," Eleanor said, sniffing her nose as she fought to hold back the tears threatening to fall. "Thank you for everything you are doing for me. If it wasn't for you, I would probably be dead by now. You are my guardian angel, and I thank God for you every day."

Mama Pearl and the wives began to tear up.

"To the rest of you, thank you for allowing me to stay here with your mother and for taking me into your lives. I know you had reservations, but I'm happy that you took a chance on me. I promise I won't ever betray that trust."

By now there were no dry eyes around the table. The men sniffed and twisted uncomfortably in their chairs, while the women blatantly allowed the tears to flow. If Eleanor wasn't already embedded in their hearts, she certainly was then.

"You are welcome, baby," Mama Pearl said through her tears. "You will always have a place in my home and in my heart."

Now Eleanor cried.

"Okay, I'm about to faint from hunger," Omar finally exclaimed, wiping his eyes with the back of his hand. "I think I got something in my eyes." He tried unsuccessfully to downplay his emotions. The table erupted in laughter, and Mama Pearl gave him a knowing smile.

"Okay, Gerald. Please bless the table so we can eat," Mama Pearl said with her too sweet smile.

"Oh, man," Gerald groaned, and another round of laughter reverberated around the room.

Chapter Twenty-two

Eleanor perched on the edge of the couch in the living room, staring at Robert like he was an alien from Mars with two heads. "Why . . . Why are you asking?" she stuttered.

Robert sighed loudly. "Eleanor, I'm not trying to get into your business. I can tell by how articulate you are that you have had some education. I'm just trying to get you back in school for the new school year which begins in September," he explained. "That is just a few weeks away. As a professor, education is very important to me, and I want you to get a good education." Robert was a mathematics professor at the University of the West Indies.

Eleanor stared down at her entwined fingers in her lap, kicking her legs nervously. Robert had just asked her where she had gone to school. This was one question that she could not and would not answer. It would reveal where she was from, and that information could not be made known.

"I can't say, Robert," Eleanor whispered as she looked at him with pleading eyes. "I know you are trying to help me, and I would like to go back to school, but my past has to remain exactly that way. My past. It's best for a lot of people."

Robert saw the fear in her eyes and relented. "Okay. I was only going to send for your school records so we can get you into another school," he said. "I assume you never finished high school?"

An image of the baby flashed into Eleanor's mind. She shuddered. "No, I was one year away from graduating."

"Really? Eleanor, that's awesome," Robert said enthusiastically. "I knew you were a smart girl."

Eleanor blushed and looked away.

"Well, Sydney and I are going to have to call in some favors to see if we can get you into a school," Robert said in reference to his brother, who was the principal of Calabar High School for boys.

"Thank you, Robert," Eleanor said excitedly. "I would really love to take my CXC exams. I know I'll pass them." The Caribbean Examination Council examinations (CXC) were usually taken by students after five years of secondary school to mark the end of it and for those who wished to continue their education at the tertiary level.

"All right, kiddo. Let me get to work," Robert joked as he stood to his feet. "I'll keep you posted."

Eleanor stood to her feet and walked with him to the door. "Thank you," she told him again. "I'll tell Mama Pearl that you stopped by." Mama Pearl was visiting a church sister in the hospital.

"She knew I was going to stop by." Robert grinned and gave her a wink before he strolled off toward his car parked in the driveway.

Eleanor shook her head and smiled. Earlier that evening Mama Pearl got dressed and hurried out of the house so fast, Eleanor wondered what was the rush. Now she knew.

"Yes! Yes! Yes!" Eleanor screamed as she danced around the room. "I'm going back to school," she sang happily.

Mama Pearl, Omar, and Robert laughed as they watched her. It was refreshing to see a young girl that enthusiastic to continue her education.

"I know it's just evening classes, but that's the best we could do under the circumstances," Robert said once they were all sitting down. "These are CXC preparatory classes at Ardenne High School for one year."

Robert went on to explain that the vice principal of Ardenne High School, Mr. Pryce, was a colleague of theirs. He had tried to get Eleanor into the regular day classes, but with no school record or birth certificate, it wasn't possible. However, he pulled a few strings and got her in the evening classes instead.

"That's even better, Robert," Eleanor said with a wide grin on her face. "I can do all my chores around the house before I go to class."

"Now don't you be worrying about no chores," Mama Pearl remarked. "You are going to study hard, do your homework, and pass those exams."

"I can do both, Mama Pearl," Eleanor told her. "Aunt Madge used to say I'm a little genius."

The room was arrested in total silence as three pair of curious eyes stared at Eleanor. Eleanor folded her lips and looked down at the floor.

"Aunt Madge sounds like a smart lady," Mama Pearl said to break the awkward moment. "I hope one day you will tell us some more about her."

Eleanor nodded, her eyes blinking rapidly, still refusing to make eye contact.

"Looks like we now have a little schoolgirl in the house," Omar said jokingly to clear the air.

"Shut up, Omar." Eleanor rolled her eyes at him, smiling. Mama Pearl and Robert shook their heads at their antics. The subject of Aunt Madge was left alone, at least for now.

The next week Eleanor sat in the back of the bus, clutching her book bag tightly to her chest as it headed up Half Way Tree Road toward Hope Road. Looking through the window she passed some of the places she had wandered while living on the streets. There was the restaurant where the owner had chased her out with a broom after he caught her taking leftovers off the tables. She saw the large commercial garbage bin in the plaza where she had found a half-eaten mango. A shiver ran down her spine as she passed the park where she had awakened to see the naked man running away from her.

"Thank you, God," Eleanor muttered under her breath, her vision becoming blurry from unshed tears. "Thank you for rescuing me."

It was Eleanor's first evening attending classes. She was excited, though a little apprehensive. Her life had changed so much since the last time she sat in a classroom. Would she be able to pick up where she had left off? What if she didn't understand anything that was being taught? What if she failed her exams? Those were some of the questions that flooded her mind. Just then, Eleanor heard Aunt Madge's voice playing in her head as if she was sitting right there beside her.

"Baby, you are a special gift from God. He will never leave you nor forsake you," Aunt Madge had told her one morning when she had reservations about taking a final exam. "Just remember to pray and turn everything over to the Lord. He will do the rest."

And that's exactly what Eleanor did after she entered the classroom and took a seat at the back. She breathed a word of prayer, leaving it all in God's hand.

Chapter Twenty-three

"Can you believe that it's Christmas already?" Mama Pearl asked Eleanor as they made dinner together one Saturday afternoon. "The year is almost gone." Not getting a response, Mama Pearl stopped peeling the yam. She turned to look at Eleanor with concern. "Eleanor, are you okay?"

No response.

Eleanor's mind was miles away in Falmouth, Trelawny. Holding a green banana in one hand and a knife in the other, she stared through the kitchen window with a deep sense of emptiness in her soul. *This will be my first Christmas without Aunt Madge,* Eleanor pondered silently. *It will also the baby's first Christmas.*

It took time, but as the days ran into weeks and weeks into months, the little scary creature was gradually becoming a baby in Eleanor's thoughts. For the life of her, Eleanor just couldn't understand why she had had that reaction to her baby. She just knew she had lost her mind. Yes, it was temporary insanity. Thank God she ran away when she did because as crazy as she was, she would definitely have hurt that child. "I'm glad I didn't hurt you, Dupree," Eleanor whispered aloud. "You are better off with Aunt Madge than you would be with me."

"Who is Dupree?" Mama Pearl asked in a baffled voice, resting her hip against the kitchen counter, giving Eleanor her undivided attention.

Eleanor's neck snapped around to Mama Pearl in a flash, her mouth forming a big "O." Good God, she'd just said that aloud. "Dupree?" she asked Mama Pearl stupidly.

"Yes, you just said you were glad you didn't hurt Dupree," Mama Pearl said calmly. "So who is Dupree, and why would you want to hurt her?"

Eleanor stared down at her feet for a few seconds before she looked up and made eye contact with Mama Pearl. "Mama Pearl, there are a lot of things in my past that I am running away from. Things I'm too embarrassed to even think about at times," Eleanor said slowly. "Sometimes I wonder why I didn't just die in that old car, so I wouldn't have these demons riding my back."

"The devil is a lie," Mama Pearl replied in a voice that sounded so much like Aunt Madge. She put the piece of yam she held in her hand on the kitchen counter. She walked over to Eleanor and pulled her into her arms. "I rebuke every thought of death that comes to your mind," Mama Pearl said as she squeezed Eleanor tighter. "I rebuke the voice of the devil telling you that you cannot be forgiven. Baby, God is a forgiving God. If you ask Him for forgiveness, He will wipe all your sins away."

Eleanor clung to Mama Pearl as if her life depended on it. Tears and snot dampened the front of Mama Pearl's blouse. "Maybe one day I'll be free," Eleanor mumbled into Mama Pearl's bosom. "The day when I can finally say 'Amen.'"

"You will, my dear," Mama Pearl told Eleanor with confidence. "It's the day you will realize that God has spoken."

So Christmas came and went in a fog for Eleanor, as did the New Year of 1980. She participated in all the festivities that Mama Pearl and the family had, forcing herself not to be a spoiled sport. She went to church for

Christmas and also for watch night service, to ring in the New Year. But as much as she tried, Eleanor knew it would be a long time before she ever really enjoyed the holidays.

Then there was today. January 25th, 1980. Baby Dupree's first birthday.

Eleanor had sat up in bed the night before, looking up at the big round clock mounted on the wall before her. Each ticking sound seemed to hit a nerve in her head. Round and round it went, seconds into minutes, minutes into hours, until it stuck 12:00 a.m.

"Happy birthday, Dupree," Eleanor whispered into the night. "May God forever hold you in His arms and protect you from the evil of this world." Tears rained down her cheeks. "I hope one day I'll see you again and you will be able to forgive me. I'm sorry for everything."

Eleanor rolled over onto her stomach. Burying her face in the pillow to muffle her cries, she wept for a long time. Finally exhaustion sneaked up on her and she fell into a deep restless sleep, plagued by nightmares. She dreamed of cuddling Baby Dupree in her arms and suddenly she changed into the scary creature with long teeth, lashing out at her face.

Eleanor woke up screaming and gasping for breath, her body soaked wet with sweat. She looked around the room frantically before she remembered where she was. Then her eyes flew to the door in alarm. Had she wakened Mama Pearl and Omar? She hoped not because she didn't want to deal with the questions. She knew they cared for her, and she felt like she was betraying them by not answering their questions.

Eleanor swung her legs over the side of the bed and stood up. Noticing the sheet laying on the floor, she reached down, picked it up, and threw it back on the bed. She softly opened her bedroom door halfway. Looking up and down the hallway, she neither saw nor heard anything.

On tiptoes, Eleanor crept hurriedly into the kitchen. Her body stumbled back sharply as she collided with a wall of flesh and bones. Recovering quickly, Eleanor grabbed ahold of the door before she fell. Almost simultaneously two arms reached out and grabbed her arm. Too wrapped up in her thoughts, she had failed to see Omar standing in the kitchen.

"I'm so, so, sorry," Eleanor apologized, her face flushed with embarrassment.

"Are you okay?" Omar asked with concern as he searched her face.

Eleanor nodded and looked away in an attempt to hide her red, puffy eyes. "Yes, I'm okay."

Omar strolled over to the dish drainer and took out a glass. Walking over to the kitchen sink, he turned on the tap and filled the glass with water. "Here you go," he said to Eleanor as he handed her the water.

"Thank you," Eleanor said before she thirstily drank some of the water. "I needed that." She took a quick peek at Omar before looking away.

"You are welcome." Omar smiled as he tried to put her at ease. "I actually came to get some water to bring to you."

Eleanor's eyes opened wide as she looked at him. "Me?"

"Yes, I heard you screaming in your room," he replied in a low voice. "I knew you were having those nightmares again."

"I'm sorry I woke you up." Eleanor covered her mouth with her hand. "I was so hoping that I didn't wake you or Mama Pearl."

"I know we have been asking you this since you came to live with us, but do you want to talk about it?" Omar asked kindly. "I won't say a word to anyone if you don't want me to. I promise."

Eleanor looked at him silently. *Maybe it would help if I have someone I can talk to about all this. But then I would have to tell him of my scandalous behavior with Officer Gregg, and he might not look at me the same again.*

"I won't judge you," Omar said as if he had read her mind. "Only one person can judge you and that's God Almighty. I know I'm the man, but I must confess, I'm not *that* man," he joked.

Eleanor gave a small laugh. "You are something else, you know that?" she smiled at him. "Thank you for offering. If and when I'm ready to talk, you will be the first person I'll turn to." She gave him a kind smile.

"I'll hold you to that." Omar returned the smile. "You are like my little, naughty sister now, you know?"

"Shut up, Omar." Eleanor laughed. She waved her hand as if to throw the rest of the water in the glass on him.

"Hey, watch it now." Omar laughed as he ran to the door. He paused and turned around to look at Eleanor. "With God's help, you will be all right," he said before he walked away.

Eleanor stared at the empty doorway for a moment, allowing Omar's words to penetrate her soul. "Yes, I'll be all right. Aunt Madge and the baby will be all right, also. I have to believe that."

"Dupree, leave that cake alone," Aunt Madge remarked with a smile from the living-room doorway as she watched Dupree trying to hook her small, chubby legs around the chair to reach the cake on the table.

Dupree giggled and took a few quick, unaided, wobbly steps toward Aunt Madge.

"Wow, be careful now," Aunt Madge said as she quickly reached down and lifted the baby in her arms. "Look

at you, trying to run." She kissed Dupree on her cheek.
"Happy birthday to you," Aunt Madge sang and tickled
Dupree's side.

Dupree giggled and wiggled happily in her grandaunt's
arms.

"We are waiting for Mother Sassy and her grandkids to
come, then we're going to have a little party for you." She
kissed the baby all over her face. "Who is one-year-old
today? Dupree!" Aunt Madge placed her hands under
Dupree's stomach and held her up in the air. Dupree
squealed as she waved and kicked her legs contentedly.

"Sister Madge? Sister Madge, we're here," came Mother
Sassy's low voice from outside.

Aunt Madge walked to the door with Dupree and saw
Mother Sassy and her five grandchildren coming down
the narrow dirt track that led to the house. The noise
level went up as the kids ran ahead of their grandmother,
laughing and talking as they hurried toward the house.

Dupree began twisting and turning excitedly in Aunt
Madge's arms.

"Oh, so now you have company you want to get down,
huh?" Aunt Madge said as she carefully walked down the
steps into the yard. She put Dupree down on the ground
and soon the baby was engulfed in other arms as the
kids passed her from one hand to the other, kissing and
tickling her. Dupree laughed and giggled uncontrollably.

Aunt Madge and Mother Sassy carried the small kitchen
table out to the yard, positioning a chair in front of it for
the birthday girl. They placed the birthday cake that Aunt
Madge bought from the bakery in town, in the middle.
Tasty fried chicken, corn beef sandwiches, slices of hard
dough bread, and lemonade decorated the table.

The kids gathered around Dupree, who stood on the
chair, staring excitedly at the cake. A few times she
reached out to grab it but Aunt Madge caught her hand.
The other kids laughed in amusement.

"Well, let us bless this food and the birthday girl so we can eat," Mother Sassy said as she joined hands with her grandchildren who stood on both sides of her. The other kids and Aunt Madge did the same. "Dear Lord, we are here to celebrate Baby Dupree's first birthday. We ask that you be with her today and for many, many more birthdays to come," Mother Sassy prayed loudly. "Give her your blessings. Hallelujah, hallelujah." By now Mother Sassy was doing a little jig, shaking the hands of her wide-eyed grandchildren rapidly as she caught the spirit. "Take her into your arms. Hallelujah, hallelujah."

Aunt Madge took a peek out of one eye and saw all the children, including Dupree, staring at Mother Sassy. But no one made a move or said a word as that was strictly forbidden.

"You are the Almighty God. You are our Savior and there is nothing too hard for you," Mother Sassy continued to pray. "This child will never want for anything. I said *anything!* Hallelujah, hallelujah."

"Amen. Amen," Aunt Madge said quickly and brought the prayer to a close. Had she not done that, Mother Sassy would have gone on for a long, long time. "Thanks for the prayer, my friend." Aunt Madge walked over to Mother Sassy who was perspiring profusely and gave her a hug. The women had been friends for years, and no matter what, they were always there for each other.

"You are welcome, my dear," Mother Sassy replied as she wiped her face with a towel that she had around her neck. "Time to cut the cake, everyone."

The kids cheered and clapped their hands.

"No, baby. Dupree. Wait until—" Aunt Madge watched helplessly as Dupree reached over and sank her hands into the cake. She was too late to stop her this time.

Dupree giggled as she tried to stuff a heap of cake into her little mouth, the icing smearing her face, hands, and her clothes. Laughter resonated around the yard.

"I think Dupree is telling us to eat," Aunt Madge said with a laugh. Soon everyone had a plate filled with food, eating, laughing, and having a good time.

Later as Aunt Madge watched the kids playing hide-and-seek and jump rope, she visualized Tiny when she was small and doing the same thing. Tears filled her eyes. "I may have lost one child, but I have another who needs me," Aunt Madge whispered to herself. "I have to carry on and be strong for Dupree."

Chapter Twenty-four

The school year went by pretty fast for Eleanor. After a few weeks, she felt as if she had never left. Eleanor decided to take five CXC exams: mathematics, English, accounting, Principles of Business, and biology. She had passed all the preparatory tests that her teacher gave her with flying colors. It was looking really good for these exams.

"I have to pass theses exams," Eleanor played over and over in her head. "I have sacrificed and lost too much to turn back now." And like an obsessed manic, she studied religiously. Eleanor did all her chores in the morning, despite Mama Pearl's objection as she wanted her to concentrate on school. She went to classes in the evenings. After getting home at night, she locked herself in her room and studied until the wee hours of the morning. Soon it was time for her first exam, mathematics.

"You are going to do fine," Mama Pearl told Eleanor as they sat on the couch in the living room that morning. "You have been preparing for this, and the Lord is going to see it through. Okay, my dear?"

Eleanor nodded reluctantly, her face etched in concern. "I'm just very nervous, Mama Pearl," she said, shaking her legs and cracking her knuckles. "I never knew I would ever get this opportunity again. Now that it's here, I don't want to blow it or let you down."

"And you won't, Eleanor," Mama Pearl assured her.

"I'm so grateful that you and the guys paid for my CXC exams," Eleanor said, struggling not to cry. "You have done so much for me. I love you all."

"And we love you," Mama Pearl replied as tears glittered in her eyes. "Come and give me a hug."

Eleanor reached over and hugged the woman who had changed her life.

"Now I know you had some difficulties with the math, but Robert helped you with that and you aced the prep test, right?" Mama Pearl said once they pulled apart and sat facing each other again.

"Yes," Eleanor responded softly. Math was Eleanor's least favorite subject. She had always found it challenging since high school. Luckily for her she had a mathematics professor on call who helped her work through the kinks.

"You better get going before you're late," Mama Pearl said with a wide smile. "Go and make yourself proud."

"Thank you." Eleanor gave her a kiss on the cheek. She stood up and grabbed her book bag that was beside her, before hurrying out the door to catch the bus.

That afternoon when Eleanor got home, she noticed the cars parked in the driveway and on the street outside the house. Worried, she hurried inside to find out what was going on.

As she entered the living room she saw Robert, Alwayne, Sydney, Gerald, Omar, and Mama Pearl sitting on the couches. They jumped to their feet when they saw her.

"What's wrong?" Eleanor asked as she looked from one face to another. "Is it Mama Pearl?" She walked over to Mama Pearl looking her up from head to toe.

"I'm fine." Mama Pearl waved off her concern. "You had your first exam today."

"*That's* why you are all here?" Eleanor asked in an incredulous voice as she looked from one smiling face to another.

"That's right," Alwayne replied lightly. "We are here to let you know how much we care about you."

"And we are supporting you now and always," Sydney added with a big grin.

Eleanor hung down her head and cried. *I am the luckiest girl on earth*, she thought. *I really don't deserve these people.*

Over the next few days, Eleanor took her other exams and felt confident about the results. *"You can only do your best, baby,"* Aunt Madge had told her a few times. *"And only your best is good enough."*

Eleanor had to wait to see if her best would give her the results that she wanted.

It was the summer of 1980 and Eleanor fell back into her old routine now that she had completed her classes and taken her exams. She woke up early and helped Mama Pearl with breakfast. She cleaned the house from top to bottom, did the laundry, swept the yard, and went grocery shopping as needed. Once her chores were completed, she would retire to the living room or her bedroom where she read books she borrowed from the public library or watched television. In the evening she prepared dinner when it was her turn to do so.

"Okay, this has to stop right now," Mama Pearl said one day as she walked into Eleanor's bedroom where she lay on the bed reading a book. "You are a seventeen-year-old girl living like a seventy-year-old woman."

Eleanor looked up at her and smiled. "I'm fine, Mama Pearl. I'm not bored at all."

"No, you need to meet some friends who you can hang out with and have fun with," Mama Pearl said to her.

Eleanor winced when she heard the word "friend." She had a friend who she had fun with, or so she thought. It was that friendship that contributed to the hell she found herself in. The same friend who later turned her back on her for a nasty, lowlife man.

"No, thank you," Eleanor replied quickly. "I don't need any friends. I have you and Omar here."

"That's not the same, and you know it." Mama Pearl frowned. "Well, how about a little part-time job to get you out of the house from time to time?"

"Really?" Eleanor sat upright on the bed. "I would like that very much, Mama Pearl."

"Okay, let me speak to the boys and have them look around for you," Mama Pearl said in a beaming voice, excited that she finally had an idea that Eleanor liked. "I'll be asking around as well."

"Thank you, Mama Pearl." Eleanor jumped off the bed into Mama Pearl's arms.

The following week Eleanor started her job as a part-time cashier for a hardware store in Cross Roads. The store owner, Mr. Kennelly, was a good friend of Alwayne. Eleanor worked from 12:00 p.m. to 5:00 p.m., Monday to Saturday. This gave her enough time to help around the house before she left for work. She loved her job and enjoyed the different people she met on a daily basis. Her boss was also a very friendly, jovial person. Eleanor knew she was blessed.

A few days later as Eleanor walked into the house after work, she saw the entire family gathered again in the living room. "What happened this time? I didn't get a promotion," she joked.

"No, but you got something else," Mama Pearl said elatedly. "You got *this!*" she waved an envelope in the air.

"Oh my God. Is that what I think it is?" Eleanor asked, stunned.

"Yup," answered Gerald. "It's your CXC results."

"I called all of them to be here," Mama Pearl said gently. "Whatever this piece of paper says, even though I already know deep down in my soul, we are here for you."

"Even if I failed them all?" Eleanor asked as she walked over to Mama Pearl and took the envelope from her outstretched hand.

"You didn't fail," Omar said confidently. "Go on and open it." He nodded toward the envelope.

Eleanor took a deep breath. Her knees felt like Jell-O. With trembling fingers, she ripped the envelope open and took out the piece of paper inside. Silence surrounded the room as everyone looked at one another expectantly.

"I can't look," Eleanor said nervously. "Here, you read it and tell us." She handed the piece of paper to Omar.

Omar quickly grabbed it out of her hand and looked at it. His brows knitted in a frown as he stared at it without saying a word.

"Man, what are you waiting for?" Robert asked impatiently. "World War III?"

"I'm sorry, Eleanor," Omar began dramatically, sniffing as if he was about to cry. "You didn't pass one—"

"*What do you mean she didn't pass?*" Mama Pearl snapped. "Boy, give me that letter."

"—You passed *all* of them!" Omar screamed. The room exploded in cheers. A weeping Eleanor was passed from one to the other as she hugged and kissed in congratulatory bliss.

"Girl, you really mashed up those exams." Mama Pearl allowed the tears to flow freely down her face. "Didn't I tell all of you that God never makes a mistake?"

Her sons nodded and grinned happily. It was truly a milestone in Eleanor's journey to success, but redemption would take a little longer.

Chapter Twenty-five

Eleanor got accepted into Excelsior Community College the fall of 1980. Again, Robert and Sydney made some contacts and called in some favors. Even though Eleanor had passed her CXC exams, she didn't have a copy of her birth certificate as required. She decided to take four preuniversity A-level courses: business management, English language, accounting, and principles of business in the evening school.

To accommodate her school schedule, Eleanor reduced her work hours from 12:00 p.m. to 4:00 p.m., Monday through Friday. Her classes were from 5:00 p.m. to 8:00 p.m. This left her mornings free to do her house chores, and Sunday was reserved for church.

"I think you're doing too much," Mama Pearl complained to Eleanor one day. "You don't have to work now that you have started school, Eleanor."

"I can manage, Mama Pearl," Eleanor reassured her. "I've reduced my time at work, and I attend school in the evening, so I have it covered. Don't worry, I can do this, okay?"

"All right, but if you ever feel overwhelmed I want you to let me know," Mama Pearl said in a serious voice. "You are too young to be taking on all of this by yourself."

But Eleanor never felt overwhelmed. It was actually the opposite. She welcomed the opportunity to be busy. The more she worked, the less time she had to think about Aunt Madge and the baby. "I don't even deserve this chance," she often reminded herself. "But for some reason the Lord sees fit to give it to me. Why? I'm not sure, but I have to make the most of it." And she did.

One of the few things that Eleanor took real pleasure in, outside of school and work, was going to church. She grew up in the church. Aunt Madge was a long-standing member of Worship and Fellowship Church of God, and as such, Eleanor spent a lot of time at church since she was a child. She attended church service every Sunday, Sunday School, Bible Study, prayer meetings, and sang in the junior choir. Her entire life revolved around church—until Dolly came along. It was then that everything started going downhill. Eleanor walked out of the presence of God into the arms of the devil.

It was different this time around. Eleanor started attending church with Mama Pearl because she wanted to make a good impression on her. However, as time went by, something got ahold of her heart and her soul. She was held captivated by the word and the power of the Lord. *It makes sense what the pastor is saying about God being a merciful God,* Eleanor thought as she sat in service one Sunday morning. *Look at what God has done for me after everything I have done. He saved my life and gave me a wonderful family to live with. There may be hope for me after all.*

So Eleanor began to read her Bible more, pray a little more, and hope for more.

Before long, after almost two years of hard work and dedication, nineteen-year-old Eleanor completed her preuniversity course at Excelsior Community College in May of 1982. She aced all four A-level exams, earning a certificate in business administration.

It was a bittersweet experience for Eleanor. The runaway, homeless teenager was elated that she was accomplishing her academic goals, but the teenage mother who abandoned her child was still held captive in despair. It was as if she was winning the battle but losing the war. At times Eleanor's mind was so consumed with Aunt Madge and Dupree, she was unable to eat or sleep. Her daughter was now three-years-old, and she had no idea what she looked like. She didn't know her mannerisms or her personality. She knew nothing about Dupree. But through it all, Eleanor knew in her heart that Dupree was well taken care of. After all, Aunt Madge raised Eleanor, so she was confident that Dupree would receive the same love and nurture.

It was a beautiful Saturday afternoon. Eleanor, Omar, and Mama Pearl were all sitting in the backyard under some big mango trees with the cool Jamaican breeze fanning their faces. As they conversed, Robert walked around the side of the house into the backyard.

"Hey, baby. How are you?" Mama Pearl greeted her son happily. "I didn't know you were going to stop by."

"Hi, Mama." Robert walked over to his mother and kissed her on the cheek. "Hello, Eleanor. Omar, how are you?" he said as he lowered himself into an empty chair beside Eleanor.

Both Eleanor and Omar returned Robert's greetings. They all noticed the big grin on his face and looked at him puzzled.

"Okay, what's going on?" Mama Pearl asked, not known for her patience. "You look like you just won a million dollars."

"This is even better." Robert winked at her. He turned around and faced Eleanor, who was watching him with a puzzled look on her face. "So are you ready for this?" Robert asked her excitedly, rubbing his hands together, beaming from ear to ear.

"Huh? I guess so," Eleanor replied hesitantly, watching his face intently for a clue to his excitement.

"You are going to give that girl a heart attack, Robert." Mama Pearl laughed and rested her head back on the lounge chair where she sat.

"He is going to give *me* a heart attack," Omar said impatiently. "Out with it, man."

Robert reached out and took Eleanor's hands into his. "How would you like to attend the University of the West Indies this fall?" he asked in a loud, animated voice.

One could have heard a needle drop in a pile of cotton.

"What did you just say?" Eleanor asked as her body began to tremble uncontrollably.

"Come again?" Omar asked almost simultaneously, leaning forward to stare at his brother.

Mama Pearl, for maybe the first time in her life, was speechless.

"You got in!" Robert yelled happily. "You have been accepted into the Undergraduate Human Resources Management Program."

"Lordy, Lordy, Lordy," Mama Pearl chanted, shaking her head from side to side. "Lordy, Lordy, Lordy."

This was too much for Eleanor. She bent over at a ninety-degree angle, rested her throbbing head in her lap, and bawled. Heart-pulling sobs pulsated throughout her entire body.

Mama Pearl, Omar, and Robert gathered around her, rubbing her back, her head, and whispering words of comfort and congratulations in her ears. But they allowed her this well deserved cry.

Minutes later the crying faded to sniffles. Eleanor lifted up her head, snot and tears staining her face. Robert handed her his handkerchief, and she wiped her face and blew her nose. "I don't deserve this," Eleanor said in a hoarse voice. "I'm grateful for this opportunity, but I can't go." She burst out in tears again before she jumped to her feet and ran into the house.

Mama Pearl, Omar, and Robert looked at one another in shock.

"What just happened?" Robert asked perplexed. "I had to jump through hoops to get her into this program. I thought I was doing the right thing."

"You are doing the right thing, my son," Mama Pearl said as she sat in the chair that Eleanor occupied earlier. "This isn't about you or even UWI. This is Eleanor's demons rearing their hungry heads."

"What can we do to help her?" Omar asked in a troubled voice.

"We *are* doing it, baby," Mama Pearl replied gently. "We just have to continue to love and support her and let the Lord to do the rest."

Chapter Twenty-six

In her bedroom, Eleanor knelt down on the floor rug, her elbows rested on the bed, her hands folded together. "Lord, why are you opening these doors for me but still can't fill the hole in my heart?" Eleanor prayed tearfully as she looked toward the heavens. "Will I ever see Aunt Madge and Dupree again? Will I ever be completely free of this ache that dominates my soul?" Eleanor hung down her head and wept, hoping that one day God would finally speak.

There she stayed for what seemed like hours, down on her knees, wallowing in her pain and grief. Slowly, Eleanor stood shakily to her feet, wincing at the cramp in her back. She walked over to the window and looked out into the now dark backyard, illuminated by the lightbulbs on the side of the house. Mama Pearl, Robert, and Omar were gone.

Walking into the adjoining bathroom, Eleanor went over to the face basin and turned on the tap, splashing water all over her face. After drying her face with a towel, she stared at her red, swollen eyes in the mirror.

"I need to go and apologize to Mama Pearl, Robert, and Omar," Eleanor said aloud. "But especially to Robert, who went out of his way to help me, only to have it thrown back into his face." Shame washed over Eleanor like a straitjacket. Taking a deep breath, she spun around on her heel and walked out of the bathroom.

As Eleanor softly approached the living room she noticed how quiet it was. Where was everyone? Upon entering the room, Mama Pearl, Robert, and Omar jumped to their feet, their faces full of worry.

"Are you okay?" Omar asked anxiously.

"I'm so sorry, Eleanor," Robert said with an uneasiness in his voice.

"Sugar, are you all right?" Mama Pearl asked sadly.

They all spoke at the same time.

"I'm feeling a little better now," Eleanor said, wringing her hands nervously. "I owe the three of you an apology. In fact—"

"No apology is necessary," Robert said quickly.

"Yes, yes, it is," Eleanor insisted, raising her right hand to stop his objections. "My behavior earlier has nothing to do with you wonderful people. It's all me."

Eleanor faced Robert and looked him in the eye. "Robert, the fact that you would think of doing something like this for me blows my mind," she said sincerely. "I love you for thinking of me and wanting to see the best in me."

Robert blinked rapidly as unshed tears filled his eyes. "You *are* going to accept it, right?" he asked her. "My brothers and I have already discussed this, and we all agreed that we want to do this for you, Eleanor. We are going to pay your tuition and take care of all your school expenses as we have been doing. Please say yes."

Eleanor practically leaped into his arms, her hands wrapped tightly around his neck in a tight hold.

"Hmmm, killing him is probably a little bit too extreme, don't you think?" Omar said jokingly.

Everyone laughed, relieving some of the tension that held the room hostage. However, the thousand-pound gorilla refused to leave the room.

"I have done some despicable things," Eleanor said after releasing Robert and facing everyone. "I have hurt people I love and who love me. For the most part, I don't feel I deserve all this." She opened her arms wide as her eyes swept the room.

"Yes, you do, my dear," Mama Pearl said in a firm voice. "You deserve God's mercy, forgiveness, and grace, like everyone else. You have gained a new family and us a daughter and sister. I am not going to stop praying until you finally break free from your past and accept your future."

"Amen," said Omar. "So you better pack your book bag and get ready for UWI."

"UWI, huh?" Eleanor couldn't stop the little smile that began to form on her face. "Me? Eleanor? Studying at the University of the West Indies?" she asked in an incredulous voice, shaking her head from side to side.

"Yes, and you are lucky you aren't majoring in math and get me for your professor," Robert said in a jovial voice. "So what do you say, are we going to do this?"

"You really think I can do it?" Eleanor asked doubtfully, her eyes moving back and forth between Robert, Mama Pearl, and Omar.

"Eleanor, you *have* been doing it," Robert told her. "You passed your CXC and A-Level exams. This will be no different because you are a brilliant young lady."

Eleanor blushed and hung down her head. "I can do it. I really can do it," she muttered as she paced the floor. "You did this for me, and I'm going to make all of you proud." She looked from Robert, to Mama Pearl, to Omar. "I'm going to UWI," she said in a low voice.

Everyone began to cheer. Eleanor was heading down the path that the Lord was making for her.

Chapter Twenty-seven

Almost four years later, Eleanor was a seasoned full-time university student. She had switched her hours at the hardware store to afternoons and reduced her working days to three days per week so she could attend classes in morning and still have time to help with house chores.

Eleanor was an A student. She studied hard, excelled in all her classes, and was just a few weeks away from completing her bachelor of science degree in Human Resources Management.

Now twenty-three-years old, Eleanor was a tall, slim, beautiful woman with a megawatt smile. She was a devoted Christian and a wonderful daughter and sister to her informal adopted family. Many people saw Eleanor as the epitome of good, and the essence of physical beauty. A role she played very well.

Eleanor had learned to function and adjust to her new life. She even had happy moments, especially around the family and at church. It was when she was alone, especially in the wee hours of the morning that her demons surfaced. Images of the aunt and the daughter she abandoned continued to eat at her soul. No matter what she did, there was always a dark cloud hanging over her happiness, and she doubted it would ever go away. It was like having God whispering in one ear, telling her that she is worthy of His love and the devil in the other ear, telling her she deserved to rot in hell. It was an agonizing, mental warfare in her head.

"Hello? Is anyone in there?" said an amused voice outside Eleanor's bedroom door, followed by a soft knock.

Eleanor quickly sat up on the bed, tucking her dress under her legs, textbooks scattered all around her. "Come in, Bighead," she said loudly with a laugh.

Omar laughed as he opened the door, stepping into the room. "I'm Bighead, and you're Dumbhead," he responded playfully.

"Oh, please," Eleanor replied with a smirk, rolling her eyes. "You are looking at an A student about to graduate from UWI *with honors.*"

"Look at you showing off." Omar smiled as he sat down on the edge of the bed, facing Eleanor. "I'm proud of you, little sis."

Eleanor returned the smile and looked at him affectionately. The tall, handsome, twenty-eight-year old was now an assistant branch manager at the Bank of Nova Scotia (BNS) and engaged to be married to a wonderful woman, whom Eleanor liked.

"I'm proud of you too, big brother." Eleanor grinned. "Rose is a lucky woman," she said in reference to Omar's fiancée.

"I'm the lucky one." he blushed. "Sometimes I can't believe that I'm getting married. Me? About to become somebody's husband." He shook his head.

"You are going to be a great husband," Eleanor said softly. "And look at the bright side. You will be moving out, and I won't have to see your ugly face every day."

Omar grabbed a pillow near his hand and threw it at Eleanor. Their laughter resounded around the room. They had grown very close over the years and had developed an awesome relationship.

"I just wanted to let you know I'm going on the road," Omar said. "Do you want to take a ride with me? Get away from the books for a while?"

"No, thanks," Eleanor replied quickly. "I need to finish this chapter and start dinner soon."

"Eleanor, it's Saturday," Omar said. "You need to get out of the house once in a while."

"I do get out." Eleanor cut her eyes at him.

"Only to go to school, church, or work," he said. "You don't go out with friends, go watch a movie, go to the mall, or do something fun."

"I don't have time for fun," Eleanor snapped. "I have to stay focused on what's important." But in her heart Eleanor knew Omar was right. She had locked herself in a shell and refused to let anyone get too close.

Omar sighed. "Okay, we will be back for dinner," he said gently. "Tomorrow, you and I are going to Devon's House after church for ice cream." He raised a hand when Eleanor opened her mouth to object. "After which we are going to take a drive up into the hills and do some sightseeing. Got that?" Omar grinned at her.

Eleanor laughed. "Okay, Daddy," she said jokingly. "Whatever you say, sir."

Omar laughed and pinched her toe before standing to his feet. "My guest and I will be here in time for dinner."

"Rose is hardly a guest anymore," Eleanor said to his back as he walked out of the room, closing the door softly behind him.

Eleanor slid down on the bed and looked up at the ceiling. As she stared up at the white blank surface, deep in thought, an image began to form. It was the face of a baby girl, faded at first but got brighter and clearer. Big, brown, sad eyes stared back at her in silence, tears running down her cheeks. Suddenly, the face contorted as if hit by a spasm of pain. In a flash, the baby's face was replaced by the ugly, wrinkled face of the creature. Huge, red eyes glared at her as it snarled its long teeth angrily.

Eleanor's breathing quickened, her heart galloping in her chest like a racing horse. Unable to move or even look away, she gazed wide-eyed at her monster, tears leaking down the sides of her face.

"You are a *fraud*," the monster said in a coarse, booming voice. "You deserve to *die*." Then it leaped from the ceiling.

Eleanor screamed in terror, jumped off the bed, pulled the bedroom door open, and ran out of the house into the backyard. Bent over with her hands resting on her knees, she hyperventilated. Struggling to suck air into her lungs, she exhaled and inhaled deeply.

"How long, Lord?" Eleanor croaked. "How much longer before all this is over?"

It took a few minutes for Eleanor to compose herself. Still visibly shaking and disturbed by the haunting images fabricated in her troubled mind, she went back inside to start dinner.

Chapter Twenty-eight

"Hey, baby," Mama Pearl said as she entered the kitchen, her hands filled with grocery bags.

"Hi, Mama Pearl." Eleanor quickly walked over and took some bags from her hands, placing them on the kitchen counter.

"Didn't I tell you to wait on me so we can make dinner together?" Mama Pearl asked her in a light voice as she put away the contents of her bags. "I thought you were studying for your finals."

"I did some studying," Eleanor replied. "I wanted to get dinner started until you get home. Don't worry, after dinner I'm back to the grindstone."

"In a few weeks you will have your degree." Mama Pearl beamed with pride. "I only wish you would change your mind about attending your graduation ceremony." She turned and looked at Eleanor who refused to make eye contact with her.

"I don't need to attend the ceremony to get my degree, Mama Pearl," Eleanor said subtly. "I don't need all that excitement."

"We wanted to come and cheer you on, take pictures and celebrate with you," Mama Pearl said with a sigh. "But we will respect your wishes. Just know we are all going out to dinner as a family."

Eleanor looked at her. "Mama Pearl! I don't—"

"No. I *don't* want to hear it." Mama Pearl put up her hand to silence Eleanor. "That's not up for debate or discussion. We are going, and that's final."

Eleanor looked at Mama Pearl in defeat. She knew when Mama Pearl made a decision, nothing or no one could change her mind. "Okay, Mama Pearl," she said finally. "I guess we can do dinner."

"Yes! *That's* what I'm talking about," Mama Pearl said happily, as if it was all Eleanor's idea. "Come on, let's finish dinner before our guest arrives."

Moments later dinner was finished and the dining table was set.

"I'm going to take a quick shower before Omar and Rose get's here," Eleanor told Mama Pearl and walked out of the kitchen.

"Oh, it's not Rose," Mama Pearl said at Eleanor's back, but she was already strolling down the hall toward her bedroom.

"Mama Pearl, hello, darling," said a strange, rich, sexy masculine voice.

Eleanor heard Mama Pearl squeal in delight from the dining room. Her brows raised in confusion. Eleanor wondered who it was. She knew it wasn't any of Mama Pearl's sons because she knew their voices.

"The big shot is here, Mama." Omar's voice made its way to Eleanor in the kitchen.

"Man, cut that out," Sexy Voice spoke again. A bout of laughter drifted into the kitchen.

I need to get out of here, Eleanor thought nervously as she looked at the open door.

"Where is Eleanor?" she heard Omar ask.

"She's in the kitchen," Mama Pearl answered. "She just went to get some more ice."

Eleanor looked down and saw the bucket of ice in her hand. She had totally forgotten about it. Great, so much for sneaking off to her room. Mama Pearl would certainly come looking for her. Taking a deep breath, Eleanor walked out of the kitchen and toward the dining room. "Hello," Eleanor said brightly as she entered the room. "Here is—" Her eyes met and locked with a pair of dreamy brown ones. They belonged to a tall, handsome, light-skinned man flashing a killer dimpled smile.

"You must be Eleanor," said Sexy Voice, his grin making his dimples even more conspicuous. In a few long strides he was standing in front of her. "Here, let me help you with that." He took the ice bucket from her hands, his fingers brushing hers lightly.

A chill ran down Eleanor's spine. She watched him silently as he placed the bucket on the dining table. In a flash he was before her again.

"I'm Dwight Humphrey," he said, advertising his thirty-two pearly whites. "It's nice to meet you, Eleanor." He stretched out his right hand toward her.

"Hi," Eleanor replied in a high, squeaky voice and took his hand for a handshake. *Gosh, I sound like a scared little mouse.* Eleanor cleared her throat and tried again. "I'm Eleanor. It's nice to meet you." *Much better. You are a grown woman, for Christ's sake; stop acting like a child.*

Dwight and Eleanor stood staring at each other, their hands still clasped together.

"Ahem," Omar said from behind Eleanor, snapping her back to the present.

"If you two would like to join us for dinner?" Mama Pearl asked sweetly from her seat around the dining table.

Dwight quickly released Eleanor's hand, both of them slightly embarrassed as they took seats around the table. Mama Pearl and Omar looked on in amusement.

"Welcome home, Dwight," Mama Pearl said after she blessed the table and everyone had filled their plates. "I always wondered if you were ever coming back to Jamaica to live."

"You knew I had to come back home, Mama Pearl," Dwight replied. "I accomplished a lot in New York, but I was ready for my island in the sun. Plus, BNS made me an offer I couldn't refuse, so here I am."

"That's an awesome position," Omar said with admiration. "Treasury manager. Congratulations, man."

"Thanks, 'O,'" Dwight replied modestly. "You aren't doing so bad yourself, Mr. Assistant Branch Manager."

"Well, you know how Big 'O' rolls," Omar said smugly, opening his arms wide.

Everyone laughed. Eleanor looked at Omar and rolled her eyes playfully. He winked at her.

"I've been living in New York for the last eight years," Dwight said to Eleanor, his eyes locked on her face. "I went there for college, got a job, and stayed a little while."

Eleanor nodded, her gaze now fixed on the food she shuffled around on her plate. She still hadn't had a bite to eat.

"Omar and I have been friends since high school," Dwight continued, undeterred by her silence. "This used to be like a second home to me. Right, Mama Pearl?"

"I should have charged you rent." Mama Pearl laughed merrily. "As a matter of fact, it's not too late." She stretched out her hand to Dwight, her eyes twinkling in delight.

Dwight and Omar laughed out loud.

Throughout the rest of dinner, Omar, Mama Pearl, and Dwight caught up on their lives and reminisced about old times, while Eleanor listened politely, nodding when necessary. She was aware of Dwight staring at her from time to time, but she refused to get caught up in his dreamy eyes again.

After dinner, Eleanor and Mama Pearl cleaned up, while Omar and Dwight retired to the living room.

"You have been awfully quiet tonight," Mama Pearl said to her while they were in the kitchen washing dishes. "Are you okay?"

"I'm fine." Eleanor gave her a strained smile. "I'm just very anxious about my finals."

"I see." Mama Pearl gave her a knowing look. "Why don't you get back to your studying and I'll finish up here."

"Are you sure?" Eleanor asked her.

"Yes, I'm sure," Mama Pearl replied. "Go on."

"Thanks, Mama Pearl." Eleanor kissed her on the cheek, happy she was escaping Dreamy Eyes.

"Here, take this with you." Mama Pearl handed Eleanor a covered plate of food and a fork "You need to get something in your stomach."

Eleanor looked at her in alarm. "Hmmm . . ."

"You're welcome," Mama Pearl said with a chuckle. "Good night."

Eleanor shook her head and walked out the door, smiling. She paused when she heard voices in the living room and thought about saying good night but felt uneasy about seeing Dwight again. So she took the easy way out and hurried to her room.

Hungry, Eleanor took the covering off the plate and dug into the brown stew chicken and rice like her life depended on it. "Thank you, Mama Pearl," she muttered with her mouth full. Eleanor had been actually planning on sneaking back into the kitchen when everyone was asleep to get some food. Thank God she no longer had to wait that long to eat something.

She brushed her teeth after she ate and changed into her nightgown. Feeling full and more relaxed, she climbed onto her bed and reached for her textbook that she left there. It was time to get back to business.

Fully engrossed in her textbook, Eleanor jumped when she heard a knock on her bedroom door. She glanced at the clock on the wall and realized she had been studying for over two hours.

The knocking came again. "Coming," Eleanor yelled. She put down her book and swung her legs over the bed. *I bet it's Omar coming to give me gripe about tonight,* she thought as she walked to the door, pulling it open. "Bighead, what do you—" Her eyes bugged in her head when they met Dwight's twinkling eyes.

"So, I'm Bighead, huh?" Dwight said with his signature, sexy grin.

"Hmmm, I . . . I thought you were Omar," Eleanor stuttered. She was mortified. "Sorry." *If only the ground could just open up and swallow me right now.*

"Nothing to be sorry about," Dwight said smoothly. "I just wanted to say good night and thank you for the delectable dinner."

"Thank me?"

"Yes, I was told that you did most of the cooking." Dwight winked at her.

"Oh, yes. Hmmm, you're welcome," Eleanor said flustered. "Well, good night."

"Okay, bye," Dwight replied softly, still rooted to the spot, staring intently at her.

Eleanor looked away shyly. "I . . . I have to get back to my studying."

"Sure, sorry," he said in a low voice. "It was really a pleasure meeting you."

"Thanks. Bye." Eleanor quickly closed the door and pressed her back firmly against it. Eyes closed, she took deep breaths, her heart pounding in her chest. "I have to stay focused on what's important," Eleanor whispered adamantly. "I can't allow anything or anyone to interfere with that." With that registered in her brain, she went back to her textbook. However, it took awhile before she was able to focus. For some strange reason, Dwight Humphrey just kept popping up in her mind.

Chapter Twenty-nine

Dwight whistled happily as he entered his four-bedroom, upscale house in Cherry Gardens, St. Andrew, one of Jamaica's elite neighborhoods. As he walked into the huge master bedroom, the telephone rang. In quick strides Dwight reached for the phone sitting on his bedside table.

"Hello?" Dwight practically sang into the phone.

"My, my, my. Aren't we in a good mood tonight," said a cold, feminine voice on the other end.

Dwight took a deep breath. "How are you, Mother?" he asked dryly. "I am actually in a good mood . . . or I was before the phone rang."

"Don't get sassy with me, Dwight Humphrey," Mrs. Eve Humphrey snapped. "You have been avoiding my calls all week."

"I wonder why," he mumbled, looking up at the ceiling in frustration.

"What was that? I didn't hear you," Eve Humphrey said impatiently.

"I have been busy, Mother. I do have a very demanding job, you know."

"Too busy for your family, huh?" Eve Humphrey replied. "Your father and I need to speak with you as soon as possible. Since you came back to Jamaica you seem to be distancing yourself from us."

"I'll stop by tomorrow after church," Dwight finally relented. "Okay?"

"After church? There you go again putting something before us," Eve Humphrey complained.

"I'm not putting something before you, Mother," Dwight said wearily. "I'm putting someone. That's Almighty God. He comes first in my life."

"Boy, you let your aunt Clover fill your head with that religious rubbish," Eve Humphrey said in reference to her sister-in-law. "I knew we shouldn't have let you stay with her in New York. That woman is as crazy as a cuckoo bird."

"Don't go there, Mother," Dwight warned in a stern voice. "Don't you dare disrespect my aunt or you won't see me tomorrow or anytime soon thereafter."

Eve sucked her teeth loudly, but she remained quiet. One thing she had learned about her only child was that he meant what he said. "Fine. I won't say anything else about your precious aunt," she replied sarcastically. "Even though it's the truth."

Dwight ignored the comment. "I have to go. I'll see you tomorrow after church." The telephone then went dead on the other line. Dwight slowly hung up the phone. "Maybe I should have stayed in New York," he said aloud as he paced the thick carpeted floor. "But my heart and spirit told me to come back home. Lord, did I make a mistake doing so?"

Dwight Humphrey was the only son of wealthy Jamaican socialites, David and Eve Humphrey. His father was the group managing director (CEO) at National Commercial Bank Jamaica Ltd (NCB), a position he held for the last twenty years. His mother, a former Miss Jamaica and international fashion model, was currently the president of Pulse Model Agency.

Dwight grew up in a small mansion in the affluent Beverly Hills in St. Andrews, Jamaica. They had servants to do just about every chore around the house. Growing up, he was only allowed to socialize with rich kids of his parents' friends. It was at Wolmer's Boys' School, considered as one of Jamaica's most prestigious schools, that he met Omar. A fast friendship developed between the two boys. His parents objected to their friendship because Omar lived with his single mother and four brothers on Molynes Road, a vast contrast to their Beverly Hills palace. However, Dwight resisted and for the first time in his sheltered life, he went against his parents' wishes. The bond between him and Omar only intensified after he met Mama Pearl. Their first meeting endeared her and her family in his heart forever.

Dwight jumped slightly as the telephone rang. "Hello?" he answered hesitantly.

"Baby, are you okay?" asked Mama Pearl.

Dwight breathed a sigh of relief. "I am now, Mama Pearl."

"I am here praying before going to my bed and you came to my spirit," she told him. "So I got your number from Omar and called you. I want you to know that I am praying for you, my child."

"Thank you, Mama Pearl," Dwight said with gratitude. "You are always praying for me."

"And I will never stop," she told him. "Don't worry about a thing, Dwight. Everything is all a part of God's plan. Okay, my dear?"

"Okay, Mama Pearl." Dwight's smile was slowly creeping back on his face. "I really needed to hear that. You know I love you, right?"

Mama Pearl chuckled. "I love you too, Dwight Humphrey. God bless you, son. Good night."

Dwight hung up the phone. "Don't worry about a thing, cause every little thing gonna be all right," he sang, nodding his head and snapping his fingers. He knew in his heart everything would be fine.

Chapter Thirty

"Please remember we have a date after church, ma'am," Omar said to Eleanor as she walked with him and Mama Pearl to his car in the driveway.

"Oh, where are you guys going?" Mama Pearl asked as Omar opened her door and she slid into the front passenger seat of the car.

"Nowhere," Eleanor said and went to sit in the back-seat. "I have to study for finals next week."

Omar walked around the car and sat behind the steering before he closed his door. "We are going somewhere, Mama." He adjusted his mirror. "We are going to Devon House, and then for a drive. She needs to get out of the house for a while."

"I totally agree." Mama Pearl laughed when she glanced over her shoulder and Eleanor gave her the beady eye. "All work and no play makes Eleanor a dull girl."

They all laughed as Omar drove off, headed for Eastland Church of Christ on Red Hills Road. The parking lot was full to capacity when they got to the church.

"You ladies go on inside," Omar said. "I'll try to find parking around the back."

Mama Pearl and Eleanor exited the car and walked up the steps to the entry of the church. They exchanged greetings with the pleasant usher waiting by the front door, who then escorted them to their seats.

"Thank God, they are just starting," Mama Pearl whispered to Eleanor.

"Welcome into the house of the Lord," the liturgist said loudly into the microphone. "This is the day that the Lord has made, so let us rejoice and be glad in it."

"Amens" rang out all over the church as everyone prepared themselves for worship and praise. Eleanor closed her eyes, forcing herself to put aside all other thoughts to focus only on the Lord. Suddenly she felt a tingling sensation creeping down her spine. Her heart began to beat faster, her breathing labored. *Oh, no! He's here!*

"Hi, Eleanor, do you mind if I sit beside you?" Dwight said close to her ear.

Eleanor took a deep breath, plastered a smile on her face, and turned her head to look at him. Big mistake. Their eyes met and held as they lost themselves in each other.

"Ahem," Mama Pearl said beside her. "Eleanor, why don't you slide over so Dwight can sit with us?"

Eleanor shook her head as if she was coming out of a trance and did as Mama Pearl asked.

"Thank you." Dwight sat down at the end of the row, his leg pressing against Eleanor's due to the tight space.

Eleanor stared straight-ahead, her body as stiff as a piece of iron. Except for the blinking of her eyes, nothing else moved. She felt Dwight and Mama Pearl throwing her looks, but she ignored them. *This is going to be a long service,* she thought. *But I just need to get through it and get back home.*

Finally church was dismissed. Everyone stood up to fellowship or to go home. Eleanor excused herself to go to the bathroom. She hustled her way through the crowd toward the back, excusing herself, slightly running and waving to familiar faces.

In the bathroom, she found an empty stall and quickly locked herself in. "This is ridiculous," Eleanor whispered angrily. "I have to get ahold of myself and stop reacting this way to that man. I don't need any more complications in my life."

With her forehead resting on the wall, Eleanor inhaled and exhaled a few times, willing her nerves to settle down. Minutes later after washing and drying her hands, she left the bathroom to find Mama Pearl and Omar.

The first person she saw as she walked out to the parking lot was Dwight. He leaned his tall, slim frame against Omar's car with his hands folded across his chest as he conversed with Omar and his fiancée, Rose. Eleanor paused and looked around for Mama Pearl, but she was nowhere in sight. Slowly she made her way over to the group.

"Hi, Eleanor," Rose greeted her in a friendly voice. "Girl, you are *wearing* that dress."

Eleanor blushed slightly. "Thank you, Rose." She felt Omar staring at her but was determined to ignore him.

"Eleanor, Dwight and Rose are going to join us on our little date," Omar told her cautiously. "Is that okay?"

"Oh, you guys can go ahead without me. I have a lot of studying to do. Go on and have fun," Eleanor rambled on. "I really won't mind. In fact—"

"Please stop, Eleanor." Omar, a look of disappointment on his face, stepped closer to her, his eyes locked on her face. "If you don't want to come, I'll just drop you off at home."

"Excuse me," Dwight said and everyone looked at him. "I don't have to come. In fact, I had told my mother I would stop by after church." He looked at Eleanor. "I'm sorry. It wasn't my intention to impose on your date. Omar invited me, and I accepted."

Eleanor felt like an eel. Here were these people welcoming her in their circle, trying to get her to have a little fun, but she was throwing it right back in their faces. "I'm sorry," she said mildly, hoping her shame wasn't visible on her face. "I'm just nervous about my finals and feel I'm wasting time when I'm not studying."

"Sis, you are going to kick butt." Omar patted her on the back. "Don't worry, you got this."

"Thank you." Eleanor smiled. "So what are we waiting for? Let's all go and get some ice cream." She looked at Dwight. "It's okay if you would like to join us."

"I would like that very much." Dwight flashed his sexy grin. "Meet you guys there? Unless you would like to ride with me, Eleanor?"

"Huh? Sure, that's fine."

"Okay. I'm parked right over there." Dwight pointed to a sleek, stylish, red Mercedes-Benz a few feet away.

"Rose and I will see you guys in a bit." Omar took Rose's hand.

Eleanor nodded and walked away with Dwight toward his car. Her legs were shaking like cooked spaghetti with each step she took. Dwight opened the passenger-side door, and she got in, tugging down her dress to cover her legs.

"Are you all right?" Dwight asked after he strapped himself in his seat. His eyes were filled with concern. "Have you changed your mind about riding with me?"

"No," Eleanor replied quickly. "I'm fine."

He stared at her for a few seconds before he started the car and drove off.

The drive to Devon House was only a few minutes, but to Eleanor, it seemed like hours. The silence that wrapped around them was uncomfortable, but she had no idea how to break it. Dwight threw her a few glances but didn't say a word. This made her feel even worse.

Soon they were parking in Devon House's parking lot. Dwight opened his door and got out, then came around to open her door. As Eleanor stepped out of the car, her shoe slipped on a little rock. She stumbled, sending her into Dwight's arms as he grabbed her before she fell.

Standing nose to nose, neither one spoke as they looked into each other's eyes. The attraction was magnetic and powerful. It was a force that was out of their control and beyond their comprehension. This was way too scary for Eleanor.

"Tha . . . Than . . . Thank you," she stuttered as she gently pulled away from Dwight.

"You okay?" Dwight asked in a hoarse voice. He cleared his throat, looking everywhere but at Eleanor.

"There you are," said Omar as he and Rose walked up to them. "I was just about to send out a search party for you two."

They all laughed, shrinking the strong tension between Eleanor and Dwight.

Eleanor was surprised at how much she enjoyed herself. The Devon House Heritage Site was one of Jamaica's leading national monuments. It created an urban panorama in a clean, magnificent, green space that was great for recreation, dining, and shopping.

They sat outside on a lush, expansive lawn, eating the popular, rich, creamy "Devon House I Scream." The conversation was refreshing as Omar and Dwight shared stories of their high school days. Eleanor found herself laughing a lot, especially when Dwight spoke. For just that moment, her demons seemed to have been exorcised, allowing her to have some fun. This was a rarity for her.

"This was so much fun," Dwight said happily as he looked at his watch. "Guys, I hate to run, but I promised my mother that I would stop by the house."

"May the Lord be with you." Omar shook his head in pity.

Dwight playfully punched him on the arm. Eleanor looked from one man to the other, curious to know why Omar made that statement. However, she was too shy to ask.

"Eleanor and Rose, thank you for the wonderful company," Dwight said as he stood to his feet. "Bighead, I'll talk to you later." He looked at Eleanor and winked.

Dwight watched as Eleanor threw her head back, her laughter sounding like a sweet melody to his ears. With the sunshine splashed across her pretty face, accentuating her dazzling smile, she looked like an angel. Mesmerized he gawked at her, his mouth slightly opened.

"You are so funny," Eleanor said as she wiped tears from her eyes. She had laughed that hard. She glanced up at Dwight and realized he was looking at her again. Blushing, she quickly lowered her gaze into her lap.

Rose and Omar looked on in amusement.

"Well . . . I . . . I'm going now," Dwight said in a high-pitched voice, clearly disconcerted.

"Bye," Omar and Rose replied, giggling.

Eleanor briefly waved her hand, still fixated on a tiny speck of lint in her lap. She only looked up a few seconds later when she knew Dwight was gone.

"Sis, it seems like you had a great time," Omar said smiling, his eyebrows rising and falling as if he had a secret that he wasn't telling.

"Shut up, Bighead," Eleanor remarked lightly, rolling her eyes at him with a big smile on her face. It was indeed a wonderful afternoon . . . But it would not be long before terror struck again, sending Eleanor back into hell.

Chapter Thirty-one

Dwight pulled up into his parents' long, marble driveway and parked. He sat in his car for a few minutes, taking deep breaths to relax the tense muscles in his body. He knew why his parents wanted to see him, and if this meeting went like the last one, it wasn't going to be a good one.

With a big sigh, he opened the car door, got out, and walked up to the front door. All around him was the familiar small paradise of acres of green, well manicured grass, small cherry, mango, and orange fruit trees, and beautiful, exotic flowers, but he saw none of these things. He just wanted to get in and get out as quickly as possible.

A loud musical chime echoed throughout the house when Dwight pressed the doorbell. Almost simultaneously it was opened by a young girl wearing a stiff, black-and-white uniform dress. This one was new, as they usually were. Very few workers stayed long with his parents. Despite the fact that they were well paid, his mother's sharp tongue, constant criticism, and rude behavior ran them all away. His father's rumored behavior with the female hires was also said to be a factor.

"May I help you?" she asked Dwight in a very pleasant manner.

"That's my son, Bella," said his father's deep voice from behind the helper. "I'll take it from here." David Humphrey came to stand beside her, a cold, hard glare directed at his son.

"Excuse me." Bella turned around to walk away.

David Humphrey reached out and slapped her on the behind, winking at Dwight as the young girl scurried away.

Dwight looked at him with disgust. "Mother would have loved to see you at work, Father," he said as he stepped inside. He stood before his father, face-to-face, matching his father's cold stare with his own. "What do you want to talk to me about?"

David Humphrey looked at the younger replica of himself and felt the anger surging through his body. The boy was as stubborn as a mule. Again, something Dwight got from him but unwelcomed now that it was directed at him. "Your mother is waiting in the parlor," he said and walked off, leaving Dwight to follow.

Dwight inhaled and exhaled a few times before he walked up the small flight of stairs into the parlor.

His mother sat crossed-legged, as pretty as her flowers, on a large, white leather sofa, sipping red wine from a crystal glass. Her long, straight hair fell heavily around her shoulders, shaping a beautiful, light-skinned, well made-up face. The chandelier overhead reflected off the huge diamonds adorning her ears and neck, complimenting the shear, long white dress that clung to her tall, slim frame. Full, bright, red lips parted in a cynical smile when her son entered the room. "Thank you for gracing us with your presence, Dwight. Your father and I are truly honored," she said sarcastically, waving a hand toward her husband who sat a few inches away from her on a matching sofa.

Dwight looked at his beautiful, fifty-eight-year-old mother, who still rivaled women half her age with her physical beauty, and felt sympathy for her instead of anger. Eve Humphrey was a very cold woman, who lived to make other people's life as miserable as her own. Unfortunately, this included her only child.

"Mother, you are looking beautiful." Dwight smiled sweetly. "It's a pleasure to see you as always." He leaned against the wall, his arms crossed. He wasn't going to sit down because he didn't plan on staying too long. Eve Humphrey looked at him, seething in anger. The fact that he was late to see his parents and walked in as if he didn't care was despicable. *No one* kept her waiting, and that included her son. "That's all you have to say when we have been waiting on you for hours?" she asked Dwight harshly.

"I went out after church," Dwight said lightly, an image of Eleanor popping up in his mind. "I had a wonderful time with great friends."

"Don't waste your time, love," David Humphrey chimed in. "This boy just don't understand the value of family. It's just like he refuses to come and work with me at the bank, so he can take over when I retire."

"Here we go again." Dwight sounded exhausted. "Father, I have told you many times that I am happy at BNS. I don't want to work with you at NCB."

"You went and took a job with the competition!" David Humphrey shouted furiously. "You were to come back from college and work at NCB. Instead, you betray me!"

"Take it easy, dear," Eve Humphrey said, scowling at Dwight as if it was his fault that his father got worked up. "Don't let him raise your blood pressure."

Dwight frowned. His family came from a long line of wealthy bankers and financial gurus. His late great-grandfather and grandfather were former group managing directors at NCB, followed by his father who currently held the title. David Humphrey wanted the family tradition to continue with Dwight taking over when he retires in a few years. But, Dwight chose instead to work at another bank, refusing to follow in his father and forefathers' footsteps. This was an ultimate betrayal to his family as far as David Humphrey was concerned.

"I'm my own man, Father," Dwight remarked firmly, not backing down. "I will be CEO of BNS one day, and on my own merit. I'm going to work hard and work my way up to the top."

"I already did that for you," his father yelled. "Now I want you to come to NCB and continue our family's legacy."

"You want me to let you control my life and do as you say," Dwight replied calmly. "That's not going to happen, Father. Sorry. I am going to live my life as the Lord see fits."

"The Lord?" David Humphrey screamed. "This has *nothing* to do with some fictitious character. This is about you making things happen for you!" he pointed at Dwight, his eyes blazing. "Was it the Lord who sent you abroad to study at an Ivy League college? Huh? What the heck does the Lord have to do with this?"

"You forced me to go to Columbia, Father," Dwight pointed out. "I wanted to stay here and attend UWI, but you refused to pay my college tuition unless I attended your alma mater."

Dwight was adamant about staying in Jamaica for college. He wanted to attend UWI with Omar, but his parents told him if he did, he was on his own. There was no way he could have afforded college without their help. He also knew that he needed a good education to get away from his parents' stronghold over his life. After discussing the issue with Mama Pearl, she advised him to go.

"We are going to miss you, baby," Mama Pearl had said. "But look at the good side of this. You need their help and getting a degree from such a reputable college abroad is a huge stepping-stone in your career. When you come back home with your degree, you can get any job you want and live your own life according to God's plan for you. Also, your aunt is there, and I know she will look after you until you come back to us."

So Dwight went and never regretted it. He enjoyed college and spending time with his only aunt, a wonderful woman of God. But most importantly, she had led him to Christ, finishing the process that Mama Pearl had started.

"I'm talking to you, boy," his father snapped, regaining Dwight's wandering mind.

"Father, I am staying at BNS. I love it there, and I'm doing well. Please accept my decision and stop fighting with me about this."

David Humphrey sucked his teeth, stood up, and stormed out of the room, slamming the door shut behind him.

"See what you have done?" his mother asked. "I don't know why it's so hard for you to realize how important this is to us."

Dwight stared at her without responding. His head was beginning to hurt, and he was ready to go.

"Melinda is in town," Eve Humphrey said, switching topics, her eyes lighting up. "She just came back from a modeling assignment overseas. She asked about you."

"That's nice," Dwight replied without emotion.

"It's time for you to settle down and give us some grandkids," his mother said. "How about dinner Wednesday night? I'll invite Melinda."

"No, thanks." Dwight frowned. "I'll be going by Mama Pearl's for dinner on Wednesday. Sorry."

His mother's face got ugly as she stood to her feet, her hands clinched at her sides. "I see you are still wrapped up with *those* people," she said with disdain, emphasis on the word "those."

"What people, Mother? The woman who has shown me more compassion than my own mother? The police officer, lawyer, principal, banker, or college professor? Do you mean *those* people?" Dwight asked irritably. "Those people are family! I love those people, and those people love me. Can you say the same?" Dwight's nostrils flared as he looked at his mother, fuming.

Eve Humphrey looked shocked as she stared at her angry son. She knew she had crossed the line again. Unlike high school days, Dwight was now a grown man with obviously a mind of his own. She didn't want to alienate her only son. "I only meant they are different from us," she mumbled, making things worse instead of better.

"Yes, I guess they are," he said sarcastically. "They are God-fearing people who love the Lord. Despite their poor background, they were able to beat the odds and become outstanding, successful, loving human beings. They are genuine people."

"I meant they—"

"Mother, if you ever want me to set foot in this house another time, please don't disrespect the people I love again," Dwight said resolutely. "I won't stand for it."

"Whatever," Eve Humphrey replied with attitude and walked out of the room without another word.

Dwight let out a long breath as he glanced about the beautiful room. Despite the expensive furniture, priceless paintings, and fabulous décor, he felt like he was trapped in a small, cold box. The room had no warmth or love. He shuddered and walked out, heading home to the place he now called home.

Chapter Thirty-two

"Is everything okay?" the elderly man asked the young lady sitting beside him on the bus, tears seeping down her face behind the thick, dark sunglasses that she wore. Eleanor nodded her head, moved the sunglasses up on her forehead, and wiped her face with a handkerchief before the sunglasses were covering her red eyes again.

"Well, I hope whatever it is, that the Lord will make a way for you," the man added and settled back into his seat, closing his eyes as if he was praying.

As the bus zoomed toward Falmouth, Trelawny, Eleanor wrapped her hands tightly across her stomach, shaking as if she was naked in a snowstorm. Her lips were folded tight to keep the bitter bile that filled her mouth from spraying out. She was feeling sick to her stomach.

Upon completing her finals, marking the end of her undergraduate studies, Mama Pearl and the family took Eleanor out for a dinner celebration. They went to an upscale restaurant in New Kingston, with a nice ambiance, finger-licking food, and good-vibes music.

As the laughter and jokes flew around the room, Eleanor laughed and conversed, but was crying inside. Each face she looked at seemed to change into Aunt Madge and Dupree. Here she was celebrating a milestone in her life, when she had run away from the woman who raised her and the child she brought into this world. She was living a lie, and until she set things right, she would never be free from this internal hell.

"I'm going to look for my aunt and daughter tomorrow," Eleanor decided on a whim. Images of Officer Gregg's gun pressed against her head flashed in her mind, and she trembled slightly. "I don't care if Officer Gregg shoots me or his wife kills me. I am going to Falmouth no matter what. He is not going to hurt Aunt Madge. He was just trying to scare me." Eleanor was trying to boost up her courage to enter into the lion's den.

For the rest of the night Eleanor gave her best acting performance. She sincerely appreciated all the love and support she was getting from these people who came to love her as she loved them, but her mind had already packed and was ready for an overdue trip.

The next morning Eleanor left home as if for work, but she had already requested the day off from her boss. Walking out to the main road, she pulled on one of Mama Pearl's big straw hats that she had hidden in her handbag and a pair of sunglasses for her disguise. Even though it had been over seven years, Eleanor didn't want to take any chances. She still had a very youthful appearance, despite the hard life she had lived, and was recognizable.

Eleanor caught a bus to Spanish Town, chanting over and over in her head that she had to do this. In Spanish Town, she transferred to the last bus that would take her into what would be a nice homecoming—or her worst nightmare.

Now here she was, sitting on the bus, trying not to puke or faint, slowly heading toward what she had run away from.

It was a long ride, almost three hours. The bus finally pulled into the bus terminal in Falmouth Square, coughing and backfiring, then coming to a sharp stop. All the passengers hurried off it, among them a nervous Eleanor.

Adjusting the big hat on her head, her hair was neatly wrapped and concealed under it. Eleanor straightened the sunglasses on her nose. She looked around at her old stomping ground with familiarity.

It was Saturday, so the streets were busy with buses and cars and vendors pushing handcarts overloaded with produce for the already full market. There were people hurrying from one place to another, some engaged in animated chatting, with children running behind their parents, laughing and screaming. It seemed as if not much had changed in Falmouth since she last lived there.

Eleanor walked out of the bus terminal, her head hanging low, toward the market. Aunt Madge would be here selling at her little stall, the fruits and produce she grew with her own hands: yams, oranges, mangoes, grapefruits, bananas, sweet potatoes, breadfruits, sweet corn, and ackees.

"I used to be here with her," Eleanor murmured as she shoved her way through the small, crowded market. "Before I played with fire and got burned." Behind her sunglasses, her eyes burned from the tears she was trying not to let fall. That would have brought too much attention to her, and that was the last thing she needed right then.

Suddenly it felt like a donkey had kicked her in the stomach. Eleanor bent over and grabbed her tummy, the tears now dancing down her face. A few people shot her quick, curious glances, but the majority scurried around her as if she was invisible to tend to their business at hand. Like a cripple she scrambled over to a light post and braced her back against it, struggling to breathe, her knees shaking like grass in the wind.

Only a few feet away from Eleanor stood Aunt Madge.

Minutes went by before Eleanor sneaked a look at her aunt from behind the light post. Her eyes soaked in the sight of the wonderful woman who loved and cared for her since she was a baby. Aunt Madge looked like she hadn't aged a day since Eleanor left. Her face was just as beautiful and warm as she remembered. Always well put together, the long, bright, floral dress she wore matched her head tie and the flat shoes she wore on her feet.

Eleanor watched as customer after customer came by, Aunt Madge greeting each one like a long lost friend. But the one thing Eleanor noticed that caused the surge of relief in her heart was the big smile on her aunt's face. Only one person could have been able to put the light back in Aunt Madge's eyes after she had put it out. Her daughter, Dupree.

By the way, where is Dupree? Eleanor spun around and around, peering at the faces of the children, trying to see if she could recognize her almost eight-year-old daughter. The last time she saw Dupree, she saw the image of a scary creature, barely a week old. Who did Dupree resemble? Her mother or her father? These were some of the questions running through Eleanor's mind as she searched the crowd for a child who might look like her daughter. *It's a shame I don't even know what my own child looks like,* Eleanor thought.

After a few minutes, Eleanor gave up looking. She did not want to walk around and risk someone recognizing her, so she focused on Aunt Madge instead. If Dupree was at the market, she would be coming back to the stall soon to help Aunt Madge.

Eleanor remembered when she did the same. It was such an exhilarating experience trying to get potential customers to come to her aunt's stall. Shouting out the produce they had for sale and the prices. Smiling and welcoming the customers. It was so innocent. So pure. Until she wanted more. Too fast, too soon.

Watching Aunt Madge, Eleanor wanted so badly to go up to her aunt and hug her. But she knew this was neither the time nor the place to lay this on the elderly woman.

She would wait until Aunt Madge got home and surprise her. Eleanor finally decided to wait at the house for Dupree and Aunt Madge. Hopefully, Aunt Madge still kept the spare key hidden under the big stone by the hibiscus trees. Nervous but anxious to reunite with her aunt and daughter, Eleanor left the market and headed toward her old home.

"Wow, nothing has changed," Eleanor said as she was walking up the lonely, country road that would take her to the narrow, dirt track to her old home. The big hat and sunglasses still in place, she looked at the familiar, small houses along the street. Mr. Bone's little zinc-fenced shoe-making shop was still standing. The Methodist church on the hill was still missing a few front windows. Miss Dorrett's tiny grocery shop still needed a fresh coat of paint. It was as if nothing had changed over the last few years.

Lost in memory lane, Eleanor walked with her head straight, greeting no one she passed. She got a few curious looks but ignored them. She just wanted to hurry and get off the main road to avoid contact with someone who might recognize her.

As Eleanor took a deep turn around a corner, where big, tall bamboo trees blocked out the sunlight, casting dancing shadows on the road, a car came out of nowhere and screeched to a stop at her feet.

Eleanor jumped back in fright. Her hand covering her mouth muffled the scream. Her eyes widened in alarm as she watched the car door open and a tall man in a stiff police uniform stepped out and walked up to her. *Please, God, anyone but this devil.*

Chapter Thirty-three

"I knew it was you," he growled. "The disguise is good and might have fooled a lot of people but not me." He came and stood within a few inches of Eleanor, looking down at her with anger and hatred in his eyes. "Why did you come back here?"

Eleanor quivered in fear. She glanced up and down the road to see if anyone was coming, but they were all alone.

"Answer me!" he screamed and bent over so they were nose to nose.

Eleanor took a small step back, her body shivering and her eyes dancing in her head like an owl. He grabbed the sunglasses off her face and tossed them over the wall that ran alongside the road, into the river below.

"Please, I don't want any trouble," Eleanor pleaded, a pool of tears forming in her eyes. "I'm on my way to see my aunt and daughter, then I'm out of here."

"My, my, my. Just look at you." He licked his lips as he looked her up and down from head to toe. "Girl, you have *grown* up." He emphasized the word "grown."

"I'm leaving now," Eleanor said quickly, backing away a few steps from him.

"Get back here!" Officer Bailey yelled, causing Eleanor to scream this time, his hand on the gun holstered at his side. "Make one more move and you'll regret it." In three long strides he was once again invading Eleanor's personal space. Officer Bailey was a huge man, approximately six feet four, weighing in at about 260 pounds.

Eleanor wrapped her arms around her body, trembling like a leaf. It was as if the educated, sophisticated twenty-three-year-old Eleanor had converted back into the petrified fifteen-year-old Tiny. "Please let me go, Officer Bailey," Eleanor whispered in deep distress. "I'll just turn around, get on a bus, and leave. This time I won't come back. I promise you, sir."

Officer Bailey threw his head back and laughed, his big potbelly jiggling in front of him. A real dirtbag in every sense of the word, Officer Bailey was the longtime friend of Officer Gregg. It was Officer Bailey that Officer Gregg had confided in and told of his affair with the minor, Tiny.

"Man, age is just a number," Officer Bailey had told Officer Gregg when he expressed concern about Tiny's age. "She may be a teenager, but she has the body of a woman." The slimeball laughed until tears ran down his face.

It was no secret that Officer Bailey was a womanizer. He liked to joke that he loved fast cars, fast women, and a faster relationship. He never got married and rumor had it that he fathered over twenty children with more than seventeen different women, half of whom were underage. But, of course, he claimed none.

It was a little over fifteen years ago when Officer Bailey transferred from the Tivoli Police Station in Kingston to Falmouth, Trelawny. Full of attitude, street swagger, and very trigger-happy, he quickly earned the name, Officer "Rude Boy" Bailey. Most of the country folk were scared of him, small-time criminals respected and obeyed him, and his colleagues at the police station admired him. Officer Bailey walked around Falmouth as if he was king of the town and he owned everything and everyone that dwelled therein.

A flashy dresser when not in uniform, Officer Bailey wore the finest and best clothes. He adorned his body with a lot of thick, expensive gold chains, watches, and rings. He changed his cars as he did his women and had a few vehicles parked up at his huge house in Clarks Town, Trelawny. It was a mystery to many of how Officer Bailey lived that well on a meager police officer salary. Even though it was suspected, only his few trusted "lieutenants," as he like to call his workers, knew for sure that he was a dirty cop. Officer Bailey was one of the biggest drug dealers in Jamaica, specializing in high-grade marijuana.

"I'm pulling a double again tonight," Officer Bailey often informed Officer Gregg.

"Man, you did a double shift last night," Officer Gregg pointed out. "In fact, you have been doing double shifts for the last few weeks."

"Remember, I'm free, single, and disengaged," Officer Bailey laughed. "Plus, I need the extra money to maintain my celebrity lifestyle."

Officer Gregg chuckled. He too had heard the rumors about Officer Bailey but chose to believe his friend instead. He had never seen the man doing anything illegal. Quite frankly, it was the other way around. Officer Bailey enforced the law, not broke it. People were just jealous that Officer Bailey was successful. But if only Officer Gregg knew that the "night shift" had nothing to do with the law . . .

Months into the affair with Tiny, Officer Gregg cornered Officer Bailey in the squad room one morning with another confession. He informed him that Tiny was pregnant.

"You know you have to take care of that, right?" Officer Bailey asked. "You have a good wife. You don't want to disgrace her or your family."

"I already took care of it," Officer Gregg said above a whisper, looking around as if someone was lurking close by.

"You did, huh? How?"

"I roughed her up a little," Officer Gregg said in a low voice, minimizing his assault on Tiny. "I told her if she ever calls my name to anyone, I'll kill her and her aunt."

"And you think she'll listen to you?" Officer Bailey asked skeptically as he stared pointedly at Officer Gregg.

"Oh, she'll listen," Officer Gregg remarked with confidence. "She was scared as heck when I was finished with her."

Officer Bailey shook his head, tsk-tsking him. "That won't work for long, man," he said. "You should have killed her."

"Ki . . . kill her?" Officer Gregg stared at his friend in shock. "Kill her?"

"Listen, if this girl tells her aunt and she reports it to 'Sup,' there is going to be an investigation," Officer Bailey explained. "My brother, they are going to send you to prison for a very long time."

Officer Gregg began pacing the floor, nibbling on his bottom lip nervously. He did have a lot to lose. His wife had recently informed him that they were expecting their first child. He couldn't afford to lose his family now. He was a lot of things, but he wasn't a murderer. He attended church regularly with his wife, and even though he wasn't living a Holy Ghost-filled, sanctimonious life as many believed, he still had some principles. He was a police officer, for Christ's sake, not a murderer.

"This will come back to haunt us," Officer Bailey egged on. "It's the only way out. Trust me, I know."

Officer Gregg paused and looked at his fellow officer funny. "Haunt us? You know? Have you been in this situation too?"

"No no no. I'm just speaking in general," Officer Bailey lied quickly. He had been in this situation many, many times. Although he never had to kill any of the girls, he made sure they would never, *ever* call his name. He was confident of his power over them but unsure of Officer Gregg's over Tiny. If there was an investigation, chances were they would start looking at the entire police department. He could not afford to let that happen. He would go to prison for the rest of his life.

"I'm not going to kill her," Officer Gregg stated in a firm voice. "I made a big mistake when I got involved with her but taking the life of an innocent girl is not the way to go about it."

"Okay. Fine." Officer Bailey held up his hand as if surrendering. "But make sure you keep a close eye on her. She could be trouble."

Eight years later, here Officer Bailey was looking at trouble. Tiny was back. This time he was going to make sure she *never* came back again.

Chapter Thirty-four

"Walk to the car," Officer Bailey barked at Eleanor. "Now!"

"No." Eleanor shook her head from side to side. "I am not getting in your car." Next thing she felt was the gun pressing hard against her temple. Her eyes bugged, her knees quivered. "Please. Please don't, Officer Bailey."

"You are not going to come back here and cause trouble for us," he growled, his mouth brushing against Eleanor's ear. He looked around to see if anyone was coming up or down the street, but they were still alone. In a flash he threw Eleanor over his shoulder and walked toward his car. Her hat fell to the road.

Eleanor screamed loudly, kicking and pounding on his back, to no avail.

Officer Bailey used one hand to open the back door of the car and tossed Eleanor on the backseat, faceup.

Eleanor jumped up and hurled herself at him, yelling loudly, but he roughly shoved her back in the car and slammed the door shut.

Officer Bailey looked around before he opened the driver's door and slid into the car. He quickly started it and sped off, ignoring Eleanor screaming and banging on the back doors.

Eleanor was thrown back against the seat after the car moved off. Quickly recovering, she moved over to the closed window, banging on it, shrieking in fright. Tears and mucus ran down her face, her terrified eyes watching the trees zip by as the car zoomed up the road, hugging the corners almost on its side. *Think, girl, think. You have to get out of this situation.*

"Help! Somebody help me!" Eleanor shouted, kicking the driver's seat in front, still pounding on the closed window, hoping to draw attention from the one or two people they passed along the road or even to break the window. She needed to get away from this lunatic.

The car swerved off the main road unto a little track, gravel flying in every direction as it headed further down the lonely lane. Eleanor rocked to and fro, side to side as they drove over the rough, unpaved path.

Soon the car came to a screeching halt. Eleanor stopped yelling and looked around her in alarm. Her eyes bounced around her head like a pin ball. Surrounding them were gigantic trees and thick, unkempt bushes. The uncut grass was as tall as a basketball player. There was not a person or house in sight. She was alone with a dirty, angry cop.

Officer Bailey jumped out of the car and ran around to Eleanor's side, his gun held tight in his hand. He pulled the back door open and stuck his head inside. "Get out!" he shouted, the gun now pointed at Eleanor.

"No, I'm not getting out." Eleanor shook her head rapidly, backing away from Officer Bailey, further into the car. "I am not going anywhere with you."

"Okay. That's cool." Officer Bailey gave her a nasty Joker grin and stood up straight.

Eleanor watched in horror as he raised the gun in the air and fired a shot. The blast sounded like the rolling of thunder to Eleanor's ears. She screamed, covering her ears with her hands, shaking like she was about to have a seizure.

Suddenly rough hands were hauling her out of the car. Weak, disoriented, and scared into a lifeless form, she was unable to fight back. She watched everything moving in slow motion as she was thrown up against the car.

Eleanor felt the heavy weight of Officer Bailey on her as they stood face-to-face, the gun now resting on her forehead. With her eyes tightly closed, she took deep breaths, unsure of what to expect next.

Just then, Eleanor felt a hand running up her bare thigh. She tried to push at the hard body on her, but she was unable to move. Officer Bailey had pinned her slim frame to the car.

"Please," Eleanor whispered through tight lips. "Please let me go."

"Why did you come back here to cause trouble?" Officer Bailey asked in her ear.

Eleanor pushed against him and tried to turn her face the other way, but he grasped her face in his big hand and held it firm.

"I told Gregg you would come back and haunt him," Officer Bailey said, spit spraying on Eleanor's face. "See, if you create problems for him that will create problems for me. We can't have that."

Things had changed in the police force over the last few years. A new police commissioner came in and was following up on the public's outrage against police brutality and corruption. Investigations into dirty cops were being carried out all over the country by special investigators assigned out of the police headquarters in Kingston.

Even though it had been years since Officer Gregg had slept with Tiny, a minor, Officer Bailey was still doing his dirt. An investigation into Falmouth police station would mean big trouble for him. He had chosen to be stationed in Falmouth for a reason. It was a small community in the country and away from the spotlight. It was a perfect cover for him all these years. Tiny coming back now had the potential of shaking up the hornets' nest.

"But I'm going to make sure this time you never come back." Officer Bailey's warm, smelly breath fanned Eleanor's face.

With her eyes still tightly closed, Eleanor began to pray under her breath. Even though she often felt unworthy of God's love and forgiveness, she knew the power of His mercy and protection. She had experienced it firsthand and was a living testimony.

"Please, Lord, help me," Eleanor's teeth rattled as she prayed. Despite the humid Jamaican air that washed over her body, it felt like she was standing in an ice rain. "All I wanted to do was to see my aunt and daughter. Please get me out of this situation, dear Lord." Her crying sounded like groans from the depth of her belly.

Officer Bailey threw his head back and laughed out loud. His booming voice echoed through the dense woods, causing the hair to stand up on Eleanor's head. "Oh, you are a church girl again, huh? Praying and stuff."

"Lord, I'm begging you," Eleanor continued to pray, ignoring Officer Bailey.

"I remember back in the days you used to leave church to meet Gregg by the high school," he laughed mockingly.

"Lord—"

"Shut up!" Officer Bailey barked as he pulled back slightly from Eleanor. "Enough of this prayer rubbish." He slapped Eleanor so hard across the face, she fell to the ground. Her back hit the unpaved track that had lots of loose gravel and sharp stones.

Eleanor howled out in pain as she looked up at the monster wearing the police uniform standing over her. This was the second time her life was being threatened by a police officer. All because of her mistake. Was she going to pay for this all her life?

"Your daughter is growing up nicely." Officer Bailey grinned as he looked down on her lying on the ground. "She is a little younger than I normally do but there is always a first."

It was as if Officer Bailey turned on the insanity switch in Eleanor's head. She jumped to her feet and leaped at him like an angry leopard. Kicking him hard in his crotch, her teeth sank into his jaw as she clawed at his eyes, growling and gnawing away at his face.

A stunned Officer Bailey stumbled back a few steps, his gun flying out of his hand into some bushes nearby. His eyes burned, his face stung, and his testicles felt like they were on fire. Eleanor had him by the balls, literally, as she kicked and swung at him like a madwoman.

"You are not going anywhere near my daughter!" Eleanor shouted as she fought him. It was like a Chihuahua fighting Godzilla. But Eleanor was too far gone to care. She had already failed her daughter in so many ways, and the thought of her at the hands of this lunatic was unbearable.

Officer Bailey quickly recovered from the unexpected attack and plucked Eleanor off of him by her hair. He then angrily flung her away from him in disgust.

Luckily, Eleanor landed in the thick, unruly grass this time around, on her back. The wind knocked out of her, she breathed deeply through her mouth, her chest rising and falling, filling her lungs with air.

Furious, Officer Gregg frantically searched in the thick grass for his gun. Unfortunately, it didn't take long for him to find it. "You are going to pay for that," he uttered as he walked over to Eleanor, his red eyes blazing in anger, blood running down his bitten up cheeks.

Eleanor tried to move, but she had no strength left. With a sigh of defeat, she looked up into the blue sky, tears leaking from her eyes. "Sorry, I didn't get to see you, Dupree. I know Aunt Madge will continue to take good care of you."

Officer Bailey stood over Eleanor, his big size twelve shoe raised high above her head. Eleanor closed her eyes tight, bracing for impact, mumbling a prayer under her breath. Suddenly, a ruffling came through the trees up ahead. Officer Bailey paused, straining his eyes to see what it was. The tall grass parted like the Red Sea, and a donkey with a farmer on its back came out of the trees onto the track. They were headed straight toward Officer Bailey and Eleanor.

Officer Bailey hurriedly fell to his knee and whispered harshly in Eleanor's ear. "You make one sound or say a word and I swear I will kill both of you. This old man's blood will be on your shoulder. You got that?" He put the gun to her face so she could see that he had it.

Eleanor nodded repeatedly, her heart racing in her chest. *Please, God, let this man help me.*

Officer Bailey quickly stood in front of Eleanor, trying to shield her with his body, the gun behind his back. It was an impossible task as she was lying down, her long legs stretched out in front of her. There was nothing more he could do without drawing the farmer's attention to them.

"Officer Rude Boy Bailey. Is that you, man?" the farmer asked as the donkey got closer. "Everything okay?"

"Great," Officer Bailey muttered under his breath. "It has to be someone who knows me." He fixed a big grin on his face. "Everything's fine. Thanks."

Eleanor groaned. Officer Bailey turned around and glared at her, shaking the gun in warning, before he faced the track, his back turned toward Eleanor still lying in the grass.

The farmer was now in front of them on his donkey. He noticed the legs of the woman on the ground and looked at Officer Bailey with a puzzled look on his face.

"Hmmm, we just wanted a little time to . . ." Officer Bailey hung down his head as if he was embarrassed.

"Oh, my bad." The farmer laughed, nodding his head in understanding. "I see I walked in on your private time with your lady."

"You know how it is." Officer Bailey chuckled nervously, the gun behind his back moving up and down as a warning to Eleanor.

"Okay, boss. I'm out of here." The farmer gave Officer Bailey a wink, a broad smile on his face. He pulled on the rope around the donkey's neck, and they were off, leaving Eleanor alone again with the lunatic.

Eleanor rolled over on her side and sobbed. That was her chance to get help, and it was gone. Again, she could not let an innocent person get hurt because of her actions. That elderly man was no match for the beast, Officer Bailey. Come to think of it, neither was she.

Officer Bailey leaned down and grabbed Eleanor by her blouse, hauling her to her feet. Her eyes shot anger and hatred at him like flaming arrows. She had gotten to the stage where she was just tired. Tired of running, tired of the guilt and shame, tired of the condemnation, tired of fighting the devil over and over, literally.

"Today is your lucky day," he said to Eleanor, his face inches away from hers. "It looks as if you are going to get one more chance to disappear. This time it better be for good." He used his index finger to tap her repeatedly on the nose.

Officer Bailey decided to let Eleanor go after the farmer had seen and identified him. He knew that killing Eleanor now could create trouble for him. Someone knew he was down by the track, alone, with a female.

"Remember what I said before. Your little girl is growing up nicely," Officer Bailey said nastily. "You don't want me to pay her a visit, do you?"

"Oh, Jesus! Leave my daughter alone," Eleanor cried, her red eyes burning like they were doused with hot pepper sauce. There were no more tears. "I told you I would leave, and I won't come back."

"You better do that. That old lady doesn't look too bad either." Officer Bailey smirked, running the gun up and down Eleanor's cheek. "I bet it's been awhile since she has gotten some good loving."

Eleanor felt nauseated. The thought of this leviathan going anywhere near her aunt and daughter was horrifying.

"I own these streets. I don't care with whom or where you have been hiding. One word from me, my people will find you and wipe out all of you. Man, woman, child, and animal. You are all history." Officer Bailey continued with his threats. "Stay away from Falmouth or pay the consequences." He fired a shot in the air.

Eleanor screamed and jumped in horror. Her ears were ringing like some high-powered firecrackers had exploded in them. "Please, I won't come back and cause trouble," Eleanor begged. "Please let me go."

Officer Bailey stared at her for a few long seconds, his face twisted as if he was sucking on sour limes, before he dragged her over to the car and shoved her in the back. He then closed the door and walked up to the driver's seat and hopped in.

Eleanor watched anxiously as he started the car and slowly backed out of the track, onto the main road. Soon they were headed toward town. With her face pressed against the window, Eleanor watched the beautiful country scenery flash by, knowing in her heart that she would never return to Falmouth.

A short while later, Officer Bailey drove into Falmouth Square. The traffic was horrible, so the car was crawling toward the bus stop.

As they passed by the market, Eleanor sat up straight, her eyes searching for a glimpse of her aunt. "There she is," Eleanor whispered when she saw Aunt Madge standing in front of her small stall, talking to someone. Just then she saw a little figure run up to Aunt Madge and wrap her small hands around her waist. "Oh my God," Eleanor muttered anxiously. "That must be Dupree. She has grown so much."

The child had her back turned toward the road, so Eleanor only got a back view of her. She drank in the sight of the little girl in her long, flower dress with her thick hair piled high on her head. Eleanor just knew in her heart that she was looking at her daughter. She hadn't been much of a mother to her but wouldn't she know? "Turn around, baby," Eleanor pleaded inside, the car edging slowly away from the market. "Please, Dupree. Let me see your face one last time."

But Dupree's back remained turned. It was almost as if she was saying to her mother, "I don't want to see your face."

Disappointed, Eleanor sat back in the car as it rolled away from the market. She blinked rapidly so she would not cry. Mixed emotions ran through her; happy she caught a peek at her daughter and sad because she never got a chance to meet her. She still had no idea what Dupree really looked like, and she may never know.

"Here we are," Officer Bailey said roughly, turning around in his seat to face Eleanor. "You are going to get on a bus and go away. This never happened. I don't know you, and you don't know me. Got it?"

Eleanor nodded, yearning to get out of the car and away from him.

"I asked if you got it!" he yelled, the veins standing up in his neck.

"Yes, yes. I got it," Eleanor said quickly. She nervously glanced out the window at the people walking up and down the street, feeling a little safer than she was before.

Officer Bailey got out of the car and opened the passenger door. Eleanor hastily leaped out and ran to the bus as if she was being chased by demons. A few people glanced at her curiously but continued on their way. Breathless from her sprint, Eleanor boarded the bus to Kingston and walked to the back. Sitting by the window, breathing heavily, she looked out at the hustle and bustle for the last time. Under no circumstances would she ever come back to Falmouth. She had to stay away for the sake of the people she loved. A deep ache settled into Eleanor's heart as she bid farewell to Aunt Madge and Dupree . . . again.

Chapter Thirty-five

"Yo, Gregg! Come here!" Officer Bailey yelled over the loud chatter in the police station, waving his hand in the air to get Officer Gregg's attention. He then walked into the bunk room at the back of the station and waited for his fellow cop.

"What's up, Bailey?" Officer Gregg asked as he walked in the room, a smile on his handsome face. The years had been very kind to him. He looked almost the same as he did eight years ago when Tiny became infatuated with him. "You need me to cover another shift for you?"

Officer Bailey chuckled. "No, I'm good for now. That's not what I wanted to talk to you about." He now had a serious look on his face.

Officer Gregg walked closer to Officer Bailey, his eyes fixed on his face. "What's up?"

"You remember that problem you had a few years ago?" Officer Bailey asked in a low voice. Officer Gregg moved closer to hear him better. "I took care of it for good this time."

Officer Gregg looked at Officer Bailey for a few seconds, wondering what he was talking about. Suddenly it dawned on him. Officer Gregg was stunned into silence. He looked at Officer Bailey in disbelief. "Wha—What do you mean you took care of it?" he finally stuttered, glancing around the room to make sure they were still alone. "Bailey, what did you do? Did you—"

"No, I didn't kill anyone," Officer Bailey said pointedly.

Officer Gregg breathed a sigh of relief. He knew Tiny had left town shortly after she had the baby and no one had heard from her since. This he knew because the few times he attended church, Aunt Madge requested a special prayer for the safe return of her niece. Finding it too uncomfortable and nerve-racking to look at his daughter every week and not being able to acknowledge her, he stayed away from church as often as possible without arousing suspicion. With too much to lose, Officer Gregg hid in his web of lies and denial, trying to convince himself that he was doing the right thing to save his family.

"What happened? I thought she left town? Did she come back? Where is she now?" he worriedly fired off one question after the other, sweat slowly dampening his face.

"Calm down, man." Officer Bailey patted him lightly on the shoulder. "You don't need to know the details. Just know that this time she's gone for good."

"So she *was* here?" Officer Gregg asked in disbelief. "In Falmouth?"

Bailey nodded. "But she is on her way to wherever the heck she was all this time. I saw to it personally."

"But—"

"Gregg, just let it go." Officer Bailey's tone clearly said that the subject was closed. "I took care of our problem. That's all you need to know."

There it is again, Officer Gregg thought. *He took care of "our" problem.* He looked at Officer Bailey's rigid face and knew he wouldn't be getting any more information out of him. *At least he didn't hurt Tiny. I better just let it go.*

"We good, man?" Officer Bailey's voice snapped Officer Gregg's attention back to him.

"Yeah, we good, Bailey." Officer Gregg reached out to Officer Bailey, and they exchanged a man hug. "Thanks, man."

The man of law nodded and briskly walked out of the bunk room, leaving Officer Gregg staring at his back, his brows knitted in confusion.

Chapter Thirty-six

It was dark when Eleanor got off the bus on Red Hills Road. Weary, she slowly walked home, her body feeling as if it was trampled on by horses. Her face felt swollen and bruised where she was slapped. She hoped Mama Pearl was asleep and Omar wasn't home. How could she explain what had happened to her today? She could not. This was yet another secret that she had to live with.

As Eleanor approached the gate, she saw a tall figure leaning up against it. The fluttering of her heart confirmed exactly who it was. Great! The last person she wanted to see her like that. Eleanor paused, contemplated her situation, and knew there was no way out. So slowly she walked up to Dwight, her eyes looking everywhere but at him.

"Hi, Dwight. What are—?"

"What happened to you?" he asked as he walked closer to Eleanor, concern splashed across his face. "My God, were you mugged? Were you in an accident? Are you hurt?"

"No, I'm fine," Eleanor said. "I was attacked, but it looks worse than it actually is."

"You were attacked, and you are *fine?* You look as if you are about to fall down," Dwight stated as he looked her up and down. "Come on, I'm taking you to the hospital so they can check you out. Then we're going to the police station to file a complaint. In fact, I think Gerald is also working tonight." He grabbed Eleanor's hand and took a step before he was pulled back.

"Dwight, please stop," Eleanor said strongly, tugging on his hand. "I don't need to go to the hospital, and I'm not going to the police."

"But why? Eleanor, you were attacked." Dwight looked worried, his eyes pleading with her. "You need medical attention."

"What I need is a . . . a . . ." Eleanor burst in tears, the stress of the day finally catching up with her. "It's just too much sometimes," she sobbed.

Dwight pulled her into his arms and hugged her. "It's going to be okay," he whispered softly. "You are going to get through this." For a few minutes he held Eleanor as she cried, his heart breaking in the process.

Dwight had stopped by earlier for a visit and was very disappointed when Mama Pearl informed him that Eleanor was working late. Extending his time until Mama Pearl and Omar were ready for bed, he finally left the house reluctantly. As Dwight closed the gate behind him, he glanced up the street and saw the woman he had been hoping to see. Feeling happy, he waited for Eleanor to reach him.

"I'm all right now." Eleanor pulled back a little from Dwight. "Sorry about that." She looked down at the ground, unable to make eye contact with him.

"Here." Dwight handed her his handkerchief.

Eleanor took it and gave him a little smile. She wiped her face and blew her nose loudly. "I should go in." She looked toward the house. "I hope no one is up because I really can't deal with this anymore tonight." She sniffled as if she was about to start crying again.

"Come with me," Dwight said and reached for her hand. "Let's take a ride so you can get yourself together."

Eleanor looked at him through red, puffy eyes and saw the compassion on his face. "Okay," she said, nodding her head. "But we can't stay too long."

"I'm parked over there." Dwight pointed to his car parked across the street. Still holding Eleanor's hand, they crossed the road, and he opened the passenger door for her to get in. After he strapped himself behind the wheel, he drove off.

The ride started off quiet, but was much more comfortable than the last time they rode together. Eleanor and Dwight kept stealing glances at each other when they thought the other wasn't looking. The chemistry between the two of them was sizzling.

As the car drove down Red Hills Road, Eleanor looked out the window lost in thought.

"You still feel okay?" Dwight asked, looking between her and the road. "Are you hurting?"

"I have been hurting for years, Dwight." Eleanor was surprised that she had shared that with him. "I have a strong feeling that I'll be hurting until I die."

"No, you won't, Eleanor," he replied. He reached over and patted the hand folded in her lap. "Not with the God we serve."

Eleanor shrugged her shoulders, staring straight-ahead.

"Okay, let's stop here and talk for a while," Dwight said moments later. He pulled in and parked in a secluded area in the parking lot of the Red Hills Mall. "I figure you wouldn't want to go anywhere with too many people."

Eleanor nodded and gave him an appreciative smile. "Thanks, this is fine."

"There's a restaurant inside. How about I grab us something to eat?" he asked. "We'll stay right here in the car. Is that all right?"

As if on cue, Eleanor's stomach rumbled loudly. She hadn't had anything to eat all day as food was the last thing on her mind. Embarrassed, she nodded without looking at him.

"I'll be right back." Dwight exited the car.

Eleanor watched him as he walked away, admiring the way his jeans hugged his firm hips and buttocks. "Oh my gosh," Eleanor muttered. "I can't believe I was just doing that. Girl, get ahold of yourself. You and Dwight are as different as cheese is from chalk. What would a man like that want with someone like you?" But in the back of her mind, she wondered at the possibility.

Eleanor knew nothing about relationships. Her only sexual encounter was an adulterous affair with Officer Gregg when she was a teenager. An exciting experience at the time that became a living nightmare. Having sworn off men, Eleanor was confused and at times resentful of the feelings she was developing for Dwight. It was said that "once bitten, twice shy."

"Here you go."

Eleanor jumped a little as she turned around to see Dwight sitting in the car beside her, handing her a large plastic container. So caught up in her thoughts, she never saw him return.

"Thank you." She took the food from him. He then handed her a plastic fork and some napkins from a bag in his lap.

"I'll put our drinks right here," Dwight said and placed them in the drink holder.

Eleanor opened the container and almost drooled when she saw the stew chicken, rice and peas, and fried plantains. The aroma was enough to cause her mouth to water. Famished, she held the food closer to her mouth and dug in. Dwight was temporarily forgotten.

Dwight peeped over at Eleanor as he ate, noticing how fast she was devouring her food. *It looks as if she hasn't eaten all day. I wonder what happened.* He waited until Eleanor cleaned the container and gulped down almost all of her drink before he spoke. "Want to tell me what happened today?" Dwight asked as he put his half-filled food container and Eleanor's empty one in the plastic bag by his feet. "Where were you attacked, and do you know who did it?" He turned in his seat to face her.

"Dwight, thank you for being here for me, but there are a lot of things going on in my life that I can't share with anyone," Eleanor told him. "Not even you. Sorry."

"You have to talk to someone, Eleanor," Dwight said gently. "You are carrying too much. If not me, then pray some more. Talk to God and allow Him to work it out for you."

Eleanor smiled sadly. "Don't you think I have been doing that? I have rededicated my life to God, attend church regularly, pray and fast, yet I'm not free. My mistakes are always dangling over my head," she told him, her eyes filled with tears. "Do you know the worst part? I don't think I deserve God's forgiveness."

"Look at me." Dwight used his hand to lift her chin until she was looking him in the eye. "God's mercy supersedes any mistake and every failure."

Eleanor stared at him solemnly without a word.

"I'm not going to stop until you finally realize that," Dwight told her. "I like you, Eleanor. I like you a lot."

Eleanor blushed and looked away. "There is not much to like, Dwight. Trust me on that."

"I think I prefer to trust God and follow my spirit." he grinned. "There is something about you that drew me to you from day one. Do you feel it too?"

Eleanor ignored the question and asked instead, "Has anyone told you how I came to live with Mama Pearl and her family?"

Dwight shook his head. "Mama Pearl called me in New York and told me she has an adopted daughter and Omar constantly bragged about his naughty little sister."

Eleanor laughed out loud with Dwight joining in. For a few seconds they just laughed freely, as if it was the most natural thing in the world.

Dwight watched how Eleanor's countenance lit up and her eyes sparkled when she laughed. Despite the swollen face and puffy eyes, she was so beautiful. Unable to stop himself, he leaned over and kissed her.

Eleanor froze when she felt Dwight's lips on hers. Her eyes widened in alarm. She had never kissed a man before. During her fling with Officer Gregg, not once had he kissed her. This should have told her something, but her young, immature, impressionable mind just never got it. So she sat there as stiff as a straitjacket.

Dwight felt Eleanor's body stiffen and her unresponsiveness. Ashamed, he drew back from her, lay his head back on his headrest, his eyes tightly closed. "I'm sorry," he whispered. "I shouldn't have done that. Please forgive me."

Eleanor looked at him and felt even worse for the way she reacted. "There is nothing to forgive, Dwight," she said softly. "It's not you. It's me."

Dwight opened his eyes and looked at her questioningly. "You're not mad at me?"

Eleanor shook her head and smiled at him. "Not at all. In fact, it was very nice hanging out with you. Thank you for the food, the encouragement, and for just being here for me. I appreciate it."

Dwight smiled. "You're welcome. Can we do this again soon? I mean get out of the car and go somewhere where we can stretch our legs?"

Eleanor punched him lightly on the arm, their laughter echoing into the night. This seemed to be the beginning of something beautiful. However . . . It would get worse before it got better.

Chapter Thirty-seven

Over the next few weeks Dwight did everything in his power to spend more time with Eleanor. Everywhere she turned, there he was with his fine self.

It was almost Christmas and Eleanor was still working at the hardware store, now fulltime as the assistant manager. It was a busy day, and the store was crowded. Eleanor was wearing a few hats that day, from cashier to store clerk, running from one end of the store to the other, attending to their customers' needs. Suddenly a hush fell over the store. Eleanor looked up from the register to see what was going on. Her mouth popped open in surprise.

Dwight strolled into the store with swag, wearing one of his many expensive business suits that molded to his long frame, nicely muscled body. He was sporting the biggest smile, carrying a large bouquet of exotic flowers. Gorgeous colors burst from them. Like the Red Sea, the crowd parted for him, watching in fascination as he made his way to Eleanor.

Eleanor watched him approach almost as if in a daze. Her face flushed, her heart raced. His captivating eyes met hers and held, almost in a hypnotizing spell.

"Hello, beautiful," Dwight greeted when he was standing in front of her, separated by the counter, his dimples winking at her. He held out the flowers to her.

"Hi," Eleanor responded in a low voice and took the flowers from him. "Thank you."

"You are welcome. Anything for you," Dwight replied, resting his elbows on the counter and staring at Eleanor through those love-filled, dreamy eyes.

There were "oohs" and "ahhs" from some nosy customers who stepped closer to listen to the private conversation. "Girl, if you don't want this fine thing, I'll take him," one brave woman volunteered.

Eleanor blushed. If she was light skinned, she would have been red in the face. She leaned over and whispered to Dwight, "See what you did, Mr. Humphrey?" with a gigantic smile on her face, showing all thirty-two sparkling teeth. She felt special, a feeling that had evaded her for many years.

"What did I do, gorgeous?" Dwight was laying it on thick, determined to let Eleanor know how he felt and that he wasn't going anywhere, any time soon. "You deserve only beautiful things in your life, and I'm going to see to that." He bridged the small gap between them, leaning over to kiss her softly on the forehead.

"Sweetheart, you better not let Mr. Lover-Lover go," a customer said loudly and the store erupted in laughter.

Eleanor laughed until tears filled her eyes. She was still smiling minutes later, after Dwight left with the promise that she would have dinner with him that evening.

Over the next few weeks Eleanor and Dwight saw each other on a regular basis. Dwight still dropped by the hardware store frequently with flowers or lunch for Eleanor. They would go out to dinner after work or to catch a movie or Dwight would have dinner with her and Mama Pearl. On rare occasions when they would not see each other, they made sure to catch up on their day by telephone.

It was an exciting time in Eleanor's life but just as frightening. She knew things were getting serious between them and therefore, she needed to tell him about her past—all of it. What would he think of her then? Would he still want to be with her?

The New Year of 1987 came with lots of optimism for Eleanor. She had sent for and received a copy of her birth certificate from the Registrar General's Department and had even obtained her passport. But most importantly, Eleanor had made up her mind to tell Dwight everything there was to know about her. They had continued to spend a lot of time together, but there was a pink elephant that followed them around. It would not go away until the secrets did.

Eleanor tried many times to break away from Dwight, but she had grown so attached to him. He made her feel safe and loved. When Eleanor was with him, the demons that tormented her stayed away.

She needed him, especially on a day like today, January 25th. It was Dupree's eighth birthday, and Eleanor woke up feeling depressed and heartbroken. She went to work as customary but lacked the bubbly personality that everyone came to know and love. A few people mentioned it, but she quickly assured them that she was fine.

What if I go to Falmouth without Officer Bailey finding out? Eleanor pondered as she leaned against the store's counter. *I could go and see Dupree and Aunt Madge real quick and come back.* Just then, an image of the ogre popped up in her mind.

"I have contacts everywhere," Officer Bailey had told her. *"If you ever come back here again, I'll know and your daughter and aunt will pay dearly."*

"I can't go back there," Eleanor mumbled. "I can't let that monster anywhere near Dupree and Aunt Madge."

So Eleanor dragged through the day feeling as if the world weighed down on her shoulders. Later that evening as she exited the store to walk to the bus stop, she stopped short when she saw Dwight leaning up against his bright sports car, arms crossed, eyes twinkling and teeth sparkling.

"Your chariot awaits, ma'am." Dwight waved his hand toward his car.

Eleanor stood for a few seconds looking at the man that she was falling in love with. *I'm going to miss him when he's gone.*

"Babe, you okay?" Dwight was now standing in front of her. "Aren't you feeling well?" He placed the palm of his hand on her forehead, his eyes searching her face worriedly.

"I'm fine," Eleanor said in a very low voice. "I'm just very tired."

Dwight looked at her for a few seconds before nodding his head. "Well, I have the perfect solution to take care of that." He reached out and pulled her into his arms, holding her tight.

With her face nestled in the crook of his neck, inhaling his cologne and masculine scent, tears filled Eleanor's eyes. Blinking rapidly, she tried to keep them from falling. It was not yet time to reveal everything to him.

"I'm going to take you somewhere you can relax for a while. Is that all right?" Dwight asked as he released her from his arms, separated by a few inches.

"Yes. I would like that," Eleanor said softly. "Where are we going?"

"That, my dear, is a secret," Dwight said excitedly. He walked to the car and opened the door for her. After Eleanor was in, he closed her door and skipped around to the driver's seat, grinning like a shot fox when he drove off.

Eleanor leaned back into the leather seat and closed her eyes. The soft purring of the car rocked her to sleep within minutes.

Dwight glanced at her sleeping form, a knot in his gut. Even in sleep her face was contorted in grief. "We are going to have a long conversation later," he whispered. "I think that is long overdue."

As the car ate up the road and mounted the hill to their destination, Eleanor slept restlessly, twisting and turning, mumbling incoherently. Soon Dwight pulled in the driveway and shut off the car. He got out and walked around to Eleanor's side. After pulling the door open, he reached in and gently lifted Eleanor in his arms.

"No! No! Let me go!" she yelled, waving her arms wildly, thrashing her feet. She slapped Dwight hard across the face, struggling to be released, her eyes still closed.

Dwight stumbled away from the car, his grip still tight on Eleanor in his arms, rapidly blinking his eyes and shaking his head to keep focused. "Eleanor, stop it!" he said loudly, rocking her vigorously in his arms. "Wake up. It's me. Dwight."

Eleanor's eyes immediately popped open and widened in alarm as she looked up into Dwight's worried face. "Hmmm . . . I think I had a bad dream." She hid her face in his shirt. "I'm sorry," she mumbled.

With his face still stinging, Dwight looked down at the shivering woman in his arms for a while before he walked with her up to the front door. Almost effortlessly, he lowered Eleanor to her feet, facing him, one arm still wrapped around her waist, pulling her close to his body. With his other hand he took keys from his pocket and unlocked the front door, pushing it open.

Eleanor turned away from Dwight and peered inside the house curiously. "Where are we?" she asked, walking slowly inside, her eyes scanning the beautiful living room that she had entered.

"My home," Dwight said from behind her. "I wanted to show you where I live."

Eleanor turned around and looked at him silently for a moment. A small smile on her face, she turned and began walking around the elegant room, admiring the thick, posh bronze and gold carpet that seemed to sparkle under the sunlight that poured through the high floor-to-ceiling windows. The walls were embellished with bright, exquisite paintings that complemented the soft russet four-piece leather reclining sectional.

"It's exquisite," she said as she looked out the window, staring down in the valley at the tops of thousands of houses in Kingston City.

"Thank you," Dwight replied from behind her, wrapping his hands around her waist, his chin resting on the top of her head. "I'm glad you like it. I'll show you the rest of the house after dinner."

"Dinner?" Eleanor asked with a smile. "You cooked?" *This man always knows just what I want.*

"Not exactly."

Eleanor turned around to look at him, her hands intertwined around his narrow waist. "What does that mean?" her eyes sparkled in amusement. "You ordered takeout?"

"No, my part-time helper," Dwight used his fingers to make quotation marks, "part-time cook, Adassa, made dinner for us before she left."

"Sounds good," Eleanor replied. "I'm starving. I haven't eaten all day." She gasped loudly and stared up at Dwight wide-eyed. She never meant to say that last part which she knew was going to lead to questions. Questions she didn't want to answer at the time.

Dwight's brown eyes seemed to laser through her, his brows mopped together as if in deep concentration. "We need to talk, Eleanor." He held up a hand when Eleanor opened her mouth to speak. "After dinner we will talk.

No more secrets. I've been patient, but we are getting closer and our relationship is growing. Am I wrong in this assumption?"

Eleanor shook her head.

"There are a lot of things I need to tell you also about my parents and our strained relationship," Dwight continued. "So today, we will lay all the cards out on the table, sweetheart. I think it's time."

Eleanor looked at Dwight with fear lurking in her eyes. Aunt Madge used to say "You can run, but you can't hide." She guessed the time had come for her to tell Dwight everything. Would he run or would he stay? She would soon find out.

Chapter Thirty-eight

"That was absolutely delicious." Eleanor leaned back into the chair, wiping her mouth with a napkin. "I have eaten so much food, I think I might have gained ten pounds." Eleanor was blabbering, but she couldn't help herself. Butterflies were swirling around in her full tummy, and her palms were getting sweaty. "Wow, absolutely mouthwatering." Her eyes glanced agitatedly around the dining room, conveniently avoiding contact with Dwight.

Dwight looked at Eleanor, noticing how uneasy she had become now that they had finished dinner and it was time for their "talk." He hated putting her on the spot, but they had to cross this hurdle in order to move forward. "Come with me," he said as he pushed back his chair and stood up. "Let's go back into the living room." He walked over to Eleanor's chair and pulled it out for her. He held his hand out to her, a serious expression on his face.

Swallowing hard, Eleanor stood to her feet, placing her trembling hand in Dwight's. With each step they took toward the living room, her pulse beat faster and faster.

"It's going to be okay," Dwight said as he lowered himself onto the couch, gently pulling Eleanor down beside him. He turned slightly so he was looking directly at her. "It can't be that bad. Is it?" He leaned over closer, looking at her intently.

Her eyes filling with tears, her lips quivering, Eleanor looked at Dwight and nodded. "You don't know the awful things I've done, Dwight," Eleanor said a little above a whisper. "I abandoned my aunt who raised me after my mother died in child birth and my one-week-old daughter." She covered her face with her hands and began to sob.

Dwight seemed to have frozen in his seat. His mouth hung open, his enlarged eyes gaped at Eleanor in shock. Of all the possibilities that ran through his mind of what secrets Eleanor harbored, he never once thought of this. "A daughter? You have a daughter?" he finally croaked. "How . . . I mean, where . . . Where is she?"

Eleanor's crying only intensified. To her ears, Dwight sounded disgusted with her.

Dwight scooted closer and pulled Eleanor into his arms. Tears filled his eyes as he rocked her gently, his heart breaking for her. "It's going to be fine," he said softly, running his fingers through her hair. He continued to whisper encouraging words to Eleanor until her crying dwindled down.

"I was only fifteen-years-old when I had my daughter," Eleanor said against his chest, the tears still leaking from her eyes. "It all started the night I met this police officer." Eleanor proceeded to tell Dwight about her affair with the married policeman. Hard as it was, Dwight remained quiet, but his heartbeat escalated with each word Eleanor spoke.

"He attacked me when I told him I was pregnant," Eleanor said, shivering as she relived the night. "He choked me and—"

"*Grrrr!*" Dwight growled, causing Eleanor to jump to her feet alarmed. Her eyes widened when she saw his hands tightened into fists, his nostrils flaring like a mad bull. Tears ran down his face as he trembled uncontrollably. "I'm going to kill him," Dwight spat. "Tell me who he is and where I can find him."

"No," Eleanor said, shaking her head. "Please, I'll tell you everything but not that. Too many people's lives are in danger."

"Do you think I'm scared of him?" Dwight asked angrily. "A punk who beat on defenseless young girls? Let's see what he does when he gets a worthy opponent."

Eleanor shuddered at the thought. Now she knew for sure that she could not tell Dwight Officer Gregg's name or where she was from. He would probably try to find the man and have to deal with him and the gorilla, Officer Bailey. Those policemen would do anything to keep their dirty secrets hidden, even if they had to kill to do so. She would never let that happen to Dwight.

"Oh, babe. It was my fault too. I—"

"*Your* fault? He got involved with a *child*, impregnated her and tried to kill her!" Dwight stood up and went to stand in front of Eleanor, his chest rising and falling rhythmically. "He's a monster!"

Eleanor bridged the small gap between them and hugged him tight. They clung to each other crying, bonding in the pain they now shared through their love for each other.

Dwight's strong arms around her gave Eleanor the strength she needed to resume the horror story of her life. It took a long time because she had to stop at intervals to calm Dwight down or he had to comfort her until she could continue. Tears and snot ran down their faces, her words ricocheting around them, like arrows sticking into their hearts.

Dwight screamed loudly and ran into the bathroom when Eleanor began speaking of the almost rape in the park downtown. Down on his knees with his mouth over the toilet, he threw up his dinner. His intestines felt like they were suffocating him internally. "Help me, Lord," Dwight muttered as he flushed the toilet. He sat down on the rug, leaned his head against the cool, white porcelain toilet, and wept. "How did one girl survive all that?"

Eleanor slowly entered the bathroom and found Dwight on the floor, shaking and crying. She felt bad seeing him in so much agony, but her heart leaped at the love he had for her. It was as if Dwight was experiencing everything that she had. Her pain became his as well.

"I'm sorry," Dwight said when Eleanor sat down beside him on the floor. He hugged her as if his life depended on it. "I'm sorry I wasn't there for you. I'm sorry for the hell you have been through." They cried together.

"I'll save the rest for another time," Eleanor said when their crying tapered off. She hiccupped. "It's too much."

"No," Dwight quickly replied. He moved his head back and looked at Eleanor. "Let's finish this tonight."

"Are you sure?" she asked him with concern.

Dwight nodded, wiping his wet, red eyes with the back of his hand.

So right there on the bathroom floor, Eleanor finished telling Dwight about her former life. Dwight broke down again when she relayed how she got sick in the old, abandoned car and almost died. He crushed Eleanor to his body as if he was scared of letting her go.

"I want to tell you about my relationship . . . or lack thereof, with my parents," Dwight began in a low voice, moments later. He proceeded to tell Eleanor about his childhood and the estrangement between him and his family.

Eleanor's heart broke for Dwight as she listened to the hurt in his voice as he spoke. Protectively, she tightened her hold on him, sharing his pain as he did hers.

It was a draining, excruciating, heart wrenching process that left the two of them feeling battered and bruised, like they had been trampled by a herd of elephants. They continued hugging for a long while before Dwight moved away and sluggishly got to his feet. He reached down and helped Eleanor to her feet.

He handed Eleanor a towel he took off the towel rack and nodded toward the face basin. After rinsing out their mouths and washing and drying their faces, they walked out of the bathroom into the living room. "I'll go and get us some water," he said hoarsely before he disappeared into the kitchen.

Eleanor lowered herself slowly onto the couch, her heart heavy with all that took place. She felt somewhat relieved, though, that she had shared everything with him. Well . . . almost everything. The names of Officers Gregg and Bailey had to remain a secret for now.

Dwight returned and gave Eleanor a glass of cold water, taking a seat beside her on the couch. Eleanor drank thirstily, moistening her dry, parched throat.

"You know I am going to find that animal, right?" Dwight said, and then took a sip from his glass. "Wait until Omar and the guys hear about this. He's as good as dead."

The glass almost fell from Eleanor's hand. "No," she said firmly. "Dwight, you can't say anything to them about this."

"Why not? We are first going to make sure that monster pays for what he did to you. After which we're bringing your daughter and aunt to live here in Kingston."

He makes it sounds so easy, Eleanor mused as she touched his face gently. *If only he knew everything that is at stake here.*

"Please promise me you won't say anything to Mama Pearl and the family," Eleanor begged him. "I'll tell them when the time is right. Please."

Dwight nodded solemnly, not comfortable with her decision but decided to let it go for now. "So when are we going to see your daughter and aunt? I think it's time for you to start mending that bridge."

"We are not," Eleanor replied and shivered as she thought of Officer Bailey. "Not now anyway."

"Eleanor, what are you afraid of?" Dwight asked her. "I know that slimeball had threatened you, but he can't hurt you anymore. We'll go and get Dupree and Aunt Madge and bring them here."

"Aunt Madge would never leave her home," Eleanor stated. "She always said she was born in Falmouth and she would die in Falmouth."

"So what do you plan on doing? Ignore them for the rest of your life?" Dwight asked her. "You have to stop blaming yourself for all that has happened. It wasn't your fault. I'm sure Aunt Madge will understand that and forgive you."

But Eleanor shook her head stubbornly.

Dwight refused to give up. "As for Dupree, you probably saved her life when you ran," he said.

Eleanor looked at him surprised.

"I think you suffered from something my aunt's friend had in New York when I was there. It's the extreme form of postpartum depression known as postpartum psychosis," he explained, remembering her telling him of the hallucinations she had of the little scary creature. "Had you stayed around the baby without getting help, you may have hurt her without even knowing it at that time. I'm no expert, but I think it went away on its own because of the time you were separated from the baby. That was eight years ago. I think it's time for you to see her again."

"I can't do that now," Eleanor stated.

"Why not, Eleanor?" Dwight asked wearily. "I'm trying to help you here." He got up and walked over to the window, staring out into the night, unsure of what else to say or do. He just wanted to fix all her problems and make everything right for Eleanor.

Eleanor knew that deep inside Dwight was disgusted with her. Taking a deep breath, she stood up and walked over to get her handbag that was on the other end of the long couch. Almost on tippy toes, she lightly moved toward the door.

"Where are you going?" Dwight's voice stopped her in her tracks.

Eleanor cringed and turned around to face him, unshed tears dancing in her eyes. Without a word she watched as Dwight's long feet ate up the short space between them.

"You are done running, babe," Dwight said gently. He pulled her to him and kissed her passionately. Eleanor responded fervidly.

"I love you, Eleanor," Dwight said as he looked intently into her eyes. "You are an amazing woman."

Eleanor smiled happily. "I love you too," she replied. "Thank you for being such a strong rock for me to lean on. I need you to get through this."

"I'm not going anywhere," Dwight assured her. "We'll speak some more about my stepdaughter and Aunt Madge very soon. I don't agree with your decision to stay away, but I'll leave it alone for now."

"Your stepdaughter, huh?" Eleanor asked, beaming from ear to ear.

"Yup," Dwight said with a chuckle. "I'm in this for the long haul, sweetheart."

Dwight and Eleanor's unity created a powerful bond. But it would be tested to the max.

Chapter Thirty-nine

Over the next few weeks Dwight made numerous attempts to change Eleanor's mind about contacting Aunt Madge and Dupree, but she refused. In Eleanor's mind she was not only protecting Aunt Madge and Dupree but Dwight, Mama Pearl, and her adoptive brothers. She was convinced that God would work it out for her to see her daughter and aunt when the time was right. Yes, she missed them dearly, but it was a small price to pay for their safety.

In the meantime, Eleanor plunged right ahead into her relationship with Dwight. It was one of the few lights shining through her dimmed world. They were almost inseparable. Rarely a day went by when they did not see each other.

"Looks as if Mama Pearl has other guests for dinner," Dwight said to Eleanor one Saturday afternoon after parking in front of Mama Pearl's house and saw two cars in the driveway. He had just picked Eleanor up from work and came by to have dinner with her, Mama Pearl and Omar.

"It's Robert and Gerald," Eleanor replied after hopping out of the car and joining Dwight at the gate. She took Dwight's hand in hers and they walked up to the house.

"Anyone home?" Dwight said in a singsong voice as he and Eleanor entered the living room.

Eleanor giggled.

They both froze when they saw Mama Pearl and her five sons sitting in the living room in a circle with a serious expression on their faces. The smile fell from Dwight's face and Eleanor got nervous, her eyes darting back and forth between Robert, Alwayne, Gerald, Sydney, and Omar.

"What's wrong?" Eleanor asked worriedly. "Is it Mama Pearl?" She hurried over to Mama Pearl, a feeling of despair in her gut.

"I'm all right, baby." Mama Pearl gave her a grateful smile. "This old bird is doing just fine. Please, you and Dwight have a seat." She waved her hand toward two empty chairs that were placed side by side in the circle.

Dwight and Eleanor exchanged puzzled looks before they took their respective seats.

"What's going on, guys?" Dwight asked as he perched on the edge of his chair, rubbing his hands together, his eyes bouncing from one face to the next.

"That's what we would like to know," Sydney said in a solemn voice, resting further back on the couch, his long legs stretched out in front of him. "We would like to know what your intentions are toward Eleanor."

Eleanor gasped loudly, her eyes as big as saucers. Embarrassed, she covered her face with her hands, shaking her head from side to side. "Oh, dear Lord," she muttered repeatedly, but everyone ignored her.

"You know you are like a brother to us, Dwight," Gerald said, his arms crossed. "We all love you. But we also love our little sister that God gave to us a few years ago, and we have her best interest at heart."

"We have watched your relationship growing over the last few months," Robert pitched in, "and we are happy for both of you. I personally believe the two of you need each other, but we would like to know where you see things going with Eleanor."

"Oh, dear Lord," Eleanor repeated louder this time, her eyes committing the area rug under her feet to memory. Again, everyone ignored her.

"You know you are my boy, 'D,'" Omar said, his eyes met and held those of Dwight's. "I would hate to have to hurt you, man."

Dwight laughed out loud but stopped quickly when he realized he was the only one laughing. Six pair of eyes stared at him in silence. The brothers, including his dear friend, Omar, were as serious as a heart attack.

Swallowing hard, Dwight reached over and took one of Eleanor's trembling hands in his own. Eleanor glanced over and gave him an apologetic shrug, but he winked at her, sending butterflies flittering around in her stomach.

"You are all like family to me," Dwight began in a somber tone, his face now void of any jokes, still clutching Eleanor's hand. "I love all of you and thank God for each of you every day. To be honest, I'm actually very glad that we are having this conversation."

Eleanor looked at him as if he had lost his mind, while the others stared at him in silence, all ears.

"I was very apprehensive coming back to Jamaica because of my parents, but I just knew I had to. Boy, am I glad I did. I met and fell in love with one of the most amazing women I have ever met." Dwight felt tears spring to his eyes. He paused and took a deep breath before he continued. "A strong, beautiful, ambitious, and courageous warrior." He leaned over and kissed Eleanor on the forehead as he squeezed her fingers.

"So to answer the question asked of me, I love Eleanor," Dwight said with conviction, making eye contact with these men that he loved and respected. "I want a future with her, and I'm trusting God to make that possible for us."

Tears ran down Eleanor's and Mama Pearl's faces. The guys sniffed their noses, blinking rapidly, twisting and turning in their seats.

"Hmmm . . . That's all we wanted to know," Alwayne said in a raspy voice. He cleared his throat loudly. "I couldn't ask for a better man for Eleanor." He got up and walked over to Dwight, hugging him when Dwight stood up.

Soon Dwight and Eleanor were receiving hugs and well wishes from everyone. It took awhile before they all settled down and took their place at the dining table.

Eleanor, who was sitting beside Dwight, turned toward him with a big smile. "You know if you want to break up with me now I'll understand, right?"

This time everyone laughed before digging into Mama Pearl's finger-licking pot roast, celebrating Eleanor and Dwight's love.

"I have some great news," Dwight whispered in Eleanor's ear. Her back was resting against his broad chest, their feet tangled up together as they lay cuddling on his couch.

Eleanor shifted position and turned over until they were nose to nose. Her eyes filled with curiosity. She gave him an Eskimo kiss, giggling. "What's the news?"

"I have a friend who is the tax regional director at BDO Jamaica," Dwight began, gently running his index finger up and down her cheek. "He told me about an assistant human resources manager position that is available there."

Eleanor's heart started beating faster, but she remained quiet, her eyes fixed on Dwight's handsome face.

"He scheduled an interview for you with the human resources director for next week. Babe, please hear me out." Dwight put his finger on Eleanor's lips when she opened her mouth to speak. "I hope you don't mind that I went ahead and set this up before saying anything to you. I just wanted to help, okay?"

Eleanor looked at him for a few seconds, trying to wrap her mind around what Dwight had just said. A job interview at one of the biggest accounting companies in Jamaica? He had to be kidding!

"Sweetheart, are you mad?" Dwight asked, misinterpreting her silence.

"No, no, I'm not upset," Eleanor quickly assured him. "I mean . . . I . . . I have no experience or anything. Why would they even consider me for this position?"

"You have a bachelor's degree in Human Resources Management," Dwight said, looking over her head. "You are smart and a quick learner. You will do great. You—"

"Dwight Humphrey." Eleanor stared pointedly at him.

"Okay. I told him you are my girlfriend," Dwight admitted. "But, darling, you are good for this. I meant what I said before. You graduated at the top of your class from UWI. This is just an interview. I only got you through the door, but you are going to have to get this job on your own, and I know you will."

A smile tugged at Eleanor's mouth. "You think I can do this, huh?" The doubt was quickly being replaced by enthusiasm, thanks to this wonderful man that God had blessed her with. "I have what it takes, right?"

"Philippians 4:13 says, 'I can do all things through Christ which strengtheneth me,'" Dwight replied. He leaned over and kissed Eleanor lightly on the lips. "I decree and declare that one day you, Eleanor, will be an executive at BDO Jamaica, helping to run that company. What do you say we claim it in Jesus' name?"

"I claim it!" Eleanor squealed in delight, forcing him back into the couch.

Dwight laughed and kissed her again. The kiss soon deepened as the passion ignited between them. The strong sexual chemistry was something that they fought with as their relationship intensified because Dwight and Eleanor had decided that they would date as Christians.

"You will pull me back when necessary, and I'll do the same," Dwight had told Eleanor. Easier said than done. They were two hot-blooded, sexual beings who were in love and profoundly attracted to each other.

"Okay. Okay," Dwight mumbled hoarsely after breaking the kiss, his breathing irregular. He nestled his face in the crook of Eleanor's neck, feeling her carotid pulse palpitating. "You, madam, are surely a temptation."

"Speaking of the pot calling the kettle black," Eleanor murmured dreamily. *Dear God, please give us the strength to hang in there.*

Chapter Forty

"Welcome to the BDO family, Eleanor," said Mr. Wallace, the human resource director, vigorously shaking Eleanor's right hand. He had a lopsided grin on his thick lips as he looked at her over the top of his bifocal eyeglasses that rested on his broad nose. "You are going to be a great asset to this company."

Eleanor had a "Tom the cat when he thought he caught Jerry" grin on her face. "Thank you for this great opportunity, Mr. Wallace," she replied humbly, releasing her hold on his hand. "I'm looking forward to working with you and learning from the best."

Mr. Wallace had the nerve to blush, his light, aged, freckled skin turning red around the face. "It will be a pleasure, Eleanor. So see you bright and early in two weeks?"

"Yes, sir," Eleanor replied happily. "I'll see you then."

Mr. Wallace walked over to the closed office door and opened it. "Take care," he said as Eleanor passed by him, toward the elevators.

Eleanor literally floated down Breechwood Avenue in New Kingston after leaving Mr. Wallace's office. "I just got the human resources assistant job," she sang softly on her way to the bus stop. "Thank you, Lord. I'm about to get my career off the ground."

Eleanor paused at a street corner, looking up and down the street, watching for a break in the flow of traffic so she could cross the road. Shortly thereafter she saw her chance and skipped across like a little girl, a gigantic smile on her face. Eleanor felt light-headed and giddy. "It's really happening," she said with a faraway look on her face as she turned on Dominica Drive. "Aunt Madge, I graduated college and am about to start my dream job." Suddenly, it was like someone flicked a light switch and the light was gone, plunging her into total darkness. There it was again. That obstinate cloud that was always hanging over her, ready and waiting to cover up every spark of happiness that was rained on her.

Her head now hanging low, Eleanor hastened her steps. She needed Dwight. He would make everything better, at least while she was with him.

"Yo, watch where you going, lady," a man said after Eleanor walked right into him, too preoccupied to have noticed him standing on the sidewalk.

"I'm sorry," Eleanor said softly as she looked up at the tall man. Her eyes opened wide when she saw who he was. "You?" Eleanor whispered tautly, glancing around and taking comfort in the fact that it was broad daylight and people and vehicles were going up and down the busy streets. The last time she saw this man he tried to choke her to death. He was an animal.

"Well, well, well, look who it is," Big Dread said animatedly as if he had just run into a longtime friend. "Little, is that you? Baby, you certainly ain't little no more." He swiped his long tongue across his chapped lips, his hand grabbing his crotch.

Eleanor took a few steps back, creating ample space between them, rolling her eyes in disgust. She didn't even bother to waste time correcting the idiot about her name. "Where is Dolly?" she asked, glancing at the closed door of the "Champion Girls" club.

"Hopefully dead," Big Dread said with a smirk on his face. "She would be doing the world a favor."

Eleanor looked at him in shock. "Did you hurt her?" She had a terrible feeling in her gut. "Did you kill Dolly?" Her eyes pleaded with him to say it wasn't so.

Big Dread threw his head back, his dirty, long, thick dreads fanning out behind him and hooted with laughter. Eleanor looked around self-consciously as a few passersby stared at them. "Where is Dolly?" she asked again, watching as Big Dread tried to compose himself, wiping his face with a stained, brown-looking face rag that had been white at one time.

"That old jezebel is probably somewhere selling her body so she can get high," Big Dread said without remorse, his face screwed up like he smelled something bad.

"Wha . . . wha . . . What did you just say?" Eleanor stuttered, tears swimming in her eyes as she listened to Dolly's demise. "Dolly is a prostitute?" She shook her head in denial, glaring at Big Dread. "No way. I bet Dolly left you, and you are just jealous," she said.

Big Dread chuckled and stared at Eleanor as if she was as stupid as a goose. "Do you *really* think *stripping* was all that Dolly was doing?" He emphasized the word "stripping." "Baby, Big Dread had to get that money and you better believe that heifer did whatever I told her to." His lips rolled back, exposing his long, yellow teeth.

"You are evil." Eleanor felt like she wanted to throw up. "One day you are going to get yours. You mark my words. God is going to deal with you in His own way."

Big Dread laughed out loud like he was at a comedy show. "Look at you talking about God," he said to Eleanor. "Big Dread fears no one. No man. No God."

Eleanor cut her eyes at the fool. It was time to go.

"By the way, now that Dolly was let go, Big Dread is looking for a new queen," he said, his eyebrows rising and falling as he winked at Eleanor. "You and Big Dread can make it happen, baby." He struck a pose; legs wide apart, his bulky arms across his broad chest. His head was pushed a little back, his left hand under his chin, a nasty-looking smile plastered on his face. A real candid moment.

Eleanor looked at him in disgust. "Ridiculous," she said aloud and hurriedly walked away.

"Yo! Little! Where you going?" Big Dread shouted at her back. "Baby, come back here to Big Dread."

Eleanor walked even faster, her heart aching with the news she received of Dolly. Images of when they were young in Falmouth, drinking rum and smoking marijuana popped up in her thoughts. She saw Dolly as she laughed so carefree, making plans for a fairy-tale life in Kingston, which was never to be.

Yes, in the end, Dolly had turned her back on Eleanor for a man that she now learned was pimping her out, leaving her out on the streets, exposed to all kinds of danger. Eleanor was angry for a long time as she ate scraps of leftovers she snatched from restaurants or found in the garbage. She was furious with Dolly when she slept in the old abandoned car. But look at her now. It was as if Dolly actually did her a favor.

"Merciful God, wherever Dolly is right now, please protect her," Eleanor prayed under her breath as she sat on the bus heading home. "Please do for her as you are doing for me." She quickly used her hand to wipe away the tears that sneaked out the side of her eyes. "Please send Dolly a guardian angel to rescue her from the streets as you did for me. She is your daughter. Please don't forsake her, Lord. Please, I am begging you to save Dolly and give her a chance to live a happy and fulfilling life according to your will. Amen."

Eleanor got off the bus, dragged her feet down the street, then up the driveway and into the house.

"So? Did you get it?" Mama Pearl greeted her in the hallway, a hesitant smile on her face, rubbing her hands together anxiously.

"Yes. I got it," Eleanor said in a nonchalant voice. "I start in two weeks."

"That's great," Mama Pearl said more like a question than a statement, walking closer to Eleanor, looking intently at her face as if she was trying to read her mind. "Why do you look like someone has died instead of celebrating your new job?"

"Oh, Mama Pearl," Eleanor took a deep, exhausted breath, her shoulders drooped like a withered plant. "I don't know how—"

"How you are going to do the job?" Mama Pearl finished, drawing the wrong conclusion. "That's what you are worried about, isn't it? You are questioning yourself because you have never had a corporate job before. Baby, let me tell you something." Mama Pearl placed her hand under Eleanor's chin, forcing her head up so she looked her in the eyes. "You were born for this job. You hear me? This is your destiny. God didn't bring you this far to leave you now. In a few years time, you will be a force to reckon with in that company. You are blessed, Eleanor. Don't ever question God's blessings, sweetheart. Just embrace them and give Him all the glory."

"Thank you, Mama Pearl," Eleanor whispered, hugging the woman she owed so much. "You always know what to do and say to make me feel better."

"You are welcome, my dear." Mama Pearl squeezed Eleanor tight before letting her go. "I also know that there is some other place you need to be and other people to see." Her eyes twinkled mischievously, a sly grin on her face.

Eleanor blushed. "Yes, I'm going to change and take a cab to see Dwight."

"Okay, ma'am. Don't let me stop you." Mama Pearl laughed when Eleanor ran off toward her bedroom. "Congratulations!" she shouted at her back.

"Thank you!" Eleanor yelled before she dashed into the room.

Eleanor left the house moments later and caught a cab on Red Hills Road. It wasn't long before he was pulling up in front of Dwight's house. Eleanor paid the cabdriver and stepped out of the car, closing the door. She noticed a shiny, white BMW parked behind Dwight's car in the driveway. "It seems as if Dwight has company," Eleanor muttered, feeling a little skeptical about going inside.

Straightening her red strapless dress that flirted above her knees, she flicked her hair before it bounced back into place around her shoulders. Blowing air through her glossed lips, she inhaled and exhaled before she walked up the driveway, passed the cars, up to the front door.

Eleanor was just about to ring the doorbell when she heard loud voices coming from inside. Looking closer at the door, she noticed that it was slightly ajar. Curious, she gently pushed on it and softly crept toward the hullabaloo in the living room.

Careful not to be seen, Eleanor peeked inside the room. A tall, slim, beautiful, light-skinned woman wearing a very short, white, tight-fitting dress was standing inches away from Dwight, waving a glass picture frame with a photograph of Eleanor and Dwight in his face. It was one of Eleanor's favorite photographs of them; they were sitting on the lush, green grass at Hope Gardens, having a picnic on their first real date, sporting gigantic grins.

"So this is the little black gal that you have been wasting your time on," hissed the woman as she stared at the photo. "That's why you are not interested in Melinda, huh?"

Appalled, Eleanor drew back from the doorway, a hand covering her mouth in dismay.

"Mother, you better watch your mouth," Dwight said angrily. "Or you will have to leave."

Outraged, Eve Humphrey spat, "Boy, you are giving up a pedigree for a mongrel?" Her beautiful face was now distorted like a dried prune. "What the heck is the matter with you?"

Eleanor gasped loudly, but no one heard her, too caught up in the argument. She rested her hip against the door for support, a hand still over her mouth to stifle her cry, tears running down her face.

"That's it." Dwight's face was flushed with fury. "Please leave, Mother. Now." His voice was firm and decisive.

"You are throwing me out?" Eve Humphrey placed a delicate hand on her chest, her eyes wide in disbelief. "Because of some low-class, underprivileged ghetto rat?" She stepped closer to Dwight. Standing nose to nose, their fuming eyes clashed and held in battle. "I'm your mother," she hissed, poking him repeatedly in his hard chest with her finger.

"That's why I'm asking you to leave instead of physically throwing you out," Dwight said in a low, dangerous voice. "Eleanor is a beautiful woman, inside and out, and I love her. If you can't show her some respect, you are not welcome here."

Eleanor jumped when Eve threw the picture frame against the wall, shattering it to pieces. "That's what I think about your so-called love," she said to Dwight, her chest rising and falling. "I will never accept the likes of her in my family, and neither will your father."

Dwight looked at her sadly and shook his head. "It's your loss, Mother."

Eve glared at him before she stepped over to the couch and snatched up a white, rhinestone clutch purse. Angrily she trotted toward the door on high, stiletto heels.

Eleanor was frozen in place as she came face-to-face with Dwight's mother for the first time. But instead of a smile, she got a frown. Eve Humphrey certainly didn't think it was a pleasure to meet her.

She came and stood in front of a distressed Eleanor, her hazel eyes crossed with outrage, her nose lifted up in the air like a peacock. Looking up and down Eleanor from head to toe, her face was screwed up as if she stepped in human waste. Eve Humphrey rudely sucked her teeth before she stormed off, her long, fragranced hair flying behind her.

The slamming of the door echoed in Eleanor's head. Feeling weak, she staggered back, right into Dwight's arms. "I got you, babe." Dwight lifted her up in his arms, took her into the living room, and sat on the couch with her on his lap.

Eleanor rested her head on his shoulder, shivering, tears leaking down her face.

"I'm sorry, sweetheart," Dwight whispered, stroking her hair. "I don't know how much of that you heard, but I see it was enough to really upset you. I'm so sorry for the way my mother treated you."

Eleanor sniffed her nose, raised up her head, wiping her face with her hand. "Maybe your mother is right," she hiccupped. Her wet eyes met his sorrowful ones. "I'm nobody. We should just stop fooling ourselves."

"Sweetheart, don't say that." Dwight looked at her in surprise. "I love you. We have something special."

"Your mother—"

"My mother is a bitter woman who doesn't know what it's like to love and to be loved. She thinks she has it all, but yet, she has nothing because she doesn't know the love of the Lord."

Eleanor looked at him skeptically.

"We just have to pray for her, baby," Dwight continued, eager to ease the emotional pain inflicted on her by his mother. "You are with me, not her. It's our relationship. Okay?"

Eleanor looked over at the opened window, a barrage of emotions splashing across her face. Eve Humphrey's words had sliced through like a meat cutter, shredding her dignity to threads.

"Hey, look at me," Dwight said, pulling her closer to his chest. "I love you," He spoke softly after she turned around to him, kissing her all over her face; lips, nose, forehead, eyelids and cheeks, punctuating each kiss with an "I love you."

Eleanor couldn't stop herself from giggling at his antics. Only Dwight could put her back together after coming apart. "Are you sure this is what you want?" she asked him, halting his kissing spree. "I don't want to come between you and your mother."

"I have told you everything about my parents and our strained relationship," Dwight replied. "If it wasn't you, my mother would have found something else to nag me about. They want everything to be done their way, and I won't allow it. I also won't let them ruin what we have. I hope you feel the same way." He searched her face anxiously.

Eleanor looked at him, and her heart swelled with love. "No, I won't let them ruin what we have," she shook her head. "Mama Pearl told me earlier to count my blessings, and I'm starting right now. I love you."

Dwight grinned and pouted up his lips. Laughing, Eleanor kissed him.

"Oh, by the way, you are looking at the new assistant human resources manager for BDO Jamaica," Eleanor said proudly, opening her arms wide, bowing her head.

"Yes! You got it!" Dwight stood up with Eleanor in his arms, spun around and around, both of them laughing until they got dizzy.

"You are so crazy," Eleanor said when they fell on the couch exhausted, trying to catch their breath.

"We are going to be okay, sweetheart," Dwight glanced at her. "Everything will eventually fall into place. Just wait and see."

Eleanor looked at him, praying in her heart that it was so.

Chapter Forty-one

It had been a year since Eleanor started her job at BDO Jamaica. She quickly grasped everything that Mr. Wallace taught her, combined it with her theoretical knowledge, pleasant personality, and the drive to succeed as she performed her duties in an effective and efficient manner.

Today was a celebratory day, in more ways than one. Eleanor was twenty-five-years-old, and Dwight was promoted to general manager for the Treasury Division of NCB.

Mama Pearl wanted the family to have dinner in Port Royal for the special occasions but Dwight requested that it be postponed until the weekend.

"I got plans for my baby tonight," he had told Mama Pearl. "I hope you understand." Mama Pearl understood.

So later that day, Eleanor left work early. She took a cab directly to Dwight's house. Her eyes twinkled mischievously as she walked up the empty driveway, excited to put her plan into action before Dwight got home. Taking the keys from her handbag that Dwight had given her a few weeks ago, she opened the front door.

With a puzzled look on her face, Eleanor closed the door behind her. She sniffed loudly when a delicious aroma tickled her nostrils. "Dwight?" she called as she walked slowly toward the kitchen. "Are you home?" No response.

"Surprise!" Dwight yelled when Eleanor walked into the kitchen. He was leaning against the kitchen counter, arms folded, sporting a sexy grin. "Happy birthday, sweetheart."

"What are you doing here?" Eleanor was surprised.

"Huh? I live here."

"Dwight Humphrey!"

"Okay. I came home earlier than you to surprise you," Dwight said smugly. "And I did."

"I was going to surprise you." Eleanor playfully sulked. "I wanted to make dinner, but it looks as if you beat me to it." She glanced over at the covered dishes on the kitchen counter.

"Thanks, babe, but it's your birthday." Dwight walked over to her, pulled her into his arms. "Happy birthday." He wrapped his hands around her small waist and kissed her.

"Thank you," Eleanor replied when they broke the kiss. "Congratulations, Mr. General Manager," she hugged Dwight again, "I'm so proud of you," she whispered into his ear.

"Thanks. And I'm proud of us," Dwight remarked, giving her a tight squeeze. "Do you want to freshen up before dinner?"

Eleanor nodded and walked toward the doorway. "I'll be right back," she said over her shoulder, then gave a little wave with her fingertips before she sashayed toward the bathroom, Dwight's love-filled eyes followed her until she disappeared from sight.

Eleanor returned a few minutes later. "Something smells good in . . ." She paused and looked around the dining room in amazement. The windows were closed, curtains drawn, making the tapered candles on the dining table shine brighter. The gigantic bouquet of red roses sitting in the middle of the table set for two seemed to be swaying to the soft music that permeated the air.

"Oh my," was all that Eleanor could mutter. She glanced over at her man who was leaned over on a chair that was already pulled out, watching her. The pair of blue jeans sculpted to his hard thighs, his T-shirt stretched taut over his broad chest, his dreamy brown eyes enhanced by the glow of the candles, his dimples deepened in his handsome face. He was the epitome of masculine sexiness. "Oh, my," Eleanor repeated.

Dwight smiled, pleased at the reaction he got from his girlfriend. "After you, madam." He waved his hand toward the chair.

Eleanor giggled, walked over to him, and sat down. As Dwight took his seat across from her, she took in the many saporous dishes of food, anxious to dig in. They ate in a comfortable ambiance, talking about her job and his new promotion.

Feeling like she was about to burst, Eleanor leaned back in her chair, looking at the damage that she and Dwight had done. Almost all the dishes on the table were empty. "I'm not eating another bite for at least a week," she groaned.

"I think I've heard that before," Dwight teased her. He pushed his chair back from the table and stood, his eyes gleaming mischievously. "I'll be right back." He winked at her before he turned and walked out of the room.

"Oh, Lord. What is he up to now?" Eleanor muttered under her breath. She had come to know that look very well. Dwight was up to something.

Suddenly the music changed. *"Now and forever, together and all that I feel is my love for you . . ."* crooned Air Supply, reverberating throughout the house, knocking forcefully on Eleanor's heart.

Wide-eyed and totally speechless, Eleanor watched as Dwight reappeared in the doorway, his hands behind his back. She watched him slowly approach, singing the words to the song, his eyes brimming with unshed tears. She searched his face for a clue, but Dwight had his poker face on.

He walked up behind Eleanor and pulled out her chair. Robotically she turned to him, peering at him intently. "Oh my God," she whispered when Dwight fell to his knees in front of her. Her heart pounding, she swallowed the lump in her throat, her eyes locked with his.

"Eleanor, you are the most amazing woman I have ever known," Dwight said and held up a small, square box to her. "You came into my life when I least expected it," he opened the box and the huge diamond ring sparkled. "I am so in love with you," the tears ran down his face. "I can't imagine my life without you. Will you do me the honor and be my wife?"

Eleanor sobbed. With her face buried in the palms of her opened hands, her body shook from the heavy sobs. Moments later, her face still streaking with tears, Eleanor fell to her knees in front of Dwight. "I . . . I . . . I love you too, Dwight Humphrey," she wrapped her arms around his neck, "I don't know what I did to deserve this but, yes, I'll be your wife."

Dwight threw his head back and screamed, *"Yesssssss!"* Taking the ring from the box, he slipped it onto Eleanor's trembling ring finger. Their lips met and held for a long while . . . the future Mr. and Mrs. Dwight Humphrey.

Chapter Forty-two

"I'm going to invite Sister Lola, Sister Margaret, Sister Norma, Brother Terry, and Sister—"

"Mama Pearl, stop." Eleanor laughed and moved over closer to the older woman on the couch.

"What?" Mama Pearl's face was lit up with happiness. "We have a big wedding to plan. This is going to be the wedding of the year."

"No," Eleanor said shaking her head. She took Mama Pearl's hand in hers. "I don't want a big wedding."

"What?" Mama Pearl shrieked, horrified. "But . . . But, why?"

Eleanor smiled. "I just want the family to be there," she stated. "That's it."

Mama Pearl looked at her for a few seconds. "Okay," she finally remarked, disappointment in her voice. "It's your wedding so we'll have it your way."

"I know you are disappointed," Eleanor said to Mama Pearl. "But I'm trying to make do with the only family that I can have at my wedding." She took a deep breath, blinking her eyes rapidly, her lips trembling.

Mama Pearl opened her mouth to ask Eleanor what she meant by that remark but reached over and hugged her instead. "You and Dwight are going to be happy, and I pray that one day soon your family will be completed."

Over the next few months as her wedding date approached, Eleanor felt like she was on a roller coaster.

She was excited to be marrying the man she loved, but her heart bled to know that Aunt Madge and Dupree weren't going to be there.

Dwight brought up the subject a few times, trying to get her to change her mind about contacting Aunt Madge and Dupree, but Eleanor wouldn't budge. She refused to let anything happen to the people she loved just for her own selfish reasons.

On Saturday, December 24, 1988, Eleanor and Dwight stood on the green, landscaped grass in the forest garden at the beautiful Hope Botanical Garden to get married. They were surrounded by a variety of exotic, colorful flowers perfuming the air with their enchanting scents and giant, green, shady trees, from palm to oak, their leaves blowing gently in the soft breeze, the bright Jamaican sun kissing their faces.

The stunning bride wore a beautiful, simple, long, white-laced dress, and the handsome groom, a black and white tuxedo. Rose stood up with Eleanor and Omar with Dwight. The guests, consisting of Mama Pearl, her four sons, their wives and children, Dwight's other best friend, Edward, and his wife, and his aunt Clover, who flew in from New York, sat on white chairs facing the wedding party and the pastor.

"Dearly beloved, we are . . ." the pastor's voice tapered off as he looked over the heads of the guests. Everyone turned around to see what had caused the distraction.

Dwight felt his blood begin to boil as he watched his mother and father strut toward them. "I'll take care of this, babe," he whispered in Eleanor's ear before he angrily marched toward his parents, Omar hot on his heels.

"So you think you can just walk in here and ruin my wedding, huh?" Dwight hissed in a low voice when he came face-to-face with his parents. "I want both of you to turn around and leave right now!"

"Son, we—"

"Or I will throw both of you out," Dwight said his fists folded in anger. Omar stepped closer to assist him with the job, if necessary.

"We didn't come to cause trouble, son." David Humphrey took a step closer to Dwight, tugging his wife to his side. Unbelievably, his eyes were filled with tears. "My only son is getting married, and we want to be here."

Dwight looked at him for a moment, trying to decipher the truth in his words, his face still masked with fury.

"I know we've had our differences over the years," David Humphrey began, "and we still do, but this is your wedding day. We would never forgive ourselves if we missed it. Right, darling?" He gently elbowed his wife who stood silent by his side.

"Right," Mrs. Humphrey said through her teeth, her eyes looking everywhere but at her son. Dwight had no doubt that his father had given her an ultimatum which was why she was there. He probably threatened to tighten the money bag. It was going to take more than her only son's wedding to a woman she despised to thaw out the ice queen.

"I don't want any trouble from either one of you," Dwight said tightly, his eyes going back and forth between his parents. "Say one thing out of line, do anything inappropriate, and I'll never forgive you. You got that?"

"Got it," David Humphrey said with relief on his face. His father had sat in the front row for his wedding and he was lucky after everything that was going on between them that his son was allowing him to stay at his wedding. Family tradition meant everything to him.

"Mother, did you hear what I just said or should I walk you out?" Dwight stared pointedly at his mother.

"I won't cause any trouble," Eve Humphrey mumbled, rolling her eyes.

Dwight sighed loudly. "Come and have a seat then and behave yourselves," he warned again.

As they walked back, Dwight noticed a worker hurriedly adding two chairs in the back row. He walked over to the man and whispered in his ear. The worker nodded, went, and got the chairs, placing them in the front row beside Aunt Clover.

Eleanor watched as Dwight's parents took their seats in the front. It was the first time she was laying eyes on David Humphrey, but it didn't take a genius to see that Dwight was a replica of the older man. "You are amazing," Eleanor whispered to Dwight when he took his place again beside her. "I know it took a lot to do what you just did."

Dwight winked at her. "Okay, I'm ready to marry this beautiful woman," he said loudly to the pastor. Laughter rang out, easing the tension as Dwight and Eleanor became man and wife.

Chapter Forty-three

Mrs. Eleanor Humphrey began adjusting to married life. She had moved into the large, beautiful house in Cherry Gardens with her husband, ready to settle down in marital bliss. In love and happy for the most part, there was still something missing from Eleanor's life, the presence of her aunt and daughter. So Eleanor focused all her attention on her husband and her job as the days became weeks, weeks turned into months, months into years.

In love and happy, Eleanor had worked her way up the corporate ladder. It was now five years since she started working at BDO Jamaica, the last two years she worked as the human resources manager after being promoted. Dwight also was claiming his spot among the executives at BNS, now the Group Finance and Deputy Group managing director.

Everything seemed to be working itself out except for one thing.

"It's negative again," Eleanor said sadly as she talked into the bedroom, waving the pregnancy test in the air. Her eyes filled with tears.

"Come here," Dwight said gently, patting the space beside him on the bed where he sat, his head resting against the headboard. "It's okay," he told his wife as he rocked her in his arms. "Baby, we will conceive when it's time. Stop worrying."

They had been trying to have a baby for almost five years now but no luck. But in her heart Eleanor knew exactly why she could not conceive. "It's my punishment for abandoning my daughter," she told Dwight. "The Lord has sealed my womb because I'm a pathetic mother."

"No, don't say that," Dwight remarked. "You are a good person. But now that you mention it, are you ready for us to go and see Dupree and Aunt Madge?"

Eleanor sighed and tried to pull away from her husband, but he held her tighter.

"Darling, I know you think you are doing the right thing by staying away, but I feel in my heart it's time for you to connect with your daughter and aunt," Dwight told her.

"I can't," Eleanor muttered. "Too many people could get hurt." Eleanor glanced up at her husband alarmed. It was too late to take back what she had just said.

Dwight sat up straighter on the bed and looked at her in surprise. "Who told you that?" he asked angrily. "Was it that scumbag, so-called police officer?"

Eleanor bit her lip and looked down into her lap. She had said too much.

"Eleanor, look at me," Dwight demanded. "He can't hurt you anymore," he said when his wife's terrified eyes met his. "You are not alone anymore."

Eleanor knew Dwight was referring to Officer Gregg, and she had no intention of telling him about the other demon police officer who had taken it upon himself to make Eleanor his enemy. At least not yet. Officer Bailey scared her more than Officer Gregg. She knew he was a killer and would do anything to keep his dirty, criminal life hidden. A cold chill ran down Eleanor's spine when she remembered how close she came to being killed by the madman. No, she had to protect Dupree, Aunt Madge, and Dwight.

"Sweetheart, are you listening to me?" Dwight's voice brought back her attention to him.

"Yes," Eleanor replied. "It's not yet time to go back there."

"What do you mean? Why—"

"Babe, please trust me on this," Eleanor implored him. "It's for the best."

"At least call someone and check on what's going on." Dwight refused to let go as he had done over the last few years. "Get the phone book and see if a neighbor or someone from the church is listed." Eleanor had told him that Aunt Madge had no electricity, so he knew she wouldn't have a phone.

"Okay," Eleanor relented. "I'll check—"

But Dwight was already off the bed and going through the door. Seconds later he returned with a phone book in his hand. "Here." he handed her the phone book. "Search and see who can you find."

As Eleanor searched through the phone book under the parish of Trelawny, she had a sinking feeling in her gut. Dwight sat on the edge of the bed at the opposite end, looking at her anxiously. The first name that Eleanor saw was the last one she wanted to see, Dr. Beverly Gregg, General Dentistry, Falmouth, Trelawny.

"You found someone?" Dwight asked when he saw the frightened look on her face.

Eleanor nodded. "His wife's office number is listed."

Dwight didn't have to ask whose wife, he knew. "Do you want me to call her?" he asked Eleanor. "She lives in the same community and attends the same church as Aunt Madge, right?"

"Yes, but do you think she is going to tell you anything about her husband's illegitimate child? Babe, I had an affair with her husband."

"No, her slimy husband was the one who took advantage of a child," Dwight said angrily. "If she is mad at someone, it should be the man who betrayed her, not you, and certainly not innocent little Dupree." He walked over to the telephone sitting on the bedside table beside her and took up the receiver. "What's the number?" he asked.

"I'll call." Eleanor held out her hand for the telephone. Dwight looked at her before placing the phone in her hand. Her fingers shaking, Eleanor dialed the number. As the phone rang, she looked up at the clock noting that it was twelve noon. It was Saturday afternoon, so surely the dental office was opened.

"Dental office, may I help you?" said a familiar voice.

Eleanor opened her mouth, but not a word came out.

"Darling, did someone answer?" Dwight asked, watching her face. "Here, give me the phone." He held out his hand but Eleanor ignored it.

"Hello?" Dr. Beverly Gregg said on the other end of the phone. Her receptionist had stepped out to get lunch, so she was covering until she returned.

Eleanor took a deep breath. "Hmmm, it's Tiny," she finally said. For the first time in many years, she used her nickname but knew it was necessary for Beverly to know who she was talking to. She had already told Dwight when and why she had stopped using the name.

"You?" Beverly screeched in disbelief. Talk about a ghost from the past. "What do you want?"

"I know I'm the last person you want to talk to, but I need some information," Eleanor said and looked over at Dwight. He gave her the thumbs-up, nodding his head in approval. Encouraged, Eleanor continued. "I need to know how my daughter and aunt are doing." Eleanor held the phone tightly to her ear, inhaling and exhaling, trying to calm her nerves.

"You really have some nerve," Beverly snapped into the phone. "Calling me to ask about the child you had with my husband. I should hang up the phone right now."

"But you won't," Eleanor stated. "I did what you and your husband wanted all these years. I left town and never came back. Now I need to know if my child and aunt are okay. You are the only one I know who is listed."

Beverly closed her eyes tight; she felt a migraine coming on. After all these years, Tiny had resurrected from the dead. She knew she was now talking to a grown woman and not the scared teenager she had threatened fifteen years ago. If she didn't tell Tiny what she wanted to hear, she might decide to come back to Falmouth and turn their lives upside down. "Sister Madge and Dupree are doing great," she lied. "I just saw them at the market earlier. Dupree was helping her grandaunt to sell her produce."

Happy tears leaked down Eleanor's face as she listened to the good news. She pressed the phone so hard to her ear, it was beginning to hurt. But she didn't care.

"Dupree has grown into a beautiful, intelligent young lady," Beverly continued with her deception. "She doesn't know who we are, but I see her every Sunday at church with Sister Madge. She also sings in the choir. Such a beautiful voice."

All lies. It had been a little over two years since Aunt Madge had her stroke and hadn't been to church since. Life for Dupree was very hard as she struggled to make ends meet. But Beverly could not afford for Eleanor to find out about this. She would probably be in Falmouth in a few hours, and she had to continue to protect her family.

"If you are planning on coming back to disrupt Dupree's life after all these years, you should seriously think about it," Beverly said. "She is getting ready to take her CXC exams in a few months. What do you think is going to happen when she sees her mother who had left her all these years, Tiny?"

Eleanor didn't respond. Her heavy breathing was enough for Beverly.

"You are going to turn her life upside down, causing her to fail her exams, denying her the opportunity to get into college. Don't you think you owe her *that* much? At least wait until she graduates high school before contacting her."

Beverly knew by then her son, Anthony Gregg Jr., would be going off to college, and so Tiny's reappearance would not hurt her only child, if she decided to return to Falmouth at that time.

"Thank you," Eleanor said and slowly hung up the phone. "She is all right," she said to Dwight who was now sitting on the bed beside her. "My daughter and Aunt Madge are doing okay." She relayed the side of the conversation he couldn't hear.

"Hmmm." Dwight looked at the wall, a frown on his face.

"What?" Eleanor asked him. "This is good news . . . Isn't it?"

"Baby, something doesn't sound right to me," Dwight remarked. "My spirit tells me she was lying. That woman was too willing to give you information and too quick to persuade you not to come back there."

"Well, she probably thinks I would cause trouble for her and her husband," Eleanor said. "But I don't see why she would lie about Aunt Madge and Dupree."

"Let's go and find out for ourselves," Dwight said.

"No, I won't go and disrupt Dupree's life now," Eleanor replied. "I do agree with her on this. I think we should wait until Dupree is ready for college, which is just a few months away. Who knows, maybe she will want to live with us and attend UWI."

Dwight grunted but decided to drop the subject. He still had a gnawing feeling in his gut. That night he prayed extensively for the stepdaughter he had never met and his aunt-in-law who he loved without even meeting her as yet. He made a note to speak to Eleanor again soon because he wanted to see for himself what was going on with Dupree and Aunt Madge.

But it was three years later that everything actually came to a climax. Eleanor, now the human resources director after Mr. Wallace retired the year before, walked into Mr. Chevon Brown's office, the human resources manager, and overhead his telephone conversation.

"Well, Dupree, I do appreciate your interest in BDO, but I have yet to review your application. I promise to do so very soon and get back to you. Okay, dear? Thank you for calling and have a wonderful day," Mr. Brown said into the telephone.

Eleanor's knees almost buckled under her. That was a very unique name. The name of her daughter. Quickly composing herself before Mr. Brown could see her reaction, Eleanor stood by quietly, waiting for him to hang up the phone, her curiosity piqued.

Mr. Brown hung up the phone and looked up to see Eleanor staring at him intently. "Is something wrong, Eleanor?" he asked her nervously.

"No. I'm sorry for interrupting your call, Chevon, and it seemed to be an interesting one, too. Why don't you tell me some more about it?" Eleanor said and smiled at him.

Mr. Brown breathed a sigh of relief and went on to tell her about his conversation with Dupree. "She's from Falmouth, Trelawny, and is currently attending UTech. She would like to work here in Kingston for the summer," he concluded. He watched as Eleanor gazed out the window, her lips sealed in deep concentration. "Eleanor?"

"Oh, sorry. My mind took a little walk. Well, she seems like an ambitious young lady and we could always use more people like her around here. Why don't you have her come in for an interview with me?" Eleanor instructed him. "And let's make it sooner rather than later. We need an assistant for one of our chief financial officers, and this young lady might be perfect for it."

With that said Eleanor turned around in her high heel pumps and walked back toward her office, rubbing her hands up and down her arms as if she was freezing. "That's my Dupree," she mumbled under her breath. "I can feel it in my bones. Dear God, after all these years am I about to finally see my daughter?"

Eleanor entered her office and closed the door. Walking slowly over to her desk, she reached for the telephone, her hand trembling as dialed her husband's number.

"Are you sure?" Dwight asked his wife when he answered the phone, his heart pounding in his chest. He was in a meeting with his executive management team when his secretary came and got him, telling him his wife was on the phone and was deeply upset. Dwight, now the president and chief executive officer of BNS since his promotion just four months prior, had quickly excused himself and hurried to his office to take the call.

"Well, what are the chances that it's another Dupree from the same community, same parish, around the same age?" Eleanor asked her husband. "That is too much of a coincidence, isn't it?"

Dwight nodded even though his wife couldn't see him. "Yes, I have to agree with you. It does sound like it's my stepdaughter."

Eleanor smiled. From the moment Dwight heard she had a daughter, he had endeared Dupree to him without even knowing her. Her husband was truly an amazing man.

"Are you sure you are okay?" Dwight asked his wife. "Do you want us to cut the day short and I come and get you?" Dwight and Eleanor both worked in New Kingston, so they commuted together with Dwight driving them both to and from work.

"No, no, I can wait," Eleanor said. "We just have a few more hours to go anyway. It's fine."

"Okay, I'll see you later. I love you."

"I love you too." Eleanor slowly hung up the phone. She pushed her chair away from the desk and stood up. Restlessly pacing the carpeted floor, her brows knitted in deep concentration, she twirled her ballpoint pen around her thumb, contemplating one question. What was she going to do when she came face-to-face with the daughter she abandoned eighteen years ago?

Chapter Forty-four

In bed that night, Eleanor twisted and turned, too nervous to sleep. It felt as if millions of ants were crawling over her body and she was about to jump out of her skin.

Before she left the office that afternoon Mr. Brown had informed Eleanor that Dupree would be in at nine a.m. the next morning for an interview with her. *What was she going to do when she sees her daughter? Should she tell Dupree who she was? How would she react?*

"Babe, you need to get some sleep," Dwight whispered in her ear from behind, pulling her back closer into his body, his arms wrapped tightly around her waist. "It's going to be okay."

"I know. But it's not going to be easy," Eleanor said with a sigh. She turned around and moved closer to her husband, face-to-face, their noses almost touching, their eyes locked on each other. "I'm glad I have your support," she leaned over and kissed him, "because I couldn't do this without you. Thank you, my darling husband."

"We are in this together, Mrs. Humphrey," Dwight replied, pressing his body closer to hers, her face nestled in the crook of his neck. "Let's get some rest. Tomorrow is another day."

"I can do this," Eleanor repeated over and over, walking from one end of her office to the other, then back. "I can look in my daughter's face and not break down." She straightened her jacket and pulled down her pencil skirt. "I won't tell her who I am right now. It's not the right time."

Eleanor walked over to her desk, leaned over, and took out her handbag from a lower drawer. Rummaging inside, she located her compact powder and lipstick. After taking a deep breath, one hand holding the compact mirror, she freshened up her lipstick for the fourth time that morning.

Knock! Knock!

Eleanor paused and looked at her office door as if a serial killer was trying to get in. "Oh my God, she's here," she whispered, her chest rising and falling in panic. She threw the compact and lipstick in the drawer and kicked it shut. Running her sweaty hands down her skirt, she inhaled and exhaled before she took a seat behind her desk. "Come in."

Mr. Brown entered, followed by a tall, beautiful young lady who was wringing her hands together nervously. "Eleanor, I would like to introduce you to Dupree."

Eleanor's heart slammed against her chest, her throat constricted, and her knees trembled. *Good God! It's her. She is the spitting image of her father.*

"Eleanor?" Mr. Brown was looking at her with a puzzled look on his face. "Are you okay?"

"Huh? Oh, yes, yes. I'm fine." Eleanor laughed nervously and stood up. "Thanks, Chevon. I'll take it from here."

Mr. Brown nodded, smiled at Dupree, and exited the room, closing the door shut behind him.

Eleanor came around her desk and walked toward Dupree. Without saying a word, she looked at Dupree for a few long seconds, her eyes raking over her from head to toe. Suddenly she realized that she was staring and smiled awkwardly. "Please forgive me for staring," Eleanor said, her right hand outstretched. Dupree reached out and grabbed it in a firm handshake. "You are a very beautiful young lady," she added.

"Thank you," Dupree responded shyly.

"I'm Eleanor Humphrey. Please, have a seat." Eleanor smiled and waved her arm toward the chair in front of her desk. She waited until Dupree sat before she went and took her own seat, facing the young woman.

"I love to see young ladies striving to make something of their lives, and that was one of the reasons I admired your determination to get a job," Eleanor began the interview. "So, tell me something about yourself, Dupree. Mr. Brown said you are from Falmouth?"

"Yes, ma'am." Dupree sat up straight, her hands flat in her lap. "I lived there with my grandaunt before I came here to attend UTech."

"That's wonderful, Dupree." Eleanor swallowed hard, her fists clinched tight behind her desk. "And you would like to work here with us at BDO for the summer."

"Yes, ma'am," Dupree replied politely. "This would be a wonderful opportunity for me."

"Sure you don't want to go back home and spend the time off with your grandaunt?" Eleanor knew she was fishing, but she needed some information on Aunt Madge. "She is alone now that you are living here in Kingston, right?" Totally unprofessional but nothing about this interview was professional. For Eleanor, it was personal. Very personal.

Dupree smiled. "Aunt Madge is staying with friends and having a wonderful time. She supports my decision to get this job."

There it was; the confirmation. Not that she needed it, but Eleanor felt like someone kicked her in the gut. She was sitting across from her daughter after eighteen years. It wasn't the little, scary creature that was before her now but a poised, intelligent, gorgeous young woman, and she had contributed nothing to her upbringing. Shame like she had never felt before draped over Eleanor like a bag of cement. She swallowed the bile that rose in her throat, forcing a smile on her face.

Eleanor asked Dupree a few more generic questions before she quickly wrapped up the interview, offering her the job as an assistant to Mr. Ryan Patterson, Chief Financial Officer. Dupree was scheduled to start working in less than one week, right after the school term ended.

After closing the door behind Dupree, Eleanor weakly braced her back against it and allowed the tears to flow. With her burning eyes squeezed tight, she took deep gulps of air into her lungs. "Help me, Lord," she chanted breathlessly. "I thought I was doing the right thing to protect the people I love, but why doesn't it feel like it now?

"Ahhh!" Eleanor jumped when someone knocked on the door. Quickly she bolted to her desk and grabbed a handful of Kleenex. The knock came again as she hurriedly wiped her face and blew her nose.

"Eleanor?" said the voice she needed to hear so badly. "It's me."

Eleanor threw the used tissue in the waste bin by her desk and rushed over to the door, pulling it open. Without a word she jumped into her husband's opened arms, sobbing.

With Eleanor's arms wrapped tightly around his neck in a suffocating hold, Dwight staggered into her office, gently kicking the door shut. "It's all right now, sweetheart." Dwight rocked her gently. "I knew that was very difficult for you."

"It's . . . it's . . . It's her," Eleanor stammered. "It was my daughter."

Dwight smiled. "I'm sorry I missed her. I had an appointment downtown and traffic was horrendous." Slowly he lowered his wife to the floor, his arms still locked around her waist, her face rested on his chest. "What does she look like?" he asked, his curiosity getting the better of him.

Eleanor pulled back and looked up at him with wet eyes. "She is beautiful," she replied. "Thank you." She took the handkerchief that Dwight handed her and dabbed her eyes. "She is tall, slender, smooth, flawless skin, and the most exquisite smile I have ever seen in my life." A tiny smile winked at the corners of her mouth. "She is very intelligent and speaks eloquently with good posture. She is a unique young lady."

"Hmmm, sounds like someone I know." Dwight's dimples deepened. "Her mother."

"But I have no claim to her," Eleanor said sadly. "To her, I'm now just her boss."

"We're going to fix that gradually," Dwight said tenderly. "Let's take baby steps, okay?"

Eleanor nodded.

"Okay, get your stuff and let's go." Dwight gently took her by the shoulders and turned her around to face her desk. "We're playing hooky for the rest of the day. I know Chevon will hold down the fort for you."

"All right." Eleanor's voice was low. She dragged her feet over to retrieve her handbag. She wasn't going to argue with her husband. If today was any indication of what was to come, Eleanor was in for a very bumpy ride.

Chapter Forty-five

Dupree started working at BDO Jamaica a few days later. Eleanor was an emotional mess. It was very hard being so close to her daughter and unable to tell her who she was. After a lengthy discussion with Dwight, they decided it was best if Eleanor developed her relationship with Dupree as her boss, get to know more about her as a person, before hitting her with the news that would no doubt change everything.

Eleanor made it her duty to have lunch with Dupree as often as possible at work. She used the time to subtly ask questions about Dupree's childhood and Aunt Madge but getting information from Dupree was like pulling teeth. It was as if Dupree had created a wall around herself, keeping everyone out. Eleanor wondered what had triggered this mistrust in her.

"She withdraws into herself whenever I ask her anything personal," Eleanor voiced her concern to her husband one evening over dinner. "All I was able to find out is that Aunt Madge is living with her church sisters, Mrs. Scott and Miss Angie, and she is very happy. That's all. I can't get anything else out of her."

"Well, you will soon find out for yourself, darling," Dwight told her. "I would like to meet Dupree, then we can tell her together who you really are."

"You think it's time to tell her?" Eleanor looked like a mouse cornered by a cat. "And to meet Aunt Madge?"

"Yes. It's time for you to reconnect with your daughter and aunt. I'm not too worried about Aunt Madge. From what you have told me about her, she is a very forgiving woman. Especially when she hears everything that happened to you. Dupree, on the other hand, might not be so easy." Dwight looked pointedly at her. "She is going to take some work, but I do believe, in the end, both of you will find your way to each other."

Eleanor went to work the next morning with Dwight's words ringing in her head. It was time for her to have the talk with her daughter. She would invite Dupree to have dinner with her and Dwight and take it from there.

At lunchtime Eleanor walked into the lunch room, scanning the room for Dupree. She noticed her sitting in the back at a table by herself. Eleanor had her lunch served and invited herself to Dupree's table. "Hello, Dupree," Eleanor said after she sat down. "How are you doing today?"

No response. Dupree was staring unseeingly into her plate. Her mind seemed to be a thousand miles away.

"Dupree? Dupree?" No response. Eleanor looked at Dupree worriedly. "Dupree?" She snapped her fingers before Dupree's face causing Dupree to jerk back in alarm.

"Yes?" Her eyes met Eleanor apologetically. "I'm sorry. I . . ."

"Please. No apologies are necessary; just tell me what's wrong."

With tears in her eyes, Dupree told Eleanor that she was attacked the night before when she was going home." He came out of nowhere," Dupree sobbed. "But I fought him off and managed to escape." The tears trickled down her face.

Eleanor was rendered speechless, her mouth opening and closing like a fish out of water. "You . . . You can't go back to that bad neighborhood," she hissed through her teeth. "You have to get out now and you can stay with me until we get you a place of your own," she told Dupree in an angry voice.

"Thank you, but I can't leave Jas there by herself," Dupree replied with gratitude. She had informed Eleanor when she just started working at BDO Jamaica about her friend and roommate, Jas.

"You know what? I have to go and check on something. Please come to my office after you finish your lunch," Eleanor instructed Dupree and marched out of the lunchroom without touching her food.

Eleanor was furious. Dupree was attacked! My God! What if she hadn't fought off that creep? What if he had . . .? "Thank you, Lord," Eleanor mumbled as she hurried into her office and closed the door. She grabbed the phone and quickly tapped in a number as she lowered herself into her chair.

"Hey, baby. Call to take me to lunch?" Dwight answered his cell phone on the first ring. "I'm heading back now." Earlier that morning after dropping off his wife at work, Dwight went to a banker's meeting at Bank of Jamaica in downtown Kingston.

"She was attacked!" Eleanor yelled and began to cry.

"What? Who was attacked?" Dwight asked confused. "Sweetheart, what's going on?"

"Dupree. She was attacked last night when she was going home."

"My God! Was she hurt? Where is she now?" Dwight fired off one question after the other.

"No, she wasn't hurt. She fought him and ran," Eleanor told him. "She's here at work, devastated. She can't go back to that place."

"Of course not," Dwight said angrily. His hand gripped the steering wheel tighter. "She will stay with us."

"She doesn't want to leave her friend, Jas, there alone." Eleanor said, blowing her nose loudly into the tissue. "I don't want her to do that either. Those girls are not safe living there alone. But I don't know if she will want to stay with us. I don't know what to do, babe." Then it hit Eleanor like a sack of spuds. "Edward," she said. "Babe, let me call you back in a minute."

"Okay, but what—" The line went dead.

Eleanor pressed and released the hook on the phone, before dialing another number. After speaking for a few minutes, she hung up, breathing a sigh of relief.

Wearily, she leaned back in her chair. Suddenly images of that atrocious night in the park so many years ago flooded her mind. The hands groping her, touching her, violating her. Her breathing became labored; she breathed in deeply and exhaled loudly, her fist kneading her forehead, willing the haunting memories to go away.

The ringing of the telephone snapped Eleanor back into the present. Shakily she reached for the receiver. "Hello," she answered in a weak voice.

"It's me," said Dwight. "You were going to call me back?"

"Oh, yes. Sorry, babe. I got distracted for a minute," Eleanor replied. "I just spoke to Edward. He said Dupree and her friend can use Jessica's apartment for as long as they want. Jessica doesn't want to rent or sell it."

"He did? Oh, baby, that's wonderful. I completely forgot about that apartment," Dwight replied happily. "I'm sure Dupree and Jas will like that. I'll call Edward and thank him myself. Do you want me to come and help you guys later?" Dwight asked.

"No, we can manage," Eleanor said. "I don't want the first time you meet Dupree for it to be under these circumstances."

"Okay. Call me if you need me."

A knock came at the door. "I think Dupree is here," Eleanor told her husband. "I'll call you later. Thanks, darling. I love you." Eleanor hung up the phone. "Come in," she called out.

Dupree entered and Eleanor invited her to have a seat. The anger returned as Eleanor looked at her daughter. "My husband's best friend, Edward, is a developer who builds and rents apartments all over the country," she informed Dupree. "He has a few places in Norbrook Heights, Constant Spring Road, Meadowbrook, Forest Hills, Cherry Gardens, and Stony Hill, to name a few."

Eleanor noticed Dupree looking at her as if she was crazy. Dupree's eyes had grown wider with the name of each place she mentioned. She knew the reason why. These were some of the most expensive communities in Kingston. She quickly explained. "I know what you are thinking, but let me explain. Edward's youngest daughter, Jessica, recently got married and is now living in Miami with her new husband. However, she refused to sell or rent her Oakland apartment on Constant Spring Road, which was a gift from her dad. Edward is offering you and Jas the apartment to stay for as long as you want, free of charge."

Dupree rested her head on the desk and cried.

Eleanor hurriedly got up, pulled up another chair beside Dupree, took her in her arms, and cried with her. For Eleanor, her tears were more than getting a safe place for Dupree to live. She was holding her daughter in her arms for the first time. Not as a baby but as a grown woman. "Thank you, Lord," she said quietly as she handed Dupree some Kleenex to wipe her face and runny nose, while she also did the same after they regained their composure.

Eleanor took Dupree and Jas to look at the apartment after work. After receiving the key from the security guard at the gate, they anxiously walked inside. Eleanor's heart sang with delight as she watched Dupree "oohing" and "aahing" over the beautiful, elegantly furnished three-bedroom apartment that was housed in the gated community.

Later that evening, Bullfrog, along with Eleanor, moved the girls into their new, luxury apartment. Bullfrog was a friend of Jas, who owned a van that he had used to moved Dupree from her previous apartment. Dupree had a falling out with her promiscuous roommate, Amanda, who slept with her ex-boyfriend, Suave. It was Bullfrog who came to the rescue again the night when Dupree was attacked by an unknown assailant.

After the girls were settled in, Eleanor went home smiling to her husband. "It feels so good to know that Dupree is safe." She hugged Dwight tightly around his waist, her twinkling eyes staring up at him.

"I'm happy it worked out." Dwight looked down at her, smiling. "Now we need to tell her who you are."

"Yes, it's time. I'll take you to meet her this Saturday."

"I'm looking forward to it." Dwight pulled her closer. "I can't wait to meet Aunt Madge as well." He would do so sooner than they both anticipated.

Chapter Forty-six

Dwight opened the car door and Eleanor stepped out of the Mercedes-Benz. She glanced at the strange car parked in front of the girls' apartment and shrugged. It probably belonged to a neighbor or someone visiting who parked in the wrong spot. But Eleanor should have paid more attention to that car because it belonged to Mrs. Scott.

Blissfully, Eleanor walked to the door with Dwight and rang the doorbell. After introducing a mesmerized Dwight to Dupree, they followed Dupree into the apartment where Eleanor got the shock of her life.

"Hello," Jas, Mrs. Scott, and Miss Angie said in sync. Aunt Madge was resting in Dupree's bedroom, exhausted from the trip to Kingston.

"What's going on?" Eleanor croaked. "I . . . I . . . I didn't know you had visitors." She looked at Dupree in panic.

"I wanted to surprise you." Dupree was confused.

"I'll be right back." Eleanor sprinted down the hall. She grabbed the handle of the first door she came to and rushed inside Dupree's bedroom. Slamming the door shut, she pressed her back firmly against it, taking deep breaths.

Suddenly Eleanor sensed another presence in the room and realized she wasn't alone. Her body began to tremble uncontrollably as she slowly opened her eyes and stared into the other all-too-familiar ones.

"Aunt Madge," Eleanor whispered as she crumbled to the floor in distress.

"Tiny?" Aunt Madge asked in surprise. "Tiny, is that you?"

"Yes, Aunt Madge," Eleanor answered. "It's me." She curled up on the floor, shivering, as deep sobs rocked her body.

Aunt Madge lay on her side staring at the crumpled figure on the floor, her tears seeping into the pillow under the head. While Eleanor cried tears of despair and shame, Aunt Madge cried tears of joy. The niece she had lost was now found. "Tiny. Come here, baby," Aunt Madge said in between sobs. "Get up off that floor and come to me."

Eleanor staggered to her feet and wobbled over to the bed. Tears and mucus ran down her face as she looked into the sorrowful eyes of the woman who had raised her. "Oh, Aunt Madge. I'm so sorry," Eleanor wept. "Please, please forgive me."

Aunt Madge opened her arms and Eleanor fell on the bed beside her and tightly hugged the aged, fragile body. It was at that moment all the secrets began peeling away, layer after layer, like a Vidalia onion.

Dupree, still perplexed by her boss's behavior, decided to check on Aunt Madge. As she approached her bedroom she heard muffled voices through the door. With a smile on her face, she gently opened the door and stepped inside. Shocked, she looked at Aunt Madge and Mrs. Humphrey huddled on the bed, crying.

"It's going to be all right, Tiny," Aunt Madge said. "The Lord knows best."

"Tiny?" Dupree asked in bewilderment. "Did you say Tiny?"

Eleanor jumped off the bed and stood facing her daughter, trembling. The tears were still flowing down her face as her red, puffy eyes met Dupree's horrified ones.

"No no no. It can't be," Dupree muttered repeatedly, shaking her head from side to side. Her trembling hand covered her mouth as the truth from Eleanor's expression slammed into her gut. It felt like a right uppercut. "Please, God. This can't be happening."

Dupree turned and staggered out of the bedroom as if drunk. She walked across the hall and grabbed the door handle of Jas's bedroom door and pushed it open.

"Dupree," Eleanor shouted as she frantically grabbed Dupree's left arm, preventing her from entering the room. "Please let me explain," she begged pleadingly.

"Take your hands off me!" Dupree snarled and shook off the offensive hand. With her pounding head held straight, Dupree stepped into the bedroom, slamming the door shut in her mother's face.

Dupree's anger and hurt smacked Eleanor hard in the heart. Everything became too overwhelming for her. She knew this day would come, but not like this. It was more than Eleanor could handle at the time.

Dwight, seeing his wife falling apart, promised Aunt Madge that they would be back the next day, and he quickly took Eleanor home.

Once they got home, in tears, Eleanor came clean with her husband, telling him everything about Officer "Rude Boy" Bailey and the kidnapping.

"That's who 'mugged' you that day." Dwight was livid. "Why did it take all this time for you to tell me this, Eleanor? That man was going to kill you!" Dwight paced the bedroom floor angrily.

"I knew how you would react. You would gather the guys and off to Falmouth you would go looking for him." Eleanor sat up straighter on the bed, her back braced against the headboard.

"You darn right about that, and that's exactly what we are going to do. You let this punk keep you away from

your daughter and aunt all this time? *I'm* your *husband.*
You should have trusted me enough to tell me what was
going on." Dwight was raging mad. "You told me about
Officer Gregg but nothing about Officer Bailey. Why is
that?"

"He would kill you!" Eleanor pleaded with her husband
for his understanding. "You, Mama Pearl, the guys, my
aunt, my daughter. He is a very bad man with thugs
working for him here in Kingston, Falmouth, and all over
Jamaica. Dwight, don't you see he gets away with everything? That man has been doing his dirt in Falmouth for
years, and no one has stopped him."

"Not yet. But I'm about to do just that."

"Baby, please let it go. Dupree and Aunt Madge are
here, so let's focus on that," Eleanor begged Dwight. "I
don't want to start up anything with this man. He will get
his soon."

"Yeah, I'm going to make sure that he does—sooner
than later. Alwayne knows people who have contact
with the police commissioner. Just wait until he hears
about this. Officer Bailey is about to get a dose of his own
medicine."

Eleanor knew there was no use reasoning with Dwight
at this point.

"So is there anything *else* I should know?" Dwight
asked Eleanor in a tight voice. "Any more secrets you are
keeping from me?"

"No, there isn't. I'm sorry I kept that from you, baby."
Eleanor's shoulders shook as she sobbed.

Dwight looked intently at the woman he loved, noticing
her pain and heartache. Like a punctured tire, his anger
leaked out. He walked over to the bed and lay down
beside her. "Come here." He drew her into his arms. "We
are going to figure out this mess. But right now we need
to focus on making things right with Dupree and Aunt
Madge."

It was almost twenty-four hours of crying, throwing up, sleeping on and off, and listening to her husband's encouraging words before Eleanor was able to pick herself up and go back to the apartment to see Aunt Madge and Dupree by herself. They had waited long enough.

However, as soon as Eleanor arrived at the apartment, Dupree locked herself in her bedroom, refusing to see or speak to her mother. Eleanor decided to speak to Aunt Madge first before trying to talk to her daughter again.

"I'm so sorry, Aunt Madge." Eleanor sat beside the elderly woman on the couch, her aged hands held tightly in her own. "My gosh, you can't even walk, and I wasn't there to help. I wasn't there for you or Dupree. I am so sorry for everything." Tears danced crazily down the women's faces as they tried to work their way through the maze of pain, reacquainting themselves with each other. "I had to leave, but I never knew it would be for so long."

"Why did you feel you had to leave?" Aunt Madge was confused. "And why did you stay away for so many years? What did I do that you had to run away from me and your baby?"

"It wasn't you, Aunt Madge." Eleanor reached over and kissed the weathered forehead. "You did everything right. But some things just went horribly wrong." Eleanor began to tell Aunt Madge everything that had happened from the day she walked out of her house over eighteen years ago. It took longer than expected because Aunt Madge broke down every so often, moaning and groaning at the ordeals her niece had endured. One minute she would cry and the next her hands would be high in the air, thanking God for His protection and mercy toward Eleanor. It was a painful process for both women, but Eleanor knew it was the only way for her and her aunt to reconcile and move forward.

"I prayed every day." Aunt Madge rocked from side to side, her eyes tightly closed, the tears still leaking down her face. "I asked God to send a guardian angel to be there for you. And He did. I thank Him from the bottom of my heart for sending you Mama Pearl and her family."

"I knew you were praying for me. I had beaten the odds so many times; I knew it had to be you." Eleanor wrapped her arms around her aunt's waist, resting Aunt Madge's head on her bosom. "There was not a day that went by that I didn't think about you and Dupree. Please believe me, Aunt Madge. I thought I was protecting you from Officer Gregg and then that devil, Officer Bailey. But had I known you had a stroke I . . . I . . ."

"Shhhh. We can't go back, baby. We now have to try to move forward, especially for your daughter's sake." Aunt Madge lifted up her head and scanned Eleanor from head to toe. "Look at my little Tiny. What a beautiful woman you have become. Went to college, got a fancy job, and married to a handsome fellow."

Eleanor blushed. "I owe it all to you." She put a finger on Aunt Madge's lips when she opened her mouth to speak. "You raised me for the first fifteen years of my life. You taught me everything I needed to survive and to become the woman I am today. I am sorry for not always listening to you, and I have paid dearly for that. But everything I am today is because of you, Aunt Madge."

Aunt Madge cried. "Thank you for saying that. All these years I wondered where I went wrong. What could I have done differently to change all that had happened? I worked very hard not to make the same mistake with Dupree."

"You never made any mistakes with me, and I'm sure not with Dupree either. All you did was love me uncon-ditionally. Can you ever forgive me, Aunt Madge?" Tears welled up in Eleanor's eyes. "Is it possible for you to let me try to make up for all the years we have lost?"

Aunt Madge reached up and slowly ran her hands over Eleanor's face as if she was reading Braille. "I already forgave you, baby. I'm so sorry for the hell you went through. Matthew 24:13 says, 'But he that shall endure unto the end, the same shall be saved.'"

Eleanor enfolded Aunt Madge in her arms. "Thank you. I love you, Aunt Madge."

"I love you too, my dear. Now go and make things right with your daughter."

"I will, Aunt Madge," Eleanor vowed. "I'm going to do everything in my power to make it up to Dupree."

Eleanor stood up and walked down the hall to Dupree's bedroom. She knocked and listened but didn't get a response. "I'm not leaving until we talk, Dupree," Eleanor said through the door. "We are going to talk today."

"Go away!" Dupree screamed. "*Now* you want to talk, *huh?* You are eighteen years too late!"

Shame and guilt filled Eleanor. "Baby, please let me come in and explain." Eleanor's voice cracked as she struggled to hold the tears at bay.

"I'm not your baby!" Dupree yelled. "You never wanted me in the first place. Get lost!" She began to sob.

Eleanor heard Dupree crying and turned the doorknob. Stepping into the room, she walked over to her distraught daughter lying on the bed. "I'm so sorry, sweetheart," Eleanor said as she gently ran her fingers through her daughter's hair. Dupree flinched and turned away. "I promise if it takes the rest of my life, I'll make it up to you."

Eleanor sat on the edge of the bed, staring helplessly at Dupree's back. Finally she stood up and sighed deeply. Maybe today wasn't the right time to speak with her daughter after all. "Okay. I'm going to leave now, baby. But I'm ready to talk when you are. I promise I'll explain everything to you," Eleanor said and walked toward the door.

"Wait," Dupree said.

Eleanor stopped suddenly and turned around excitedly to her daughter. She was glad that perhaps Dupree had had a change of heart.

Dupree's crying had tapered off, and using the back of her hand, she wiped her wet face. Sluggishly pulling herself up into a sitting position on the bed, she faced her mother. "Tell me something," Dupree said.

"Anything," Eleanor replied quickly as she sat down on the edge of the bed.

"Who is he?" Dupree asked.

"Huh?" Eleanor's eyes bulged out of her head. "He?" She knew Dupree would ask this question one day but she still wasn't prepared for it.

"Please don't play any more games with me," Dupree said. "You owe me that much. Who is my father?"

"Oh, sweetheart. It's so complicated," Eleanor began nervously. "It was such a long time ago and—"

"Who is he?" Dupree snapped angrily.

Eleanor flinched at her daughter's tone of voice but knew her behavior was justified.

"His name is Anthony Gregg," Eleanor whispered, her head hanging low. "Your father is Officer Anthony Gregg."

Dupree felt as if someone had thrown a bucket of ice-cold water over her head. Instead of the familiar pain, she now felt numb. Her body began to shiver, the force of the deception freezing her from inside out.

"Dupree, please let—" Eleanor halted in midsentence when Dupree held up a hand for her to stop.

"Please leave now," Dupree said in a very cold voice. Her arms were wrapped tightly around her body as she rocked from side to side.

Eleanor took one look at Dupree's face and knew there would be no more conversation that day. Reluctantly she stood up, her heart breaking at the misery her daughter was going through. "I'll be back," she informed Dupree. "And I do love you." Eleanor silently slipped out the door, pulling it closed behind her.

"Please help her, Lord," Eleanor prayed softly as she walked back into the living room. She knew Dupree was hurting very badly and it tore her up that she could not be there for her daughter. "Please touch her heart that she will allow me to explain everything to her and be there for her."

Eleanor soon found out that was easier said than done. Dupree was like a volcano about to erupt.

Chapter Forty-seven

"Dupree. Telephone." Jas's voice was very low as she waved the telephone in front of Dupree's face as she lay on the couch in the living room facing her.

"Who is it?" Dupree rolled her eyes dramatically and gave a big sigh.

"It's your mother, again," Jas whispered.

"She is *not* my mother," Dupree yelled. "She wouldn't know what to do as a mother even if it bites her on her little, cute, rich behind."

"Dupree!" Jas was appalled. She tried to cover the telephone by pressing it to her stomach.

Dupree rudely sucked her teeth, rolled over on the couch with her back now facing Jas and the offensive telephone, her eyes closed as if she was taking a nap.

Jas took a few deep breaths, and then placed the phone back up to her ear. "Hmmm, Mrs. Humphrey, she is—"

"I heard her, Jas," Eleanor sounded as exhausted as she was. "Tell her I am not going away, and one day we will have to talk. I love her."

"I'll tell her, Mrs. Humphrey."

"Thanks, Jas. Is Aunt Madge available?"

"She just went to take a nap." Jas looked at the extra bedroom that Aunt Madge was occupying while she stayed in Kingston to help Eleanor and Dupree through this rough time. "Do you want me to see if she is awake?"

"No, it's okay. Dwight and I will stop by this evening." Eleanor shifted positions on the bed that she had been spending most of her time on. It had been a week since Dupree had found out that Eleanor was her mother, and she still refused to speak to her. Whenever Eleanor and Dwight stopped by to see Aunt Madge, Dupree locked herself in her bedroom with the radio playing loud, refusing to see or listen to a word Eleanor had to say. Luckily for Dupree, Eleanor hadn't been back to work since her secret was exposed. Dupree was glad she didn't have to deal with her there. At least for now.

"Thanks, Jas. I'll see you later."

"Bye, Mrs. Humphrey." Jas hung up the telephone and jumped when almost instantaneously it rang again. "Hello?" She listened for a few seconds before she looked over at Dupree who still had her back turned. "Please hold." Jas took a few cautious steps toward Dupree. "Dupree, telephone, again."

"Tell them whatever they are selling, I'm not buying," Dupree threw over her shoulder at Jas.

"It's your father," Jas informed her. "He said he is just asking you for a few minutes of your time."

In a flash Dupree turned around and sat up straight on the couch with eyes blazing. "Tell Mr. Gregg to please not call here anymore." She had officially dropped the "Officer." "I don't want to talk to him," her rigid finger pointing, "and I don't want to see him," her neck rolling. "I don't want a darn thing from him. Tell him to get lost!"

Dupree furiously jumped to her feet, stamping them loudly as she marched with her head held high to her bedroom, slamming the door shut. Gone were the tears. Dupree was just plain mad. She woke up mad, spent the day mad, and went to bed mad. Lying crossway on her bed, with her bare feet hanging over the edge, her chin resting in her open palms, Dupree contemplated her future. *I need to go far away from them. Somewhere they can't call me or stop by to try to see me. I really need a break from those two.*

"Dupree, Tony is on the phone for you," Jas hollered from outside the door. "I told him you weren't taking any calls, but he insists on speaking with you."

"I don't want to speak to Tony. He's a traitor," Dupree screamed, curling up on the bed in a fetal position. "I wish they could all just leave me alone," she muttered, fighting against that awful pain that was buried deep inside her. Truth be told, she really missed her best friend.

"He said you both are going to talk one way or the other real soon," Jas yelled. "We have heard from all your nemeses for today, at least for now, so you can stop hiding."

Dupree shook her head at Jas's antics. "Come in, big mouth."

Jas entered with a smirk on her face. "You know I'm going to start charging you for my operator services, right?" She went and lay down beside Dupree on the bed, nudging her in the side with her elbow. "You can't avoid them forever, girlfriend."

"I know, but I'm going to run as far away as possible," Dupree replied in a cold voice as she tried to visualize herself in New York.

After Tony had found out that Dupree was his sister, he demanded that his parents pay for her to attend New York University with him, without yet revealing to Dupree that Officer Gregg was her father. He convinced Dupree to accept the generous, life-changing opportunity and to apply to NYU. Finally with Aunt Madge's blessings, Dupree did. Dupree started the fall semester at UTech in September of 1995. She wanted to attend NYU in the fall of 1996 but was instead accepted for next spring, which would begin late January of 1997.

"That's why I made an appointment to go to the embassy for my student visa on Monday." Dupree looked at Jas apologetically. "I need the break from them, Jas."

Jas was silent for a moment as she stared at her friend. "It's okay. I'm going to miss you, but this is such a great opportunity for you."

"He paid the tuition for the first semester," Dupree said in reference to Officer Gregg. "I hate to take his money, but I need it to get away from him. Does that make sense? Do you think I should tell him to take back his money and just stay here?"

"Oh, no, you won't." Jas rolled over and sat up on the bed, tucking her legs under her body. Dupree did the same. "He *owes* you this, Dupree. After all these years and everything he has done, you deserve this and so much more."

"You think so?"

"I know so. Go and get what's yours. Don't worry about me. I know I will have to move from here, but I'll manage. I can work full-time at the bank and go to school at night. With full employment I'll be able to get an apartment with a roommate in a nice neighborhood."

"We'll look for an apartment for you before I leave so I can help you move." Dupree reached over and hugged her friend. "I thank God for you every day, Miss Operator."

Jas laughed and gave her a squeeze before letting go. "I thank Him every day for the excitement that you and your folks are giving me." She ducked, allowing the pillow that Dupree threw at her to bounce off her back.

"I got it, Aunt Madge." Dupree sat down beside her grandaunt on the couch. "I got a five-year student visa. See?" She opened her passport to show Aunt Madge the visa stamped there. Dupree had applied for her student visa the day before. She just came home from the U.S. Embassy where she went to pick it up that afternoon.

"I am happy for you, baby." Aunt Madge took the passport from Dupree's hand and looked down at it with a smile. "You are going to study abroad, huh? What an awesome God."

"I'm going to call you every day, and I'll be home to see you every holiday. It's just you and me as always, Aunt Madge."

Aunt Madge closed the passport and reached for Dupree's hand. "But it's not just us anymore, sweetheart."

Dupree tried to pull her hand away, but Aunt Madge held it firmly. "Look at me, Dupree." She waited until Dupree made eye contact with her. "You have a mother who we thought was lost, but she is alive and well. You also have a father and a half brother."

Dupree sucked her teeth loudly, pushed out her lips, then shook her feet impatiently. "They don't matter to me," she mumbled.

"I am going to ignore that suck teeth business because you are hurting right now." Aunt Madge gave Dupree an earnest look. "Baby, I'm not asking you to forget everything that has happened. Nor am I telling you to just forgive your parents. I know it's going to take time. All I'm asking is that you give them a chance to tell you their side of the story, especially your mother. She has . . ." Aunt Madge closed her eyes, shaking her head from side to side, holding in the tears. "She has suffered too, Dupree. Please talk to her. I know it will make a difference toward both of you finding your way to each other." Her eyes opened and silently pled with Dupree. "Promise me you will at least think about it."

Dupree searched Aunt Madge's face and noticed the unshed tears in her eyes. Eleanor had been visiting Aunt Madge regularly, and they have talked for hours on end. Obviously, she had told Aunt Madge something that was pretty upsetting. *What could that be?* Dupree wondered.

Maybe I should hear what she has to say. But just as quickly as the thought came, so did the memories of the hell she went through growing up while her mother was alive and well. *No, Tiny can stay dead for all I care. I don't want to hear the lies she took eighteen years to make up.* "I'll think about it," Dupree replied with a nonchalant attitude. "It will probably take a lifetime before I'm done thinking, but at least you know I am."

Aunt Madge opened her arms, smiling. "Come here, my dear." She wrapped her small arms around Dupree as she would when she was a child. "God is hammering away at the ice around your heart, piece by piece. You have a right to be angry, but I'm praying that you will forgive them soon. Not just for their sake but yours. I want you to move on from the past so you can enjoy the present and embrace the wonderful future ahead of you. I want you to be happy, baby."

The tears came and wet Aunt Madge's shoulder where Dupree's head lay. "I want to be happy too, Aunt Madge. But it just seems as if I can't be for long. Something or someone always comes along and takes it from me."

Aunt Madge whispered. "John 16:20 says, 'Verily, verily, I say unto you, That ye shall weep and lament, but the world shall rejoice: and ye shall be sorrowful, but your sorrow shall be turned into joy.' Your time is coming, sweetheart. It's coming very soon."

But Dupree had many rivers to cross before she could find that happiness that she so deserved.

Chapter Forty-eight

"What is he doing here?" Dupree slammed the door shut, then marched angrily over to Aunt Madge and Jas sitting on the couch. "Didn't I say I don't want to talk to him?" her finger moved accusingly back and forth between both women, "So why on earth do you think I want to see him?" Hands folded across her chest, Dupree stared down at them with eyes blazing.

"Kindly sit down right here." Aunt Madge patted the space on the couch to her right. "And you watch that tone with me, young lady."

Dupree sat on the edge of the couch, rapidly shaking her legs, her face twisted up like she was drinking Verjuice. "I can't wait to get away from all of them," she mumbled under her breath and pursed her lips disgustedly.

"Hello, Pree." Tony leaned forward on the couch across from her. "I told you we need to talk. That's why I'm here, and I'm not going anywhere until we do."

Dupree sucked her teeth and quickly glanced over at Aunt Madge who gave her a stern look.

"I never wanted to hurt you, Pree," Tony continued, his voice fortified with grief. "You know I love you, first as my best friend, then as my sister. I did what I thought was best at the time."

"You love me, huh? Is *that* why you and your father watched me struggle after Aunt Madge got sick and neither one of you helped me?" Dupree bent forward, her eyes pinning Tony to the couch. "You introduced yourself to me like you never knew me, and all this time you knew I was your father's bastard child!"

"Dupree," Aunt Madge said loudly. "Look at me, baby. You are no one's bastard, you hear me? You are a child of the Most High God. He loves you, and I love you too."

"I love you too, Pree." Tony eyes were swimming with tears. "I love you so much that I moved out of my parents' house when I found out you were my sister."

Dupree looked at him. "So that's why you went to stay with your grandparents?"

"Yes, *our* grandparents, by the way. I found out the same night you were attacked by Deacon Livingston." Tony proceeded to tell them of getting home late that night after leaving the hospital and hearing his parents arguing. "I was curious because they rarely fought, so I went and listened by their bedroom door. My mother was telling my father that they were going to hell for what they did to you, Dupree, his daughter. My father was shocked because he never knew that my mother had known all this time of his betrayal and the child that resulted from it." As the story unfolded, Dupree, Aunt Madge, and Jas didn't say a word. "She knew that he impregnated a teenager, and she covered it up." Tony's voice grew louder. "Can you see now why I couldn't stay in the same house with them? They betrayed you." Tony stood to his feet and began pacing the floor. "They denied you so they could keep their secret hidden."

Aunt Madge groaned deep in her throat.

"Instead of helping your mother when she told him she was pregnant, my father threatened to kill her and Aunt Madge if she ever revealed that he fathered her child. Did you know that?" Tony stopped in front of Dupree, looking down at her with compassion.

Tears leaked down Dupree's face.

"I hated them for it, Pree." Tony knelt down in front of his sister, taking her trembling hands in his own. Both were crying. "It took many family counseling sessions with Bishop Chude in Clarendon before I was able to even speak civilly to them again."

"That's where you always disappeared to? With them?" Dupree said in a low voice.

Tony nodded, got up, and squeezed in beside Dupree on the couch, his leg squashed against hers. "Yes. I gave them some ultimatums as well."

"Uh-huh, such as paying the tuition for me to attend NYU." Dupree used her fingers to wipe the tears from her face. "I wondered why they were doing that for me, you know. Why would these perfect strangers do something so generous for their son's best friend? All this time they were trying to appease their guilt."

"For what it's worth, Pree, they are really torn up over what they've done. I know it's going to take some time for you to forgive them, but I know you will one day. It takes time, just like it did for me."

"Yeah, it will take some time." Dupree looked sadly at Tony. "Like a lifetime."

"No, it won't. You are just mad right now." Tony gave her a small smile. "I didn't tell you because you were badly hurt and had a long road to recovery. We thought it was best to wait."

"We?" Dupree looked at Tony with raised eyebrows.

"Yes, my parents and I discussed it. Dad wanted to tell you when everything came out after your attack, but it would have been too much for you. I did it for you, Pree, and I would do it all over again to protect you."

The siblings stared at each other. *He is as much a victim in this whole mess as I am,* Dupree contemplated, her anger toward Tony sidling away. "Maybe I should ease up on you a little." She gently elbowed him in his side, a smile flirting at the corners of her mouth. "Although you could have told me after I started college."

"I eventually would at the right time, little sister."

"Please, you and I are the same age, *little* brother."

Tony reached over and hugged Dupree, who clung to him. "I'm sorry about everything, Pree. I hate that you are hurting so much, but I know you will come out of this a stronger and better person. I'm always here for you."

"Thanks, Tony. I'm so confused," Dupree confessed. "I don't know what to do, where to turn, or who to talk to."

"For now, why don't you focus on talking to God? He'll lead you down the right path for you to follow."

In silent acquiescence, Dupree pulled back and looked at her brother. Over the last few days she had spent so much time being mad and so little time seeking God. Maybe it *was* time to get back on track.

Chapter Forty-nine

"Hi, Aunt Madge, how are you feeling today?" Eleanor walked over to the opened window in her living room, the telephone pressed to her ear.

"I'm doing all right, baby. But your daughter is another matter."

"I know she's hurting. But she refuses to see or talk to me, Aunt Madge. I don't know what else to do."

"It's going to take time but don't give up on her. Her brother is here. They have talked and are mending the gap in their relationship."

"I'm glad to hear that because he has nothing to do with all this." Eleanor gazed down the hill at the beautiful Jamaica landscape, the bright sun reflecting off the leaves of the tall trees swaying softly in the wind, sprinkling the green, luscious grass with its yellow rays.

"I'm going back to work next week. I hope to see Dupree."

"Remember to take it slow with her, sweetheart. I was also planning on calling you later," Aunt Madge added. "I have a message from Beverly Gregg for you to call her. She left her personal number and said it was urgent."

Eleanor froze. *The nerve of that . . . Lord, please hold my tongue.* "What's the number?" She wrote it down and waited anxiously for Dwight to get home from work.

"What does she want?" Eleanor asked her husband that evening as they sat around the dining table. "She lied and told me all was well with my daughter and aunt when she knew that Aunt Madge had a stroke." Eleanor indignantly threw down her fork into the plate of food that she barely touched. "Now she wants *me* to call *her?* I'll call her. Yup, I'll *definitely* call her because I have a few things to say to her."

Dwight rested his elbows on the table, his eyes fixed on his irate wife. "Did you really expect her to tell you the truth, knowing that you would probably come back to town?"

Eleanor looked at him without a response.

"After keeping her husband's secret all these years, why would she help the person she thought could ruin her life?" Dwight held up a hand when Eleanor opened her mouth. "It wasn't right, babe. But there were a lot of things that happened over the last few years that weren't right."

"You're blaming me, aren't you?" Eleanor blinked back the tears. "I should have gone and seen for myself that Dupree and Aunt Madge were okay. I honestly thought I was doing the right thing, Dwight."

"I'm not blaming you, darling. You did what you thought was best. We can't go back, so let's try to move forward for Dupree's sake."

So against her better judgment, Eleanor called Beverly Gregg.

"I'm sorry for lying to you, Tiny, but what else could I have done?" Beverly's voice broke as she struggled to speak. "The last eighteen years of my life have been one big lie; the secrets, the guilt, the inner rage at my husband. I did what I thought was best for my family."

It was those words that touched something within Eleanor. For over eighteen years she too did what she thought was best for her daughter . . . but look at the way things had turned out.

"Anthony and I would like to come up there and meet with you and your husband if—"

"*Meet?*" Eleanor practically shouted.

"Yes. I think it's time we all get together and discuss where we go from here for Dupree's sake. I know it will be a painful and uncomfortable situation for all of us, but it's a start. The Lord will get us through it."

Eleanor shook her head from side to side as if Beverly could see her. "I don't think so. I know you mean well, but this is not a good idea. I will deal with my daughter my own way."

"What about her father? You can't pretend that he doesn't exist anymore. I have a strong feeling Dupree won't."

"*He* is the problem. If my husband sees him, there is no telling what Dwight will do." Eleanor's grip tightened on the telephone. "I won't let that happen. Sorry."

"We could meet in a public place. Please discuss it with your husband and get back to me. It would mean a lot to Anthony and me to try to right our wrongs against you and Dupree."

Eleanor ended the call, and then relayed Beverly's suggestion to Dwight.

"Absolutely not!" Dwight looked at Eleanor as if she had lost her mind. "If I see that man I won't be responsible for what happens, babe. I'm telling you right now."

"Sweetheart, as much as I hate to admit it, I agree this is a move in the right direction. He is Dupree's father."

"He is a slimeball!"

"We might never be friends, but we have to coexist for Dupree's sake," Eleanor told him.

"Uh-uh, he shouldn't exist any at all," Dwight hissed under his breath.

Eleanor tapped him on the behind. "What do you say we give it a try, darling?" She draped her arms around Dwight's narrow waist, giving him the puppy dog look that always lets her get her own way. "Please, for Dupree's and my sake. I need some resolution about the past."

Dwight playfully rolled his eyes, but knew there was very little he could deny his wife, especially in this situation. As much as he hated the thought of seeing Officer Gregg, he was anxious for him and Eleanor to put the past behind them and move on with their lives. "I'll try to restrain myself, but I'm not promising anything."

Eleanor squeezed him tight in gratitude. "Now I have to tell the family what's going on. They deserve to know," she said in reference to Mama Pearl and her sons.

Dwight clicked his teeth together. "Officer Gregg might not be around for our meeting after all. You're worried about me. Wait until the guys get *their* hands on him."

Eleanor shuddered at the thought. *Lord have mercy.*

Chapter Fifty

Silence blanketed the room. Mama Pearl sat beside Eleanor as stiff as a statue, her lips folded so tight Eleanor feared they would fuse together. Sydney, Robert, Alwayne, Gerald, and Omar were rendered speechless, tears running unashamedly down their faces. To see these grown men openly crying for her touched Eleanor's heart. Dwight, who had heard the story a few times, with every time seeming like the first time, was hunched over on the chair where he sat, his face almost resting in his lap.

"So that's my story," Eleanor finally said in a teary voice. "That's how I came to be a part of this wonderful family that saved my life."

"I. Am. Going. To. Kill. Him," Omar spat through his teeth. "As a matter of fact, both of them are dead. Officers Gregg and Bailey are about to meet the devil up close and personal. I'm going to make sure of it." He took a handkerchief from his pocket and wiped his face.

"No, they are *mine*," Gerald said a little above a whisper in a deadly tone. "I'm going to show these lowlifes the penalty for abusing young girls and dishonoring the badge I have proudly worn for over twenty years."

"Let me take care of it." Robert blew his nose loudly into his handkerchief. "I know people. I'm going to make a call now and by tonight they are dead."

"No, I got—"

"Enough!" Mama Pearl's voice sounded like rolling thunder as it ricocheted around the living room. "I raised law-abiding, God-fearing men, not murderers. Now if I didn't have the Holy Spirit dwelling in me, I would say those men deserve all that and more. But Romans 12:19 reads, 'Dearly beloved, avenge not yourselves, but rather give place unto wrath: for it is written, Vengeance is mine; I will repay, saith the Lord.'"

"Well, I'm going to help out the Lord." Omar peeked at his mother's austere face before quickly looking away.

Mama Pearl tugged Eleanor closer to her side, her arm around her shoulder. "My heart aches for you, baby." She kissed Eleanor's forehead. "I wish all those things hadn't happened to you, but you probably wouldn't have been in our lives had they not. See, what the devil meant for evil, God turned around for your good. I know you are a stronger, wiser, and better person because of it."

Eleanor leaned closer and hugged her. "I am, Mama Pearl. Thanks be to God." Just then Eleanor's cell phone rang in her handbag that sat in her lap. She reached in, pulled it out, and flipped it open to answer the call. "Hello? Yes. Okay, my husband and I will be there shortly." Eleanor ended the call and noticed every eye was trained on her. "That was Beverly Gregg. Dwight and I are going to meet her and her husband at the Wyndham Hotel."

"What?"

"Like heck you are."

"You must be crazy."

The five brothers were speaking at once, their outrage splashed across their faces. Even Mama Pearl was staring at Eleanor as if she had lost her mind. Omar and Gerald got up and began pacing the floor angrily.

"Baby, do you think that's wise?" Mama Pearl leaned her head toward Dwight, her eyebrows rising and falling questioningly. "I can understand why you want to do this but . . ."

"I'm going with my wife, Mama Pearl." Dwight's face seemed to be carved in stone. "We are in this together all the way."

"I know, Dwight, but you might not be able to control yourself."

"We are meeting in the hotel's restaurant. I don't want any witnesses around, so I won't kill him today," Dwight replied as serious as a judge.

The other men smirked with satisfaction, nodding their approval.

"We'll get him when he least expects it, my friend," said hot-tempered Omar. "He won't even see us coming."

Mama Pearl peered from face to face, giving them the evil eye, but her sons turned their attention elsewhere, not ready to give in to their mother's admonishment.

"You guys are going to behave yourselves." Eleanor stood to her feet and placed her handbag over her shoulder. "There won't be any killing going on here." She walked from one stiff-postured man to the other, kissing one cheek after the other. "I love you," she repeated to each of them. "I loveeee you," she said as she kissed Mama Pearl good-bye.

Dwight gingerly got to his feet and took his wife's hand in his. "Well, let's get this over with."

"Good luck," Mama Pearl called as the couple walked out the door, leaving her with her furious sons.

Chapter Fifty-one

Eleanor's knees felt wobbly as she walked with Dwight behind the waitress escorting them across the restaurant, through mazes of tables and chairs, her hand clutched tightly in his. Breathing deeply through her mouth, her heart felt like it was doing somersaults in her chest. "I can do this," Eleanor muttered under her breath. She felt Dwight's hand tightened on hers and gave him a reaffirmed squeeze.

Then there they were: Officer and Mrs. Anthony Gregg seated around a table for four in the back of the restaurant. They quickly jumped to their feet when they saw Eleanor, Dwight, and the waitress approaching.

"Here is your party that has been waiting for you." The waitress waved her hand toward the Greggs. "I'll give you a few minutes, and I'll be back to take your orders." She sashayed away on high stiletto heels, leaving an awkward silence behind her.

After nineteen years, Eleanor and Officer Gregg came face-to-face. The two stared at each other as if the meeting was a figment of their imagination. Dwight slipped his arm protectively around his wife's waist, pulling her closer to his side. *This is the man I was infatuated with as a teenager,* Eleanor thought as she looked at the now older, still handsome, Anthony Gregg. *The man who got me pregnant and almost killed me when I told him about it. The man who is responsible for me running away from my daughter for all these years.* But where was the anger?

Officer Gregg took a few slow steps toward Eleanor with Beverly right on his heels. Dwight stepped before Eleanor with his fists clenched and stood face-to-face with the man he wanted so badly to punch in the face.

"I'm so sorry," Officer Gregg said in a very humbled voice, tears wetting his eyes. "I was a monster."

"Do you know how badly I want to get at you—*huh?*" Dwight took two long steps and bridged the small gap until he was nose to nose with Officer Gregg. "I want to wipe up the floor with your pathetic—" Dwight stopped when he felt Eleanor's arm around his waist.

"You promised," she whispered to him, poking him a little in the side. "Why don't we all sit down and talk," she said to the Greggs.

Relieved, Officer Gregg and Beverly both hurried back to the table and took their seats. Eleanor gently tugged on a red-faced Dwight, who reluctantly dragged himself over to the table. He pulled out Eleanor's chair for her to sit before he threw himself in the other, his chest rising and falling in anger.

"You both have every right to be angry." Beverly's pain-filled eyes went back and forth between Eleanor and Dwight. "Tiny, what we did to you and Dupree was despicable."

"It's Eleanor now. I left Tiny behind when you both ran me out of town."

"You must hate me, and you have a right to." Officer Gregg stared down at his hands clasped together on the table.

"I used to but surprisingly, not anymore." Eleanor looked at him sincerely. "The Lord has made a big difference in my life. So has this wonderful man that He blessed me with as my husband and my adopted family that rescued me from the streets. It took many years, many nightmares, and a lot of work, but I'm in a better place. It will only get better when my daughter forgives me and welcomes me into her life."

"Tiny . . . I mean, Eleanor, I'm so sorry. If I could go back and do it all over again, I would." Officer Gregg wiped the tears that escaped down his face. "I was a different person back then. Please believe me. I'm sorry for the way I treated you and our daughter. You both deserved better."

"Me too," said Beverly. "I'm not making excuses for what I did, but the devil played us like a flute. I'm a better person now. I know you probably regret ever knowing us, but—"

"I don't." Eleanor leaned back in her chair, her eyes locked with the older woman. "If I should say that I regretted everything, that would include Dupree, and that's not the case. I love my daughter. What I regret is everything bad that happened to separate us and the hurt and suffering Dupree endured."

"I won't give up until Dupree gives me another chance. It will take her some time, but she is a kindhearted young woman." Officer Gregg's eyes shone brightly like a proud father. "I don't deserve her, or even your, forgiveness, Eleanor, but I am hopeful. I would also like to ask yours as well, Mr. Humphrey." He stole a glance at Dwight who had been silent all this time, listening and watching what was going on.

"Let's keep the focus right now on my stepdaughter," Dwight replied in a hard voice. "By the way, where is that other creep *Officer* Bailey?" The "officer" was emphasized with disdain.

Officer Gregg's mouth opened wide as he looked from Dwight to Eleanor. "Bailey?"

Eleanor nodded and told them of her horrifying encounter with him.

Beverly sobbed silently, Dwight's nostrils flared dangerously, and Officer Gregg was rendered speechless.

"My God, *that's* what he meant," Officer Gregg said after a few seconds. "Dear Lord . . ." He closed his eyes tightly but not enough to stop the tears from pouring out. "I . . . I . . . I'm so, so, sorry, Eleanor. It's my fault."

Officer Gregg admitted that he had confided in Officer Bailey and told him about his affair with Tiny and her being pregnant. He also told him of the threats he made against Tiny to keep her quiet. "He told me I should have shut you up permanently." Officer Gregg looked at Eleanor with remorse. "I told him I wasn't a killer, and I just let it go. It wasn't until about nine years later that he came to me and told me you had come back to town, but he took care of you for good this time. At first I was scared that he had harmed you, but he assured me he never hurt you. He refused to give me any details, only that he had put you back on a bus to Kingston."

Officer Gregg felt his wife's accusing eyes on him but refused to look in her direction. This was the first time Beverly was hearing about this. He hung down his head in shame.

"No wonder he died the way he did," Beverly said through her teeth. "He was actually going to *kill* her!"

"Died?" Eleanor looked at Officer Gregg for an explanation. "Officer Bailey is dead?"

"You mean someone beat me to it?" Dwight sat up straight in his chair, ignoring the stern look that his wife threw his way.

Officer Gregg informed them that two years ago, Officer Bailey had failed to turn up for work. This was unusual because if he wasn't going to work, he would have had someone cover for him, which he didn't. Two of his concerned colleagues went to his house to check on him. They found Officer Bailey in the bedroom. He was naked, tied to the bedpost, a bullet hole in his forehead, his neck cut from ear to ear, and his severed penis stuffed into his mouth. Officer Bailey died with his eyes wide open.

Eleanor felt sick to her stomach. Astounded, she pressed her hand over her mouth to keep down her breakfast from that morning. Thank God she hadn't yet eaten lunch.

Dwight turned away his head in disgust. The man was a beast, but did he deserve that? It was obvious someone thought he did.

"The house was stripped of everything, except the four walls and his deathbed," Officer Gregg continued. "In a hidden cellar in the kitchen, the police found tons of marijuana. I guess his killer or killers missed that. None of us knew exactly where he came from and no one came forth to claim the body, so four of us got together and buried him in the local cemetery. Except for us, no one else attended the funeral. There was an investigation, but we got no leads. The case is still open, but I seriously doubt it will ever be solved. No one is saying a word."

Instantly, Galatians 6:7 came to Eleanor's mind. "Be not deceived; God is not mocked: for whatsoever a man soweth, that shall he also reap."

Eleanor began, "What a horrifying way to die. I mean—"

"*There* he is!" came Omar's angry voice before all hell broke loose in the restaurant.

Chapter Fifty-two

Officer Gregg's head snapped back as Omar's fist made contact with his jaw, knocking him out of his chair, onto the floor. Surprised, Eleanor, Beverly, and Dwight jumped up out of their chairs and away from the table, the ladies screaming loudly.

In a split second the five brothers were on Officer Gregg like a pack of wolves. The table and two chairs were flipped over, sending glasses of water and utensils flying.

"Stop it!" Eleanor shouted as Gerald picked up Officer Gregg by his shirt like a rag doll, setting him on his feet. Officer Gregg had blood pouring from the side of his mouth. His left eye was blood red and was already getting swollen.

Robert rushed forward and took the opportunity to punch Officer Gregg in the gut. He doubled over in pain but was snapped back up by Gerald who now held him in a neck hold.

Screams echoed around the room, chairs and tables turned over as panicked customers fell over each other, hurrying to get out the door when Gerald pulled out his gun and held it to Officer Gregg's head. Soon the restaurant was empty, except for the brothers, Dwight, Eleanor, Officer Gregg and Beverly.

"So you like to threaten young girls, right? You like to get them pregnant and intimidate them, *Officer* Gregg?" Gerald hissed in Officer Gregg's ear.

"Please, please, don't do that," Beverly begged, snot and tears running down her face. "He regrets everything and is now a better man."

"Kill him, Gerald," Omar shouted, his fists folded, moving his head back and forth as if he was in a boxing ring.

"Gerald, man, you don't want to do this." Dwight moved closer to him. "You are the good cop."

"I'll get you off, my brother," Alwayne said with confidence. "I am one of the *best* lawyers in Jamaica. Shoot the fool."

Officer Gregg whimpered in pain as he struggled to breathe but surprisingly he never made a move in his defense or even tried to break away from the man who held him. It was almost as if he felt the assault was justified.

"You are a disgrace to the police force," Gerald bellowed. "I should just pull the trigger."

"What are you waiting—?"

"Stop ittttttttttt!" Eleanor's voice reverberated around the empty room, bouncing off the walls, slamming into everyone's eardrums. The room was stunned into silence, all eyes now focused on her. Slowly, one small step at a time, she walked over to Gerald and Officer Gregg. "Let him go, now." Low but firm, no questions asked, only a swift response required.

Gerald dropped his hands to his sides, his mouth slightly opened as he stared at Eleanor. Officer Gregg bent over, his hands resting on his knees, coughing loudly. Beverly ran over to him, rubbing his back as he sucked air into his lungs.

Eleanor angrily peered from one face to another, her eyes were narrowed to a slit, her eyebrows almost meeting in the middle of her forehead. No one had ever seen her this mad before, including her husband. "Kill him? Really? Kill him?" She eyeballed Omar, who met her eyes, still fuming. "That's *not* who you are," Eleanor said as she turned to Gerald. "You are a great father, husband, cop, son, and brother. You can't throw all that away."

"What's going on in here?" a short, heavyset man ran in, breathing heavily. "Why are you destroying my place?" he yelled, stomping his stubby feet, his eyes bugging out of his head as he quickly scanned the mess in the restaurant. "I'm calling the police right now to arrest all of you."

"Hi, Mr. Pamoody," Alwayne said as he calmly strolled over to the restaurant manager, who was actually one of his clients. "Sorry about the mess."

"Alwayne? *You* did all this?" Mr. Pamoody took a closer look at the faces of those who remained. His mouth dropped open in surprise when he saw Gerald. "I guess I don't need to call the police, huh? What do you know? I already have one at the crime scene!"

"Calm down, Mr. Pamoody." Alwayne moved closer to the owner. "This was all just a big misunderstanding. My brothers and I will pay for all the damage that was done."

"Oh, really?" Mr. Pamoody nodded his head as if in agreement, a cynical smile on his face. "Tell me something, Counselor. Who is going to defend *you* when I sue your behind for destroying my place and running off all my customers?" he shouted, his nostrils opened up like a funnel.

"Mr. Pamoody." Dwight strolled over to the angry man. "We will definitely compensate you for your losses."

"Well, well, well. If it isn't Mr. CEO himself." Mr. Pamoody looked Dwight up and down, the dollar signs almost transparent in his greedy eyes. "I really should call the police." He briefly glanced at Gerald. "Ones that are not pulling out guns in public restaurants and threatening to kill a civilian in front of dozens of witnesses. But I think we might be able to work this out among ourselves."

"Thank you." Dwight shook the man's hand. "We will get together next week and take care of it."

Mr. Pamoody nodded happily. "I'll go and get some workers to come and clean up all this mess." He hurried away as pleased as a puss in boots.

"I'm going to take him up to his room," Beverly announced, drawing everyone's attention to her and Officer Gregg. "Eleanor, can we call you tomorrow?"

Eleanor crossed over to them in a couple of strides. "I'm sorry about what had happened. I didn't know they were coming."

Officer Gregg waved off her apology, peeking at her through his distended left eye, the right one was swollen shut. "They have a right to be angry at me. We'll speak some more on how to deal with this situation with Dupree. Is that okay?"

"Yes, that's fine."

Officer Gregg shot a quick glance at the men before he and his wife slowly exited the room, her arm around his waist and his around her shoulders for support.

All the men were silent as they looked at Eleanor, trying to gauge her mood. The brothers knew she wasn't pleased with what they had done. And it would only get worse after Mama Pearl got wind of what had happened.

"I'm upset with all of you." Eleanor pointed her index finger at each of the brothers. "You all need to repent and ask God for forgiveness. Wait until Mama Pearl hears about this."

The men groaned. Dwight grinned.

"Let's get out of here before Mr. Pamoody changes his mind and calls the police." Eleanor reached for Dwight's hand.

"Please. He is so busy calculating how much we are going to give him, the police are the last thing on his mind right now," said Alwayne. "Greedy bastard. Wait until he needs my services again. I am going to charge him ten times the regular price."

The other men smirked before they followed Eleanor out of the restaurant, each vowing within himself to be in church the next day. They did need to repent and start to forgive as Eleanor seemed to have done.

"She loves you very much." Dwight sat beside Dupree on a bench under a big lignum vitae tree, out in the court-yard. "If you could just give her a few minutes to explain everything to you, I know it will make a difference."

Dupree shrugged her shoulders, her eyes staring straight-ahead. It had been over two months since she found out the identity of her mother and father. But she still hadn't taken the time to speak to either one of them. Eleanor had returned to work. Trying not to push too much, she gave Dupree her space. It was Dwight who was trying to get Dupree to listen to her mother. He stopped by the apartment frequently to see Dupree and called to check up on her both at home and at work.

"You both have so much in common," Dwight noted. "What do you say, Dupree? Can you do this for me?"

Dupree turned her head and looked at Dwight. She actually liked him very much. "You never give up, huh?" She smiled at him.

"No, not when it comes to you and your mother. I loved you before I even met you, Dupree. I want what's best for my girls."

"I'm just so angry with her." Dupree's eyes met Dwight's. "Every time I think about what she and Mr. Gregg had done, it infuriates me."

Dwight took her small hand into his. "I understand. But to move past this anger, you need to get answers. You need to know why they did what they did."

Dupree looked at him, contemplating what he had just said. "I even hate the fact that he is paying my tuition for NYU. Jas and Tony think I deserve it but . . ."

"What if I pay for it? Would that make you feel better about going?"

"Really? You would do that?" Dupree's face lit up in astonishment.

"Your mother and I would be happy to." Dwight held on to her hand when she tried to pull away from him, the joy on her face instantly gone. "Dupree, whatever is mine is also my wife's and vice versa. We are a team."

Dupree remained quiet.

"In fact, I have another suggestion for you. Instead of staying in a dorm, why don't you stay with my aunt? I know Aunt Clover would love to have you. She lives by herself on Seventy-second Street in Manhattan. You can even have my old room." He lightly nudged Dupree in her side.

Dupree couldn't keep the smile off her face. "Really?"

"Yes, you are family now. You jump on the subway and NYU is right there. You'll be in the heart of New York City with everything close by; stores, restaurants, libraries, museums. Plus, you will feel more at home in the Big Apple with Aunt Clover."

"Can I think about it and let you know?"

"Sure. So what do you say about dinner tomorrow at our house?" Dwight grinned when Dupree playfully rolled her eyes at him.

"Okay, but I'm not making any promises as to how I'll react when I see her," she said in reference to her mother.

Dwight gaped at her. "Huh? Really?"

"Well, if you are not sure—"

"Come here you." Dwight hugged Dupree, his smile stretching from ear to ear. "Wow, wait until your mother hears this. She won't sleep tonight."

Dupree released Dwight. "Remember, no promises."

"Got it. I'll come and get you around 6:00 p.m."

Dupree nodded her head, trepidation moving into her gut. Was she ready for tomorrow?

Chapter Fifty-three

Eleanor had spent the night before and all day on edge as she waited for Dupree to come to dinner. She tried to imagine how the evening would end but came up blank. She made an attempt to rehearse what to say to her daughter but gave up. Finally, she decided to just tell Dupree the truth, leaving nothing out. Dupree was an intelligent, young woman, and hopefully, she would understand.

"We'll have dinner first, after which we will talk," Eleanor said aloud to herself as she paced their home, waiting for Dwight to return with Dupree. But that went out the window real fast.

"I don't understand why you never wanted me. What did I do so wrong that you had to run away from me?" Dupree asked her mother as soon as she entered the house, crying. She'd been holding that question in for so many years that she just exploded. "For heaven's sake, I was just a baby, Tiny!"

Dinner was put on hold as Dwight quickly excused himself and went into the bedroom, leaving mother and daughter to finally have that long, overdue talk.

Eleanor invited Dupree into the living room. "Please have a seat, Dupree." Eleanor pointed to the couch, waited until Dupree sat, before taking her seat on the other couch across from her. Without hesitation Eleanor began her story, starting with her friendship with Dolly and recounting her experience with the dazzling Officer Gregg.

Dupree cried silently for the most part of Eleanor's story. With her eyes tightly shut, her arms wrapped snugly around her belly, she listened intently to the hell her mother had gone through. But it was the near rape in the park that eventually pushed her over the edge.

"No no no, please don't tell me they . . . they . . ." Dupree fell to her knees on the thick carpet in Dwight and Eleanor's living room, her forehead brushing against it as she wailed. Loud, piercing cries rocked her slender frame.

"No, they didn't, sweetheart." Eleanor got up from the couch and knelt down beside her daughter. "I think it was the police who came and rescued me. All I know was shots were fired, and they released me." Eleanor pulled Dupree up off the floor and into her arms, both women crying hard.

"If Brother Bunny hadn't come when he did, he would have raped and killed me too." Dupree rested her head on Eleanor's shoulder and cried.

Eleanor froze, her eyes bugged out of her head in shock. "Who was going to rape you?"

"Deacon Livingston."

This was the first time Eleanor was hearing about Dupree's attack. All the time she spent catching up and reacquainting with Aunt Madge, she'd never said a word. But being the wise woman that she was, Aunt Madge knew this unfortunate incident would be a glue to bond the mother and daughter together after hearing Eleanor's story. Both women had escaped similar fates by the grace of God.

"Deacon Livingston? He was like a father to me. He was a friend of Aunt Madge and your grandmother. *He* attacked you?" Eleanor felt as if someone had just reached in and ripped out her heart.

Between sobs, Dupree told her mother of the most horrendous experience of her life. The women's cries were like howls, boomeranging around the house. Dwight ran from the bedroom into the living room in alarm. He found Eleanor and Dupree huddled together on the floor, bawling. Their pain was so intense, he began to cry himself. Without a word Dwight knelt down beside the ladies and pulled both of them into his arms.

"Heavenly Father, if there is a time this family needs you, it is now," Dwight prayed, gently rocking both his girls. "Please heal Eleanor and Dupree's aching hearts. Please, I am begging you to erase the pain of the past and help them to create new, wonderful memories today and forever. You are the only one who can bind them together, Lord." Dwight prayed until their crying tapered off to sniffles. "I'm going to get us something to drink."

Dwight sluggishly rose to his feet, reached down, and helped his wife, then Dupree to their feet. The women staggered over to the long couch and wearily sat down beside each other. Eleanor reached for Dupree's hand and held on to it tightly. She still had so much to tell her daughter.

"Here you go." Dwight returned with two tall glasses of water. He gave one to each woman, peering intently at their still damped faces. He crossed the room and got a box of Kleenex from a side table, returned, and handed sheets to Eleanor and Dupree. "Do you ladies want to take a break and get something to eat?"

"No." Dupree turned to look at Eleanor. "I want to hear the rest of it."

"Are you sure? We can continue another day. I know that was a lot for you to absorb." Eleanor stared at Dupree with concern.

"I'm sure." Dupree nodded with determination. "Please, go on."

"Babe, why don't you go ahead and eat without us?" Eleanor said to Dwight. "Dupree and I will have something later."

Dwight agreed and left the room. It took a few more hours, many more tears, and over eighteen years of pain and heartache before Eleanor concluded her story.

"So that's why I stayed away but never a day went by that I didn't think about you, my daughter." Eleanor's eyes pleaded with Dupree, the tears creeping down her face. "I thought I was protecting you."

Dupree's wet eyes locked with her mother's. "You came back?"

"Yes, I did. But I just got a glimpse of your back."

"May God forgive me but I'm not sorry that monster is dead," Dupree said, alluding to Officer Bailey. "As for Mr. Gregg, it's going to take a long, long time—"

Eleanor leaned over and placed her index finger over Dupree's lips. "No. Please. I don't want it to take a long time for you to be free. I want God to help you to forgive us so you can finally step into your future."

Dupree nodded. "It all makes sense now. You were forced to do what you did. I do wish you had told Dwight or your adopted brothers what was going on and maybe they could have helped us, but on the other hand, who knows what might have happened with that lunatic."

"I pay for my sins every day, Dupree. I was such a bad mother to you that the Lord decided I would never be a mother again, so He shut my womb."

Dupree looked at her mother in shock. "What?"

"The one thing my husband wants so much, I can't give him; a child of his own. It's my punishment for what I did to you." Eleanor shivered as if cold, crying. "I accept my fate and I have you, but I can't help feeling the pain for the man I love. It's all because of my sins."

"That's not true. You know God doesn't work like that." Dupree stood up, without a word she knelt down in front of Eleanor and placed her hand on her mother's tummy. "Dear God, my mother is ready now to be a mother again.

Please grant her and Dwight the desire of their hearts and bless them with a child of their own."

Eleanor wept, her eyes closed.

"Lord, please make it a girl and not a boy. I don't know if I can deal with another bigheaded brother."

Eleanor smiled through her tears, stealing a peep at Dupree. To her surprise Dupree had a serious look on her face, her eyes closed in deep concentration.

"I will try to help change diapers when I come home on school breaks, but I'm not going to make any promises right now. Who knows, they might get a nanny and let me off the hook."

Eleanor bit her lip, happiness overtaking her body.

"So, please I am asking this of you in your holy name I pray. Amen."

"Amen." Eleanor's mouth was stretched wide with a huge grin on her face.

"It's going to be okay, Mother," Dupree said as she stood to her feet and sat by her mother's side. "Just wait and see."

Eleanor crushed Dupree to her bosom and began praising God in a loud voice. Dwight ran in again, expecting the worse. But this time it was cheers instead of tears. "She called me 'mother,'" Eleanor told him over Dupree's head. "She prayed that we will have a baby. A girl though."

Dwight placed a hand to his cheek, nodding his head repeatedly. "I . . . I . . . I love girls," he stammered, his wife's happiness reflecting in his own eyes.

Chapter Fifty-four

A week later, Eleanor stood outside the offices of BDO Jamaica waiting on Dwight to come and pick her up from work, beaming from ear to ear. Usually she stayed inside until Dwight got there, but she was just too happy to be confined to the office. The last few days had been some of the best for Eleanor. She had been spending a lot of time with Dupree, getting to know her daughter and vice versa. Eleanor was surprised at how much they had in common. With her eyes fixed on the ground, a smile on her face, her thoughts were consumed with Dupree.

"Can you spare some change, ma'am?"

Eleanor's eyes swept over two dirty, skinny, sore-infested feet swallowed up by a pair of grimy flip-flops. Moving upward, she took in the small, stained, raggedy dress torn in multiple places, falling off the skeletal frame. Sympathy filled Eleanor's heart as she stared at the yellow, sunken eyes in the bony face, decorated by big pimples and acne scars. Suddenly Eleanor's breathing sped up. "Dear God," she muttered, her eyes widened in recognition. "Dolly, is that you?"

"Tiny? Girl, I didn't even know it was you in your fancy clothes and things." Dolly smiled, revealing a mouth full of rotten teeth as she scratched at some sores on her arms.

"Oh, Dolly." Tiny moved closer and hugged her, fighting against the tears that threatened to fall. "I'm so sorry."

Some people stared in surprise, others in fascination at the contrast of the expensive business suit enfolding someone wearing dirty rags; the business executive embracing the stinky junkie.

That was the sight Dwight saw as he pulled up alongside the pair. Quickly parking the car, he hopped out and approached his wife and company.

"This is my husband, Dwight," Eleanor made the introduction, her hand around Dolly's bony waist, not fazed by the strong odor emanating from her old friend. "Baby, this is Dolly."

Dwight's eyes enlarged with shock. "Huh? Hmmm, hello, Dolly." He stretched out his hand and shook hers, before releasing it. It felt like a piece of dried stick.

"Tiny, you done got you a fine man here, high yellow with pretty hair and colored eyes." Dolly winked at Dwight, who looked away embarrassed. "From the looks of the two of you, he has money too. Handsome, beg you a few dollars to buy something to eat." Dolly stretched out her hand to Dwight.

"We are not giving you a cent to go and buy drugs," Eleanor told Dolly. "But we can help you if you want us to." Eleanor had taken one look at the fidgety Dolly and knew that she was on something other than marijuana. It had been on the news for the last few months about Jamaica being infiltrated by cocaine and heroin. Jamaica's National Council on Drug Abuse (NCDA) vowed to intensify its drug law enforcement and increase drug arrests and seizures.

Dolly hung down her head in shame. She had been hooked on cocaine for almost a year, doing a little heroin also when it was available. In order to get her daily fix, she sold her body. But as the poison took its toll on her once curvaceous body, even that was hard to do now as no one wanted her. She was homeless and walked the streets begging for a few cents to get the monkey off her back. "Why would you want to help me, Tiny? I left you on the streets when you came to me for help."

"I was mad at you for a while, but now I'm glad you did. Now that I look at it, you actually did me a favor." Eleanor's voice was filled with kindness. "I had to follow

my own destiny, Dolly. It was all a part of God's plan."
She felt Dwight take her hand and gave it a squeeze.
"Just like you running into my wife today," Dwight
added. "It's God's will for us to help you."

Dolly looked down at her grimy feet in the beat up
flip-flops. "God don't deal with the likes of me. I have
done too much dirt."

"It's just the opposite, Dolly." Eleanor moved closer to
her. "Look at me," Eleanor demanded and waited until
Dolly's wet, sunken eyes met hers. "God specializes in
people like you; people who need Him."

"So are you ready to make a change, Rockin' Dolly?"
Dwight grinned at her.

Dolly threw her head back and laughed out loud,
Eleanor joining in. "I see you told your man all about me,"
Dolly said to Eleanor. "I'm not rocking anymore, but I
sure would like to again," she told Dwight.

"Good. I have a client who has a big inpatient reha-
bilitation center in Portmore, St. Catherine. He started
it here in Jamaica about two years ago and has a few in
the USA after his only brother overdosed about six years
ago," Dwight told Dolly. "I know it's full to capacity, but
maybe I can call in a favor."

"Dolly, please do this." Eleanor's eyes pleaded with her.
"This is not the way for you to live. You know that."

Dolly looked from Eleanor to Dwight with uncertainty,
rocking back and forth on her heels. "I'm not so sure . . ."

Eleanor stepped closer to her, a determined look on
her face. "Not sure, huh? I thought you wanted to be a
performer. What happened to those dreams?"

Dolly's face lit up. "I used to perform in my own show."

Eleanor shuddered at the thought, forcing the image
from her mind. "Not those shows, Dolly," Eleanor said
dryly. "I meant the Pantomime."

"Really? You think I can still do that?"

"First you need to get clean and get your life back on
track," Dwight informed her. "My wife and I will pay for

all your expenses. We will also help you get a job when you finish the program."

Dolly went and wrapped her arms around Dwight, her tears wetting his jacket. Dwight awkwardly patted her on her bony back and waited a few seconds before untangling himself. They both turned to face Eleanor.

Eleanor smiled. "We will visit often. I'll also take my daughter to meet you."

"You had a girl. I left before you had the baby, and I never even asked you the last time I saw you. I was so nasty to you. Sorry for what Big Dread did to you, Tiny. I'm sorry for everything."

"That's okay. Come on, let's take a drive over to Portmore." Eleanor got ahold of Dolly's hand and moved toward the car.

Dwight opened the doors for the women to enter the car. Dolly sat in the back, with Eleanor in the front passenger seat beside him. After strapping himself in the car, he drove off, headed toward St. Catherine. As they drove to Portmore, Dwight called his friend and informed him about Dolly and that they were on the way. Meanwhile, Eleanor and Dolly caught up with each other. It was apparent that they both had been through some tough times. Eleanor made a promise to herself to help Dolly get back on her feet.

"Here we are," Dwight announced as he pulled up to a tall, iron gate. A massive, white, multistoried building stood behind it. The rehab center had high fencing all around it and was isolated, the nearest property miles away.

Dolly hung her head out the car window and stared in awe, hope plastered across her face. *It's almost like looking up at heaven,* she thought, tears swimming in her eyes. This place represented a new life for her. "I'm going to do this," Dolly stated loudly. "Rockin' Dolly will be back, mark my words."

Eleanor and Dwight looked at each other happily. Everything was finally falling into place.

Epilogue

"Get up off my bed, Bighead." Dupree grabbed a pillow off the bed and threw it at Tony, hitting him in the stomach. "You know you don't live here, right?"

Tony laughed and returned the favor, the pillow bouncing off Dupree's head, landing on the floor. "Aunt Clover says I'm family too, and I'm always welcome, thank you very much."

Dupree laughed and went to lie down beside her brother. "Well, you practically took over the guest room so what else was she going to say?"

It had been a little over a year since Dupree started attending New York University the spring of 1997. As Dwight promised, she lived with his aunt Clover in Midtown Manhattan instead of staying in a dorm. A wonderful Christian woman, Aunt Clover reminded Dupree a lot of Aunt Madge. Tony, wanting to spend a lot of time with his sister, had practically moved in, spending more time at the apartment than at his dorm. Dupree loved having her brother around. It made adjusting to the Big Apple so much easier.

"You know you love me being here," Tony teased just before his cell phone in his jeans pocket rang. He took the phone and answered it, shooting a sideway glance at Dupree. "Hi, Dad, hmmm, hold on a second." Tony got up off the bed and stood up. "I'll be right back," he said to Dupree and walked toward the door.

"Where are you going?" She stopped him in his tracks. "It's okay. Come back." She patted the space beside her on the bed.

Tony looked at her hesitantly for a few seconds before he walked back over to the bed, sitting on the edge of it. "Dad? How are you and Mom?" Tony listened for a while. "Yes. I'm with her."

As Tony talked to their father, Dupree's mind travelled back to the talk she finally had with Officer Gregg last Christmas. While it was easier for her to forgive her mother, Dupree held a lot of resentment for her father. "If he hadn't threatened you but had taken responsibility for what he had done, our lives would have been different," Dupree had told Eleanor when she begged her to speak with her father before she left to study abroad. "I don't want to deal with him now. I'm still praying about it but not now."

Dupree also refused to let Officer Gregg pay her college tuition, so Eleanor and Dwight did. "He saw me when I needed money and never offered. So I don't want his money now."

True to her word, Dupree left for New York without seeing or speaking to Officer Gregg or his wife. Getting settled in a new country, in a new school, took up a lot of her time, but Dupree's relationship with her father weighed heavily on her mind. She tried to ignore it, but it was like a big zit on her forehead full of pus that wouldn't go away.

"Fast, pray, and ask the Lord to wash away all the anger and malice, baby," Aunt Madge had told her. "You can do it. You are a young lady of great faith. You know God for yourself."

So Dupree did as Aunt Madge suggested. She began attending church with Aunt Clover, feasted on the words of God by reading her Bible frequently, but most importantly, Dupree prayed. There were some prayer sessions when all she could do was bawl. The pain of her past felt like open wounds, still bleeding, still hurting.

She never got a miracle of forgiveness instantaneously, but she had gotten to a place that when she went home for Christmas, she finally met with her father. Sitting between Eleanor and Aunt Madge on Mrs. Scott's verandah in Falmouth, her hands tightly clasped in both women's, with the Greggs sitting across from them, Dupree finally listened to Officer Gregg's story.

"I went to church almost every Sunday. I was the perfect husband, the perfect son, the perfect man in everyone's eyes but God's. I wasn't saved, Dupree. I went through the motions but I never knew God," he began, his eyes filled with tears as he looked at his daughter. "So when I saw your mother, lust filled my heart and I gave in to it. I didn't think about my family, my job, or anyone but myself. I mean, I felt flattered that this beautiful, young girl wanted to be with me. I was just a selfish man."

Dupree stared at him without saying a word.

"At first it was exciting. You know the thrill of doing something forbidden without getting caught. So when Tiny told me she was pregnant, it was like someone threw a bucket of ice water over my head and woke me up. It was then that I realized what was at stake for me. Again, I was only thinking of myself. My wife would leave, and I would disgrace my family. But, the worst was that I could go to jail for being involved with a minor." Officer Gregg paused and took a deep breath. His face was stained with tears.

"Something snapped in me. Dear God, I acted like an animal." He bent over with his hands resting on his knees, his face fixed on the floor. "I attacked the poor girl and almost killed her so I could keep my dirty secret hidden. Lord, help me, but I also thought denying you as my daughter would make everything better for me. Again, I was just a selfish bastard."

Officer Gregg stood up and walked over to Dupree. He knelt before his daughter, crying. "I wish I could go back and do it all over again, Dupree," he sadly concluded, his eyes pleading with his daughter for understanding, "but I can't. I can only move forward and try to be the best father I can be to you from now on. Please let me try."

Dupree stared at him silently, her head slightly tilted to the right, as she studied the face that looked so much like her own.

"Being good Christians now makes a big difference in our lives, Dupree," Beverly said softly. "Second Corinthians 5:17 says 'Therefore if any man be in Christ, he is a new creature: old things are passed away; behold, all things are become new.' Your father and I have asked the Lord for His forgiveness, which I know He gave us. Your mother and Aunt Madge have given us theirs. Now we are begging for yours."

"Well, I'm not that mad anymore." Dupree felt Eleanor give her hand a reassuring squeeze. "I no longer wish you would drop dead, so that's progress, right?" Dupree looked at her father.

Officer Gregg nodded his head. "Yes, that's a step in the right direction."

"I don't hate you, Mrs. Gregg. To be honest I don't even resent you that much anymore," Dupree stated. "So by the grace of God, I'm trusting that it will get better with each day."

"Thank you. I'm so happy that you are willing to give it a chance." Officer Gregg's face lit up eagerly. "Your eyes see the best in people, your heart forgives the worst, and your faith is anchored in God. So we can do this, my daughter. I know we can."

Dupree gave her father a little smile in agreement. They had certainly come a long way.

The next day Dupree was hit with another test of forgiveness. As she sat in Mrs. Scott's living room with Mrs. Scott, Aunt Madge, Miss Angie, Eleanor and Dwight watching television, Dupree felt her heart leap in her chest. The room got quiet before Eleanor jumped up and rushed over to the television to turn it off.

"No! Please leave it." Dupree's eyes were fixed on the face of the man that had haunted her for years. A face that was slowly but surely becoming a very distant nightmare.

"I'm here at the maximum security St. Catherine's Adult Correctional Centre," the pretty reporter said into the camera. "Today I am interviewing Deacon Livingston, a man who was sentenced to fifteen years in prison for brutally attacking a teenage girl. Now you may be wondering why. Well, Deacon Livingston has formed a Christian ministry here in the prison. It has become one of the largest that prison officials have ever seen in Jamaica. Every Sunday, dozens of prisoners gather in the prison yard to listen to this man tell them about God."

"Can you believe this?" Miss Angie looked at Dupree, but she was absorbed in the news.

"Deacon Livingston, many people are wondering if this is a scam for a possible early release from prison or are you for real," the reporter said.

Deacon Livingston smiled and looked directly into the camera. "A few months ago I wanted to die for what I had done to an innocent, young girl and the shame I brought my family. I prayed for death every second of the day. But one night God spoke to me and said He has work for me to do here. I mean, why would God want to use me? I still don't know, but that night has changed me. I was just like Saul on Damascus Road. I was converted into Paul. For years I faked being a Christian, but today, I can say that I am a child of God. Hallelujah!" Deacon Livingston rocked to the right, then to the left, before he began to do a little jig as he spoke in tongues.

The interview continued for a few more minutes with prisoners who had gotten saved giving testimonies and praising Deacon Livingston for bringing them hope in their dismal situation. "The man is a prophet," said one prisoner. "He showed me that all is not lost when you have Jesus. Yes, man, I love him for that."

After the interview, the room was lulled into silence. Every concerned eye was on Dupree, unsure of what to do.

"It's good to see Deacon Livingston doing something worthwhile, isn't it?" Dupree glanced from one face to another. "He seemed genuine. If he is, I'm glad that he has found the Lord so when he comes back to society, he will do some good and not harm anyone again."

"Chile, you know you are a little too grown for your age," Aunt Madge remarked, breaking the tension in the room.

"I'm almost twenty-years-old, Aunt Madge."

"As I said before, too grown for your age."

Dupree and the others laughed. This time there were no tears, only laughter. Dupree was getting there.

For the rest of the Christmas holiday, Dupree had a blast. She alternated her time between Falmouth and Kingston, spending a few nights with her mother and Dwight and the rest at the apartment with Jas and her new roommate, Vanessa, a coworker at NCB. Before Dupree had left for New York, Eleanor had informed Jas that not only could she stay in the apartment but she was free to get a roommate so she would have some company. Dupree and Jas were super thrilled.

"Dupree? Dupree, are you hearing me?" Tony reached over and shook Dupree's leg.

"What?" Dupree looked at him as if she was surprised he was there. She was so consumed with her thoughts that she actually forgot about Tony.

"Dad would like to speak to you?" Tony posed it as a question. He knew that his father and Dupree had been communicating ever since she came back for Christmas break, but there was still a little tension between the two of them. It was best to play it safe.

Dupree took the phone from Tony. "Hi. Yes, I'm doing fine, thank you. How are you and Mrs. Gregg doing?"

"We are doing well, my dear." Officer Gregg was happy to be talking to Dupree. "I wanted to tell you that Beverly and I will be coming up in a few weeks for my in-laws' fiftieth wedding anniversary."

"Really? Please bring some roasted breadfruits and ackee. Also, ask Miss Angie to bake one of her delicious potato puddings for me. Tell Mom to make some grater cakes and drops for me too."

Tony began to laugh. "Bring the entire Jamaica, Dad," he shouted.

"Shut up, Bighead." Dupree rolled her eyes at him. "Father, don't listen to him. Also, please bring some sugar cane for me."

Officer Gregg's grip tightened on the telephone, a big grin on his face. "She called me 'Father,' sweetheart," he whispered to Beverly who was standing close by, as Dupree continued listing items for him to bring from Jamaica.

Beverly smiled and kissed him on the cheek. "One day she'll say 'Daddy.' I can just feel it."

Officer Gregg beamed. He felt it too.

A few days later as Dupree entered the apartment the telephone rang. She hurried and picked up the phone in her bedroom. It was more than likely her call anyway. She got one almost every night from her loved ones in Jamaica.

"Hello, darling. I'm so glad I got you," Eleanor said excitedly when Dupree answered the phone.

"Hi, Mom. I was planning on calling you later as well." Dupree let her backpack fall to the floor and found a space to lie on her bed among the books covering most of it.

"I wanted to call before Dwight's parents get here for dinner."

"Really? Dinner?" Eleanor had told Dupree of the strained relationship Dwight had with his parents and their dislike of her.

"Can you believe it? Last week they invited Dwight and me to their house for the first time," Eleanor replied as if she was still in shock. "Things were a little tense at first, especially between his mother and me, but it turned out to be a pleasant enough evening. That's a start, right?"

"Yes, it is." Dupree was happy for Dwight and her mother. "How is my favorite stepdad doing?"

"You only have one stepdad." Eleanor and Dupree laughed. "He is right here anxiously waiting to talk to you. How is school going?"

"School is great! New York is out of this world," Dupree gushed happily. "But I miss you guys too," she added soberly.

Eleanor laughed. "I know you do, sweetheart. I'm happy you are happy."

"Aunt Clover is spoiling me rotten, and I love it," Dupree squealed, waving her hand in the air as if her mother could see her.

"So when are you coming to visit?" Eleanor asked.

"Mom, I was just there for Christmas." Dupree giggled, switching the telephone to her other ear. "Aunt Madge called last night and asked the same thing."

"What if we have a special reason to celebrate?"

Dupree sat up straighter on the bed. "What reason? Come on, tell me now."

"You are going to be a big sister!"

"Yay!" Dupree jumped off the bed, screaming and dancing around her room. "Yes, yes, yes."

Aunt Clover knocked on the door after hearing the noise from Dupree's room.

"Come in, Aunt Clover," Dupree shouted animatedly. "Dwight and Mom are having a baby," she informed Aunt Clover when she entered the bedroom.

"Oh, thank you, Lord." Aunt Clover lifted up her hands to the heavens. "God certainly does things in His own time." She took the telephone from Dupree and congratulated her nephew and his wife while Dupree was still dancing.

"Congratulations, Mom," Dupree said after she had settled down. "You and Dwight are going to be the best parents ever."

"Thank you, sweetheart. You do know this baby will not be replacing you. Dwight and I love you so much."

"I know. I asked God for her, remember?" Dupree replied softly. "But, just so you know, I'll be okay if I get a brother too."

Eleanor laughed, her joy tickling Dupree so many miles away. "I'm so happy, Dupree. My life has definitely come together, and all praise belongs to God. The devil put us through hell, but we got the last laugh, my daughter."

"We won, Mom." Dupree was smiling happily as the tears trickled down her face. "We beat the odds because finally God has spoken."

Discussion Questions

1. After reading Tiny's story, do you feel more sympathetic toward her now? Can you understand why she ran away? Why she stayed away all these years from her daughter and aunt?

2. Dolly had a lot of influence over Tiny. Do you think Tiny succumbed to peer pressure? If you were in that situation, what would you have done differently?

3. Dolly and Tiny drank alcohol and smoked marijuana. What are your views on underage drinking? Do you think marijuana is a drug that affects teenagers negatively? How? Why?

4. Do you think Tiny seduced Officer Gregg? Can an underage girl seduce an older man? Who is to blame for the affair?

5. Tiny stopped using her pet name and began using her birth name, Eleanor. Do you understand the significance of the change? Do you think this was a way for Tiny to forget her past? Was it symbolic of a fresh start for her?

6. What do you think about Mama Pearl? Was she a guardian angel sent to take care of Eleanor aka Tiny? Why? Do you believe in guardian angels?

7. Do you believe that Eleanor should have told Mama Pearl and her five adoptive brothers about Dupree and Aunt Madge? Would that have made a difference in her life as well as Dupree's? How?

8. The rich financial guru fell in love with the once homeless woman. What are your views on Dwight and Eleanor's romance? Do you think her past made a difference in their lives? In what way?

9. It is said that love conquers all. Dwight still got married to Eleanor after hearing the secrets she kept. Do you think their marriage is stronger because of this? Should Eleanor have listened to Dwight and contacted her aunt and daughter? Why? Why not?

10. What are your impressions of Officer Bailey? What do you think of his reasons for getting involved in Eleanor's life? Do you think he would have hurt Dupree and Aunt Madge if Eleanor had gone against his wishes? Was Eleanor's fear of him validated? Did she do the right thing by staying away to protect her loved ones? Were you surprised at his demise?

11. Dwight had a strained relationship with his bourgeoisie parents. What are your opinions of David and Eve Humphrey? Did you agree with Dwight's decision to not follow in his father's footsteps? With Dwight eventually becoming the CEO of BNS and his father the Group Managing Director of NCB, will this competition help or hinder their relationship? Why? Why not?

12. Eve Humphrey disliked Eleanor for Dwight because of her dark complexion and her poor background. Do you think she will ever truly accept Eleanor? Will David Humphrey? Why? Why not?

13. Deacon Livingston resurfaced briefly in the story. What do you think of his proclamation? Is he for real? Were you surprised at Dupree's reaction to this?

14. Do you think Dupree should have forgiven Mrs. Humphrey, Officer Gregg, and Tony? Why? Why not?

15. If you were Dupree, would you find it easier to forgive your mother or father? Please state your reasons.

16. Are you happy with the way the story ended? Was there anything you would have changed in the end? What? Why?

About the Author

Theresa A. Campbell is the author of the intriguing novel *Are You There, God?* She was born and raised in Jamaica, West Indies. She received her associate's degree in business administration from Bronx Community College, a bachelor's degree in business administration from Baruch College, and a master's degree in business administration from Fairleigh Dickinson University.

Theresa has had a deep passion for reading since she was a child. It is her desire to inspire readers by writing stories from the heart to uplift their faith in God.

Theresa would love to hear from her readers! Her contact information is below:

www.theresaacampbell.com
https://www.facebook.com/theresaacampbell
https://twitter.com/theresaacampbel
http://theresaacampbell.blogspot.com
www.linkedin.com/in/theresaacampbell

UC HIS GLORY BOOK CLUB!

www.uchisglorybookclub.net

UC His Glory Book Club is the spirit-inspired brain-child of Joylynn Jossel, Author and Acquisitions Editor of Urban Christian, and Kendra Norman-Bellamy, Author for Urban Christian. This is an online book club that hosts authors of Urban Christian. We welcome as members all men and women who have a passion for reading Christian-based fiction.

UC His Glory Book Club pledges our commitment to provide support, positive feedback, encouragement, and a forum whereby members can openly discuss and review the literary works of Urban Christian authors.

There is no membership fee associated with UC His Glory Book Club; however, we do ask that you support the authors through purchasing, encouraging, providing book reviews, and of course, your prayers. We also ask that you respect our beliefs and follow the guidelines of the book club. We hope to receive your valuable input, opinions, and reviews that build up, rather than tear down our authors.

What We Believe:

—We believe that Jesus is the Christ, Son of the Living God.

—We believe the Bible is the true, living Word of God.

—We believe all Urban Christian authors should use their God-given writing abilities to honor God and share the message of the written word God has given to each of them uniquely.

—We believe in supporting Urban Christian authors in their literary endeavors by reading, purchasing and sharing their titles with our online community.

—We believe that in everything we do in our literary arena should be done in a manner that will lead to God being glorified and honored.

We look forward to the online fellowship with you.

Please visit us often at *www.uchisglorybookclub.net*.

Many Blessing to You!

Shelia E. Lipsey,
President, UC His Glory Book Club

Printed in the United States
by Baker & Taylor Publisher Services